ISBN-13: 978-0615771618
ISBN: 0615771610

Published 2013 by Pulpwork Press, New York. Information for bookstores and web retailers available at PulpWork.com.

Special thanks to Master Scott Irey for martial guidance and sword expertise!

The Gantlet Brothers: Sold Out

Joel Jenkins

Chapter 1

Three women strutted through the Foxboro Stadium tunnel. They wore miniskirts and Spandex, hair teased out, and laminated all access passes dangling from their necks. The sound of the sold out concert was muted here, beneath the stage, but the bass reverberated through the stone and steel.

A very large black man with a Mohawk stood guard halfway down the tunnel, making a secretive phone call on his cell phone. His dark eyes viewed the backstage vixens with jaded suspicion and he abruptly ended the call. The first woman had shoulder-length brown hair stiff with hairspray, and despite the attractive features, there was a certain hardness to her expression. Beneath the makeup, the guard could detect the tracing of a scar that stretched from the right corner of her mouth to just below the lobe of her ear, which dangled with a golden hoop.

"Sorry girls," rumbled the guard. "Ever since the incident in Tallahassee, the Gantlet Brothers have banned all groupies."

The brunette laid a hand upon the guard's broad chest and glanced at the name embroidered in his heavy leather jacket. "But Mr. Hawkins—can I call you Blake?—we're not groupies," she cooed, her voice held the hint of a German accent. "We're artist reps from Arista."

"Really," said Blake, but he didn't seem convinced. He grabbed her laminated pass and flipped it over to examine the back. It didn't have the guns and guitar hologram that the Gantlet Brothers were using for this leg of the tour. "This is a fake and the Gantlet Brothers are no longer with Arista."

"We're not here to see the Gantlet Brothers," said the brunette. "We're with Entropy. The Gantlet Brothers are old news. We're with the up and coming band."

"You're here to see the opening band? I doubt that very much," said

Blake, and he was about to turn the women away when Sticks Anderson, the drummer of Entropy, wandered from a side door carrying a case of beer, a towel draped around his neck.

"Hey, Sticks!" called the brunette. "This muscle bound oaf won't believe us that we're with Entropy."

Sticks's eyes widened when he saw the array of feminine pulchritude down the corridor. "Oh, yes, Angela! We'd been wondering when you'd arrive. It's okay, Blake. The girls are with us."

"You sure about that?" growled Blake.

"Absolutely sure," said Sticks. "Send 'em on down!"

"Fine," said Blake and he smacked one fist into a meaty palm. "But there will be hell to pay if you let them anywhere near the stage."

Sticks leered at the women strutting down the hallway. "Don't you worry about that. I promise, I won't let them out of my sight."

Angela smiled sweetly at Blake and then brushed past him, her fingers trailing across his chest and beginning to sweep back the corner of his jacket, revealing the jutting dragon-engraved handgrips of a .44 magnum revolver. Blake knocked Angela's hand away. "Watch those fingers, sweetie."

Blake pegged Angela to be in her mid-thirties, but the second girl past couldn't have been much beyond her eighteenth birthday—a svelte, glacial blonde with an icy gaze. She wore a Gantlet Brothers tour jacket—the sort that sold for two hundred bucks in the vendors booths outside the arena. Blake highly doubted that she worked for Arista, unless it was in the capacity of a call girl.

The third woman was a buxom redhead in her mid-twenties, clutching a tiny handbag and drowning in an oversized tour jacket which fell to mid-thigh. Beneath, she wore a low-cut Spandex top and a belt that was cinched with a pair of handcuffs. Her stiletto heels clicked on the concrete floor as she retreated down the corridor.

Though Blake was a married man, she was worth a second glance. She was the last through the door into Entropy's private den of iniquity beneath the stage, and that was when Blake noticed a splotch of crimson on the collar of the woman's jacket.

"Hey, you! Stop!" bellowed Blake.

The redhead turned, her hand dipping inside her clutch. Blake wasn't sure just what she was removing from her clutch, but his hand slipped inside his jacket and found his pistol. He heard a pin clatter to the floor and then saw a spring flip away from her hand, then the redhead skipped a concussion grenade down the hallway.

Blake knew that he had about four seconds from the time the spoon was released before the grenade exploded. He didn't waste a moment of that time firing at the redhead; instead he turned tail and ran as fast as his massive legs would carry him. He heard the redhead slam the door shut and he started counting at two. "Two one thousand, three one thousand," he muttered, and then at about twenty yards distance he threw himself on the ground. The concussion grenade exploded into a fiery blossom of over-pressure that swept down the hallway, then picked him up and rolled Blake down the corridor like a leaf before a hurricane. Darkness engulfed him.

As the tremor of the concussion grenade shook the den of iniquity, Razzle Harmon, lead singer for Entropy, pushed off a pair of fawning groupies and leaped to his feet, his glass of bourbon sloshing its contents on the ground. His face was smeared with stage makeup. "What was that?"

Angela smiled. "I guess the Gantlet Brothers are bringing out the heavy pyrotechnics."

Ripper Bogs lay back on a couch, his face barely visible from beneath the mop of curly hair, upon which rested his top hat. An empty syringe lay nearby and a vacant smile spread across his face. "That's wild, man."

The redhead pulled a device about the size of a garage door opener from her purse.

"What's that?" asked Sticks Anderson.

"It's a remote detonator," said Angela.

The redhead activated the trigger and the three women waited expectantly for a few moments.

Angela cursed. "Nothing, I'll kill that Bosnian son of a ..."

The redhead interrupted her. "The detonator must be on the same frequency as some of the wireless guitars."

The glacial blonde spoke now. "Then wouldn't they trigger the thermite bomb?"

"No," said the redhead. "They are just causing interference. The remote has to receive a specific sequence to trigger."

"Bomb?" said Sticks, who seemed to think that the trio of beautiful women were doing some sort of playacting. "You three are the bomb, if you're asking me."

"Wait," said Razzle and he guzzled down the remaining contents of his bourbon glass. "Who are you three?"

"Why, they're from Arista," winked Sticks. "Right, 'Angela'? Or maybe they're three spies out to destroy our arch-enemies, the Gantlet Brothers."

Ripper Bogs chuckled manically. "Arch-enemies? That's like something out of a comic book, man. If they are our arch enemies, how come Fritz let me borrow his rig after mine blew at last night's show?"

Razzle jabbed a finger at Ripper Bogs. "You know that they purposely had their crew plug your rig into too high of a voltage. They wanted it to explode. You saw them laughing!"

"But I was the one who plugged it in," said Ripper.

"They must have switched the voltage," spat Razzle.

"If we want to trigger the bomb, we've got to get closer to the stage," said the redhead.

"Right," said Angela. She reached beneath her miniskirt and jerked free a mini-pistol loaded with .22 magnum rounds. She fired three rounds into Razzle's chest, saving the last two for the shrieking groupies that stood behind him—one for each, right in the head.

A slender blade appeared from the sleeve of the glacial blonde's Gantlet Brothers tour jacket and she sliced Sticks Anderson's jugular. He went immediately to his knees, grasping his throat in a futile attempt to staunch the flow of blood that was drenching the towel draped around his neck. The blonde watched impassively, putting a stiletto heel to his chest and pushing him to the floor when he tried to grasp her legs.

The redhead smiled at the blonde's cold efficiency. "Nice work, Killingsworth." She set aside her detonator and drew out a short-barreled Ruger .357 revolver. Ripper Boggs hadn't even moved from the couch, his drugged stupor not allowing him to discern whether he was experiencing a hallucination or reality.

"You're not going to shoot me, are you?" asked Ripper. "I mean, fire away. This is all a dream, anyhow? Right?"

"Wrong." The redhead pulled the trigger twice and Ripper Boggs convulsed on the couch, blood seeping into the cushions.

"The room's clear," said Angela. "We've got to get closer to the stage for the detonator to work."

"Out the back, then," said Killingsworth, who paused only long enough to wipe away the blood on her knife. She resheathed it and headed out the rear door.

The redhead arched her brow in a quizzical expression, as if wondering why the youngest member of their group was giving the orders. She glanced at Angela, who nodded. "Move on—"

Her order was interrupted as a great weight threw itself against the outer door. The door frame splintered, but did not come out of the wall.

Angela swore. "It must be the security guard—Hawkins."

The redhead frowned and turned her .357 toward the door. "No way. I hit him with a concussion grenade. That thing would stop an elephant in its tracks!"

Angela reloaded her magnum mini-pistol. "Maybe you're not as good as they say you are, McDonagh!"

Normally the redhead would have replied with a bullet, but she was saving the four she had left. A great force struck the door again, and this time it lurched free of the wall, one part of the frame pivoting around and striking McDonagh even as she fired at the massive black man that burst through the opening.

McDonagh, red hair flying, went tumbling to the floor, and the trajectory of her bullet went awry, striking Angela just above the temple and blowing out the other side of her skull. Blake Hawkins made a dive for the red-haired assassin, but McDonagh fired her last three bullets point-blank into his chest, so that he fell, two hundred eighty pounds of dead weight upon her legs.

Smoking pistol still in hand, she carefully extricated herself, climbed to her feet and found the detonator where she had set it, amidst a tray of mostly empty vodka and whiskey bottles. Instead of picking up the detonator, she first took hold of a bottle of Tyrconnell single malt whiskey and took a healthy swig that drained the dregs of it. She wiped her red lips with the back of her forearm and picked up the detonator.

Monica Killingsworth wound through the labyrinthine corridors beneath the stage, passing crewmembers who were too intent upon performing their various jobs to give the attractive blonde more than an admiring glance. They saw her backstage pass and didn't hassle her—at least until she reached the steps to the stage. Here, a grizzled ex-cop leaned against a railing. His Gantlet Brothers tour jacket clearly delineated him as Harold Ostkopf, Chief of Security, and he wore a taser at his belt alongside a well-worn police issue Smith and Wesson .40 caliber.

His eyes wandered from the glacial beauty of her features to the backstage laminate clipped to her jacket. Ostkopf's hand went to the butt of his Smith and Wesson. "There's blood on your backstage pass. Turn around slowly and put your hands on the back of your head."

Up above, colorful lights strobed and the sound of crunchy guitars and shrieking solos washed through the air. The bass rumbled the supports of the stage and the drums clattered in a rhythm steadier than any machine gun. Killingsworth neither turned around nor put her hands on the back of her head. "Money is mightier than the sword."

"So it is," growled Ostkopf and he glanced around to see if there were any witnesses to his interaction with the young blonde. When he was satisfied that they were alone and that the crew was otherwise engaged, he spoke again. "This wasn't part of the deal, Blondie. I'm never supposed to see you."

"Your understanding is correct," answered Killingsworth and she pointed with her left hand, into the shadow of the corridors where a curvaceous ginger-haired woman emerged from the shadows. "There will be no witnesses."

For a moment Ostkopf was distracted by the disheveled appearance of the redhead. Her hair-sprayed coiffure was wild and tangled and her jacket torn. Killingsworth used this moment of inattention, and her right hand dipped toward the small of her back where she kept a brace of .45 Glock pistols. She fired from her waist, the muzzle flash lighting up the dim corridor and the bullets chewing through Ostkopf's tour jacket. The sound of the gunfire mingled with the staccato of the drums, and suddenly Matthias Gantlet, the lead singer, halted mid-verse—and he shouted a warning through the Public Address system.

The Gantlet Brothers had heard the missed beats, and realizing that it had not been the sure-handed Mitz, the drummer, who had bungled the rhythm, they recognized the gunshots for what they were.

Ostkopf slumped on the stairs, one hand grasping at the rail. Then that hand fell loosely to his bloodied chest, where a half dozen bullets had stitched his jacket with crimson blossoms. He croaked out an epithet and his eyes glazed over.

There was the hum of feedback as guitars were thrown aside, cartwheeling and spinning across the stage. The crowd roared at the spectacle of it, thinking that it was part of the show. Firearms were secreted about the stage and in a few moments each of the Gantlet Brothers was carrying pistols of various makes and calibers.

Beneath the stage, Killingsworth's icy demeanor was beginning to crack. "Hurry, McDonagh. Trigger the detonator!"

McDonagh hurried forward, repeatedly pressing the trigger of the detonator. "I'm trying! I'm still getting interference!"

A beefy man with long yellow hair and a dark beard appeared at the top of the stair, moving through a spectral haze pumped out by the fog machines. He carried a massive Desert Eagle .44 magnum in his fist, and his keen eyes narrowed as he saw his head of security lying lifeless on the stair—an icy blonde and a curvaceous redhead standing over him.

This was Sly Gantlet, lead and rhythm guitar player of the Gantlet Brothers, and as soon as he recognized the firearm in the blonde's hand, he jabbed his pistol in her direction, the crimson laser dot appearing on her low-cut blouse, and he pulled the trigger. Just a moment before, one of McDonagh's repeated attempts at detonating the hidden explosive breached the interfering signal of a wireless guitar, triggering the detonator cap inside one of the eight pyrotechnic wells that stretched across the front of the stage. Here McDonagh had installed five blocks of C-4 plastic explosives, six-and-a-quarter pounds in total that detonated, blasting apart the stage from beneath.

Bass player, Otto Gantlet, stood at the proscenium of the stage, just beyond the pyrotechnic wells, scanning the crowd for trouble, a chromed Mossberg Persuader shotgun in his hands. The explosion pulped flesh and bone, picked him up and hurled him two hundred feet into the crowd, where he landed, still aflame. Three security guards manning the barrier between the stage and the crowd died instantly, and the wave of pressure crumpled the barriers and pushed back the crowd, toppling them like dominoes.

Only the fact that the plastic explosives were installed so deeply beneath the stage and inside a canister with quarter-inch metal walls saved the lives of the rest of the Gantlet Brothers. Stage planks and struts erupted and rained across the set. A beam pierced Mitz's bass drum and shot past his chest, even as the rest of his drum set was obliterated and he went hurling backward, his fall cushioned by the great curtain that screened the backstage.

Splitting stage left and stage right in an effort to locate the source of the gunshots, Fritz and Matthias were already off the stage when the explosive detonated. Great banks of speaker cabinets were torn from their stabilizers and toppled down with bone-crushing force. Matthias rolled with the debris, narrowly escaping being crushed, and Fritz was picked up by the erupting stage and tossed ten feet into the air. He landed amidst a mound of splintered guitar cabinets had been hurled through the stage ramps.

Sly Gantlet's aim was thrown awry as the explosion pushed him into a rail and cracked a rib. His gunshot tore through the rail next to Killingsworth, sparing her life. The massive concussion caused the guitar player to black out, and he lost his grip on his Desert Eagle, so that it tumbled away.

Even with so much steel and wood between the bomb and the rear of the stage, Killingsworth and McDonagh were tossed from their feet, feeling the heat of the explosion as it rushed past Sly and down the aluminum steps of the stairwell. Killingsworth regained her feet first. There was no sign of Sly Gantlet any longer. Whether he had been swept away or obliterated by the explosion, she didn't know.

McDonagh picked herself up off the ground, a devilish grin across her face and spouted a bit of Irish slang. "That was a holy show!"

"Right," said Killingsworth. "Things are going to get a little hot around here. I say it's time we disappear."

Both McDonagh and Killingsworth had memorized the stage layout prior to the execution of the assassination. Now they made good use of the knowledge, and in the chaos they made their way into the crowds, and were lost in the braying tumult of confusion and injury.

Chapter 2

Blake Hawkins groaned and peeled back his Gantlet Brothers tour jacket, revealing massive bruising across his chest and torso. "Feels like I was sucker punched with a sledgehammer."

"The Kevlar lining saved you worse," said Matthias. "You going to be all right?"

Hawkins tossed the jacket aside and reached for an ice pack. "Don't worry none about me, I've taken worse beatings from my Pappy when I was a whippersnapper."

"Some upbringing you must have had," said Matthias. His face was crusted with blood from a gash he'd taken on the head during the explosion.

"I earned every one of those beatings," said Hawkins. "And more."

Matthias fell into silence, the heavy burden of grief falling on him once again.

Sly sat in the corner, bare-chested, ribs wrapped to reduce movement. He was uncharacteristically quiet, his face smudged with charcoal, except where his bulletproof Gargoyle sunglasses had protected him. When he did speak, his voice came harsh and cracked. "I can't believe that Otto's gone."

Fritz's curly hair spilled around his features, which were frozen into a frowning mask of grief and bitterness. "It was inevitable. We've tempted fate for so long. Did we think we could dodge every blow, every bullet that was fired in our direction?"

"I've caught my fair share of bullets," said Sly, "but ..."

Mitz rolled a pair of drum sticks between his palms, the muscles in his abnormally large forearms writhing like snakes beneath the skin. "But you thought we were invincible—just like I did. You thought that ultimately, nothing could touch us. We started to believe our own hype. We're the Gantlet Brothers: we escaped over the Berlin wall, we've defeated every enemy that life has thrown at us."

Matthias threw off his heavy jacket and glared at the pair of massive pistols holstered in the lining of the Kevlar jacket. "I don't know why Otto was at the front of the proscenium ..."

"It was a tactically poor position," said Fritz. "We all know that, but there must have been something that he saw in the crowd."

Mitz hurled his sticks across the room and they splintered against the wall. "What?"

"That's what we need to find out," said Fritz. "Jemandem vor die Büchse kommen."

It was an uncommon German idiom, but they all knew it well enough. They had come into someone's gun sight, and they needed to figure out just who it was that was targeting them for destruction.

Sly jacked a round into the chamber of his charred Desert Eagle. "We won't let Otto's death go unpunished."

A sharp rap came at the door and Sly lowered his .44 magnum, targeting the center of the door. "Come in."

A broad-shouldered man just a bit shorter than Fritz, and in his early fifties, entered the room. The skin around his jowls hung loosely, and the salt in his dark hair had spread since the last time Sly and Matthias had seen him. He was followed by a studious-looking man, at least three decades younger, wearing an ill-fitting suit.

"Well, if it isn't Cromwell Jensen," growled Sly. "To what do we owed the pleasure of a visit from the CIA?"

Jensen's partner sniggered at the mention of his senior companion's first name. "I thought your first name was Cole."

"Sly has done some research since we last met. Cromwell's my given name. I'm not particularly fond of it." Jensen turned his attention back to the four remaining battered and bruised Gantlet Brothers. "I should think it is obvious enough why I am here." Jensen laid a sheaf of papers on the table, shoving aside various beverages and a platter of hors d'oeuvres to make space. "Please do accept my condolences. I'm sincerely sorry to hear the news about your brother. He was a good man and has provided reams of valuable information for our intelligence operatives."

Mitz's face twisted into a quizzical expression. "What?"

Jensen turned to face the blond-haired drummer. "You didn't know?"

"Know what?" asked Matthias.

"He's been monitoring various wavelengths and keeping tabs on illicit communication on the World Wide Web and providing intelligence to the CIA for years."

"That actually explains a lot," said Mitz. "He'd hole himself up in his loft for weeks at a time just listening to shortwave recordings and doing stuff on his computers. I knew he had an obsession with being wired in—didn't realize he was saving the world."

"Thanks to Otto, we've been able to head off a number of very bad situations," said Jensen.

Mitz squinted. "So you think that someone he uncovered got hacked off and planted that bomb?"

Jensen shrugged. "It's a possibility, but Otto's surveillance was much more discreet than the usual activities of the Gantlet Brothers. You have no idea how much effort it takes to cover up some of your fiascos. We've got a full-time team spinning the news that gets out—all paid for by the taxpayers."

"We pay a lot of taxes," grunted Sly. It was clear from his demeanor that he was in no mood to debate politics or argue with Jensen. "What do you want from us?"

"I want to help you. We've got four dead security guards, forty-seven concert-goers with injuries ranging from cuts and bruises to broken bones. Three out of four members of the band Entropy are murdered: Ripper Boggs, Sticks Anderson, Razzle Harmon—and then we've got your brother, Otto, blown off the stage in front of fifty thousand witnesses. There's no covering this one up. We're going to spin this one as an act of terrorism—and ostensibly it is."

"The question is who is responsible," said Fritz, his gray eyes were hard as flint.

"That's why I'm here, to see if we can get you pointed in the right direction."

Matthias flexed his fingers, the joints cracking. "The US government is giving us a license to kill on this one?"

Jensen cast a glance over one broad shoulder. "Officially? You've got to be out of your mind. This is strictly off the books. However, having dealt with you before I know full well that you won't stop until you've brought the perpetrator of this to some sort of justice. There's less red tape if you handle it—and as an employee of the federal government, I can tell you that I'm drowning in red tape."

Sly pushed aside the grief for just a moment, glad to be distracted from his anguish, by focusing his attention on finding Otto's killers. "I laid my eyes on two of them. They shot Ostkopf down. One was a hot young blonde—willowy figure—and carrying a .45 Glock, and the other a red-head with some killer curves. It was the redhead who had the detonator, but it was hidden in her hand and I didn't realize it until too late."

"You think you could recognize either of them?" asked Jensen.

Matthias saw that Jensen's CIA compatriot carried a thick binder, filled with photos. "Do you have full-body mug shots? Sly never forgets a figure."

Sly grabbed the binder away and spread it out on the table, knocking over a pair of eponymously titled bottles of Sly Beer that he had downed after the tragedy. "I can recognize their faces. Who have you got in this book?"

"It's a compilation of known female terrorists and assassins," said Meriweather, the younger CIA agent from which Sly had torn the hefty volume. "You are positive that these were female assassins that you spotted below stage?"

"I can tell a man from a woman," snapped Sly, and he grimaced as his cracked rib sent a pain lancing through his torso.

"I'm just asking, because there are some reported incidents of ..."

"Shut your hole and let me concentrate!" Sly fell to examining the photos with an intensity so deep, that it seemed the pages might catch fire from exposure to the burning gaze of his red-rimmed eyes.

Meriweather reeled back from the rebuff, as though Sly had physically assaulted him, but he kept quiet—glancing at Jensen as if expecting his mentor to defend him.

It was long minutes before Sly halted at a photo of an attractive red-head with a sullen expression. He jabbed a finger at the photograph. "This is the woman that I saw tonight."

Jensen leaned closer. "That's Sorcha McDonagh—an IRA bomber."

Matthias inspected the photograph. "What does the Irish Republic Army want with us? I don't think we've tangled with them before."

Jensen's face furrowed and he turned to Meriweather. "What's the background on Sorcha McDonagh?"

"C-can I speak now?" stuttered Meriweather.

Matthias sighed. "Yes, you can speak."

"Sorcha McDonagh is the younger sister of the infamous McDonagh Brothers—Aengus and Fergal—who were responsible for at least three bombings that resulted in twelve deaths. Before Aengus and Fergal were tracked down and killed in an exchange of gunfire, they taught their sister the art of bomb-making. She is rumored to have followed in her brothers' footsteps for a time—and is linked to at least four bombings—but just when her capture appeared imminent, she left Europe and began to sell her skills abroad."

Sly finally holstered his Desert Eagle. "So, it's your opinion that this bombing has nothing to do with the IRA. This Sorcha McDonagh is working freelance."

Meriweather raised a finger as if to interject something, but then halt-ed, glancing tentatively toward Jensen.

"If you've got something pertinent, then out with it," said Mitz. With his drumsticks out of his hands, he beat an anxious rhythm on the bench with his palms.

Meriwether swallowed hard. "McDonagh is suspected to have worked with at least three different organizations since leaving the IRA. She's reported to have built a pair of bombs for the Abu Nidal Organization—a group that splintered from the PLO in 1974. McDonagh has been tied to three bombings for the ETA ..."

Matthias scratched at his stubble, his gray eyes narrowing. "Isn't that the Spanish Marxist group—Basque Fatherland and Liberty—that's trying to break off from Spain?"

"They've got close ties to the IRA," said Meriweather, "so it's no surprise that she would wind up doing some work for them. Then we've got a couple of unsubstantiated reports of her working with the Manuel Rodriguez Patriotic Front in Chile. They mainly target international corporations and churches. They've blown up a few Mormon chapels and a couple of McDonalds."

"Pretty scattershot," said Fritz. "It's not much of pattern, but it does give us a few places to start."

"What have you got on the blonde?" asked Sly, and he added a few choice words of description.

"Not much," said Jensen. "She goes by the alias of Monica Killingsworth, and there's diverging reports of her coming out of South Africa or perhaps being involved in some inter-cartel drug killings in Colombia."

"Any specific cartels?" asked Matthias. "We need more to go on."

"She's a ghost," said Jensen. "All we've got are rumors. People she work with have a nasty habit of ending up dead. There's not a whole lot of eyewitness corroboration."

"We had crews filming the show," said Matthias. "I've already got them reviewing the footage to see if they can spot anything. How about the security cameras?"

Jensen pulled a handful of tapes out of his case. "The CIA has already laid claim to these, and we'll have our guys go over them with a fine tooth comb. If we turn anything up we'll let you know. I'd suggest you get a good look at the film your crew shot, because it won't be long before the CIA thinks of it and decides that should be confiscated for evidence, also."

Meriweather shot a surprised glance at Jensen, that suggested he couldn't believe what he was hearing. Still, he kept his mouth shut.

Mitz raised an eyebrow. "I thought you were the CIA."

Jensen smiled broadly, his grin almost lost in the folds of loose flesh. "Just a cog in the machine, my friend. But you are correct. If I wait too long to suggest confiscating that film for evidence it will look, rightfully so, as if I'm incompetent. So, if you think the film might have some value, I suggest that you make a copy of it immediately. You should expect a pair of agents to visit tomorrow morning to collect that film. Make good use of your time."

Mitz ceased the rhythm he was drumming on the table. "Thanks for the heads up. Is that all?"

"No," said Jensen. "Meriweather has spent some time doing background checks on your stage crew and other employees."

"We do a background check on everyone on our tour," said Matthias. "They're all clean."

"They were clean," said Jensen, "but things change. Meriweather, tell them what you discovered."

Meriweather cleared his throat and looked toward the long-haired and muscular lead singer of the group. "As you said, everything was turning up clean—until I took a look at your head of security, a Mr. Harold Ostkopf. He recently came into the sum of one hundred thousand dollars, which he moved into an offshore—Bahamanian to be precise—account. There were some papers to indicate it was an inheritance from a distant relative, but it was a simple matter for me to discover that no such distant relative died, or even ever actually existed."

Sly scowled. "Ostkopf sold us out."

Meriweather continued. "It takes no real leap of logic to presume that it was Ostkopf that allowed Sorcha McDonagh access to the stage after the pyrotechnics were rigged, so that she could place the bomb."

"At least Ostkopf won't be able to spend his blood money in hell," growled Sly. "The scum got what was coming to him, paid in lead."

"Ostkopf's wife was suffering from cancer and they were running some huge medical bills. That's probably how the assassins got to him."

Matthias's face tightened. "If he was having trouble making the bills, all he had to do was ask us for help."

"He was a proud man," said Fritz.

"His pride cost us our brother," said Matthias.

"That's the truth of it." Jensen dropped the security tapes back into his bag while Meriweather moved to gather up the binder of mug shots. Sly closed the book, moving his body so that Meriweather couldn't see him slip the photograph of Sorcha McDonagh out of its sleeve and drop it into his lap beneath the table. He glanced at Jensen, and by the sharpness of his gaze it was clear that his petty theft had not gone unnoticed by the senior CIA agent. Still, Jensen, made no comment on the purloined mug shot of the Irish assassin.

Sly waved. "See you later, Cromwell."

Jensen cast a glance over his shoulder as he departed. "Two can play at that game, Slatko!"

Despite the tragedy of the situation, Matthias couldn't help but chuckle. Slatko was his brother's given name, and Sly merely a nickname given by American students while their father served as a diplomat to the United States. Sly had adopted the moniker and the public was entirely unaware of his birth name.

Jensen and Meriweather passed from the room and into long corridors that existed beneath the stadium seats.

"They had no respect for me or the fact that I'm a CIA agent," said Meriweather.

"They grew up in communist East Berlin—and killed at least a half dozen soldiers escaping over the wall into West Berlin. If you're looking for respect for authority, don't look to the Gantlet Brothers."

"They made a few pokes at you," observed Meriweather, "but they actually seem to respect you. Why didn't you defend me?"

Jensen chuckled. "You don't earn the Gantlet Brothers respect by having someone else fight your battles for you. If you want to gain their respect, you demonstrate your value, and you demonstrate that you're willing to fight and die for what you believe."

Meriweather ducked his head and scowled. "You didn't have to die to earn their respect."

"No," said Jensen, "but I came close enough. Don't worry, they're not blind to your skills. They'll see you as a resource now, but nothing more until you've proven you're willing to fight the good fight."

Inside the chamber in the bowels of Foxboro Stadium, Matthias shrugged his heavy Kevlar-lined jacket on. "How about that Meriweather? He's like a walking encyclopedia."

"He might be helpful," agreed Mitz. "Otto was always the go to guy if we needed to dig up intel, but now that Otto's gone ..."

Fritz scowled. "Meriweather might be helpful if we can trust him ... but he's CIA indoctrinated. I'm not sure how much we can rely on him— and it's risky letting him know too much."

Matthias opened up the door. "Jensen's a good man, and he's giving us a head start."

"Head start on what?" growled Sly. "Making the funeral arrangements?"

"Otto's burial will wait a few days," said Matthias. "We're making funeral arrangements for someone else."

Mitz was right on Matthias's heels. "I know Otto spotted something. Just before the bomb went off, I saw him looking up into the second level of seats on the south side of the stadium."

They navigated a series of dim, dank corridors before finally emerging behind the stadium where a quartet of eighteen-wheel trucks sat silent, a waning moon hanging overhead and gray clouds drifting past its face, the air chill and pavement damp from a recent cold rain. "The Gantlet Brothers: Agents of Oblivion Tour" logo was splashed across the side of the cargo containers on the back. Normally the stage crew would already be dismantling the set and packing up the trailers so they could head to the next engagement, but the entire set was taped off for investigation. The tour wouldn't be going anywhere for quite some time—not that there was much left of the stage to pack up, and not that they would continue without Otto, anyhow.

To the left of the trucks was an oversized van, which had a bundle of cables running in through the side door. This was the audio-video feed that piped in the footage from the concert. At any given time there were seven cameras running. One camera was devoted to each of the five Gantlet Brothers, the sixth camera was taking wide angle shots of the stage and the seventh camera was taking footage of crowd reaction. This way, they could intercut back and forth, splicing together the prime footage so they could release a concert video—or perhaps use the footage for an MTV video.

The interior smelled of sweat, Cheetos, and smoke, so Matthias left the door open when he joined the two technicians inside. Ronny, an over-large fellow with a bulbous nose and shaggy blond hair tied into a ponytail, was a technical wizard with video. Jermaine was the slight black man with the foot-tall afro, and a reputation for being the best live audio tech in the business.

Matthias coughed out some of the sickly sweet smoke and knew it wasn't tobacco. "What have you two been doing in here? You know full well we don't allow the crew to ..."

Jermaine threw up his hands in surrender. "I know, I know. It's just we—we didn't know how to take it when we saw Otto get blown to bits. Ronny happened to have picked up a little weed when we were in Vegas last week, so we lit up a couple in Otto's honor."

Matthias glanced at his brother, Mitz, who shrugged slightly. "Getting stoned out of your gourd is not how Otto would want to be honored."

Matthias softened his voice. "I'm going to overlook it this once. Don't let it happen again."

"Never will, never will," said Ronny.

"That's cool," said Jermaine. "I'm swearing off the stuff, anyhow."

Matthias suspected Jermaine's resolve would soon fade, but there was no point in firing them. With Otto's death, they were out of a job anyhow. If they hadn't realized it yet, they would soon. "We need to look at the crowd footage, particularly anything that sweeps the south side of the stadium."

"What we're looking for is probably on the second level," said Mitz.

"Where do you want to start?" asked Ronny.

"Right from the beginning," answered Matthias. "We could be here for a couple of hours."

"It may not take that long," said Ronny. "I can fast forward past any non-relevant footage. Craigster was shooting the reaction camera tonight, so he spent an awful lot of time getting shots of hot girls."

"That doesn't surprise me," said Mitz, who knew that the reaction camera was a coveted position for just that reason.

Ronny cued up the tape. "Are you still going to want all this stuff edited down?"

"I don't know," said Matthias.

"We can burn it all," suggested Jermaine with a wave of his hand. "Destroy it so that there's no chance of it getting out."

Matthias began to watch the monitor as a panoply of faces, and slender and curvaceous figures began to flicker across the screen. "I'm inclined to go with your suggestion, but the CIA would be quite displeased—accuse us of destroying evidence."

"They'll be along tomorrow morning to collect the tapes," added Mitz.

"How do you know that?" asked Ronny.

Mitz nodded toward his brother. "Matthias has got a friend in the CIA."

"I didn't know Matthias had any friends," said Ronny, with a lopsided grin. "Besides Blake Hawkins. That's all the friend anyone needs. No one in their right mind would mess with that mean s—"

"Blake took a concussion grenade tonight and still managed to kill one of the assassins," said Matthias.

Jermaine's eyes widened. "They killed Blake?"

"Nothing can kill Blake," answered Mitz, but his eyes stung as he said the words—for he'd thought his brother, Otto, just as invincible.

The reaction footage lingered on a curvy woman in black spandex and a string-strap tank top and then the view was obscured by several crowd members and the camera's eye veered into the south end of the stadium.

"Slow it down," ordered Matthias.

Ronny took it off fast forward and brought the replay down to half speed so they could get a good look at the faces that passed. On the second level, a man dressed in casual attire stood at the rail. He did not move to the rhythm of the music, instead he stood perfectly still, holding a pair of binoculars to his eyes.

"Back it up and let's take another look at this guy," said Matthias.

"It's tough to see much of him," said Mitz. "Those binoculars obscure his face."

They went through the footage frame by frame, but never did he lower the binoculars.

"Check out the crowd behind him," said Mitz. "There's two other guys dressed similarly, and they don't seem to have much interest in the music."

"They look like bodyguards," agreed Matthias. "Not too tall, maybe Asian extraction."

"I'm guessing Vietnamese, by the features," said Mitz, who had a good eye for physiognomy.

"Can you capture that image and get us prints?" asked Matthias.

Ronny flicked a couple switches on his board. "Not a problem. So it's the faces of the bodyguard dudes that you want, right?"

Matthias nodded. "Yeah, now let's see if Craigster got any other shots of this guy later on."

Ronny shifted his bulky frame and began fast forwarding the footage. Craigster, however, wasn't much interested in filming footage of a trio of men who made no reaction to the music, and continued to focus most of his camera work on nubile females of all shapes and sizes. Finally, the camera once again panned into the eastern section of the stadium and toward the second tier. There was a bright flash that lit up the stadium and the expressions amidst the crowd ranged from shocked and horrified to confused and fearful.

The man at the rail lowered his binoculars and a wicked smile spread across his broad face. His eyes were as cold as a glacier.

"Hold it right there," said Matthias.

Ronny flicked a switched and froze the image.

Matthias studied the features of the man and noted the scar on his chin. Just as the bodyguards that flanked him, he was of Vietnamese lineage. "Look at his expression. He knew the explosion was coming. He wanted to see it for himself."

"I know that face," said Mitz. "That's Quan Tang. Fritz tangled with some of his lackeys last year in Czechoslovakia—dismantled some smuggling operation that was bringing in slave labor from Vietnam. Fritz gave him that scar on his chin—sliced him with his sword."

Matthias rubbed at the stubble growing on his face. "Czechoslovakia? How did he get tangled up in that?"

"A woman," said Mitz.

"Of course," muttered Matthias. "The Achilles' heel of the Gantlet Brothers."

Mitz idly drummed out a pattern on the console with his index finger. "It wasn't like that. Her sister got snatched off the streets in Can Tho, and so Fritz went to work tracking her down."

Ronny and Jermaine exchanged glances.

Matthias gestured with his left hand. "How come I didn't know about any of this?"

"You and Blake were caught up with that Ikarian thing in California ..."

"And you just neglected to mention that Fritz took down a slaving operation?"

"Well, I helped," said Mitz. "I didn't bring it up, because it didn't end well and I didn't want to open up any wounds—"

Fritz stood at the door, the round lenses of his sunglasses pushed into the curly hair on top of his head. Leaning against the frame of the van, he looked haggard beyond his years. "He didn't want to open up any of my wounds. That's what Mitz means."

"What happened?" said Matthias.

"Quan Tang's men killed Ket Nien in retribution. Diu blamed me for her death."

"And you were seeing Diu?"

"Engaged to be married," said Fritz. "It seems I botched her rescue in more ways than one. I chopped off the tail of the snake, but I left the head—and that head turned around to bite me. If I had tracked down Quan Tang and killed him, then Otto would still be alive." He almost choked on the words that he said next, and he hung his head in misery. "It's my fault that Otto is dead."

The anguish was palpable, and Matthias could even taste the bitterness of it on his own tongue. "The blame isn't yours, brother. One man is responsible for this and we know that three hours ago he was right here in Massachusetts. Maybe we can track him down before he gets too far."

"Normally, we'd have Otto handle that end of things," said Mitz.

Matthias stood up. He knew that the best antidote for grief and self-pity was action. "I'll grab a cell phone and call Jensen. Maybe we can put the resources of the CIA to some use."

Matthias clapped his oldest brother on the back. "Come on. We'll get through this."

"It was my job to look out for him," said Fritz. "Ever since they imprisoned mother and tortured her to death, it's been my job to look out for the family—and I've failed."

Matthias embraced his brother. "No you haven't. You've been the best big brother that anyone could hope for. If not for you, we'd be rotting in an East German prison at best—or every one of us would be like Mutter und Vater."

On the tour bus, Matthias found the large cell phone on the dashboard. He dialed Jensen's number and the CIA agent answered on the fourth ring.

"Jensen here."

Matthias didn't bother with a preamble. "There's a Vietnamese crime lord named Quan Tang who attended the show tonight with two bodyguards. We need you to check for flights out of Massachusetts—possibly something connecting to Vietnam or Czechoslovakia."

"So I take it that footage turned up this piece of information?" probed Jensen.

"Yes, it did. We're done with it now. You can pick it up any time that you like."

Jensen's rough voice came through a patch of static like gravel on a washboard. "Can I reach you at this number?"

"We'll keep the phone handy," said Matthias.

"I'll have Meriweather do some checking and we'll get right back to you."

The phone went dead and Matthias set it on the alcove table. "I don't like depending on someone else for our intel."

"Especially the government," said Mitz. "It would be easy enough for them to lead us around like a cow with a ring through the nose."

Fritz said nothing, buried in his own morose thoughts.

Matthias tried to prod him out of the darkness into which he was descending. "What do you know about Quan Tang, Fritz?"

It was a few moments before Fritz spoke. "He's involved in everything from human trafficking to racketeering, extortion, theft, prostitution, and weapon smuggling. He likes to employ devotees of the Vovinam martial art as his enforcers."

"Vovinam?" asked Matthias, whose formal martial training extended only as far as Bruce Lee's Jeet Kune Do, which he found efficient and flexible.

"It is Am-Duong," muttered Fritz. "Vovinam seeks to find the balance between the negative and positive; the hard and the soft."

"The yin and yang," said Mitz.

"Correct," said Fritz. "*The iron hand over the benevolent heart* is the Vovinam salutation."

Matthias snorted. "How benevolent can they be, working for a slaver and murderer?"

Fritz picked his guitar off the stand and idly strummed a few sad chords on the unamplified strings, he wheedled a few more mournful notes from the fretboard. "The founder of Vovinam died twenty-five years ago. It does not take even a generation for a good cause to be perverted or those less principled to splinter away and seek power."

A screech of tires came to their ears and a canary yellow Ferrari 328 GTS skidded to a stop on the damp pavement in front of the tour bus. The car was built at low slung, flat angles, the rear window louvered and the ceiling panels removable. Matthias made a grab for his Desert Eagle at the sudden appearance of the vehicle, but left it in its holster when he saw Sly pile out of the driver's seat. "Where did he get that?"

"Must have gone on a shopping spree this afternoon," said Mitz. "He disappeared for a few hours."

Fritz wrenched the handle and opened the bus door for Sly, who came barreling through. "Where are we going? I can get us there fast."

"You can get two of us there fast," replied Mitz as he observed the limited seating space. "Unfortunately, we don't know where we're going yet."

Sly pounded his fist against the sheet metal wall of the bus in impotent rage, leaving behind a dent and causing himself bloody knuckles. "Give me something—just give me something ..."

Matthias knew it was a long shot, but he also knew that he needed to provide Sly's rage some sort of direction before his anger and futility exploded into a chiasma of self-destruction. "A couple of years back I picked up some LAW rockets from an ex-IRA fighter named Brannon O'Leary. He's actually quite a talker once he's had a few drinks."

Mitz raised an eyebrow. "You drank with him?"

"It didn't seem to bother him that I was drinking soda water. He had a heavy conscience and he needed to tell somebody."

Fritz bit at the inside of his cheek. "Before or after he sold you the black market Light Anti-tank Weapon?"

Matthias ignored the comment. "Back in the day, O'Leary had quite a few IRA connections. He might be worth looking up, just in case he knows something about Sorcha McDonagh and might have some way to locate her."

Sly narrowed his left eye. "And just where might I find this Brannon

O'Leary?"

"He frequents a tavern called Coogan's Bluff on Milk Street. At least, that's where I found him," said Matthias. "Buy him a couple of drinks and hear what he's got to say."

"So you're telling me the best way I can help is to go drinking? Because that's right down my alley—especially if it involves punching somebody afterwards."

Matthias grimaced. "Not exactly what I had in mind. O'Leary should be the one doing the drinking. You should be asking questions and listening."

"Milk Street, is that in Boston?"

"Yep," said Matthias. "About a half-hour drive from here."

Sly shook the blood from his knuckles. "Fifteen minutes in my Ferrari. It's time I broke that sucker in."

Fritz exchanged glances with his younger brother. "Keep an eye on him."

Mitz responded and clattered down the steps after Sly. "I'm going with you."

"Hah," laughed Sly. Given some direction, his spirits were already lifting at the prospect of some action. "I knew you couldn't resist the opportunity for a lift in my sweet ride."

Mitz pulled open the passenger door. "I'm driving on the way back."

Sly slipped into the driver's seat. "If you think I'm going to let you behind the wheel of Rosabel, you've got another thing coming."

The drummer's oversized forearm flexed as he flipped the door closed. "Rosabel, eh? You've already named your car?"

Sly patted the dash. "Rosabel's a good girl. Now let's see what she can do."

Chapter 3

In a bit over five seconds, they hit sixty miles an hour and Sly gave the wheel a spin as they went sliding out of the parking lot. They got on the Boston Providence Turnpike, blew through the intersection at Pine and raced onto I-95 in a minute flat. Sly sent the Ferrari 328 speeding down the highway, passing other cars as if they were standing still. He threaded through traffic, buffeting the other automobiles with the hurricane wake of his passing. The engine alternately whined and moaned as Sly deftly guided his vehicle, bringing it into the outskirts of Boston in nineteen minutes.

Here the traffic became denser and Sly was forced to give up his high-speed maneuvering for a more circumspect pace, which he augmented by weaving through the traffic and defying stale yellow traffic lights in sudden burst of speed which he easily coaxed from the responsive V8 engine.

He left I-95 and wheeled down the John Fitzgerald Expressway to make a quick left onto Summer, then Devonshire Street. Here the discombobulated layout of the Boston streets left Sly facing a one-way street coming the opposite direction. Instead of following traffic to the left, Sly gunned it down the one-way street from the wrong direction, causing no end to the consternation of other drivers, before turning right onto Milk Street and entering with the proper flow of traffic, horns and voices still wailing behind him.

Mitz settled back into his seat. "I'm definitely driving next time."

Sly gunned the Ferrari and slipped into a parking spot before a sports utility vehicle could parallel park into the narrow space. "You don't like the way I drive, then you can walk home."

Mitz motioned to the angry driver getting out of the SUV ahead. "It's not me that has the problem with your driving. You might want to apologize to that fellow for stealing his parking spot."

The Boston driver hurled a few choice epithets and was bracing himself to kick in the fender of the Ferrari when Sly popped open the door and stepped onto the street. The Bostonian halted, foot cocked back, when he saw the rock guitarist hoist his Schwarzeneggerian bulk out of the low-riding sports car, long blond hair falling around his cannonball deltoids, and dark beard masking his ruddy features.

A brief appraisal of his nemesis caused the Bostonian to rethink his strategy, and he retreated to the relative safety of his SUV, and quickly pulled back into traffic to seek a less contested parking space. Sly shook his scabbed fist after the fleeing driver. "Come on back and I'll serve you a helping of this!"

Mitz slammed his door shut as he joined Sly on the street. "Leave him alone. He had just as much right to this spot as you—probably more. Save that fist for Sorcha McDonagh and Quan Tang."

Sly glared at his younger brother. "Maybe it's you that needs a beat down."

"That's good," said Mitz. "You think beating up one brother will bring back the other one you lost? Get a grip."

"I've got a grip," snarled Sly, then he bowed his head to hide his emotions. "It's just ..."

Mitz clapped his arm around his brother and led him down the street, past the brick-faced shops of the financial district. "I know. I don't know what to do, either."

The lettering for Coogan's sign jutted out from the bricks of the building. The interior was smoky and strobing with multi-hued illuminations from the stage lights of the cover band. The place was mostly filled with college students taking advantage of the dollar drafts, and the incongruous appearance of the two long-haired and leather-clad rockers attracted a fair amount of attention.

Mitz sidled up to the bar. "We're sticking out like a sore thumb."

Sly's dark melancholy slipped away, replaced by a vicious grin. "Yes, yes we are."

A surly bartender appeared, speaking from behind three days of stubble. "What'll it be?"

The big guitarist lifted an eyebrow. "You got Sly Beer?"

The bartender scowled and motioned to a chalkboard that exhibited a variety of options. "This is an Irish pub. You won't find German imports here, but I've got a fine selection of Irish ales and lagers."

"Fine," said Sly. "Give me a Beamish Stout."

It was only a few moments before the bartender had a frosty bottle uncapped and on the bar in front of Sly. "And what will it be for …"

The bartender stopped short when he saw a pair of hundred-dollar bills resting on the bar, extending from beneath Mitz's hand.

"I'm looking for Brannon O'Leary. Is he in tonight?"

"Usually he's in the corner drinking himself into a stupor." The bartender deftly removed the hundreds from between the countertop and Mitz's fingers. "Not tonight, though."

This fragment of information didn't seem worth two hundred dollars to Mitz. "Any ideas where we can find him?"

"Couldn't tell you." He folded the bills between two fingers and dropped them into his shirt pocket, then jerked his head in the direction of a brunette wearing the waitress uniform of Coogan's Bluff—a white blouse and a knee-length skirt of green. "You can ask Molly. She keeps close tabs on him."

Sly leaned in toward his brother. "You just got ripped off."

Mitz scowled, mostly because he figured his brother was probably right and he shouldered his way toward the diminutive waitress, who was in the midst of taking an order and fending off the lewd comments of the frat boys she was serving. "We'll see."

Molly finished taking her order and backed away from the hand of a drunken frat boy that was reaching out to slap her posterior. Mitz caught the hand before it connected and took the index and middle fingers and bent them back, so that in less than two seconds the frat boy was on the floor, begging for Mitz to let go.

"I didn't mean anything by it!"

Mitz bent the fingers back just a bit further. "That's not what it looked like to me. Now, I'm betting that the lady would like an apology."

"I'm sorry, I'm sorry, I'm sorry!" yelped the frat boy.

Mitz relinquished his grasp and followed the waitress, who retreated to the bar and began pouring the requested drafts.

"Thanks for that," she said, "but it happens all night every night. It will help for an hour or two, but as soon as you leave it will go back to the same old groping and pinching. I've learned to fend for myself."

"Maybe it's time for a new line of work," said Mitz.

"I make a hundred plus in tips a night, plus minimum wage. You know of any other jobs that will pay as much to someone who never graduated high school?"

"Not off the top of my head," said Mitz, who withdrew a pair of hundreds, "but I can certainly make a contribution to your nightly tips if you can tell me where I can find Brannon O'Leary."

Molly tilted her head and appraised Mitz with long-lashed eyes of green. "You one of his customers?"

"I'd like to be," said Mitz. "My brother bought some merchandise from him."

Molly reached and snatched away the hundreds. She tucked them into a small pocket on the breast of her ruffled smock. "I don't know what merchandise Brannon sells, but I do know that he gives me a nice bonus anytime I take a message for him."

"I see why you don't want another job. You're making a healthy living in this dive."

She reached into the lower pouch of her smock and came out with her notebook and pencil. She licked the tip of her pencil. "Give me your phone number and I'll have Brannon give you a call."

Mitz shook his head. "I need to talk to Brannon tonight. That two yards you just tucked away was for telling me where I can find O'Leary—not for you telling him where he can find me."

Molly raised her eyebrows and taunted Mitz. "What are you going to do, drummer boy, throw me over the bar and take your two hundred dollars back if I don't come through?"

Mitz didn't rise to the bait. Obviously Molly recognized him and she had arrived at the erroneous conclusion that he would be afraid to make a public spectacle. "I had something a little less subtle in mind, but I don't think there's any need to go there, do you?"

The brunette frowned. "I suppose not, but I'm not opposed to a little rough housing now and then."

This, Mitz realized, was no less than a thinly veiled invitation—a temptation he had no intention of succumbing to. Still, if Molly thought he was amenable to her offer she might be more willing to part with Brannon O'Leary's location. "When you write me O'Leary's address, be sure to leave me your own phone number."

Molly fluttered her lashes at Mitz. She had just found her ticket out of this dive and planned to use every bit of the considerable feminine allure she possessed to make it happen. It was a part she played often in order to extract larger tips from customers, and she knew just how to turn on the charm and flirtation. She scribed an address in loose, looping cursive, wrote her name below O'Leary's address, and then added the inscription of a heart. "I hope to hear from you soon, Mr. Gantlet."

Glancing at the note just long enough to assure himself that there was indeed an address on the paper, Mitz folded it and shoved it in his jacket pocket. "Thanks, Molly."

"I get off work at 2:30," she said. "If you're done with your business ..."

"If I'm done with my business, I'll give you a call," said Mitz, who couldn't by any stretch imagine that his business would be concluded this evening.

Sly had returned to his ale while he let Mitz pump the waitress for information. His leather jacket and long blond hair made him less than inconspicuous in a tavern full of college students dressed in Izod, Calvin Klein and expensive loafers. Bravery bolstered by many shots of liquid courage, the friends of the fellow Mitz had levered to the floor made the egregious mistake of concluding that the big man at the bar might be easier prey than the drummer.

The dark-bearded guitarist downed the last of his drink when he found himself surrounded on all sides by four frat boys looking for a fight. The frat boy on Sly's left wore a BU letterman jacket with a wrestling insignia. The frat boy on Sly's right wore a baseball hat on backward and was rubbing the knuckles of his closed fist as if anticipating hitting something. Sly found two more frat boys standing behind him with their arms folded across their puffed out chests. This, Sly observed, was an intimidation tactic but also a serious error. When going into combat, never close up your hands so they couldn't be readily used.

The frat boy with the letterman jacket thrust his face into Sly's personal space. "I won first in my weight class in the CAA wrestling tournament."

"Congratulations," said Sly, his hand sliding up toward the neck of his empty ale bottle. "Now get out of my space before I wipe the floor with you and your pansy boyfriends."

The wrestler sneered. "Is that a threat?"

Sly grinned. "One last warning. Back off before things get ugly."

Coogan's bartender turned away from mixing a colorful drink with an umbrella and saw that trouble was brewing. "Leave 'em alone, Charlie. You and the boys go make trouble somewhere ..."

Before the bartender could finish his sentence, Charlie jabbed Sly hard in the chest. "Come on, hippy. I'm betting I can pin you in ten seconds flat."

"Pin this," said Sly. He swung the beer bottle, breaking it across the crown of the wrestler's head. Charlie went down bleeding and dazed.

Sly discarded the jagged neck of the bottle and hauled back to deliver a hard right to the jaw of one of the frat boys behind him. If the frat boy's arms hadn't been crossed, he would have been able to react to the assault on Charlie and either attack or defend himself, but Sly's fist broke his jaw and he went reeling into the arms of a passing sailor. The third frat boy was just untangling his folded arms when Sly hit him with a left and right combination that knocked him onto his posterior.

That was all Sly could manage before the frat boy with the backward baseball cap tackled him. Sly tripped over Charlie's fallen form, and he and his assailant went crashing onto a bar table, upsetting the table and drinks and sending a quartet of beer-spattered college students scurrying for safety. Sly found himself lying amid puddles of beer and fragments of broken glass while a college student who weighed as much as he did wailed away with both fists.

The college student, however, scored only a few glancing blows and Sly grabbed him by the sweatshirt and heaved him aside, then landed an elbow in the frat boy's windpipe that effectively ended the fight. Sly rose to his feet, brushing off the broken glass and surveying the wreckage with a grim satisfaction. He paused above Charlie, who still lay on the ground, clutching at his bleeding scalp.

"I'm kind of glad you started that," said Sly.

"Get away from me, you maniac!"

Sly professionally surveyed the wound he had inflicted. "You're going to need at least twenty stitches for that cut. Next time you better watch who you pick a fight with."

"I'm calling the police," shouted the bartender. "You and your friend better clear out of here."

Mitz ignored the bartender's warning and jerked his head in the direction of his brother's sprawled and groaning assailants. "They're just a bunch of dumb college students, Sly."

"They're bullies, and they got what was coming to them—in spades."

"The bartender is right. Explaining this to the cops will be a delay we can't afford. Let's get out of here."

Sly got a smug smile on his face. "Four to one. I'd say I have a clear cut case of self-defense."

Mitz grabbed his burly brother's arm. "But we don't have time to plead a case tonight. I've got Brannon O'Leary's address. Let's go pay him a visit."

Sly grunted his assent and followed his brother out of Coogan's Bluff and into the cool night air.

"You feel better now?"

Sly spotted the yellow Ferrari down the street and headed toward the sport's car, which was being admired by a gaggle of passersby. "I thought I would—but I don't really. Those poor suckers picked the wrong night to start a fight with me."

"As if there was ever a right night to pick a fight with you," muttered Mitz. "How are those ribs?"

"Nothing a few more drinks won't cure," said Sly.

Brannon O'Leary's apartment was three blocks over, and Mitz persuaded Sly that they should go for a walk instead of trying to find another parking place. O'Leary's apartment was at 61-63 Chatham Street in a fifth-story apartment and office building with a brick face and steep tin siding that surrounded the fifth story. A striped awning overhung the doorway and marked the address. Mitz caught the door as a resident departed and, ignoring the dirty look of the matronly resident, they moved inside—bypassing the door code that restricted entrance. They moved past a placard displaying the names of various businesses within the building and bypassed the elevator, climbing the stairs to the fifth floor.

"What are the chances that we find O'Leary home?" asked Sly. "Probably Coogan's Bluff isn't the only bar that he frequents. There's one right next door."

Mitz wasn't sure that barhopping was the best way for Sly to spend the evening. He was in a foul mood and he had a penchant for drinking too much, as it was. Already he'd been in one bar fight. In Mitz's mind's eye, he envisioned a string of bars and a wake of broken tables, bottles, and bodies. "If O'Leary's not home, we'll let ourselves in and wait for his return."

Sly tromped up the stairs. "He's Irish, right? Maybe his larder is stocked with some tasty whiskey."

"Maybe," said Mitz, but his voice was doubtful.

The hollow echo of footsteps in the cavernous shaft of the stairwell gave way to the carpeted halls of the fifth floor, which were given over to residences. Mitz checked the address that Molly had scribbled for him in looping cursive and they took a corner, halting in front of door 507. Mitz thought he scented a lingering perfume in the air, something with a slight musk and the odor of crushed flower petals. The moping wail of Thin Lizzy's "Shades of a Blue Orphanage" came filtering through the closed door."He likes Irish rock," commented Sly. "He must like Irish whiskey."

Mitz rapped four times on the door and there was the sound of movement and the tinkle of glass from within. Then a whiskey-brined voice with an Irish brogue spoke through the door. "What is it you want?"

"Molly sent me," replied Mitz.

The door came open a crack, but the chain was still attached from the frame to the slide hasp on the door. A five-day stubble stood out on Brannon O'Malley's seamed face, which had seen more than its fair share of hard living in its forty years on earth. He spoke in a low tone. "What is it ye are looking for?"

"Rocket-propelled grenades, anti-tank weaponry ..." replied Mitz. "Anything with a bit of a punch."

Mitz was not talking loudly, but O'Malley outstretched his hand and pushed it toward the floor. "Hush! First, I need credentials."

"My brother sent us," said Sly. "He's done business with you before and recommended we pay you a visit. Now why don't you invite us in and share some of that whiskey you've been hoarding."

O'Malley's eyes narrowed. "How do you know that I have any whiskey?"

"I can smell it on your breath, for one," said Mitz.

"I can see the family resemblance now," said O'Malley. "Your brother is a good man. Let me make some calls. Come back tomorrow and we'll share that drink."

"I'm thirsty now," growled Sly.

The vinyl popped and hissed and the record on the player began to play the sleepy ballad "Sarah."

Mitz reached into his jacket, slowly, so as not arouse any fear or gunfire on the part of the Irishman, and withdrew a folded piece of paper. "You can also help us with something else. Matthias told us that in the old days you had a few connections with a certain group." He unfolded the paper and revealed the black and white security camera capture of Sorcha Mc-Donagh. "Would you have any ideas to the whereabouts of this woman?"

O'Malley's eyes widened and he swallowed hard.

"You know her, don't you?" said Sly.

O'Malley stammered a response. "W-w-well, yes. She used to be my oul doll."

"Oul doll?" questioned Mitz, he was unfamiliar with the term.

"My girl," explained O'Malley, "but that was years ago. We've gone our separate ways since. I found I had a conscience and she found she didn't need one."

Sly scowled even more deeply—for he's scarcely worn any other expression since Otto had been killed. "When's the last time you saw her?"

"About a year ago," said O'Malley. "She sometimes pays me a visit when she swings through the colonies."

Sly leaned on the door frame. "I think we need to have that drink now."

O'Malley sighed and reached up to release the chain. "What has she gone and done now?"

The lights were dim and the air reeked of cigarette smoke. An open bottle of Green Spot whiskey sat on the coffee table next to a glass and an ashtray with smoldering cigarettes. Mitz thought he detected the musk of perfume mingling with the cigarette smoke, but he could not be sure.

O'Malley shut the door behind them and secured the double dead bolt. He motioned to the couches, which were sagging and threadbare. "Take a load off."

Sly surveyed the apartment. The kitchen and the living space were separated by just a counter, that was empty, but for a couple bags of partially consumed Chinese take-out, which rested next to a few copies of the *Irish Times*. A broad window overlooked the neon and amber of Chatham Street and if he craned his neck, he could even see the centuries old architecture of Faneuil Hall, where Samuel Adams rallied the citizens of Boston to the cause of independence and where George Washington raised his glass to celebrate the first birthday of the United States. "What's in the back of the apartment?"

O'Malley entered the kitchen and took down two glasses from the cupboard. "The bathroom and my bedroom. The accommodations aren't anything to write home about, but the view is deadly."

Mitz took a seat on the couch as O'Malley returned to the living room and began pouring from the bottle of Green Spot. This distracted Sly from his suspicions. "Make it a triple."

Thrusting his hand into the crack between the cushions of the couch, Mitz found a handgun shoved beneath. O'Malley was an arms dealer, so he suspected that this pistol was not the only weapon hidden about the apartment. He pulled the gun loose and found that he was holding a Belgian FN High Power that fired 9mm rounds. "What else have you got in the couch cushions?"

"You'd be surprised," said O'Malley, and he shoved a drink toward Sly.

Mitz dumped the pistol on the coffee table, still within easy reach. "Oh, I don't know. I'm not easily surprised. However, a man who can come up with a couple of LAW rockets might have an interesting thing or two stashed around the apartment."

O'Malley shifted in his seat. "A connoisseur of weapons, like yourself, would certainly appreciate some of the firearms I've collected over the years, but really I've been trying to distance myself from this sort of work."

"Selling weapons?"

O'Malley tossed back a dangerous quantity of Green Spot. "It's the quality of the clientele—and what they might do with the weapons that bothers me."

Not to be outdone, Sly guzzled down his healthy portion of Irish whiskey and slammed the empty glass on the table alongside of O'Malley's. "A conscience is a pesky thing, isn't it?"

"I think it would be easier if I could get rid of it," admitted O'Malley. "It takes a lot of whiskey to blunt its edge."

Mitz pondered the cigarette that still smoldered in the ash tray, watching smoke curling up into phantom wisps that dissipated in the twilight of the apartment. "What do your clients do with the weapons you sell them?"

O'Malley shrugged. "I find it better not to ask. Ignorance is bliss, and all that. Very few of my clients are like Matthias Gantlet and can be trusted to use them responsibly."

Mitz made a face. "I don't know if responsibly is the word."

"But he's going to use those weapons to do some good—not shoot up some innocent family in a parking lot to steal their jamjam."

"You ever thought about coming clean?" asked Mitz.

Sly clearly wasn't interested in this line of conversation. He poured himself a refill. "Call the Police" was next on the record—a more raucous and strident song than the previous. "If you were going to contact Sorcha McDonagh, where would you start?"

"Why are you looking for her?" asked O'Malley. "Has she done something?"

Sly downed another stinging slug of Green Spot and hurled the glass across the room. It shattered against the wall. Sly's face twisted in anger. "She blew up my brother. That's what she did!"

O'Malley pushed out a long breath and stared at the floor. "I've still got some acquaintances in Ireland that are involved in the IRA. She may have been in touch with one of them. Her mother lives in Belfast. That might be a good place to start."

Mitz leaned forward and plucked up the smoldering cigarette so that the lipstick stain on it was clearly visible. "You don't look like the type to be wearing lipstick, Brannon. So let's start by having you bring out the guest you're keeping hidden in your bedroom."

O'Malley spread his hands in front of him. "Honest, I didn't know she'd be coming here tonight … and I had no idea what she'd done."

At that moment the door to O'Malley's bedroom flew open and Sorcha McDonagh emerged, wearing a scoop neck top and tweed pencil skirt and holding a short-barreled Ruger revolver, which she began firing the second she could ascertain her targets.

Mitz was expecting trouble and he threw himself to the side as a .357 round skipped by, slicing through the stuffing on the couch and turning the glass in O'Malley's hand into glittering shards. As Mitz dove, he plucked the Belgian high power off the coffee table and shook loose the holster. He flipped off the safety and jacked a round into the chamber, while the red-haired assassin fired two shots into Sly's chest.

The Kevlar plates in Sly's tour jacket absorbed the velocity, so that they did not penetrate. The impact of the bullets felt like hammer blows, but instead of falling down, Sly rose to his feet, his hand emerging from beneath his coat with a .44 magnum Desert Eagle.

Sorcha's attention was diverted by the blond-haired giant that she hadn't been able to take down and she adjusted her aim to the middle of Sly's forehead. She failed to notice Mitz until it was too late. He hurled himself across the kitchen counter, scattering Chinese food, and got an arm around Sorcha's neck, pushing her head into the door frame, so that she was momentarily stunned. Her trigger finger jerked and sent a bullet through the front window, and then Mitz shook the assassin so that the pistol fell from her hands. He put the Belgian high power to her temple.

"Well, if it isn't the woman that killed my brother. You're going to answer a few questions for me."

Sorcha was still woozy from having her head slammed repeatedly into the wall, but she managed to form a few words. "Sure, I'll answer your questions."

Mitz adjusted his grip upon the Belgian high power. "Let's start with this: was it Quan Tang that hired you to kill Otto?"

Sorcha squirmed just a bit. "It seems as though you've got it all figured out, hardchaw. Why bother asking me any questions at all?"

"Then tell me this," said Mitz. "Where can we find Quan Tang?"

"That I can't help you with," said the assassin. "I'm supposed to meet with one of his intermediaries tomorrow to collect the rest of my payment. Perhaps you can come with me, and then we can put the screws to him. It shouldn't take you long to work your way up the food chain."

"Just where are you going to meet this underling?"

"Why, I'll be happy to show you," said Sorcha, "but if I tell you outright than you'll no longer need to keep me al ..."

Sly's Desert Eagle rocked in his hand and the back of Sorcha's head exploded in a gout of blood and brains. Sorcha's body fell from Mitz's arms and the drummer turned angrily upon his brother. "We needed her alive!"

Chapter 4

It was two o' clock in the morning when the call came in on Matthias's cell phone. The ringing awoke Matthias from his fitful sleep and he grabbed the brick-sized phone and answered. "This is Matthias. What have you got for me?"

"This is Jensen," came the gruff voice, "but you already knew that. Take notes, because I'm on a secure line and I'll only be able to say this once."

Matthias scrambled for a pen and flipped open a notebook of musical liner paper which contained the chord progression for a song in progress—for the best outlet and balm they had for their sorrow was the musical expression of it and they had drowned their impotent grief in a wash of mournful notes while they waited. "Go ahead."

"We've found a private jet that's scheduled to depart the Logan International Airport in about thirty-five minutes. It's registered to a French company called *Corp Internationale*, which has ties with several Czech criminal organizations. Best as we can tell the company serves to launder illegal funds by treating them as investment returns."

Matthias scrawled down the notes as fast as his fingers would allow. "Does Quan Tang's organization happen to be one of those criminal groups?"

Jensen's voice crackled over the weak connection. "Meriweather is sure of it. Whether or not this particular flight is related to Quan Tang isn't clear, but it seems a likely possibility given the circumstances."

Without hesitation, Matthias marked down the flight number and the hangar where the private Learjet was being kept. "We'll take a look."

"Make it quick," said Jensen. "I'll be turning this bit of information in to my superiors in the next couple of minutes. If they decide to act on it, and can mobilize quickly enough, you may have the CIA hot on your heels."

"Got it," said Matthias. "And, Jensen?"

"Yes?"

"Thank you. I owe you one."

"That's one debt I'll be collecting," replied Jensen, and then the phone line went dead in a burst of static.

Fritz had overheard the bulk of Matthias's conversation. He removed a gold-plated 1908 Lang pocket watch—an heirloom passed from his grandfather to his father and again to him, the oldest son—from his breast pocket, where he habitually carried it, and consulted the time. Then he fired up the tour bus. The thing was a monstrosity with turbo-charged gas engines, steel-plated walls, and bulletproof windows. It wasn't much for off the line speed, but once it built up a head of steam it was as unstoppable as a train engine. "Where are we off to, little brother?"

Matthias buckled into his seat and reached for a road map. "Logan International Airport. We've only got about thirty minutes to get there and find Hangar 614."

Fritz jammed through the gears, doing his very best to the get the incredible bulk of the tour bus rolling. "What's my best route?"

"Get on I-95 and then ride east on I-93 all the way through Chinatown."

By liberal use of the gas pedal and the horn, Fritz navigated the highway, barreling down the fast lane and shoulder—when necessary—at eighty to ninety miles an hour, which was the most he could milk out of the massive steel block V8 engine.

The Massachusetts Turnpike took them beneath the dark waters of Boston Harbor and into the ruddy light of the tunnel that passed beneath its churning surface. They looped into the airport at dangerous speeds, the bus leaning on its heavy chassis—the only thing keeping it from toppling over on its side.

Matthias pointed to an off-ramp that descended to rows of private hangars. "Take this exit."

Fritz sent the logo-emblazoned "Agents of Oblivion" tour bus hurtling down the decline and past rows of massive hangars, designed to accommodate the luxury planes of wealthy travelers. "We're not exactly inconspicuous in this."

Matthias tossed aside the map and peeled back a section of spined rubber flooring, revealing a compartment hidden beneath. "I don't know that we have time for a stealthy approach. What's your weapon of choice?"

"My weapon of choice is the *katana*," said Fritz as he watched the numbers on the hangars spin by, "but we may not get close enough for that."

Matthias withdrew a scabbarded blade from the hidden compartment where it was nestled amidst machine guns and pistols and bricks of ammunition. It was a thirty-three-inch Koyama Munetsugu *katana* forged in 1847 and of the finest workmanship. Then Matthias produced a brace of mini-UZI machine pistols. He jammed thirty-two-round magazines into the handles. The mini-UZIs were primarily intended for use with a twenty-round magazine, but at 950 rounds per minute, a magazine of twenty didn't last too long.

Neither did a magazine of thirty-two, for that matter. Matthias slid one of the UZIs onto the dash next to Fritz, adding a quartet of spare magazines should they be needed.

Fritz laid on the horn and rumbled past a pair of slow moving automobiles. "You think we'll need this much firepower?"

"A Vietnamese crime lord? He's bound to have security that is loaded for bear. Better to be over-prepared than underprepared."

"If we had a little more time we could approach this with some subtlety," said Fritz, but he shrugged on his tour jacket nonetheless.

A half mile ahead of them a Learjet eased from the brightness of a hangar and into the shadowy wilds of the night. A trio of men with flashlights waved the Lear out, streetlights gleaming against the silver skin of the sleek aircraft. Through his John Lennon glasses, Fritz could make out the insignia of Corp Internationale scribed on the tail of the plane. "That's our quarry."

"We've got him," said Matthias. "He's just starting to taxi out to the runway."

On the straightaway, Fritz brought the tour bus back up to ninety miles per hour. He pushed open the wing window on his left and the cold night air howled in. "At least it's still dark. We may be able to get close before they see it's the Gantlet Brothers tour bus bearing down on them."

Indeed, the nose of the plane had turned toward them and they came within a hundred yards before the ground crew tossed away their glowing red flashlights and began blazing away at the bus with pistol fire. Bullets pocked the windshield and ricocheted away from the armor plating and the bus rolled forward unhindered.

"One hundred thousand dollars of retro-fitting," said Fritz, "and worth every penny."

Matthias's eyes narrowed when he saw the whirling Garrett double turbines of the jet, and that it was picking up speed and on a collision course with the bus. "Do you think we can take a direct hit from a Learjet?"

"There's only one way to know for sure," said Fritz, the odds calculating in his head. He kept the tour bus on course, nose to nose with the oncoming Lear.

"There's no way it can get any sort of lift-off in a hundred yards," said Matthias, who had some experience behind the yoke of a Learjet himself. "You need at least 2,500 feet to even have a shot at it."

Fritz watched other traffic scatter onto the sloping shoulders of the road as the thirty-nine-foot wings swept toward them. "If he can make it far enough down this road, he'll have enough space."

Bulletproofing and armor aside, Matthias began to think that their chances of surviving a head on collision with the jet were minimal—but still Fritz kept dead on. "Maybe we want to rethink this."

"It's all about who loses their nerve first," said Fritz. "I'm not going to let Quan Tang fly out of here without meeting the edge of my sword."

Second by second they drew closer, but neither the pilot of the Learjet nor the driver of the tour bus budged from their disastrous course. Matthias braced himself for the impact and at the last moment the pilot of the Lear veered. Metal shrieked and moaned as the top of the tour bus sheared off the plane's left wing. The bulletproof windshield turned into a web of lines, but the buttressed frame stayed intact. However, the bus caught in the jagged metal and twisted to the side. At high speed, this was more than the heavy, and not very maneuverable, bus could take, and it flipped over on its side, spinning along the asphalt in a trail of sparks and a fury of sound.

The Learjet didn't fare much better. It left the roadway and plowed into a chain-link fence, that took off one of the fuselage-mounted engines, which continued to whirl and moan as it sucked in twigs and gravel and spat them out the other side.

Fritz was buckled in, so he survived the impact with nary a scratch. Matthias was jarred loose from the spot where had braced himself and thrown against one side of the bus before gravity and momentum took hold and slammed him into the other side of the bus. The breath was forced from his body and for a moment he lay stunned, lungs heaving as he tried to regain his air.

In a moment he found his brother peering down at him, through the round lenses of his polarized glasses. "You in one piece, Matthias?"

Matthias hoisted himself onto one elbow and found that he was still able to move. "So far so good."

Through the front window they could see the ground crew running toward the bus. They had equipped themselves with some heavier weapons now—automatic rifles, some of which might have enough velocity to penetrate the bulletproofing.

The muzzle of the first crewman's rifle flashed a staccato of light, which was accompanied by the rattle that indicated it was a 7.62-mm Soviet PK machine gun. The already damaged windshield began to cave in under the assault as the crewman chewed through a hundred-round belt, and empty brass scattered at the feet of the shooter.

Matthias hoisted himself to his feet, still hanging on to his UZI. "That window is not going to last for long."

Fritz's UZI was lost somewhere among the tumult of guitar cases and sheet music. So instead of spending precious time searching for it, he went to the still open secret compartment, walking across windows and seats to reach it in the overturned bus. Still strapped securely inside was a Swiss made SIG 710-3, one of the finest machine guns ever made—even if it was one of the least popular because of its high pricing and the severe exportation restrictions imposed upon weapons by the Swiss government. It was the most reliable of any machine gun due to its precision parts and expert design. Truly, it was a martial work of art—much like Fritz's *katana*. A case of five hundred-round belts sat next to the SIG and Fritz pried this loose so it dropped onto the windows where he stood. He erected a tripod next to the ammunition box and set the machine gun on it. "You go out the back. I'm going to provide some cover fire."

The stutter of the Soviet PK began again and the milky white windshield vibrated and danced beneath the incessant impacts of machine gun fire. While Matthias negotiated his way to the back of the bus, climbing over broken mini-amplifiers and suitcases, Fritz lay on the ground and fed the first hundred-round belt into the SIG.

A couple of Soviet rounds punched through the windshield, whistling over Fritz's head and ricocheting around the interior of the bus. That was the problem with a bulletproof bus, mused Fritz. Once a bullet made it inside it didn't want to leave. Anyhow, this was Fritz's signal to return fire and he concentrated his bullets in a small area about a foot wide, quickly clearing a firing hole, so he could see the three ground-crew members who had set up about fifty yards away. One of them was firing the Soviet PK while a second was feeding the belt in so that it wouldn't jam. The third of the ground crew was laden with a half dozen hundred-round belts and he was reloading the magazine of a Chinese-made pistol.

With fragments of bulletproof glass flying around, Fritz paused his firing so he could sight in on his targets without the interference of the muzzle flash in front of him. The ground crew wasn't interested in such matters of accuracy. They were firing blind, counting on the sheer quantity of fire power to punch through the windshield and kill anything inside of the bus. A handful more of Soviet bullets made it through the windscreen and one nicked Fritz's calf as it ricocheted around the cabin.

Fritz sighted in on the machine-gunnist and pulled the trigger. In four seconds the SIG cycled through the rest of the belt, throwing the empty brass around the cabin. When Fritz's vision cleared, he saw machine gunnist and one other of the ground crew laying dead upon the ground. The third of the ground crew fled toward the safety of the hangar, casting aside belts of ammunition as he ran.

The rock guitarist cleared the chamber and fed a second belt into his machine gun, then he carefully sighted in on the shrinking form of the fleeing ground crewman. The crewman paused just a moment to fire his Chinese-made pistol back in the direction of the bus. His shots were hurried and from a long distance and they careened off the plating of the bus, leaving scores in the paint job. Fritz almost felt bad as he squeezed off a six-round burst that leveled the last of the ground crew. Still, it wasn't tactically sound to let the gunman live. If Fritz left him alive he might return and cause trouble when they least could afford it.

While Fritz provided cover fire, Matthias kicked open the rear door of the bus and ducked behind the wall of the bus in case there were gunmen waiting for him at the rear of the bus. A couple of Soviet rounds blew through the front windshield, traversed the length of the bus and sliced past Matthias and out the back door. Then Matthias rolled through the door and onto the pavement. He regained his feet in a single movement and then ran low toward the Learjet that was still entangled with the chain-link fence.

Traffic continued to roar by on the elevated highway, though a few gawkers had pulled to the side and come to the railing to peer down at the wreckage of aircraft and tour bus below.

The hatch was opening on the far side of Learjet, and Matthias saw dark clad forms dropping into the grass. The occupants of the plane weren't waiting for the stair to lower. They knew they were easy targets if they were trapped within the jet. They immediately turned and began firing machine guns in the direction of Matthias. Bullets spattered the pavement and Matthias took refuge behind the housing of the still-spinning turbine which had been ripped from the fuselage of the Lear. It was whining so loudly that Matthias couldn't hear anything else.

From around the edge of the turbine, he saw the muzzle flash of gunfire from within the fuselage of the Lear. A trio of Quan Tang's gunmen had taken up the job of providing cover fire for the three gunmen that were advancing on him from below. Bullets pounded into the turbine housing and pelted the pavement, throwing up flecks of asphalt as they gouged holes. Matthias was effectively pinned into place, and the other gunmen would move into flanking positions and shoot him down.

.

Chapter 5

Sorcha McDonagh's body crumpled from Mitz's grasp and he wiped away the bloody gore from his face with the sleeve of his tour jacket. "What did you do that for? We needed information from her!"

Brannon O'Leary gave a strangled cry of grief and bounded toward the fallen woman. She was still beautiful from the front, despite the red blossom on her forehead. It was the back of her skull that was a ghastly ruin of bone and brain. He cradled her and moaned. "It wasn't much … but she was all I had."

Mitz fixed his brother in his gaze. Sly still held the smoking .44 in his grip. "I had her dead to rights. Why did you shoot her?"

Sly raised his eyebrows. "She killed Otto. Isn't that reason enough?"

"Maybe," raged Mitz, "but did you have to blow her brains out when you could have just as easily hit me?"

"Check her left hand," said Sly. "I thought she was making a move for something."

"Something?"

Mitz crouched alongside of Brannon who rocked back and forth with the ghastly form of his erstwhile girlfriend in his arms. There on the floor, by Sorcha's left hand, was a stiletto dagger. Mitz picked it up. In expert hands it could make short work of a man, and in the dim light he could make out a sticky substance that was spread on its razor surface. "It's poisoned."

O'Leary broke out of his grief long enough to speak a coherent sentence, though it was still garbled in grief. "She had a fancy for fly agaric—red mushrooms that are hallucinogens. She said that six milligrams of muscimol extract from the mushroom would cause a man to go into seizure."

Mitz saw the sheath for the knife protruding from beneath McDonagh's tweed pencil skirt and he unstrapped it, then carefully pushed the poisoned blade back into its scabbard where it could do no harm. "I'm sorry, Sly. I shouldn't have doubted you."

"Not a problem, Mitko. Now go get yourself cleaned up."

When Mitz disappeared into the bathroom, Sly pulled up a chair across from O'Leary. "You wouldn't know it, but my brother's a bit of a softy—but you and me, we're going to have a heart to heart."

"I don't blame you," choked O'Leary. "I knew what sort of things she was involved in. She had no conscience and sometimes it seemed as though she had no heart—but still I loved her. Sorcha would never say when she was coming, she'd just show up two or three times a year and we'd pick up where we left off ..."

"So you're telling me that you know absolutely nothing about her employer—the man who hired her to kill my brother?"

O'Leary shook his head. "Sorcha already told you more than I knew. Except, she did mention she was going to be checking out 'giant baby heads' tomorrow."

"What?"

O'Leary shrugged. "That's what I said, but she said that some people consider it fine art."

Sly slapped the barrel of his Desert Eagle in his palm. "That's it?"

"I swear, that's all I know."

Sly glared at the Irishman. "If I find out that you've been lying to me, I'll hunt you down and kill you."

"You'd be doing me a favor," replied O'Leary.

Chapter 6

Matthias crouched down behind the turbine, while a storm of bullets rattled against the casing. He dropped the magazine from the handle of his UZI and pocketed it for future use. Instead, he fitted a specially packed magazine that alternated with steel-jacketed armor piercing and incendiary bullets, which were loaded with nitrocellulose and a small steel ball to ensure ignition. From his own experiences flying the 36A model of the Lear, Matthias knew that it carried 2,500 pounds of fuel between its wing and fuselage tanks.

The fuselage tanks were four blisters located at the aft of the fuselage, and so when Matthias came around the opposite corner of the turbine, where he could shoot without being in the line of fire of the occupants of the jet, this was the area he targeted. It took him three seconds to empty his magazine into the blisters and the aft of the Lear erupted into a fiery ball that ripped apart the skin of the jet and sent flaming shrapnel flying in all directions. All that was left was the cockpit, which flipped forward on the fulcrum of its landing gear. The cockpit crumpled and flame licked along its belly, while black smoke belched from the superheated inferno of the jet fuel.

Everything within a radius of thirty yards was scorched black. The grass that had been growing at the roadside was nothing but ash and scorched earth, and through the drifting clouds of smoke Matthias could see the scorched bodies of the gunmen that had been fanning out from beneath the belly of the Lear. They hadn't gotten far enough.

Matthias backed away from the turbine as he saw the wind shift and send flame in the direction of fuel that had been spilled on the roadway when Fritz had clipped off the larboard wing of the Lear. He retreated to the bus in just the nick of time, because flame sprang up and raced along the roadway, then burst up around the turbine where Matthias had been hiding.

Fritz kicked out the windshield of the bus and emerged, carrying the Swiss SIG, a fresh hundred-round belt in the feeder and the other end dragging along the ground. He gave way as he felt the heat of the inferno against his face. "You get all of them, Matthias?"

The vocalist's face was grim, his eyes slitted against the blazing light and the stinging smoke. "I think so, but it's hard to be sure."

Fritz went belly down on the pavement, the tripod of the machine gun in front of him while he sighted through the flame, searching for any sign of movement among the raging flame. "Your penchant for blowing things up is going to get you in trouble someday, *kleiner bruder*."

Matthias jacked a fresh magazine into his UZI. "It saved my life today. They had me pinned and in a few moments they would have had me flanked, too."

The brick phone began ringing from somewhere inside the battered tour bus. "I'll get that," said Matthias. He disappeared inside the bullet-scored interior and came out two minutes later.

After fruitlessly searching for any sign of movement among the wreckage, Fritz glanced back. "Was that Sheila looking for her hubby? Wasn't she coming into town?"

"No, it was Mitz. Seems that he and Sly tracked down Sorcha Mc-Donagh."

"And?"

"Sly shot her in the head."

"I'll be curious to see how the CIA covers this one up," said Fritz.

Chapter 7

Morning light was barely seeping over the horizon when a knock came at the door of the penthouse suite of the Black Cemetery Apartments—an exclusive Boston hotel which catered to the celebrity and the wealthy, and was not even known to exist by all but a select few. The Black Cemetery Apartments had a reputation for discretion and went to great measures to protect the privacy of their clients. Some guests may have found it distasteful that the slate walls and gothic windows of the hotel overlooked a graveyard, but for others it was part of the morbid appeal. Besides, there were plenty of amenities and activities, which did not depend upon gazing through those tinted windows.

Fritz sat on the ground in the wide vestibule of the hotel room, feet tucked beneath him and sword at his waist. The moment the knock came at the door he commenced the Seitei kata of the venerable sword art of Iaido. The kata was designed for two opponents sitting and facing each other and Fritz rose to his knees even as his *katana* leapt from its sheath, delivering a slice across the temple of his imaginary opponent. This was followed by an immediate downstroke meant to cleave the crown of his enemy. He rose to his feet, and completed his kata, finally sheathing the sword blade.

When he answered the door, he found the concierge—a sharp-eyed man in his seventies—of the Black Cemetery holding a copy of the Boston Globe. "Sir, as you requested."

"Thank you ..."

"Arturo Sippo, but most everybody calls me Doc."

"Are you a medical doctor?" asked Fritz.

"I am," replied the concierge. "In fact, I once extracted a bullet from Keith Moon's posterior in this very chamber."

"Why not do it at the hospital?" asked Fritz, but he suspected he already knew the answer.

"Because of the circumstances it had to be done quite discreetly. I wouldn't even mention it now, were you not a man of discretion—and if Mr. Moon wasn't long dead, may the Lord rest his wild soul."

"So you've been concierge at the Black Cemetery for quite some time."

"Thirty-one years, and it was quite by accident that I fell into the job. I've seen all kinds of saturnalia and strangeness during those thirty-one years. Now, if you need anything else, please don't hesitate to ring me. Locating a Boston Globe requires only a brisk walk to the corner newsstand. Next time, perhaps, you'll think of something more challenging."

Fritz watched the concierge retreat down the wide corridors which were flanked with shielded sconces. "I'll work on that."

Matthias was awake and trying to shake a headache brought on by his ringing ears. He pressed a mug of hot chocolate to his temple, while he drowned among the leather-clad cushions of a recliner. He grunted when Fritz dropped the Boston Globe on the table in front of him. The headline read: Faulty Fuel Line Causes Jet Explosion.

Matthias raised an eyebrow. "Learjet Corporation is going to love that. Their stock must be plummeting."

"Dropped five dollars already," said Fritz. "I was on the phone to the Benny this morning and had him divest all of our Learjet stock before the news got out."

"How did you know what angle the CIA was going to take on this?"

"I didn't," said Fritz. "But anytime a plane explodes it doesn't reflect well upon the manufacturers—no matter the real reason."

"You mean, getting hit by a tour bus and taking thirty-two rounds of armor piercing and incendiary rounds in the fuselage tanks."

Fritz produced a paper bag. "Bagels and lox? I've got some orange juice in the fridge."

Matthias found that he was ravenous, and eagerly helped himself. "Thanks, I hadn't gotten around to ordering up room service. Still thinking about Otto."

"That pain isn't going to go away any time soon," said Fritz, his own gray eyes haunted by the too fresh memories. It seemed like a nightmare, except he knew that there was no waking up from the horror. This he was sure of, for he'd seen far too much horror with his own eyes.

Matthias started to speak, but broke off. "Do you think …"

Fritz reached for his guitar case and unlatched it. "Do I think what?"

"Do you think this is it—or is there some other existence after this life?"

Fritz fiddled with the tuning knobs of his Fender guitar, bringing the strings into tune. "Maybe … or maybe we live on in the memories of people that knew us, or through our music."

Matthias gnawed on a bite of bagel. "That's not what I'm talking about. Sure, that would be nice to be remembered by historians or musicians a hundred years from now, but are we just wiped out of existence once our bodies are destroyed or do we actually have a soul of some sort?"

"Mom was secretly a Protestant," said Fritz. "She used to read her Bible after we went to bed, but she couldn't say much. The East German government officially endorsed scientific-atheism and since Dad was an ambassador, she couldn't risk church attendance."

"So she thought that each human had a soul and that soul could be saved?"

Fritz nodded. "Through the redemption of Christ."

"And what do you think?"

Fritz gently strummed his guitar. "I'd like it be true. I'd give anything to see Otto again."

Matthias pulled himself forward, his forearms resting on his knees, his head bowed and his long hair shielding his features. "Me, too—but if each person has an eternal soul, how many people have I sent to an eternal hell?"

"A lot, but I'm no priest," said Fritz. "I know the sword and the guitar, and neither one of those will bring salvation."

"Maybe damnation, though. Live by the sword and die by the sword, right?" Matthias rose, temporarily shoving aside thoughts of eternity. "Does the article mention us?"

"The plane struck our empty tour bus while it was taxiing to the run-way—according to the paper."

"Before or after the fuel line malfunction?"

"The article isn't really clear on that point."

Matthias gave a rueful smile. "Of course not. What about *Corp Internationale*? Won't they refute the reports?"

Fritz noodled out a lead melody on the fretboard of the Fender. "Ha! Not likely. They're a money laundering front for various criminal organizations. Do you think they'll come out and announce that it was actually the Gantlet Brothers that blew up their plane to kill an international slave trader that was fleeing the country?"

"No," said Matthias, chagrined that he hadn't thought this line of reasoning through before speaking the question. "There were some eyewitnesses, though."

"Not unlikely," agreed Fritz.

"No, I actually saw two people standing at the rail of the elevated road. They pulled over and were watching."

"I wonder if Jensen knows about that," mused Fritz.

The battered, but still functioning, brick phone rang and the rock vocalist picked it up. "Matthias here."

Jensen's gravelly voice came across the connection. "We've had our men combing through the wreckage of the *Corp Internationale* Learjet. Couldn't you have taken care of things a little more quietly? My superiors are extremely unhappy about the large mess you left."

"They had me pinned down," said Matthias. "I didn't have much choice in the matter."

Jensen sighed. "That seems to be the excuse every time."

"It was effective, wasn't it?"

"If you were trying to get attention, yes," replied Jensen. "If you were trying to get Quan Tang, then not so much."

Matthias sat bolt upright. "What are you saying?"

"I'm saying that Quan Tang wasn't in the wreckage. We identified seven bodies—all known henchmen of Quan Tang—but no Quan Tang."

Matthias pushed back his tangled hair. "So where is he?"

"That seems to the question of the day. The pilot of the Lear was still alive, but trapped in the cockpit, when we arrived —a fellow named Asante Gille who's on the payroll of *Corp Internationale*. Turns out that he's also known as Jerard Jupin, and used to make flights into Colombia for the Sinoloa cartel until he beat a local woman to death and decided a change of identity might be wise."

"Did he know anything about Quan Tang?"

"It seems that Quan Tang received a phone call and, after that phone call, insisted on a change in plans. He sent all but two of his henchmen home without him, on the plane you blew up, and he said he would arrange for some other transportation home."

"So he still may be in the United States," concluded Matthias.

"It's likely … unless he already had a second plane standing by as a contingency."

Fritz had ceased strumming the guitar and was alongside of Matthias so that he could hear Jensen's voice. "Quan Tang is a sharp fellow. I wouldn't be surprised if he did have a second plane standing by, or maybe a flight booked under an alternative identity."

"Was that Fritz?" asked Jensen.

"Recognize the accent?" chuckled Matthias. "It's more deeply ingrained in him than the rest of us."

"I'm proud of my accent," protested Fritz.

"Let Fritz know that we've got the CIA checking the identities of foriegn travelers. At any rate, it's likely out of our hands now. We'd need presidential approval to go after Quan Tang in Czechoslovakia. It could happen, but in order to even make the case it will take some time to cross all the t's and dot all the i's."

"Got it," said Matthias. "We appreciate all your help."

"You'd better," said Jensen. "I'm taking a lot of heat for this Learjet incident."

"Do you know there were a couple of witnesses on the elevated road-way that were watching over the rail?"

Jensen muttered an imprecation under his breath and drawled out an answer. "No. Who were they?"

"They had their Ford Explorer pulled over to the side. I think it was a man and a woman, but it was dark and I was a bit preoccupied."

"We'll put a call out for witnesses and swear them to secrecy," said Jensen. "We'll tell them it's a matter of national security or some such thing."

"One other thing," said Matthias.

"What now? You've got some other hole to poke in my boat?"

Matthias did not smile. "You do have a leak. Who besides us knew that Quan Tang had a private jet standing by to take him out of the country?"

Jensen's voice was hard and Matthias could tell that Jensen didn't like what he'd just said. "Just a handful of intelligence guys. I can follow the chain of hands through which the information was passed, but why don't you take a look at your own end? I'm working with good men who have all passed extensive background checks. You're the one who's got an ex-drug dealer and killer on the payroll. Why don't you take a hard look at him before you start pointing any fingers in my direction?"

"He's come clean," said Matthias. "I trust him enough that I have him watching my wife and kids."

"A tiger doesn't change its stripes," said Jensen. "His phone logs show he's been talking with some old drug associates." The phone went dead.

Matthias dropped the cell phone onto the side table and scowled.

"I didn't catch that last part," said Fritz.

"Jensen thinks Blake tipped off Quan Tang that we were going to be coming for him."

Fritz raised a bushy eyebrow. "Hawkins? What do you think?"

"Ever since Blake and I had it out on the beach during that Ikarian mess, he's had my back and he's played completely straight with me and everyone else. I think he's clean."

"But?"

"But Jensen is right. Compared to a bunch of squeaky clean CIA agents, Blake does look like the most obvious suspect."

Chapter 8

The Boston Museum of Fine Arts was located across the Back Bay Fens from the War Memorial and on the corner of Fenway and Forsythe Way. Constructed with Greco-Roman architecture as inspiration, a pillared terrace met a broad stair which was flanked on either side by a massive child's head that protruded weirdly from the closely-cropped turf.

Mitz idly tapped a drumbeat on the dashboard of the Chevy Silverado. They had traded down from the Ferrari, for a less attention-drawing vehicle. The Silverado didn't have the off-line capability or speed of a Ferrari, but a truck was fairly inconspicuous. "I wonder what the sculptor was on when he came up with that bizarre idea."

Sly peered through a pair of binoculars at a curvaceous redhead in sunglasses that loitered near the giant head on the south side of the steps. "You've read some of Matthias's lyrics, right?"

"Well, of course." Mitz studied the foot traffic coming up the walk. It was mostly families and couples, young mothers pushing strollers and retired couples enjoying the sunlight.

Sly adjusted the binoculars and studied the line of people filtering into the museum. "No, I mean the stuff that doesn't make the cut. Strange stuff. Proof that there are no drugs required for weirdness."

"But you and I both know plenty of bands whose weirdness is drug-derived. What about the guys from Condemner and their whole Satan worshiping schtick?" contested Mitz.

Sly wasn't ready to concede the point. "They were weird to begin with. The drugs just augment their natural weirdness—and I'm not convinced the Satan worshiping thing is a schtick."

"Legion Tate seems okay," said Mitz, referencing the band's guitar player.

"Yeah, but even he's messed up. Did you know he spent some time in Frankham Mental Institution? And he's gone into self-imposed exile for the last couple of years."

"That hard-core place in Switzerland where they sent that Calvin Klein model after she stabbed herself in the wrist with a dinner fork?"

"That's the place." Sly shifted his binoculars as a slight Vietnamese woman pushed a stroller across the grass and knelt down to attend to her baby next to the redhead who stood at the oversized features of the brass infant. The Vietnamese woman set her diaper bag on the ground next to the stroller and through the binoculars Sly could see her mouth moving, even though she was faced away from the redhead. "They're speaking."

Mitz reached forward and adjusted the receiver he had wired beneath the dash. He turned up the volume and they could hear the two women.

"My employer isn't pleased," said the Vietnamese mother as she adjusted the blanket. "You were contracted to plant enough explosive to kill all five of the Gantlet Brothers."

"Holy crap," murmured Mitz. "We guessed it right and the contact is falling for it."

The redhead leaned against the sculpture. "There was a problem with the remote trigger. They were in position when we triggered the remote, but some stage equipment interfered with the frequency."

"My employer has provided one-fifth of the contracted price. It's in the diaper bag. I'll leave it when I go."

"And the rest of my payment?" inquired the redhead.

"Kill more Gantlet Brothers if you want the remainder of the money."

The redhead's hand wandered to her purse. Sly knew that she kept a snub-nosed .38 Colt revolver with a threaded barrel in the outside pocket. "Is this coming from you or is it coming from Quan Tang?"

For a moment the Vietnamese mother lost her composure. She glanced sharply behind her, before returning her attention to the infant in the stroller. "It's coming from Quan Tang. He won't be pleased to learn that you know his identity."

"It helps to know the identity of my clients in the case that they fail to pay me. Then I make an example of them."

"Are you threatening Quan Tang?"

"Nothing of the sort," replied the redhead. "I killed only one of the Gantlet Brothers, so fair recompense is one-fifth the contracted price for killing all five."

The mother fussed with her baby's covers. "You seem reasonable about this."

"You've got to be in this line of business," said the redhead. "You've also got to be persistent. How do I get a hold of you when I kill the rest of the Gantlet Brothers?"

The mother removed a card from her purse, which was slung across the handles of the stroller. She shoved this into the pocket of the diaper bag. "Contact the man on that card and he'll know how to get the message to your employer."

"So it's back to calling Mr. Tang my employer, is it?"

The Vietnamese woman rose and faced the redhead, her eyes hard beneath the veil of her lashes, and her mouth set tightly. "We're in a public place, Mrs. McDonagh. Do you like it when I use your name?"

"Point taken," said the redhead. "I'll be in touch, after I've killed another or all of the Gantlet Brothers."

"Despite your failures, our employer was quite entertained to see Otto Gantlet splattered across the stadium. He appreciates your work. It just needs to be more encompassing." The Vietnamese mother pushed the stroller through the crowds and headed north on Forsythe.

Sly opened the door of the Silverado. "I'm going to kill her."

Mitz put his hand on Sly's wrist before it left the steering wheel. "You think she won't be watching to see if someone is following her? You're going to stick out of the crowd like a white guy at a Black Panther rally."

"I don't care if she sees me coming," said Sly. "No one talks about my brother like that!"

"What about the baby? You going to shoot her down while she's strolling her baby down the street? We've got a contact point," said Mitz. "It's not her that we want. Besides, it looks like that redhead is intending to collect on a bounty for two more of the Gantlet Brothers." He jerked his thumb into the street. The redhead was striding toward them, diaper bag slung over her shoulder and legs moving at a brisk pace, her hand thrust into the pocket of her purse.

Mitz opened the door and stepped out. The redhead brushed by him with just a glance and climbed into the cab of the truck. As the drummer climbed back onto the seat beside her, she ripped off her red wig, revealing the glossy mane of black hair pinned beneath, and shoved it into her purse. "I hate that thing, it itches like crazy."

"I don't know, Sheila," confessed Sly. "I kind of like it."

"You got a thing for redheads, too?" asked Sheila. "Have I mentioned that I'm the jealous type? Because I know where you live and I've got a collection of very sharp knives."

"Yes, I know," said Sly. "They're underneath the bed next to your Mossberg and a brace of gold-plated Desert Eagles that belong to me."

"Share and share alike—isn't that part of being married?"

"I'm only into redheads when you're the redhead," said Sly, "just so you know."

"That's not what I've heard." Sheila disconnected the miniature lapel mike and transmitter that had been hidden in her blouse and dropped them into the empty ash tray. "It seems to me that you've always had a weakness for redheads."

"I don't think it's just redheads," said Mitz.

Sheila turned her sloe eyes upon the blonde-haired drummer and graced him with a withering glance. "Did I ask for your input?"

Sly raised his hands in surrender. "I don't know what you're talking about."

"Let me refresh your memory," said Sheila. "Perhaps you recall a certain strawberry blonde Russian belly dancer that lured you into an alley in Egypt?"

Mitz stroked his chin. "Really! I haven't heard this story."

"But, but only Matthias knew about that," protested Sly.

Sheila gave a smug smile. "And he's normally so tight-lipped that you thought the story would stay a secret forever, didn't you?"

Clearly Sheila had her husband on the ropes. "Well, yeah," he answered.

"Did you forget that you're married to a woman who has been trained in interrogation techniques by John Velvet, director of the American Intelligence Machine, and spent years undercover perfecting my craft?"

Sly raised an eyebrow. "You tortured Matthias?"

"No, Sly. You see, he trusts me and I started asking him questions about various adventures you and he had. Pretty soon I had him painted into a corner and he had nowhere to go, but to tell me just how it was you managed to get yourself surrounded and weaponless in a rat-infested alley."

"That was years ago," protested Sly. "I only have eyes for you now."

Sheila grinned. "I do love to see you squirm. Now let's see what we've got in this bag."

Sly fired up the Silverado's engine. "Let's go after the woman. I think we can get her to talk."

"What about the baby?" repeated Mitz.

"There is no baby," said Sheila. "She had one of those hideous Cabbage Patch Dolls wrapped up in a blanket."

Sly pulled a screeching U-turn to go after the faux-mother.

"Leave her alone," said Sheila. "She bought into my cover identity hook, line, and sinker. We've got the contact that we need. If she fails to return they'll know something is wrong and close-up shop before we can make our move."

Horns honked and driver's gestured rudely in Sly's direction. He ignored them and continued down the street. However, he turned right on Fenway instead of following the Vietnamese contact. He could see her as she folded her stroller, Cabbage Patch Doll still inside, and dumped it into a shrub. In quick, smooth movements she stripped off her jacket, reversing it so that the color was a day-glo orange instead of the muted brown which she had worn when she encountered Sheila. She pulled on a knit beanie cap of equally outrageous coloration and continued down the street, scarcely breaking her stride as she accomplished this transformation.

"She's paranoid," observed Sheila. "We'd never be ever to trail her without her noticing."

"Are you kidding?" said Sly. "With that getup she changed into, satellites could pick her up from outer space!"

"Would you have known it was her, if you hadn't caught her in mid-change?" asked Sheila.

"Maybe," said Sly, and despite his desire to trail the messenger he continued down Fenway in the opposite direction. "You sure that she didn't pass off a bomb instead of a cash payment?"

"No," said Sheila. She reached under her jacket and a three-inch curved blade appeared in her hand. She ran the sharp tip along the seam of the bag, slitting open the side instead of opening it from the top. Amidst diapers and baby clothing of disparate sizes she found ten packs of well-worn hundred-dollar bills. There was no sign of any explosive. "We're safe."

Mitz rifled through one of the stacks. "Looks like real currency—roughly a thousand bills per stack."

With mercenary precision, Sly figured the payout. "That's a million bucks. Our Cabbage Patch mother said Sorcha was getting a fifth of the payout she had been contracted for. That means that Quan Tang was paying out a million for each of us." Sly's face twisted in grief as thoughts of Otto settled upon him in a dark cloud.

"Quan Tang must really want us dead," said Mitz.

"Why so much?" asked Sly, still deep in his grief. "There's any number of cutthroats who would attempt the job for a lot less."

Sheila put her comforting hand on her husband's knee. "Quan Tang was paying that much for a whole team of assassins. The payout got bigger for Sorcha McDonagh when she was the only one coming forward for payment."

"The payout got bigger for the fake Sorcha McDonagh," observed Sly. "I wonder why the other assassin and the blonde chick, Killingsworth, hasn't laid claim on the payment."

"Maybe she's lying low," suggested Sheila, "or maybe she doesn't feel she's earned her money, yet."

"Yeah, right," snorted Sly.

Mitz plucked the protruding business card from Sheila's breast pocket, and examined the embossed ridges and ornate patterns. "Thinh Dai Leathery: Custom apparel. Thinh Dai, Proprietor."

"We've got a couple of ways that we can go about this," said Sheila. "We can fake your death ..."

"Fake my death?" said Mitz. "Why my death?"

Sheila waved away the drummer's objection. "It's not important whose death we fake as long as it's one of you brothers. The important part is that Thinh Dai believes that Sorcha McDonagh has killed another of the Gantlet Brothers. If he believes that, he may let his guard down."

Sly hunched over, his massive arms draped over the steering wheel. "Where is this leathery?"

Mitz examined the card. "Utica Street. I believe that's east of Chinatown."

The dark-bearded brother tromped on the gas and the engine roared as they barreled through traffic.

"Or," said Sheila, "we can just smash down the door—guns blazing—and see if we can intimidate Thinh Dai into telling us what we want to know."

Chapter 9

It was a three-hour flight from Boston to the Fort Lauderdale International Airport, but Matthias didn't bother bringing his Bell 222 into the airport. Instead, he continued toward a gleaming twenty-three-story building that thrust up along the beach front, and brought the copter down upon the concrete heli-pad which stretched out on the highest portion of the building. Matthias shut down the systems, but the overhead blades continued to whirl, whipping his dark mane into a tangle as he made his way to the edge of the heli-pad that overlooked a sparkling swimming pool which was shaped in a stylized G.

This was the Gantlet penthouse apartment that spanned the width and breadth of the Croxton Building. After an unfortunate helicopter attack, the place had been fortified with sheaths of steel and six-inch-thick polarizing bulletproof windows. Once the brothers had shared the spacious penthouse, but eventually it became obvious that they each needed their own distinct and separate space, especially after the close proximity of being on the road. So the apartment had become a catch-all—a place to crash if needed, a place to store automobiles, band gear, and guitars, and a place for Mitz to hold an occasional soiree.

Now, with its reinforced concrete walls, ceiling, and floor, it seemed like the ideal place for Matthias's family to take refuge from danger. The downside to the penthouse was that it was well known, but Matthias felt that its fortifications more than made up for its notoriety. Still, each time he was here he couldn't help but remember the night a stolen military Sikorsky had lifted from beneath the concealing face of the Croxton Building and unleashed havoc and death with triple M60 machine guns. That was the night Arabella VanSciver died in his arms. She was beautiful, utterly charming, and oh so vain. Though, in retrospect, Matthias could see what a mistake it would have been to marry the socialite, that her life had been snuffed out in her prime—before age and wisdom could polish the rough edges of her character—seemed unfair and arbitrary.

Matthias climbed down a steel ladder and onto the pool deck. Here, the windows were polarized, and the only thing he could see was his reflection—a hard-faced man with a long brown mane that was singed around the edges. Is this what he was to become? A man drowning in the sorrows of bitter losses and mistakes that cost the lives of others? Would his wife and children end up paying for all the blood that he had spilt?

Shielding the number pad with his body, so that no telephoto lenses from nearby buildings could discern the combination, he punched in an alphanumeric code on the pad alongside the sliding doors. The doors slipped open, hidden machinery humming. As the door slipped open, it revealed the steel frame which was lagged with three-foot bolts into the concrete above and below. Matthias shoved his bulletproof Gargoyle glasses onto the top of his head and entered the cool interior of the penthouse, his eyes adjusting to the dimness.

A deep voice rumbled out of the darkness. "Hold it right there, sucker—unless you want a forty-five-caliber lobotomy."

Matthias couldn't help but break a smile. "That's supposed to be my line, Blake."

A hulking form emerged from the darkness, head shaven except for a Mohawk stripe down the center. Blake was holding .44 magnum Smith and Wesson revolver with gilded inlays in the form of a dragon, which he didn't yet lower. He glanced suspiciously behind Matthias as if assassins might swarm through behind him. "I came up with that line, that night we were hanging with that cat named Dillon."

"Uh uh, it was me. Remember, you were the one competing with Dillon to see who could crush the most empty beer cans flat in sixty seconds."

"How were we crushing them?" asked Blake.

Matthias made no sudden movement. "With the palm of your hands."

Blake still did not lower his gold-plated Smith and Wesson. "And?"

"To make your point, you smashed the last one with your forehead."

The six-inch-thick blast-resist door closed behind Matthias. Blake released a blast of pent air from his cavernous lungs and lowered the golden

.45. "It's a good thing I've sworn off drinking, or I never would have been able to beat that cat."

"You had a half bottle of Demerara edge."

"That's right! That's what I like about you, Matthias. Clean living gives you that edge—and now I've got the edge, too."

The voices in Matthias's head kept whispering suspicions to him. Who was it that had tipped off Quan Tang that he and Fritz were intercepting the Learjet? "What was with the fifth degree?"

"I wasn't expecting you so soon. I was worried that someone forced you to open up the penthouse at gunpoint. Figured you'd tip me off during the questions, if that was the case."

"Where's Courtney and the kids?"

"I've got them in the vault. Put 'em there when I heard the helicopter coming in." He paused. "They're just fine, but they're worried sick about you. Did you track down Quan Tang?"

Matthias scowled. "No, somebody tipped him off that we were coming. He wasn't on the Learjet."

The hint of a grin twisted Blake's broad face "Would this happen to be the same Learjet that had a fuel leak in Boston and mysteriously blew up before reaching the runway?"

"One and the same," said Matthias.

"So who do you think leaked the information?"

"I think that somebody in the CIA told Quan Tang that we were coming. Jensen thinks it was you."

Blake reversed the grip on his dragon-engraved Smith and Wesson and slapped it into Matthias's palm, the barrel pointing in the giant black man's direction. "And you thought enough of Jensen's suspicions that you gave off chasing the man who killed your brother to come down here and check on me?" He jabbed a finger at his temple. "If you don't trust me, then put a bullet here—right now! I won't stop you. The friendship—and trust—of you and your family means everything to me. It was the only thing besides Vera that pulled me out of my spiral of destruction, made me a better man. If you can't trust me, then finish it now."

Matthias turned the pistol and put it back in Blake's hand. "I trust you, Blake—but you've got to come completely clean with me. Why have you been contacting some of your old associates? I thought you'd left that behind."

"So did I," said Blake, "but I can't seem to leave my conscience behind. The men I killed when I was carving out my drug empire were no-good lowlifes like me—and a lot of 'em worse than me. The world was a better place without 'em, but I started to think about all the people whose lives were ruined by the cocaine and crack that I was selling them. I made a fortune off their misery and pain. I know there's nothing I can accomplish that will undo all of that, but I've been talking to a few associates that have reformed."

"What are they up to now?"

"They're putting together some rehab clinics and I've been funding them."

Matthias shucked his heavy jacket, revealing the massive 454 Casull that was holstered beneath. "So why keep all this a secret?"

"Because I'm embarrassed, Matthias. Anna and Jacobbe actually look up to me. Your kids actually think I'm something. What if they knew the real me?"

"Why keep it a secret from me and Courtney?"

"And let you know that guilt is eating me up from the inside? Have you wonder if I can cope with the job of protecting your family?"

Matthias clapped Blake on the shoulder. "I'm sorry I ever doubted you."

"Nah, it's my fault. I should have known better than to keep any secrets from you."

They headed deeper into penthouse, climbing out of the sunken living room, past the granite countertops of the chef's kitchen, where Fritz liked to work his culinary magic, and down a corridor emblazoned with posters and artwork from various Gantlet Brothers tours, and rows of framed platinum albums. At the center of the penthouse was a large recreation room with a full-sized pool table, foosball and air hockey tables, and a complete Olympic gymnasium with punching bag and sparring floor. A niche at the back of the gymnasium contained shelves filled with boxing gloves, medicine balls, and other workout paraphernalia. Matthias flipped open a hatch that was cleverly disguised to look like part of the molding. He pressed his index finger against a scanner and then punched in a different alphanumeric code than the one he had used to enter the penthouse.

A section of wall slid away, revealing a six-inch steel plate and a large armory which was concealed within the vault. The scent of oil and gunpowder filled Matthias's nostrils. Bricks of ammunition were stacked high against the wall and pistols, rifles, and machine guns from dozens of different countries were slotted into built-in racks. Additionally, there were shelves of food supplies, water, a range, and a microwave.

"I still can't believe the stuff you've got in here," said Blake.

"It never hurts to be prepared," replied Matthias. "You never know when a million rounds of ammunition might come in handy."

It was not the weapons or ammunition, however, that Matthias was interested in. A beautiful woman with raven hair sat at the table in the center of the room, a mini-UZI submachine gun clutched in her hands. Hiding behind her were a pair of similarly dark-haired children—a boy and a girl of three and four years of age. Matthias smiled when he saw them, and the dark-haired woman set aside the UZI on a high rack and ran to greet her husband. She ran into Matthias's open arms and he held her closely, wrapping his arms around her lithe waist, while she clutched him tightly.

"I heard about Otto," she whispered in his ear. "I'm so sorry."

"Do the kids know?" asked Matthias.

Courtney nodded.

"How did they take it?"

"Not well. Anna's been crying for hours. It was only a few minutes ago that I was able to distract her with a game of Connect Four. I've been letting her win."

"She doesn't like to lose," commented Matthias. "I can't figure out where she gets her competitive streak from ..."

Courtney gave her husband a squeeze. She was a two time Ms. Fitness champion, but had finally abandoned the competitions when it became clear that the judges were leaning more and more toward freakish muscularity than feminine symmetry. "Why, I don't know what you're talking about, Matthias."

Anna and Jacobbe, both named after Matthias's deceased parents, shrieked in happiness when they saw their father. They swarmed around their parents, clutching Matthias's pant legs until he hoisted them up, one in each arm.

"I heard the helicopter," said Courtney. "Is it safe to leave the vault?"

"That was just me flying in," said Matthias.

"Why didn't you give us a warning?"

Matthias left the vault, carrying Anna and Jacobbe into the recreation room. "In case somebody was monitoring the airwaves. I preferred to keep everything on the down low."

Courtney punched in a code as they left the vault and the six-inch steel portal slid shut, seamlessly merging with the architecture so that it appeared to be part of the closet wall, populated by racks of equipment. "Good. I'm not certain that the vault is a great place to hide the children. It's got about every type of weapon you could imagine—even a box of grenades and a couple of those bombs you shoot."

"Rocket-propelled grenades?" asked Matthias.

Courtney shrugged her shapely shoulders, and Matthias noticed the sprinkling of freckles that indicated she had been out in the Florida sun with the children. "I don't know what they're called, but can you imagine what would happen if Jacobbe got a hold of one of those grenades and pulled the pin?"

"Got it," said Matthias. "You think a separate vault might be a good idea?"

"We could convert one of the bedrooms," suggested Blake, but then he abruptly shut his mouth instead of continuing. Otto kept a spacious room within the penthouse, and he hadn't meant to imply that it wouldn't any longer be needed.

Matthias frowned, but didn't seem to take offense to Blake's suggestion. "Maybe, but once we get all this sorted out I'm tempted to buy a private island somewhere in the Bahamas—some place where old enemies won't come looking."

"You can buy it under a false name," said Blake, who had plenty of experience making purchases under aliases. "It's not that hard to manufacture an alternate identity. I've done it dozens of—" He broke off as he noticed that Jacobbe and Anna were intently listening to him. "I've seen other people do it dozens of times."

"So you still don't have all this sorted out?" asked Courtney. "After I heard about the plane explosion in Boston, I wondered if that might have been connected."

"It was," said Matthias. "Last year, Fritz tangled with a Vietnamese warlord by the name of Quan Tang who was working out of Czechoslovakia. He hired a hit team to kill us. Blake took care of one of them, and Sly and Mitz got the explosives expert who planted the bomb. We thought we had Quan Tang cornered but someone tipped him off and he wasn't on the plane. He had a squad of gunmen ready for us, but he wasn't there."

"What about that blonde hit woman?" asked Blake.

"Killingsworth? We haven't seen hide nor hair of her. She seems to have disappeared like a ghost."

"She's no ghost. I got a close look at her," said Blake, who thought that now might not be a good time to mention her ice-goddess good looks. "Let me know if I can be of any help."

Blake's cell phone rang and he picked the blocky device from his belt, grinning when he saw the incoming phone number. "It's Vera."

"Hey, sugar pie. How's my sweetie doing?"

Courtney cocked her head to one side and bit at her lower lip. "It always amazes me how Vera can turn a tough, trash-talking giant of a man into a sweet-talking cuddle-bear."

"Women serve as a civilizing influence upon the male population," said Matthias. "Otherwise we'd all be running around fighting and brawling."

Courtney pushed her fingers through Matthias's long brown hair. "Apparently, I'm not having that much effect upon you. You're still fighting and brawling."

"Only by necessity," sighed Matthias.

Courtney's expression was wistful. "You won't be staying for long, will you?"

"Just tonight. Sly and Mitz are following up a lead in Boston, and Fritz and I will be heading to Czechoslovakia to see if we can intercept Quan Tang before he gets back."

"You can't go there," objected Courtney. "Czechoslovakia is under communist rule. If they get a hold of you they'll send you to the gulags, or something."

"Probably nothing so pleasant as that," said Matthias. "But if we let Quan Tang get away with killing Otto, then it sends a signal to everyone else who holds a grudge against us that it's open season on the Gantlet Brothers. We can't let our enemies think they can hit us and then retreat to safety behind the Iron Curtain."

Courtney put her hand on her husband's shoulder. "So you'll be here just one night?"

Anna and Jacobbe began to groan when they heard these words. "Just one night?" groaned Anna.

"Yes, but it's going to be a great night!" roared Matthias. "Who's up for caramel corn and Connect Four?"

Anna Gantlet and Blake Hawkins both raised their hands and spoke in unison, one in a high-pitched soprano and the other in a rumbling bass. "I am!"

Chapter 10

In the early morning hours as sunlight began to creep over the horizon, leaking life-giving light into the leaden skies, Matthias met Fritz outside Hangar 612 at the Fort Lauderdale-Hollywood International Airport. The air was brisk, but comfortable, and the scent of the bright yellow spot flower, which dotted the surrounding fields, sweet in the air before the onset of the coming heat. They climbed the stair into a Learjet that the brothers mutually owned—the spoils of a gunfight with a pirate warlord in Somalia—and Matthias entered the cockpit and began the pre-flight sequence.

Fritz stowed his sword blade and rucksack in an overhead compartment and plopped into the co-pilot's seat, leaning back with his hands behind his head. "Where we headed to, little *bruder*?"

Matthias flipped on the master switch and checked the fuel gauges to make sure that they were indeed full. "Czechoslovakia."

Fritz pushed his round-lensed glasses into the curly hair atop his head. "Yes, of course, but if we fly this Lear into Czechoslovakia under the radar, we'll never see it again—unless you have some contact there I don't know about who owns an abandoned air strip?"

Matthias lowered the flaps, and turned the fuel valve. "I figure we'll make a pit stop in Austria first and find something more suitable—and far less expensive."

"What do you have in mind?"

"A couple of years after we blasted our way out of East Berlin a guy named Ivo Zdarsky flew out of the Czechoslovakian countryside and into Austria in an ultralight powered by a Trabant engine."

Fritz sat up, because he had seen plenty of the poorly built East German cars and had the displeasure of many aborted trips due to frequent breakdowns. "A Trabant? That piece of junk? He actually made something out of a Trabant engine that could fly?"

Matthias fired up the engines of the Lear. "The guy's somewhat of a genius. He's living in California now, making a fortune selling adjustable props."

Fritz closed his eyes. "I wish we would have had a handful of ultralights to take us out of East Germany. Would have saved us a lot of trouble. If only I were genius enough to make a Trabant engine fly—who would have thought?"

Matthias radioed the control tower to let them know they were ready for flight.

Chapter 11

Sly drove the Silverado through the back wall of the Thinh Dai Leathery, while Mitz and Sheila entered through the front door and found themselves flanked by expressionless mannequins dressed in leather pants, jackets, and corsets. A few startled customers glanced up from their perusal of leather accoutrements when they felt the impact shake the building, heard the roar of a revving engine and the shriek of rending metal as the truck tore through the rear wall of the building. They couldn't know what happened, but when the gunfire started they fled past Mitz and Sheila, through the front door along with a petite almond-skinned Vietnamese sales clerk dressed in a red leather skirt and silk blouse. Mitz caught the sales clerk by the arm before she exited the store.

"Where's Thinh Dai?"

She jabbed a slender finger toward the back. "In his office! He's in his office! You'll help him?"

Mitz scowled and raised a dubious eyebrow. "There may be no helping him, but I'll see what I can do."

The salesclerk wriggled free from Mitz's grasp and headed out the door. "You see what you can do!"

Halfway through the wall and into the back room, the Silverado was buried in a layer of rubble, shattered two by fours, insulation, and broken plaster board. Sly tried to kick open the driver's door, but it was blocked shut by the wall. He threw the truck into reverse and found that it was inextricably jammed into place. Through the screen of plaster dust and brick, Sly could see a pair of suited men running down the aisles of the stock room and toward the Silverado.

Sheila had been able to push Thinh Dai's name through the CIA databases via a contact she had made while an agent for the John Velvet-helmed American Intelligence Machine. Thinh Dai's name came up in connection with a couple of agencies that ran call girls and cocaine. This connection was confirmed for Sly when a couple of Thinh Dai's business associates pulled guns from the jackets of their Pierre Cardin suits and began firing into the Silverado. Sly ducked into the footwell of the Chevy, counting on the engine block to give him some protection against the bullets that ripped through the radiator. One of the gunmen was aiming higher and putting a barrage of lead through the windshield, spraying Sly's broad back with glass.

Sly reached up with the toe of his boot and unlatched the passenger door of the truck and then gave it a hard kick with the sole of his shoe. It came open about a foot, not wide enough for Sly to slide out of the truck. He could knock out the back window and escape across the bed of the truck, but this would expose him to the hail of bullets coming through the front windshield, and so Sly found himself stuck inside the cab—just as the Silverado was stuck in the back wall of the leathery.

For a moment the gunfire ceased—maybe because the Vietnamese mobsters had emptied their magazines, or maybe because they were peering through the haze of plaster dust to see what damage their gunfire had done. Sly took this moment to change the direction he was facing in the footwell and he thrust the snout of his Desert Eagle between the hinges of the partially opened passenger door. Unfortunately, sighting along the edge of the front fender limited his line of sight, but for a moment one of the gunmen stepped into that line of sight in order to better survey the mess that his bullets had made of the grill and engine.

The gun barrel was propped against the hinge so when, for a moment, Sly's laser sight appeared on the Pierre Cardin jacket, he was able to hold steady and deliver a pair of 240-grain hollow points, which expanded and tore through the gunman's side. The gunman spun and crumpled to the ground, his pistol rattling across the stock room floor. A volley of bullets resumed from the other corner of the truck's hood, rupturing metal and spraying oil and coolant. Then the remaining gunman shifted his aim and sent a trio of bullets through the driver's door. These struck the seat just above Sly's hip, and one bullet took off the heel of his boot.

"This is getting a little too close for comfort," muttered Sly, but he was pinned down with nowhere to go but the next life, should the Vietnamese mobster get a fraction more accurate with his aim.

Sheila made good time down the back hall of the Thinh Dai Leathery, especially considering the ridiculous high heel shoes that she wore. Now that she wasn't impersonating the assassin Sorcha McDonagh, Sheila had abandoned the red wig and wore a diamond-studded earring in the shape of an S in her upper piercing, and a gold hoop in the lower. Her dark hair was sleek and long, swinging to the left as she pulled loose her .38 snub-nosed Colt—not an accurate weapon at long distances, but efficient when you were up close and personal, and a low enough caliber that it didn't kick like a wild horse.

Mitz came hard on her heels, a pair of .45 Double Eagle Colts in his hands. Firing two guns at a time was a ridiculous proposition for most men—but thousands of hours behind the drum set had given Mitz a degree of ambidexterity that allowed him to hit close targets in unison. Thinh Dai's office was halfway down the hall, and a prune-faced, diminutive man in his fifties emerged from the office when the sound of gunshots resonated from the stock room at the back of the facility. When he saw the dark-haired woman and long-haired drummer running down the hall toward him, he ducked back into his office and locked the door.

He dropped the Levelor blinds and they were still swinging when Sheila reached the door. She wasted no time putting a .38 bullet through the locking mechanism. Metal fragments sprayed her arm and face, and the wreckage of the lock hung jumbled and torn in the door. She was about to give the door a boot, but she remembered she was wearing high heels and backed away. She turned her dark gaze in Mitz's direction. "You mind giving this a kick for me?"

"Next time we assault a leather shop, you might want to throw on a pair of running shoes," said Mitz. He put his foot against the door and it flew open with so much force that it bent the hinges upon which it hung. The prune-faced man was dipping into his office drawer and his hand emerged holding a silver-plated and highly engraved semi-auto pistol.

Mitz and Sheila simultaneously moved through the doorway, their trio of guns aimed at his chest.

The stubby barrel of Sheila's .38 did not waver. "Thinh Dai, I presume?"

"Who wants to know?" blustered the prune-faced man, but he let go of his pistol, so that it dropped back into the drawer. He raised his hands in front of him.

Sheila strode toward Thinh Dai and fired a bullet at point blank, just past Thin Dai's face, so close that powder burns formed on his cheek. "All you need to know is that I will kill you at the count of three—unless you tell me everything you know about Quan Tang. One … Two …"

Thinh Dai blinked, his reddened eyes stinging and watering from the close proximity of the muzzle flash from Sheila's snub-nosed .38. "Wait! Wait! I'll tell you everything you want to know. Just don't hurt me!"

The sound of yet more gunfire resounded through the walls. Sheila spoke to Mitz without diverting her attention from the Vietnamese leather broker. "You want to go check on my husband and make sure he hasn't bitten off more than he can chew?"

"Already on my way," replied the drummer as he slipped outside the office and toward the stock room at the back.

A couple of stock room workers nearly collided with Mitz as they ran away from the gunfire as fast as their legs would take them. When they saw that Mitz carried a pair of Double Eagles, they backpedaled in fear. Mitz raised up his guns toward the ceiling. "Go past me. As fast as you can!"

They hesitated for just a moment, fearful to get anywhere near the long-haired gunman in the hallway, but even more fearful of retreating back into the stock room where the front end of a Silverado was hanging through the wall and being pelted by gunfire.

"Now!" ordered Mitz.

Ducking low, as if this would help them pass unnoticed, they slipped by Mitz and then the drummer burst into the stock room. The Silverado was gushing coolant from a dozen holes in the radiator, the front tires hanging loosely and the rest of the vehicle jammed through the wall. A gunman in suit and tie was quietly clambering onto the bumper, pistol in hand, and about ready to fire in through the windshield at an angle that indicated he was firing at somebody who was taking cover in the footwell of the cab.

Mitz took aim and fired his Double Eagles alternately, putting a half dozen rounds into the back of the gunman and sending him pitching forward. Hidden in the footwell, Sly heard the flurry of gunshots and then saw a body impact on the windshield above him, blood spattering from between the gunman's lips as his face smashed against the glass. Still, there was a spark of life within the gunman. The dying gunman could see Sly crammed into the footwell, and with the last vestiges of life, he brought the muzzle of his gun against the glass, so that it pointed at the body of the hidden guitarist.

Sly fired his Desert Eagle three times, blowing laminated glass through the body of the gunman, and the force of the bullets pushing the body off the windshield and hood.

Mitz did a thorough survey of the stock room. "It's safe to come out, Slatko!"

"Is that you, bro?"

"No, it's your grandma," said Mitz. This was a shorthand code that the brothers had developed to identify themselves. If Mitz had responded to the inquiry with any other phrase that did not include grandma, then Sly would have known that it was not safe to emerge. They changed up the code occasionally, so that enemies wouldn't get wind of it.

Sly climbed onto the bullet-riddled bench seat and put his back against the vinyl. "I'm coming out." He tucked his legs in and kicked with his boots. It took Herculean effort, his ribs screaming in pain with every single thrust of feet, but eventually Sly was able to knock out the webbed and mangled windshield and climb out onto the hood. He jumped to the floor and coolant splashed the legs of his Levi's. "How much of a trade-in do you think we can get for the Silverado?"

Mitz overlooked the still-twitching gunman that had taken six bullets from his Double Eagles and another three .44 rounds from Sly's Desert Eagle. "Maybe a hundred bucks if we tow it to the junkyard."

Sly narrowed his eyes and sucked at his lower lip. "I think I'll let Thinh Dai keep it."

"What are we going to use for a getaway car?" asked Mitz. "I thought we agreed on a distraction, not driving the truck through the wall."

Sly shrugged his brawny shoulders. "Distraction? I thought you said 'destruction.' Where's Sheila?"

"She's questioning Thinh Dai."

"You left her alone?"

"She can take care of herself," said Mitz. "Besides, I was rescuing your sorry hide."

Sly spotted a row of thousand-dollar leather boots and began prying off his own damaged footwear. "Go check on her, while I get myself some new kicks. It's the least Thinh Dai can do for me after his henchman shot the heel off my snakeskins."

Chapter 12

"Now tell me," said Sheila, "where can I find Quan Tang?"

"He was blown up on a Learjet when he was trying to leave the country," stuttered Thinh Dai.

Sheila fired a bullet that notched Thinh Dai's ear. "Don't lie to me! Now, tell me—the truth this time. Where is Quan Tang?"

Thinh Dai clutched at the gristle of his ringing ear, blood seeping between his fingers. "He—he got a phone call that told him not to take the Lear. Instead he took a helicopter into international waters and boarded a freighter for Puerto Rico."

"What's he doing in Puerto Rico?"

Thinh Dai glared at Sheila, fixing her in an evil glare that could kill insects and small animals. "He's got business there."

"You're going to have to do better than that," threatened Sheila. "My next shot will take off your entire ear."

"He's selling, ah … selling weapons to the FALN. Stuff stolen from European stockpiles."

Sheila's brown eyes gave no sign that she believed or disbelieved the story. "I see, and what is the name of this freighter?"

"*Rogue Trader*," said Thinh Dai.

"I've got a problem with your story," said Sheila. "I happen to know a few of the fellows who dismantled the *Fuerzas Armadas de Liberación Nacional*. It's defunct." She adjusted the aim of her gun so it was pointing at the base of the ear, which he still clutched. "If you don't move your hand this bullet is going to take off your fingers as well as your ear."

"I tell the truth!" protested Thinh Dai. "There were a few separatists that weren't arrested. They plan to put the FALN back on the map. You can't completely kill a movement like that. They are like cockroaches."

Sheila seemed satisfied enough by this answer that she let Thinh Dai keep his fingers and his ears. "One more thing. Who tipped off Quan Tang that his plane would be stopped?"

Thinh Dai shrugged. "He didn't tell me, but I heard him call the man by the name of that clown, that advertises hamburgers."

"Krusty?"

"No," said Quan Tang. "The one with the Hamburglar."

"Ronald," said Sheila. "It figures that the Hamburglar's the only one you could remember. Where's your car?"

"Around the corner." He reached into his jacket pocket and eased out a set of keys to a Mercedes Benz. "Take it. You can have it!"

Sheila plucked away the keys with her left hand. "Thank you for your generosity. This way we don't have to tie you into the truck bed. Your trunk will do nicely."

An expression of fear flickered across his face. "You're taking me with you?"

"We'll be keeping you somewhere safe until we've determined that you've been telling us the complete truth."

Mitz burst into the office. "Thin Dai managed to call in his enforcers. We've got three cars of gunmen in front of the shop.

All of a sudden, Thinh Dai seemed to recover his composure. "Please take my car, but I suggest that it will be safest for you if you leave me here."

Chapter 13

The moon was obscured by the gray of overhanging clouds, so the pair of ultralights crossing the Austrian border into Czechoslovakia navigated by compass in the tarry umbra of night. The darkness obscured the view of the guards and the check posts, so they did not see the dark wings of the intruders as they passed from Austrian airspace and across the patchwork quilt of the Czech fields.

Matthias took the lead, steering away from populated centers, skimming low over the fields, and then rising just enough to clear the copses of trees. They veered west to avoid the dark shapes of the buildings of Dolni Dunajovice which, in their eyes, rose in sinister clusters against the starless sky. Soon they crossed the sullen ribbon of the Dunajovicky potok that cut a furrow through the land, and then passed over the slate gray waters of the Nove Mlyny reservoirs.

The air was brisk and they could feel the moisture of the falling dew in their faces as they winged across the waters, the motors of the ultralights humming and the propellers beating the air. For a few moments, it was enough to make Matthias forget that if they were discovered they would be thrown in a gulag at best, or just shot out of hand. The communists would like nothing better than to get their hands on a pair of Gantlet Brothers.

Several small islands rose from the reservoir, most of these little more than patches of earth thrusting up from the waters, upon which a few trees found just enough purchase to thrive. One contained a solitary home, enclosed by stands of trees and they gave this island a wide berth, praying that the noise of the ultralights would not alert the resident. They rose higher to clear a thick forest of trees that grew up at the water's edge, and once they passed over the leafy tree tops, they cut their engines and glided into a potato field. Matthias descended first and jounced across the mounded potato hillocks, the impacts rattling his teeth. Finally, the momentum of the ultralight was spent and he came to a stop at a cock-eyed angle that barely spared the wings of the craft.

Fritz's landing was not as smooth as Matthias's, and the wheel caught a ridge in the field and upended the ultralight. The propeller struck the earth and threw up a haze of dirt into Fritz's goggles, and then he found himself hanging upside down, still strapped into the mangled ultralight. Matthias released himself from the seat of his ultralight and sprinted over to his brother, just in time to see Fritz drop into the potato field on his hands and knees.

Matthias pulled aside a snapped wing to allow his brother room to crawl out. "You still alive?"

Fritz pulled himself from the wreckage and cut loose a rucksack of gear. "I take back what I said about wishing we had a fleet of ultralights to escape East Germany. In fact, I never want to see one of these things again."

Matthias took this to mean that all of Fritz's limbs were still intact and functioning. "Let's get these things dragged into the forest, so that they're not in plain sight when the sun comes up."

A strip of trees hid the field from a paved road that ran alongside a tributary to the reservoir, but a farm road circled the potato crop. Fritz knew that ninety-five percent of the Czech farming was government owned and run under something called the Unified Agricultural Cooperative, meaning that the government owned the land and would take the fruits of your labors and redistribute them as they saw fit. This meant that party leaders got the lion's share of the workers' labors and the farmer would never have anything to show for their work except a meager subsistence. It also meant that the farm workers didn't have much incentive to excel; nevertheless, someone would probably be out in the day to check the field. It wouldn't do to have a pair of ultralights sitting in plain sight and arousing the suspicions of local authorities.

However, the Czech government was generally more concerned about unhappy citizens attempting to leave the country, rather than anyone trying to sneak into Czechoslovakia. That might cause a bit of confusion, but not for long. Matthias and Fritz righted the broken ultralight and dragged it from the field and through the brush and into the forest. While Fritz cut branches and camouflaged its hiding place with a screen of boughs,

Matthias started the engine of his still-functioning ultralight and used the propeller to pull the craft into the brush. He cut the engine again and Fritz helped him conceal the craft.

Fritz pulled on a heavy jacket which concealed a Mini-UZI and his Colt .44 Anaconda. Then he hoisted his duffel bag, which contained his *katana*, a collapsed metal detector, and some basic survival gear. "You think the farmer will notice the spot we gouged out of his field?"

"Eventually," said Matthias, who pulled on a similarly drab jacket, which was designed to avoid attracting attention, and conceal the pair of pistols that were strapped beneath. "Hopefully, we'll be long gone by that time."

Fritz's iron-gray eyes took on a grim cast. "I guess that depends on how long it takes for us to dismantle Quan Tang's operation."

It was about a mile, trudging along the tributary road, past scraggly trees and dewy sward, before they reached the low bridge which took them across the tributary and into the town of Ivan. Fritz patted his pockets and noticed a tear along one of them. "My satellite phone is missing."

Matthias noted the tear in Fritz's jacket. "You must have lost it in the crash."

Fritz frowned. "It's probably too late to go back for it now."

"Assuming we could even find it," said Matthias.

"You've still got your satellite phone, right?"

Matthias checked and found that he did indeed have it tucked away inside a zipped pocket. "Yes, right here."

As the sun broke over the horizon, it shed its yellow rays on a daffodil-colored church that rose four stories and bore a cross upon its steeple. In-set arches formed or framed the door and windows. Its entrance was also flanked by a pair of crosses which were proudly displayed, despite the fact that communist authorities did everything they could to discourage worship and blacklisted known members from ever rising in work opportunities or political power.

The town of Ivan was still asleep and in the roseate haze of the sunrise there were just a few signs that it was awakening: a truck bed full of sleepy workers that drove toward the fields, a man watering his garden before the onset of the sun, and a few automobiles that crossed the dusty thoroughfares in the distance. Sunlight gleamed from the overhead power lines and a bit of warmth began to seep into the bones of the brothers who, despite their brisk walk, were still chilled from their nighttime flight across the border.

"This is the church," said Fritz.

They entered the portico through the arch, crossing into the dim interior. Fritz tested the double front doors and found them securely locked. A knocker, engraved with the sign of the cross, was attached to the door on the left and Fritz lifted it, letting the fall of it resound through the interior of the chapel.

Matthias watched the street while they waited. A woman in the cracker box house across the street pulled back her checked curtains and peered through the window. "This priest—you feel like you can trust him?"

Fritz lowered his heavy rucksack to the ground. "He was a great help to me when I was here last. He's part of an underground religious network. The Czech constitution claims that freedom of religion is guaranteed, but it is tightly controlled by the state. They've got their fingers in all the churches."

"So this underground movement ..."

"It's an effort to practice their religion without interference from the government. Miloslav also prints tracts against prostitution. Prostitution is illegal, of course, but the state condones it because the officials get a cut, as well as free services. So when I was looking for Ket Nien, he helped point me in the right direction." Fritz lifted the knocker again, and let it fall three more times.

Finally, the sound of footsteps came to their ears. The door came open a crack and a dark-eyed woman in her early twenties peered through the space, auburn locks spilling down her forehead. "What do you want?"

She spoke in Czech, but Fritz knew a smattering of the language so he responded. "We're looking for Father Miloslav Lada."

Apparently, Fritz's German accent was plain enough. "What does a German want with a Czech priest?"

"He was very helpful to me a couple of years ago, and I need his help again."

"He's spent all his years helping people, but when he needs help who is there to reach out their hand? No one. Now good-bye." It was easy enough for Matthias to hear the bitterness in her voice, even though he didn't speak a word of Czech.

She started to shut the door, but Fritz inserted the toe of his boot before it could shut. "I'll help Father Miloslav, if you'll let me."

"It's too late," she said. "They have taken him away for reeducation."

"Reeducation?"

"They have found him guilty of clerico-fascist ideology. They claim that he is in league with the bourgeoisie—even though it is they that are they bourgeoisie."

"How do you know Father Miloslav?" asked Fritz.

"I am Otka, his daughter, and now that you know he is beyond your help, leave here. It is because he associated with people like you that the authorities have taken him away. It is your fault!"

Fritz put his open palm against the door. "If you can tell us where to find your father, we'll release him."

Otka narrowed her dark eyes, her brows turning down at the center. "Anyone with authority enough to do that would not come skulking at the door of the church at dawn."

Fritz opened up his jacket with his left hand and revealed the UZI and Colt Anaconda that were holstered beneath. "I have an authority of a different sort."

Otka's mouth dropped open and then she opened the door wide enough to usher them inside the shadowed chapel. "Come to the vestry. There, we can speak in private."

Matthias shot a hard glance at his older brother. "What did you just promise her?"

"We're springing her Poppa from prison," said Fritz.

Chapter 14

Mitz grabbed Thinh Dai by the collar of his jacket and bodily hauled him through the front door of the office. "We're not leaving you behind. You're our ticket out of here."

Sheila plucked Thinh Dai's pistol out his desk drawer, released the magazine and noted that it was full. "I agree. Mister Dai will serve as our insurance, or at the very least a shield against bullets."

"You're making a big mistake," said Thinh Dai. "My men will become very angry if they see you mistreating me."

"Maybe a gag would be in order," said Mitz.

"Good idea." Sheila ripped a frilly sleeve from her blouse, spun Thinh Dai around and pulled it between the crime boss's teeth, knotting it at the back of his skull. "That's a two-hundred-dollar Girbaud blouse, but if it gets him to shut up it'll be worth every penny."

Mitz pushed Thinh Dai out of the office ahead of him. "Let's go."

Sheila glanced down the hallway. "Where's Sly?"

"Picking out a pair of boots."

"What was wrong with the pair he was wearing?" demanded Sheila.

Sly appeared at the end of the hallway, wearing new alligator skin boots, his freshly-loaded Desert Eagle in his right fist. "You looking for me, babe?"

"Just wondering what the holdup was. We're on a tight schedule, darling—and nice boots!"

Sly grinned. "I think they're illegal in forty-seven states, including Massachusetts."

"That's the least of our concerns. We've got cars full of Thinh Dai's gunmen coming to his rescue. He must have triggered a general alarm before we got to him."

"The Silverado's not going anywhere," said Sly. "There was an err … an accident."

Sheila dangled the keys to Thinh Dai's Mercedes. "Already on top of it. Mr. Dai's got his ride waiting for us in the alley."

Sly reached forward to snatch the keys. "I'm driving!"

Mitz, however, was a little quicker. He plucked away the keys before his brother could get his fingers on them. "The last car you drove is hanging through the back wall. Why don't you let someone drive who knows how to avoid buildings?"

"But I drove through the back wall on purpose!" protested Sly.

Sheila gave her husband an acid look. "I thought you said it was accident."

"Well, it was an accident that I got stuck inside the cab."

They hurried through a series of hallways that passed by offices, a few of which contained cowering clerical workers who stared goggle-eyed as they saw their gagged boss being ushered past by a trio of gunmen. Sly smiled and waved. "Everybody gets the day off!"

Mitz let himself out the back door into a dead-end alley of brick walls and barred windows. There were a half dozen parking slots, all marked by signs that designated them reserved for upper management of the Thinh Dai Leathery. It wasn't hard to spot Thinh Dai's vehicle, the only Mercedes in the lot—a sleek black 560 model with the logo imbedded in the center of the grill.

Mitz climbed in the driver's seat and fired the engine while Sheila pushed Thinh Dai into the front passenger seat and slammed the door shut behind him.

She slipped into the backseat, directly behind Thinh Dai and pushed the snub nose of her revolver against the back of his skull. "Don't let those gunmen forget that we've got their boss."

Sly stood in the crook of the open door as Mitz backed the Mercedes out of the slot and eased toward the street. Six different gunmen in Thinh

Dai's employ had taken up positions on the street. He bellowed out to them. "We've got your boss. If you fire on us, we'll shoot him. If you want to see him alive again, hold your fire!"

A pock-faced gunman returned Sly's demand. "Show us Thinh Dai or we'll fire!"

It was only natural that they would want some proof that Thinh Dai was indeed captive, and so Mitz used the controls on the arm rest to roll down the front passenger window to reveal Thinh Dai sitting and gagged in the front seat, with a snub-nosed pistol shoved against the back of his skull.

Once the pock-faced gunman witnessed this, he waved off his men. "Hold your fire! They have Mr. Dai!"

Fortunately, Thinh Dai appeared to have some loyalty among his men— or at least, no one wanted to appear to be disloyal by being the first one to pull the trigger. Sly withdrew into the relative safety of the cab and slammed the door shut, then Mitz threaded the gauntlet of traffic. The Vietnamese gunmen stared intently at the Mercedes, trying to pierce the veil of the tinted windows. If they opened up on the Mercedes, the Gantlets would be sitting ducks with little protection against the bullets. Of course, Thinh Dai would be just as likely die and this was the only factor that was keeping them safe at the moment.

Once clear of the gunmen, Mitz rapidly accelerated, anxious to put some distance between him and the enemy. Given a few seconds to think it over, the gunmen might try and follow and that might prove disastrous as well.

Sly prodded his wife. "Does the American Intelligence Machine have any safe houses near here where we can stash Dai?"

Thinh Dai's eyes widened when he heard this, but Sheila shook her head. "Velvet's going to have a kitten when he hears what unsanctioned activities I've been involved in. Besides, I haven't been an active agent since we married."

Mitz couldn't tell whether this bit of information relieved Thinh Dai or worried him more. "I've got a place where we can hide Dai until his information proves true or false. I'm told that the personnel there are very discreet. Better blindfold our prisoner."

Chapter 15

Arturo Sippo, concierge for the Black Cemetery, slightly raised his eyebrow. "So let me get this clear: you would like me to detain a Vietnamese crime boss as a prisoner in one of our suites until further notice?"

Mitz tapped his fingers on the highly-polished counter in the lobby of the Black Cemetery, which resembled how one might imagine a drawing room in a Victorian men's club, complete with over-stuffed leather chairs with hand-chiseled legs and bookshelves stocked with curious reading material. The only thing the lobby lacked to complete the ambience was a blue haze of cigar smoke. "Precisely."

"Very well," said the concierge. "I believe I understand your instructions."

"Are you comfortable with this?" asked Mitz.

"Our guests' demands are usually somewhat more self-indulgent, but this won't be the first time I've accommodated such a request."

Mitz's interest was piqued. "Really?"

"You understand that I am the epitome of discretion, but considering this guest has long since passed, I feel that I am able to share this particular event."

"I appreciate your discretion," said Mitz. "Otherwise I wouldn't even be asking you to host our Vietnamese friend."

"Well, once John Bonham kidnapped Keith Moon from backstage at a Who concert in Boston. In order to win his freedom, Moon challenged Bonham to a drum duel that went on for five hours and demolished three drum sets."

"Really? I would have liked to have been in on that."

"I thought you might appreciate that story." The concierge consulted one of several monitors hidden behind his desk. "The rear drive is clear. Bring your guest around back and we'll see that he's well taken care of."

"Give him whatever he wants," said Mitz, "but make sure he doesn't leave here—or contact any of his associates on the outside."

Chapter 16

Otka moved aside a panel of still burning candles, revealing a narrow stair that wound into a secret basement beneath the chapel. She turned, brushing back wisps of her auburn hair from her face, then motioned down the stairs. "This used to be a fruit cellar dug by the owners of the house that stood here before the church was built."

"Handy," said Matthias, who noted that the mechanism was built cleverly enough that it would be difficult to discover the moving panel without a concerted effort.

Otka motioned them forward. "We keep a printing press in the cellar now—for publishing religious tracts without the interference of government officials who want to edit any thoughts that might run counter to party thinking."

Fritz moved onto the dark stair and began to descend. Matthias was a couple of inches taller than his brother, so he had to duck as he descended the stairs. Behind him, he could see Otka's sylph-like figure limned in the soft light from the chapel. She pulled a lever that pushed the wall back into place, and then secured a pair of hasps which would keep the wall from being opened from the outside, should it be discovered.

"The Party is opposed to anything that recognizes that there is a higher power than themselves. They only tolerate religion because they realize they cannot completely quash it. Instead, they have decided to co-opt the churches by installing leaders who swear loyalty to the party."

Fritz reached the bottom of the steps and in the blackness he felt something brush against his face. He reached up and caught hold of a string and pulled. A pair of overhanging bulbs flickered to life in the chamber, revealing uneven wooden floors and a Platen printing press that was at least fifty years old. A number of tracts were stacked beside it, and he picked one up. Though he could speak a smattering of Czech, he had difficulty making much sense of the content; his vocabulary was more mundane, dealing primarily with subject matters like the location of bathrooms, restaurants and black market gun dealers rather than theological subjects.

Otka motioned to the printing press. "They will torture my father until he tells them where he printed those tracts. He will make a valiant effort to resist, but the torturers of the state are too skilled. No man or woman can resist for long. I can't stay here at the church for much longer. When they return and find the printing press, they will accuse me of being an accomplice and take me for reeducation, too."

"Where will you go?" asked Fritz.

She shrugged her shoulders, her features showing only sadness. "I can go to relatives living in Ostrava, but then I will put them in danger. The first place the authorities look for fugitives is with their relatives. I really have nowhere to go. Perhaps, it is best if I just stay here and take my medicine."

Fritz dropped the tract back into the pile with the others. "There are other options."

"You can request asylum in Austria."

Otka pushed chairs in their direction and then sat down at a well-crafted wooden table, the scarred and scratched table top which was spattered with ink of various colors. "The borders are too heavily guarded."

Fritz hoisted his rucksack onto the table and sat down. "We came across the Austrian border early this morning and the guards didn't even see us."

"How is that possible?"

Here in the light, Fritz could see a light sprinkling of freckles across the bridge of Otka's nose. Even roused from slumber in the early hours, she was an attractive woman. Apparently, she got her looks from her mother, because Fritz had met Father Lada and he was not a particularly handsome man. "It's better that I don't say."

"It doesn't really matter," she said, and even Matthias—who could understand little of what was being said—could detect the mournful quality of her voice. "I cannot leave my father in the hands of those butchers. It would be better for him to die a quick, merciful death than be a subject for their experiments."

Matthias pulled his chair up to the foot of the stairs and rested where he could keep an eye on the entrance to the chamber. The entrance was also the exit, because there appeared to be no other way out of the former fruit cellar.

"If you help us find someone," said Fritz, "we can rescue your father."

This was the second time Fritz had offered to help her father, and Otka seemed to take some reassurance in it, as though she had been concerned that she had imagined the offer the first time. "Who are you looking for?"

"A man named Quan Tang. He's a crimin—"

"I know who he is," interrupted Otka. "My father helped two of his girls escape—found families for them to live with in the country."

"Girls that Quan Tang brought in from Vietnam?"

"Yes. They are anxious to escape the poverty of their own country and he promises them jobs and tells them that they will work for him until they pay off the debt they owe him for smuggling them across the border. Quan Tang doesn't tell them that they will be working as prostitutes and that they will never work off their debt, because he keeps adding to the total by charging for food, clothes, and room and board."

"I'm aware of how it works," said Fritz.

Matthias thought he heard a noise in the shadows of the stair and he eased his Casull from the shoulder holster beneath his jacket. A moment later a dirty, gnaw-eared kitten, fuzzy and splotched with patches of orange fur, came bounding down the steps. It pounced on Matthias's boot, and without reholstering his pistol, Matthias reached down with his left hand and stroked the kitten's head. The kitten rewarded him for his kindness by sinking his claws into Matthias's hand and chomping on his finger. Matthias jerked his hand away, but continued to listen, straining to catch any tremor of movement that might be lurking in the umbra of the stairwell, while the feline attacked his boot strings. When his ears could catch no hint of anything else, he turned to Otka.

"How did this kitten get into the cellar?"

Otka's beautiful features took on a blank expression as she turned her attention to Matthias. Matthias pointed his bleeding hand at the kitten that was rolling over, one end of Matthias's boot string caught between its paws.

Fritz translated Matthias's question for Otka and she responded in a rapid staccato that Matthias caught only a few words of.

"She says there's an old rabbit warren that runs from the stairs to a spot underneath the altar in the chapel," translated Fritz. "And Otka speaks some German. You might want to try speaking to her in the mother tongue."

Instead, Matthias responded to his brother in English. "I don't know, Fritz. You seem to be building a nice rapport. I don't want to mess with your mojo."

At first Fritz seemed chagrined by Matthias's comment, but then he grinned and took a page from Sly's playbook. "Nothing can mess with my mojo, little brother."

"Is she still expecting us to rescue her father?"

Fritz's expression was resolute—cleft jaw set like granite in the face of Mount Rushmore. "I promised that we would."

Matthias sighed and switched to German, speaking directly to Otka now. "Where is your father being held?"

Otka seemed relieved that they were again talking about her father. She responded in German so that Matthias could understand, but directed her gaze toward Fritz. "They are holding him at Pankrác."

"Pankrác!" choked Matthias. Even in Germany, as a child, he'd heard whispers of Pankrác. It was built in the late 1800s and designed to house around nine hundred prisoners, though there were many times when its population far exceeded that. When the Nazis invaded Czechoslovakia, they took over the prison and used it as temporary housing for anyone they deemed a danger or unacceptable. Thousands were shuffled through and sent to killing fields for execution. Finally, for the sake of expediency, the head executioner, Alois Weiss, installed a guillotine in the prison itself and sent over a thousand people to their demise. That wasn't even counting the Jews he had killed in the hook room. "That's practically a city. They must have a staff of over five hundred people."

Otka did not refute this. "Not all of them are armed."

"That's comforting," said Matthias, but he did not seem at all relieved by the pronouncement. "If we were in the US and had our full resources, and the time to plan an escape, I think it might be possible—but we're in a communist country with just a handful of guns and two people."

Fritz frowned. "Actually, just you. Once we spring Father Lada or take out Quan Tang's criminal organization, we're going to be hunted by the entire Czech military machine. We'll have to leave the country as quickly as possible. We won't have time to do both operations separately. We're going to have to do them simultaneously."

Matthias's face twisted in dismay, but again he saw Fritz's resolute expression. "Okay, but how am I going to get past the guards on the wall, into Pankrác and out again, with Father Lada, without being discovered?"

"I know somebody who holds a high position at the prison," said Otka.

Matthias holstered his Casull. He was listening but his expression was one of skepticism. "Who is that?"

"My boyfriend," answered Otka.

Fritz did his best to hide his disappointment at discovering Otka had a boyfriend. Of course she would have a boyfriend, she was a beautiful woman. Still, that changed nothing. In exchange for Otka's help locating Quan Tang, he had promised to deliver her father. "We must meet your boyfriend, immediately."

Otka checked a cheap watch which she wore on her slender wrist. "He'll be off his night shift in just two hours. He usually comes by after the shift and visits me."

Matthias was bold enough to ask the question that Fritz didn't dare ask without seeming jealous. "If your boyfriend has access to Pankrác, why doesn't he arrange for your father to escape?"

Otka's face expressed no emotion at first, but at the last her lip trembled and tears glistened in her limpid eyes. "He is not brave enough to do the deed himself. However, the two of you are the answer to my prayers."

Two hours later, Matthias sat in the spire of the chapel eating a *rohlik* with jelly, alongside a slice of cheese and salami which Otka had provided him, and he was watching when Budek Benes pulled up to the door of the chapel on a battered Jawa motorcycle produced at least twenty years earlier.

He removed his helmet, revealing a predatory visage framed by a shock of disheveled hair. Budek unstrapped a bouquet of wild flowers, plucked from a nearby lot, from the back of his cycle.

A moment later he disappeared inside the vestibule that covered the doorstep. Matthias picked up his jacket and empty plate and descended the stairs. Below, Otka took the proffered flowers and kissed Budek, pulling him into the flickering candlelight of the chapel.

"I have good news!" she said.

Budek's dour face turned in a hopeful smile. "You've finally agreed to marry me?"

"I've told you that I'll only marry you after my father has been freed from Pankrác. My father must be the one to perform the marriage."

Budek's forehead creased. "Yes, I'm working on doing that through legal channels, but you know it takes many bribes and a long time. It may be years. You won't make me wait that long, will you?"

"No, because my father will be freed within a matter of days!"

Only now did Budek notice that the door to the chapel had shut behind him, blocking out the sunlight. He turned and saw a stolid man with cleft chin and brown, curly hair that descended to his shoulders. "Who is this?"

"This is Fritz Gantlet. He's going to help us free my father."

"But ..."

Otka clasped Budek's hand and looked into his eyes. "You'll do this for me, won't you? When my father is free, then I will be free to marry you."

At that moment, Budek saw the long-haired Matthias emerge from a side corridor and pass through the licking shadows. He wore a T-shirt stretched over his muscular torso, but it was the two hand-cannons strapped to the musician's body that he noticed most. "And who is this?"

"This is Matthias Gantlet," beamed Otka. "Isn't it wonderful!"

Though an employee of the state, Budek had bought his fair share of black market albums. "You mean the Gantlet Brothers from the band Gantlet?"

Fritz extended his hand. "One and the same. Otka tells us that you will be able to sneak Matthias into Pankrác and provide directions to find her father. Your help will be critical to the success of our operation."

Budek ran a hand through his spiky hair. "Of … of course. It's just that I didn't expect—Otka never told me that she knew the Gantlet Brothers, or that they were coming to help free her father."

"It was a surprise to me as well," said Otka, "but an answer to my prayers. My father helped Fritz when he was last in the country and that is why he came by the chapel."

Budek shook his head in disbelief. "I didn't realize that Father Lada kept company with Western rock musicians."

"Oh yeah," said Fritz with a straight face. "When Iron Maiden and Van Halen are in the area, they always drop by to visit Father Lada."

Budek blinked and turned to Matthias. "If I get some of my albums, would you be willing to sign them for me?"

"He doesn't speak Czech," explained Otka, when Matthias opened his palms in a gesture of incomprehension.

"That's perfect," said Budek. "The upper management at Pankrác usually ignores the janitorial crew. They don't like to speak to them and never want to hear from them. We'll smuggle Matthias in as a janitor and he won't have to speak a word to anyone."

"One other matter," said Fritz. "I need help locating Quan Tang."

Budek's eyes shifted. "I don't know of him. Is he a Vietnamese immigrant?"

Otka put a hand on Budek's shoulder. "I've heard of him, but he's moved his operations since Fritz was last in Czechoslovakia."

"Where to?" asked Fritz.

"He's relocated his headquarters from Cheb and into Prague—little Hanoi, they call it. His son, Duoc, still runs the business in Cheb."

"Little Hanoi, that's the Malesice District in Prague District Ten," said Budek.

"My father says he's got a heavily guarded mansion in the Malesice

District, surrounded by a high stone wall with a gate."

"Good," said Fritz and Budek noticed that the guitar player glanced at the long rucksack that rested nearby. "I'll be dropping by to see if Mr. Tang has returned from his journeys abroad."

Chapter 17

Mitz was jarred from sleep when the Gulfstream III bounced down the runway in San Juan, Puerto Rico. The landing was too fast and the deceleration pulled Mitz forward, his head banging on the head rest in front of him.

He rubbed his forehead and grumbled. "Who is piloting this thing?"

When finally the private jet came to a halt, Mitz unbuckled himself and staggered up to the cockpit. The door was open and he found Sly unbuckling himself from the pilot's seat. The pilot was sitting in the copilot's chair a wide grin upon his pasty face. "Wait'll I tell my buddies that Sly Gantlet landed my plane!"

"It doesn't handle quite the same as an F-14," said Sly, "but I like it. I might have to buy one of these suckers. What do they run?"

The pilot straightened his cap. "Thirty-seven million, brand new. You might be able to pick one up used for a little cheaper."

Sly shrugged. "I prefer new. You never know how somebody's been treating a used plane. They might have been letting former Navy pilots land them ... or something."

"No kidding," scowled Mitz. He directed his attention to the pilot. "And if you want to keep your job, I'd suggest that you keep your mouth shut and don't tell any of your buddies about letting Sly land the plane. They might frown on you lending out a thirty-seven-million-dollar aircraft to whatever rock guitarist happens to be on board."

Sly reached for his jacket as the pilot took control of the plane. "I'm not whatever rock guitarist. I'm the premiere rock guitarist in the world, and if I can handle landing an F-14 on an aircraft carrier, I can handle landing a Gulfstream on a strip that's nearly half a mile long."

"Two thousand four hundred forty-three, to be precise," replied the pilot.

"Whatever," snapped Sly. "My point is that it's a lot longer than the deck of an aircraft carrier."

Mitz jabbed a finger into Sly's chest. "The problem is you're flying the Gulfstream as if you were landing it on the deck of the aircraft carrier."

"Get that finger out of my chest, before I break it off," growled Sly.

Mitz removed the finger but waved it front of Sly's face. "Next time I'm taking a nap, I had better not have my face slammed against anything or I'm holding you personally responsible."

Sly chuckled, his mood shifting like the wind. "Is that why your forehead's so red?"

Mitz made his way back into the cabin. "I don't want to hear it, Sly! Remember, I'm holding you responsible."

A moment later Sheila poked her head into the cabin. "Mortimer, what was with that landing? If I hadn't been buckled in I might have been thrown through a window!"

The pilot turned around, wincing as he took the brunt of Sheila's wrath. "Don't look at me, Mrs. Gantlet. It was your husband that did the landing."

If Mortimer thought that this would turn away the storm, he was sadly mistaken.

Sheila unleashed her displeasure. "You should know better than to let a customer take over the stick, and if you know anything about Sly you should never let him take over when you're landing the plane!"

"I'm sorry," said Mortimer. "I'll never let it happen again!"

Sly groaned. "Sheila, are you trying to ruin all my fun?"

"I still have fresh memories and scarring from that crash landing in Bangkok!"

"The scar on your ..."

Sheila leveled a deadly glance at her husband. "Don't even start with me, Sly."

Sly clamped his jaw shut and, glad that the storm was lifting, Mortimer taxied toward a hangar where his passengers could safely disembark. When they descended from the plane, they were greeted with a blast of humid air and a drizzle that fell from hazy skies. The Luis Muñoz Marín International Airport was located in the capitol city of San Juan, which was the largest port on the island. Whether or not the *Rogue Trader* had chosen to dock in San Juan's port or the directly adjacent Puerto Nuevo was another matter. An island provided lots of coastal access and the *Rogue Trader* could literally be anywhere. The ship didn't necessarily have to dock in order to make an exchange of weapons and money.

"Let's inquire with the harbor master and see if the *Rogue Trader* had docked," said Mitz. "It might be a good place to start."

Despite the haze that obscured the brightness of the sun, Sly slipped on his Gargoyle sunglasses and his blond mane rippled around his shoulders as he lifted his face to the sputtering sky. "Sounds reasonable. Let me do the talking, though. I understand that the native Puerto Ricans have a cultural distrust of foreigners with red foreheads."

"Very humorous," replied Mitz, though his acid tone made it clear that he was not amused.

Sheila lifted an oversized purse to her shoulder. She wore a corded crimson tank top, a floral skirt, and a pair of designer sandals on her carefully manicured feet. "I think you two can handle a couple of inquiries at the port authority. I'm going to run into town and do some shopping."

Sly kissed his wife. "Just don't break the bank."

Sheila smiled ran her fingers through her husband's dark beard. "Remind me. Who was it that went and bought a Ferrari 328 in Boston and named it Rosabel?"

Sly's eyes narrowed. "You know about that?"

"I know about everything, darling. Remember, you married one of the top spies in the American Intelligence Machine. Just because I'm retired doesn't mean I don't have friends who can trace bank activity or even access satellite photos."

"You took satellite photos of me?" questioned Sly.

The corners of Sheila's lips turned up in an enigmatic expression. "I will keep my precise methods confidential."

"I told her," said Mitz.

Sly burst out a loud, "What?"

"Maybe next time you slam my head into something you'll be a little more apologetic," suggested Mitz.

"I can't believe my own brother is ratting me out to my wife."

"Remember how Mom used to catch you every time you'd sneak a cookie out of the jar?"

"Yes," said Sly. "It was like she had a surveillance camera on that blasted thing."

Mitz smiled. "That was me, too."

"I get it. You don't appreciate my flying skills. Still, if we run into a dead end we may want to consider doing a surveillance run around the coast of the island."

Mitz hoisted a gym bag with a few items of clothing. It was the bricks of ammunition hidden underneath that caused the double-sewed straps to strain at the canvas. "In the Gulfstream? Because Mortimer can do the flying."

Sly began a loping stride that took them toward an automobile rental agency at the outskirts of the airport. "The Gulfstream wouldn't be well-suited to the task; besides, I think Mortimer has got to do a run from New York to LA tomorrow. I think we can rent something more appropriate."

"Just as long as you promise to avoid anymore aircraft carrier landings."

Sly clapped his brother on the back with enough force to knock over a lesser or less-prepared man. "Just for you, Mitko. Just for you."

It was just a short jaunt in their rented black five-liter Mercury from the airport to the seaport—just around three kilometers—and it took longer to negotiate the cobbled streets of old San Juan, with the high stone walls of Fort El Morro looming on the coast, than it would have taken on foot. Sheila spotted a swimwear shop she wanted to explore and stepped out, leaving the two brothers to their own devices.

"If we would have just walked, we could have been talking with the harbor master already," said Mitz.

"Yeah, well, live and learn," said Sly.

Finally they located the Port Authority and they found a narrow stall where they parked, scattering a few black-beaked terns that were squabbling over a greasy wrapper still retaining a few gobbets of nourishment. The port facilities consisted of three military terminals and a number of other berths of varying drafts which accommodated tankers, Liquified Petroleum Gas carriers, and cruise ships. Sly grunted as he hoisted himself out of the Mercury, his ribs sending pain shooting up his side and down his arm. He and Mitz were dwarfed by the massive vessels as they strode along the wharves, mingling with sailor and tourist alike as they made their way to the modest structure that served as the office for the Port Authority.

Sly and Mitz kept an eye on the hulls of the vessels, reading the names of the ships as they passed, but none were marked with the name of *Rogue Trader*. Inside, the air-conditioning kept the office at a frigid sixty degrees and a Puerto Rican with neatly parted hair and a trimmed mustache met them at the counter. Appraising his guests' most likely language, he spoke to them in English.

"What can I do for you gentlemen?"

Sly looked over his shoulder. "Gentlemen? I thought maybe you were talking to somebody standing behind us."

The harbor master smiled. "I always assume the best until I know otherwise." He looked at Mitz and pointed to his own forehead. "What happened?"

Mitz glanced sharply at his brother. "Someone made a very poor landing at the airport."

Sly's reply was nonchalant. "What can I say? I'm used to landing in under four hundred feet."

Mitz steered the conversation away from the red spot on his forehead while the harbor master was still cooperative. "We're trying to locate a vessel called the *Rogue Trader*."

"Ah, yes. A Czech freighter, I believe. I'm sorry, you just missed them. They came into port this morning, refueled without any of the crew disembarking and they were on their way."

Mitz did his best to appear perplexed. "I don't understand. We were supposed to meet with one of the passengers while they were still in port."

The harbor master gave a slight shrug. "I saw them sailing down the coast—in the direction of Rincon. Perhaps they thought they were meeting you at one of the smaller ports. Mayaguez might be large enough to accommodate a ship the size of the *Rogue Trader*. Who were you meeting?"

Sly saw no harm in telling the harbor master exactly who they were looking for. "A Vietnamese fellow by the name of Quan Tang."

"There was a Vietnamese man who accompanied Captain Pavlik— hard eyes like flint, and a scar across his chin."

"That would be him," said the harbor master. "What sort of business would you have with a man like that?"

"He killed our brother," said Sly.

The harbor master's face became grave. "Then that is a matter for the *policia*."

"We'll let them know," said Sly, though he had no intention of informing the police.

Chapter 18

An hour later they were buzzing down the verdant Puerto Rican coast-line in a canary yellow, two-man Robinson R22 helicopter. Sly had his hand on the T-bar mounted between the seats and he had the copter up to its cruising speed of 110 miles per hour. The haze was beginning to lift and spears of sunshine slipped through the overhanging gray, so that here and there radiant beams scintillated from the heaving oceans.

They spotted a number of fishing vessels trawling for tuna, and the reefs showed a darker indigo in the blue-green of the sea. They reached the clustered houses of Isabela and the surrounding farmlands which stretched around the outskirts, bordered by thick green jungle foliage, but still they encountered no freighters as they circumnavigated the island.

"You think the freighter could have reached Mayaguez already?" shouted Mitz, so that he could be heard above the din of the rotors.

"I doubt any of these smaller ports would have the depth to be able to take a ship that size in," said Sly. "So, yes. Probably they've reached Maya-guez … or they've headed out to sea and we missed them."

"They could have off-loaded whatever weapon they're carrying when they were docked in San Juan," suggested Mitz.

"Maybe," agreed Sly, who knew there were ways to bypass customs and security even in the most conscientious of ports. "But for now we'll have to go on the harbor master's word that they were in San Juan only long enough to refuel—and that nothing but the captain and Quan Tang left the ship."

At the tip of the island, they passed a golf course upon which a few in-trepid players were braving the still-damp greens that were steaming as the sun began to suck up the moisture. Rincon rose up on their left, a village built into the side of the hilly terrain which marked this portion of the is-land. Homes clung to hillsides, alongside bakeries, hotels, and gas stations which were nestled into the hollows and rills. Narrow roads twisted like snakes among the hills and cars moved at reckless speeds around hairpin corners, heedless of meeting another intrepid driver doing the same from the opposite direction.

Just beyond, in a slip of flatland along the coast, a small airport lay, and then the coastline dropped into a hollow where the port of Mayaguez made its home. Deeper into the bay, the azure waters turned muddy and well out from the coast they spotted a medium-sized freighter anchored away from the traffic lanes of the other boats.

"Is that the freighter we're looking for?"

Sly made a wide arc around the ship while Mitz focused a pair of binoculars on the rusty hull of the freighter. Finally, the flaking name of the ship came into view.

"That's the *Rogue Trader*," Mitz confirmed.

"Anything interesting?"

"Well, they've got open crates of Soviet machine guns on deck."

"Really?"

Mitz replied in a monotone. "No, but they do have a security detail walking the deck. I'm counting at least eight."

"They armed?"

"Not openly, but there's one climbing the stairs over there that's clutching his rib cage. He's got something strapped under his jacket. He's looking at us. We seem to have attracted some attention."

Sly adjusted the course of the helicopter, steering it inland toward the *Maria Eugenio De Hostos* Airport. "I wonder if they've already made the exchange."

Mitz peered at the superstructure and he saw the guard, black-haired and missing a chunk out of his left ear, who had raised the alarm ducking into the captain's cabin. He briefly caught sight of the captain, a severe man with graying temples and a flat broad nose. He barked something and Mitz could not read his lips. Probably the order had been in Czech. "Why would they be sticking around if they already off-loaded their merchandise?"

"I don't know. Maybe they have an actual legal cargo to off-load?"

Mitz caught a glimpse of something being lifted from a crate inside the captain's cabin—a two-piece unit of steel tubing that fitted together. One end was flared and on the other was inserted a bulbous device which came to a narrow tip. "They've got a rocket-propelled grenade."

"What sort?" asked Sly without changing his course.

"Hard to tell, but it looks like an RPG-7."

Sly knew that though the RPG-7 was initially a Russian design, that at least six other countries, including Iran, made their own versions. However, they were uniformally poor at long range and when shooting at fast-moving targets. "At this distance, we've got nothing to worry about."

Mitz continued his surveillance of the *Rogue Trader*. "They haven't brought it out in the open yet. I think they're waiting to see if we approach the ship."

Sly kept on course for the small, private airport that stood about a mile inland. "We're going to have to disappoint them."

As they passed over the shoreline, Mitz was no longer able to see within the captain's cabin. "They're going to be looking for a canary yellow helicopter now."

"We're just sightseers—nothing more, nothing less," replied Sly innocently.

"Where are we going to sightsee from, if our helicopter is going to stay grounded?" asked Mitz.

Sly pointed to a public park along the coastline that was thick with trees. "I think, we set up some surveillance right over there. We've got everything we need in the back."

"The problem is that we'll be in a public park." Mitz stressed the word public.

"Hey, just bird or babe watching—nothing more, nothing less," recited Sly.

"This surveillance assumes that they haven't made the weapon exchange yet."

Sly shook his head, blond hair splaying about his shoulders, and smiled assuredly. "They ain't done the exchange. They're too nervous. They're waiting until dark and in the meantime their nerves are gnawing out their guts—or else they wouldn't be so ready to blow a passing helicopter out of the sky."

"An exchange under the cover of night does make more sense," agreed Mitz. "They're sitting right out in the open. Too bad we didn't bring the infrared lenses."

"Sheila's got that stuff in the trunk of the Mercury, and she's already on her way."

Mitz seemed skeptical. "Yeah, but she's got to drive all the way across the island. You think she'll be here before dark?"

Sly laughed. "Haven't you seen her drive? That woman's got a lead foot. She makes these crazy Puerto Rican drivers look sane by comparison!"

"That's saying something," muttered Mitz.

"That she makes Puerto Rican drivers look sane?"

"No, it's saying something when you think any driver is crazy, because you're the most lunatic driver that I know."

Sly radioed the airport to let them know they were coming in for a landing. Since the airport was small and little-used, and since they didn't require a runway to land, there was little delay. A half hour after they finished taking care of their landing fees, Sheila screeched up to them in their rented black Mercury.

She rolled down her window and Sly leaned in for a kiss. "Hey, babe. What took you so long?"

"Pesky toll roads," she complained, her thick lashes fluttering. "I never seem to have the correct change."

"As if you bothered stopping for the tolls," said Sly. He hissed as he straightened, his ribs reminding him that they were not well.

"You must have been doing a hundred miles an hour in between toll booths," calculated Mitz.

"A hundred twenty on some stretches," bragged Sheila. "Sly tells me that you've found your missing ship."

Sly's eyes glittered with a dangerous intensity and he held his thumb and forefinger just a fraction of an inch apart. "We're this close to killing Quan Tang."

"Did you see him?"

"No," admitted Sly, "but we did spot a crate full of RPGs. Now we know just what weapons Quan Tang is selling the FALN."

Sheila opened her door and swung long, dark legs out of the cab of the Mercury. "Rocket-propelled grenades? How did you get into their hold to take a look?"

"We didn't. We spooked them enough that the head of their security team went running for the cabin, pulled one out and gave some serious contemplation to shooting us out of the sky—or trying to. He didn't have a chance of hitting us at that distance." Sly sounded confident in this, though he had occasionally assayed and triumphed in some long shots where he had a ridiculously small chance of success.

Sheila regarded the canary yellow helicopter sitting on the tarmac. "So using that helicopter again is out of the question. They'll spot it coming from miles away."

"Not necessarily," said Sly.

Sheila didn't appear convinced. "If they've still got the RPGs onboard, it's not too late to set up surveillance from the shoreline. There's got to be an empty building or a hotel room that we can confiscate for a few hours."

"You retired from the American Intelligence Machine," Mitz reminded Sheila. "You don't have legal authority to confiscate anything."

Sheila patted her purse. "I did keep the badge."

"It won't be necessary to use it," said Sly. "The weather is good and there's a small park along the shoreline. You can do some sunbathing and Mitz will do some bird watching."

"What are you going to do?" asked Sheila.

Sly smiled. "I'm making a trip to the hardware store."

Chapter 19

Just beyond a stand of coconut and palm trees, Sheila reclined on a beach towel emblazoned with the Puerto Rican flag—a solid blue triangle with a singular star of white in the middle, offset by three stripes of red and two of white. She made a quick change into a sleek, black, one-piece swimsuit, which she pronounced more practical than a bikini should their surveillance require some quick action. Nearby, Mitz shoved his sunglasses up into the mop of his unruly hair and looked through the large telescope, examining the security detail that patrolled the deck of the ship.

Once again, the dark-haired Czech who was missing the lower part of his left ear appeared on deck. He talked to each security detail and directed them with broad gesticulations and a bit of harshness.

"I wish I could speak Czech," muttered Mitz. They had staked out a spot on the hillside which was populated by some low foliage that screened them from the view of suspicious eyes on the *Rogue Trader*. There was a gap between the shrubbery through which an enterprising salamander scrambled, and this is where Mitz trained his telescope on the freighter.

"That wouldn't be good enough," responded Sheila, without opening her eyes behind the large lenses of her Rayban sunglasses. "Unless you had a bug planted on the ship, we'd never be able to hear them. No shotgun mic I know of can pick up dialogue at this distance, let alone over the roaring of the ocean."

"In that case, I wish I could read lips in Czech," modified Mitz. "I met a Czech model after a show in Switzerland. I could read her lips just fine."

Sheila reached for her diet soft drink which was planted in the grass next to her. "I'd keep stories like that to myself if I wanted to stay in a committed relationship with one supermodel named Cindy Warner. I do have her on speed dial."

Mitz glanced over at Sheila who was propped up on one elbow and taking a sip of her cola. "Just forget I said anything."

"My lips are sealed. I spent years undercover. I'm very good with secrets. Did I ever tell you about the time that I blackmailed the president of Moldavia into allowing the US to run some covert operations along his border?"

"I'm not liking where this conversation is heading," said Mitz. "Are you saying that you intend to blackmail me?"

Sheila settled back onto her blanket. "Not at all, Mitz. I'm just pointing out to my brother-in-law that secrets have a certain power when an enemy knows them."

"Thanks," said Mitz in a very dry tone. "Did your government connection run my description of the head of the *Rogue Trader*'s security team?"

"I took the call when I was visiting the ladies room," said Sheila. "He can't be a hundred percent sure without examining a photograph, but the description fits that of a Tomik Korda who is now known to be in Quan Tang's employ, so I'd say that it's a pretty sure bet we've got the right man."

"What's his story?"

"He came up through the ranks of a couple of different Czech criminal outfits, mostly because he was willing to do absolutely anything. He's got a reputation for torturing and maiming enemies who fall into his hands, and he's suspected in at least twelve different murders. The Czech authorities don't do anything about it because they've been well paid to bury the evidence—and Tomik Korda has made a point in burying anybody who shows a willingness to testify against him."

"Sounds like a nice guy. How did he get hooked up with Quan Tang?"

Sheila rolled onto her belly and exposed her bared back to the sun. She moved aside her dark hair so that it wouldn't interfere with the tan on her shoulders. "Don't know. Probably Quan Tang made him a lucrative offer. Maybe he had a falling out with his old boss and the only way he could get protection was take a job with Quan Tang. Whichever it was, Quan Tang must have been impressed with him, because usually he's got a squad of his Vovinam trained martial artists surrounding him."

"I tried to have Fritz explain the whole concept of Vovinam as a martial art, but it still doesn't make sense to me. He says it's all related to Âm-

Duong. I'm not sure if I even pronounced it correctly."

Sheila seemed only vaguely interested. "I have no idea what that's supposed to mean."

"Fritz says it's yin and yang, hard and soft and that the difference between Vovinam and other martial arts is that Vovinam does not prefer the hard or the soft, but they are used equally to adapt to every situation."

Now Sheila sounded vaguely interested but still unimpressed. "Leave it to some martial arts master to confuse common sense with something profound. They have a way of complicating the obvious and presenting it as though it has the deepest of meaning."

Mitz didn't disagree with his sister-in-law's assessment. "Whatever the philosophy, Fritz says the best of the Vovinam are dangerous men."

Sheila yawned. "Yeah, well, I find the best way to deal with martial artists is to stand clear and shoot them from a safe distance. I have yet to find a martial artist that can stop a bullet—without dying, that is."

The sun began to sink and the sweltering heat began to subside. The croak of the coqui frog swelled into a cacophony. Sheila pulled on a light jacket to protect against the mosquitoes that appeared out of nowhere looking for flesh to feast upon. Once the last roseate ray of sunlight sank beneath the heaving bosom of the ocean, Mitz fitted an infrared lens to the telescope and resumed surveillance of the *Rogue Trader*. Even though the world was bathed in darkness, by using the lens he could see the bulk of the freighter rising from the sea and make out orange-hued figures patrolling the deck.

Sheila handed Mitz a spray can of mosquito repellant to help ward off the avaricious pests and they took turns watching the freighter. As the night wore on, the one who was not surveilling the *Rogue Trader* would drop into a light doze, until it was their turn to take watch. Nothing much happened, but an exchange of perimeter patrols on board the deck of the *Rogue Trader*, until about two in the morning when Mitz heard the buzz of a boat engine over the incessant murmur of the waves rolling upon the shore.

He turned his infrared lens away from the massive freighter and across the luminescent gloaming of the rolling ocean until he spotted a boat striking out from the Punta Boca Morena up the coast—a network of docks that connected beneath a large red-roofed marina. It was an oversized powerboat of some sort, which lay low to the ocean, but still Mitz counted five distinct figures crouched in the craft. The powerboat crossed the Bay of Mayaguez on a direct path to the freighter, so Mitz became rapidly convinced that this was no coincidence and that the men on the speedboat were the FALN terrorists coming to purchase the crate of rocket-propelled grenades from Quan Tang and his Czech bodyguards.

Sheila was lying on a beach towel with a blanket pulled up over her. Mitz reached over and shook her gently by the shoulder. Her lashes flickered open and adrenaline cleared her vision as she reached for her snub-nosed pistol. "What's up?"

"We've got a boat headed for the *Rogue Trader* with five men on it. They launched from the Punta Boca Marina."

Sheila threw aside the blanket and leaped to her feet. "What are we waiting for? Let's get up the coast and set up an ambush."

Pausing just long enough to scoop up the telescope, their cooler, and other evidence of their occupation, they loaded their gear into the trunk of the Mercury and they both headed for the driver's side door, reaching for the handle at the same time.

"I'm driving," said Sheila.

"You're still groggy," said Mitz. "You ride shotgun."

Sheila scowled and reluctantly conceded. "Fine, but next time I'm taking the wheel."

"Fair enough," said Mitz and Sheila opened the door and climbed in the driver's seat. At first Mitz figured that Sheila was going back on their freshly struck bargain but she gave him a smile that dared him to say something and then scooted across to the passenger seat.

In a few moments the Mercury was roaring down the Avenue Jose Gonzales Clemente with Mitz behind the wheel. Three blocks later they crossed the bridge over the river and immediately peeled down an off-ramp. Mitz sent the Mercury sliding around the corner in a left-hand turn that put him on the San Pablo, until he reached the Heyliser which took them along the coastline until they reached the point.

As they drew nearer the marina, Mitz shut off the lights of the Mercury and drove the last half mile by the light of the moon. He stopped the vehicle well short of the marina and shut off the motor. They sat in the darkness for a moment and Mitz lifted a pair of binoculars, scrying the darkness, trying to sift shape and shadow. He spotted the flicker of a cigarette lighter down by the end of the docks. For a brief moment it illuminated a face with Puerto Rican features partially concealed by a thick mustache and sideburns. This man in a painter's cap leaned against the rear bumper of an olive-green delivery van and sucked on a cigarette until he had ignited the tobacco. Then his face returned to the shadows and Mitz could only see the cherry at the end of his cigarette, when the fellow pulled the tobacco fumes into his lungs.

"We've got a van down by the docks," said Mitz. "There's a man standing guard at the rear."

Sheila screwed a silencer onto the threaded snub nose of her .38 Colt, a custom job with very tight tolerances to keep the gases escaping from between the barrel and the cylinder at a minimum. "There's another in the cab—just lit up a cigar with the dashboard lighter."

"I guess it's a good thing they're both smokers," said Mitz, "or we never would have spotted them."

"Do you have anything to keep those Double Eagles of yours quiet?" asked Sheila.

"No, I left all my silencers at home."

Sheila arched an eyebrow. "Then, if it comes down to it, you'll have to let me do all the shooting. We're going to need to keep this quiet."

Mitz toggled the dome light of the Mercury so that it wouldn't illuminate the interior of the car when they opened the doors.

"You ready to go?" asked Sheila.

"I was born ready," said Mitz. He eased open his door and slipped into the cool night air. They left the doors to the car slightly ajar so they didn't risk the click of a latch alerting the FALN men guarding the van. Then, staying low, they ran from shadow to shadow, taking advantage of benches, shrubs, and automobiles to provide them cover.

Mitz ducked beneath the projecting rearview mirror on the side of the van and edged along the vehicle. The guard at the rear was just finishing his cigarette as Mitz completed his approach. He exhaled a plume of smoke and threw the cigarette onto the ground, grinding it out with the toe of his shoe. He heard the crunch of gravel beneath Mitz's footstep and turned, only to have Mitz club him over the head with the butt of his semi-automatic pistol.

It was a savage blow that knocked off the guard's cap, and the guard gave out a croak as he sank to his knees. Mitz clubbed him again, knocking him flat on his face, unconscious and bleeding. Kneeling, Mitz heaved the guard over and removed a magnum pistol that was shoved into the front of the fellow's pants.

On the other side of the van, the driver heard the croak and the collapse of his companion through his open window and called back in Spanish. "Fernando? What's going on back there?"

The driver saw a sudden shifting of shadows and then a woman stood just outside his door, thrusting a silenced revolver through the open window so that it pointed at his temple. "Fernando's taking a *siesta*. Unless you want to take a permanent *siesta*, you're going to do exactly what I tell you."

The bill of the driver's cap turned, and the driver saw that it was a woman who was holding him at gunpoint. "You are just a *poco chica*! You wouldn't dare pull that trigger." He kicked the door open, sending Sheila sprawling. Instead of dodging or bracing herself against the blow, she kept her eye on the driver and pulled the trigger.

When Mitz came around the corner, he found the driver slumped over, brains leaking out a bullet hole. Sheila was picking herself up off the ground and dusting off the dirt from her legs. "He didn't want to cooperate."

Mitz reached in and hoisted the driver out of the van, throwing him heavily on the earth. "The one in back is still alive. Maybe you can find something to tie him up and gag him with."

Something sharp flickered into Sheila's hand. "I've got something more efficient in mind."

Mitz had killed plenty of men, but cold-blooded killing made him squeamish. "You and Sly are a perfect match—if you don't end up killing each other, that is. Tying him up will be good enough."

The stiletto rasped back into the handle. "If you insist."

"I insist," said Mitz.

An old Caddie rested in the nearby parking lot and Mitz grabbed the dead driver by the collar and dragged him across the lawn and the pavement until he reached the trunk—one large enough to hold a pair of bodies. He slipped a tension bar and pressure lever into the lock and in a few moments he had the trunk open. There was jack and some other odds and ends in the trunk, but Mitz figured the driver wouldn't mind the discomfort of a few odd things poking into his back. He squatted and hoisted the body into the trunk, then quickly returned for the guard he had knocked unconscious.

This one was still breathing as Sheila crouched over him, cinching zip ties around the guard's limbs. "Zip ties. Never leave home without 'em."

Mitz was about to protest when the stiletto again appeared in Sheila's hand. The blade stopped just short of the man's belly as Sheila lifted the guard's shirt and sliced a section away. She glanced up at Mitz with a wry smile. "What? You thought that I was going to cut up my own clothes to make a gag?"

"No, I thought you were going to eviscerate him."

"I know what you thought," said Sheila. "I just like messing with your head."

"Sometimes you scare me."

"I like to keep things unpredictable," said Sheila. "That's one reason why John Velvet was happy to accept my resignation from the American Intelligence Machine. I had my own ideas about how missions should be run."

Once the unconscious fellow was gagged and zip-tied, Mitz hoisted him over his shoulder and made the trek to the still-open trunk of the Cadillac. After depositing the body, he carefully pushed the trunk closed, listening for the click of the latch. Though the murmur of the ocean might well cover the sound of a slamming trunk, he didn't want to take any unnecessary risks that the occupants of a returning speedboat might be alerted to their presence.

Even as he returned to the van he heard the whine of the speedboat, and peering into the night he thought he saw a glimpse of the boat's white belly as it plowed through a swell, then disappeared in an intervening trough.

Sheila stood, an hourglass silhouette in the dim light of the moon. She gazed out at the ocean. "They're on the way back."

"We can set up flanking positions at four and eight o'clock," pointed Mitz. "That way we won't catch each other in the crossfire. Think we can take out all five of them before they get wind of the ambush?"

"We've got a pair of UZIs in the Mercury," said Sheila. "That might help even the odds."

"No time," said Mitz. "They're coming in fast."

Indeed, the speedboat emerged out of the darkness, sloughing to the right and throwing up a white froth that rolled along the waves. Now it eased alongside the covered docks amidst the moored yachts and fishing vessels. Shadowed forms leaped from the boat and cinched the boat to the cleats. With great care they eased two crates from their craft. A stiff breeze picked up, blowing out to sea, so that it seemed that the very elements were conspiring against the terrorists bringing their weapons ashore.

Sheila plucked out her cell phone and speed dialed a number while she and Mitz split into the shadows. The cover consisted of a few benches and shrubs, nothing concrete enough to afford them any real protection against gunfire. Mitz threw himself down behind a shrub and began to burrow into the soft earth of the garden bed, trying to give himself as much protection as he possibly could. He sucked in his breath when he saw that the speedboat had returned with two extra men.

Four of the Puerto Rican terrorists were occupied with carrying the first crate. A squat and wild-haired Puerto Rican led the way, his left eye roving the darkness. In the wan moonlight, Mitz could see that the terrorist's right eye was a milky white, and a scar extended from his brow to his cheekbone. This was Normando Abrego, a small-time FALN lieutenant who had suddenly found himself in charge when CIA sweeps had somehow missed him, while managing to arrest and incarcerate everyone who outranked him.

Flanking the nearest side of the crate came Tomik Korda, cradling a 7.62 Czech machine gun. This gun was generally meant for firing from a fixed position, but Korda had a metal ammunition box hanging awkwardly from the right side of the gun, which contained a fifty-round belt of ammunition.

In the flanking position to the left of the crate was one of Korda's Czech henchmen carrying a second vz59 machine gun which was identical to Korda's, except that he had opted to wrap a 250-round belt over his shoulders. There was a lot of firepower on the flanks of the crate, and to make matters worse, the bushy-haired Puerto Rican at the point pulled out a mini-MAC submachine gun as he approached the open doors of the van.

"Fernando, Pedro! Start the engine," ordered Abrego.

To Mitz's surprise, the van started up and he saw a dark shape sitting in the driver's seat of the van. Instead of taking position, Sheila had climbed inside the van. This meant that Mitz was left to take out three machine gun toting terrorists all by his lonesome—unless Sheila had some other plan up her sleeve.

The four Puerto Rican crate bearers began wrestling their burden into the back of the long-bed van, pushing it forward to make room for the second crate that they would be momentarily retrieving. Mitz rested the butt of his Colt Double Eagle on the ground, aiming at Tomik Korda through the shrub—wondering if he should take the first shot. Without Sheila firing from the other flank, he had little chance of being able to take out all three gunners before they located his muzzle flash and chewed him up with a storm of lead.

Mitz heard the thumping of a helicopter's blades in the distance. He wasn't the only one who heard it. Tomik Korda and his henchman looked to the sky, hoping to spot the aircraft. The moment that Tomik Korda lifted his machine gun to the sky was the moment that Mitz flicked his laser sight on and fired. He put a pair of bullets into Korda's chest, staggering the Czech terrorist but not taking him down. Mitz muttered a curse. He hadn't recognized it in the cloak of darkness, but Korda's shirt was far too bulky and unnatural in form. Korda was wearing a bulletproof vest, and now the Czech terrorist unleashed a torrent of lead in the direction of

Mitz's muzzle flash.

At that moment, Sheila dropped out of the driver's seat of the van and strode toward the back. With the silencer still on her pistol, the sound of her unleashed bullets was unheard amid the cacophony of hellfire that Korda unleashed upon Mitz, empty brass spewing high into the air and reflections of the foot-long muzzle flash stuttering against the glossy panels of the van.

Sheila's first shot hit the Czech right at the sternum, but he didn't even seem to notice. This was when Sheila realized that the pair of Czechs were wearing Kevlar vests. Before the Czech could adjust his aim, she worked her way upward, putting a second bullet mid-chest with equally feeble results, and then a third bullet just above the clavicle and through the Czech's throat. He pulled the trigger of his vz59 and it immediately began chewing through the ammunition belt at a rate that would devour all 250 rounds in a matter of twenty seconds.

The third bullet Sheila fired had clipped the Czech's spinal cord after passing through his esophagus. He was gasping for air, choking on his own blood, and his knees buckled beneath him so that he pitched backward as his machine gun poured torrents of lead into the air. Still, this alone would not have been enough to save Sheila. The Czech had a death grip on his trigger and as he collapsed, the barrel of his gun began to fall toward Sly's wife. Suddenly the barrel was jerked from its course as the ammunition belt that was wound around his shoulders slipped off and tightened around his neck and arm, twisting the Czech around so that his gun barrel pushed into the earth and the ammunition belt pulled from the guides, the receiver jamming and the firing ceasing.

Twenty rounds spat out of Korda's machine gun, clipping off branches and spitting up dirt. One round took the sunglasses off the top of Mitz's head and another furrowed his shoulder. It was a combination of factors—the cover he had managed to eke out by burrowing into the earth, that Korda could not see his target, and that the vz59 machine gun pulled to the right, off-balanced by the hanging ammunition box—that saved Mitz's life. For if the snout of Korda's machine gun had lingered on target for just a moment longer, surely a round or two would have found Mitz.

Korda began to swing around when, out of the corner of his eye, he saw his companion pitch to the ground. He saw the dark-haired woman, smoking pistol in hand. She spun, bringing the silenced snout of that pistol toward him and he pulled the trigger of his machine gun in anticipation of bringing her into his sights. He pulled the trigger a fraction of a second too early and sent a trio of rounds into the back of one of the FALN terrorists who was scrambling away from the rear of the van. That terrorist pitched onto the paving, while Normando Abrego, the glassy-eyed Puerto Rican cell leader, jammed his thick body past the crate of rocket-propelled grenades and into the driver's seat of the still-running van.

With the crate firmly inside the van, a pair of the terrorists thought it best to join the cargo, but a third terrorist turned, pulling a magazine pistol from the waistband of his baggy jeans. He thrust the barrel in Sheila's direction, but Mitz had already risen up from his shallow grave, firing alternately from each hand in a rapid staccato accompanied by the licking tongues of muzzle flash from his Colt Double Eagles.

Mitz didn't like splitting his targets, but that didn't mean that he couldn't—and he really had no choice in the matter. He sent a pair of bullets into the FALN terrorist's chest, so that the terrorist fell, striking his head on the bumper of the van even while the tires began to smoke and spin as Abrego jammed the vehicle into drive and stomped on the gas. Another pair of bullets found Tomik Korda, one passing through the back of his neck. Korda pitched to the ground and his machine gun clattered from his hands.

Sheila and Mitz turned their attention to the fleeing van. Abrego was behind the wheel and one other terrorist was firmly ensconced inside next to the crate, but a third leaped to the bumper and hung onto the door frame as the vehicle squealed away. Muzzles flashed as the terrorists fired from the back and bumper of the van, and bullets spat and whined against the pavement.

While Mitz holstered one of his pistols and dropped the magazine from his other, Sheila returned fire and a terrorist toppled from the bumper, landing face first on the pavement, then rolling in a tangled heap of limp limbs.

A formerly canary-yellow helicopter, now sprayed with patches of green and black that effectively camouflaged it in the darkness, swooped low, its runners threatening to strike the van. If Normando Abrego was unnerved by the sudden appearance of the copter hurtling toward him, he didn't show it. He kept his van on course, standing his ground in the high stakes game of chicken.

Sly pulled the copter up just enough so that he cleared the top of the van by at least a foot, but gunfire erupted from within the van, puncturing the roof with a hail of lead as the occupants tried to hit the swooping helicopter. They fired a fraction of a moment too late to hit the speeding helicopter, which didn't slacken its pace. Instead, Sly sent the aircraft speeding over Sheila's and Mitz's heads, washing them in a sea of sound and rushing air, which tore at their hair and clothing as if they stood in a hurricane wind.

Mitz would not be distracted. He shoved a magazine of incendiary bullets into his pistol, jacked back the slide and took careful aim at the receding van. He had time enough for only one shot, and so he made it count. A moment later the rocket-propelled grenades went up in a fiery blossom that turned the van into shrapnel and reduced it, Normando Abrego, and its other occupants to pulp. Grenades hurtled hundreds of feet in all directions, and some of them exploded, leaving pockmarks in the asphalt and landscaping of the marina.

When finally the tumult had died down, Sheila turned to Mitz. "Well, that was spectacular. We should have the police here in about four or five minutes."

Mitz checked the burning furrow in his left shoulder. It was ugly, but not serious. "I only regret that Quan Tang wasn't in that van."

She looked to the sky and the shrinking shape of the camouflaged helicopter. "That must have taken about a hundred cans of spray paint."

"The rental agency will love it," said Mitz. "Any idea where Sly's headed?"

Sheila pointed to the sea, and amidst the waves, the moonlight temporarily revealed the outline of a motorboat heading back out to sea. "It looks like one of our terrorists decided to take the last crate back to the *Rogue Trader*."

Mitz surveyed the bodies strewn about their feet. "Where's Tomik Korda?"

Sheila was sure that Mitz was mistaken, and that Korda's body was being overlooked. Yet, when she searched the tarry umbra of the landscape, she did not see Korda either. "I thought you put him down!"

Mitz shone a flashlight on the ground, revealing splatters of blood where Korda had fallen, and a trail of crimson that led back to the docks of the marina. "Down but not dead, apparently. He must be aboard that boat as well."

Sheila scowled. "Sly's going after the motorboat, but he's on a collision course with the *Rogue Trader*."

Chapter 20

The homemade camouflage on the helicopter helped Sly approach the fleeing jet boat, but even though cloud cover was beginning to move in on a gusting westward wind, he became a clear target when the shadow of the copter blotted out the rays of the moon.

The Czech driver called out a warning to Korda, who sat in the bottom of the boat. Korda left off clutching at the crimson bullet wound in his neck and lifted his driver's vz59 machine gun so that the tripod was propped on the seat in front of him. He already had a 250-round belt lined up in the receiver of the machine gun's feed and he leaned back, yellow muzzle flash strobing his craggy features as he unleashed a torrent of lead at the chasing helicopter.

Sly juked the helicopter from one side to the other, but bullet holes poked through the floor of the cockpit and out the roof, just missing the trio of M14 grenades he had dangling from the overhead visor. The holes whistled as air gushed through them and though Sly had managed to avoid the vast majority of the bullets, he realized that the helicopter could not sustain another burst of fire from Korda's machine gun. He could see Korda scrambling to feed a second belt into the machine gun and he realized that he had just a few moments to turn the helicopter around and make his escape, or to make his move.

Demonstrating the kind of snap decision making that had resulted in Sly being discharged from the Navy, he opened the cockpit window and swooped over the top of the boat. He matched velocity with the craft and pulled an M14 grenade from overhead. The M14 had a thermite core which turned the casing to molten iron when it exploded. It wasn't designed for massive casualties like a fragmentation grenade, but it did a great job of destroying things in a short radius and had enough juice to melt through an engine block. Praying that his timing was right, Sly shoveled a grenade out the wing window, then veered away as the grenade hit the chrome rail of the speeding boat and ricocheted in, coming to rest next to the second crate which had never been transported to the now-destroyed van that had been waiting at the marina.

Korda just finished attaching the second belt when he heard the clank of the grenade and saw it roll across the bottom of the boat and stop next to the crate. "The nerve gas!"

At Korda's shout, the driver glanced back and fear washed across his face as he realized what was happening. He abandoned the wheel and dove from the boat even as Korda threw himself forward in an effort to grab the grenade and toss it overboard before it could detonate.

Korda was a fraction of a second too late and the grenade detonated, melting through flesh and destroying everything within the boat. Sly heard the sound of the detonation and then close on its heels came a second explosion that lit up the waves and the sky for a brief instant. Sly struggled to keep the helicopter from being tossed end over end as a shockwave hit the aircraft.

Once Sly brought the helicopter under control, he wheeled it around. Where there once had been a speedboat, there was nothing but wreckage and an oil slick. A great cloud rose from the spot where the boat had once grappled with the waves and the gusting wind picked up the cloud of deadly gas and sent it rolling toward the dark bulk of the *Rogue Trader*.

Chapter 21

The sun was just rising over the swelling and falling ocean, bringing light and hope to the new day when a haggard and fatigued Sheila stood on the deck of a Villa Del Carmen hotel room. The gusts of the evening had died and a light rain had given way to scant cloud cover and the sun which warmed the vibrant red blossoms of the majestic trees outside. She had Cromwell Jensen on the phone and he wasn't very happy.

"You've really put your foot in it this time. I expect you'll be hearing from your old boss, before this thing is sorted out," growled Jensen.

"Velvet? If you let him on this, he'll take all the credit."

"Listen," said Jensen. "I'm trying to spin this thing so you, Sly, and Mitz come out heroes, but the fact is that Sly detonated a Soviet-made Scud 17 warhead equipped with a VR nerve agent right off the coast of a US territory. If the wind had been blowing the other way, there would have been massive casualties. As it is, we've got seventeen crew dead on the *Rogue Trader*, including the captain."

"Look at it this way," said Sheila. "If the FALN had gotten their hands on that Scud, it would have ended up being detonated in a major population center. What would the casualties have looked like then?"

"Tens of thousands," admitted Jensen. "In fact, we've rounded up a couple of accomplices and they've admitted they planned to blow off the Scud in Times Square."

"What did they plan to do with those rocket-propelled grenades?"

"Heaven knows," growled Jensen. "A couple of years ago they got their hands on just one of them and one night they fired it into the FBI offices in Puerto Rico. Lucky for the agents on duty that night, the grenade went through the window and through the roof without detonating and then landed in the nearby parking lot of a shopping center before exploding."

Sheila pushed her fingers through a tangle of her dark hair at her scalp. "Anyone hurt?"

"Just a few cars and a few windows. The place was closed and empty. The FBI agents don't turn on their overhead lights anymore. Instead they use desk lamps. It makes it harder to target the right floor."

"What about this VR gas?" asked Sheila. "Is it headed toward the Dominican Republic?"

"The winds are dying down," said Jensen. "Our meteorologists predict that it will dissipate before making landfall. The VR nerve agent is composed of two less toxic components that are meant to mix during flight. In this case there was no flight, so the components didn't mix adequately."

"Adequately enough to kill seventeen on the *Rogue Trader*," said Sheila.

"It's deadly stuff," said Jensen. "Nothing's sure, but given the current wind directions our experts think the Dominican Republic is safe."

"Nothing we can do about those sailors on the *Rogue Trader*, though," said Sheila.

"Look," said Jensen. "When you jump into the middle of situations like this without full intelligence, these things will happen. You've been in this business long enough to know that sometimes collateral damage is inevitable, besides—the crew of the *Rogue Trader* wasn't exactly a bunch of altar boys.

"Captain Pavlik hired strictly ex-convicts. His crew is made up of rapists and murderers from a half dozen different countries. There is even some indication that they've been indulging in piracy. A pleasure yacht disappeared from the Balearic Sea earlier this year along with its owner, Alexander Thomasine ..."

"The millionaire financier?"

"Yes. He disappeared along with his wife and daughter. The path of his yacht intersected with that of the *Rogue Trader*. We can't prove anything, of course, but Thomasine's body washed up on the shores of Monaco. We may have a line on the yacht, but it's repainted and renamed the *Grimme Ouvre*."

"Thanks for easing our consciences, Cole, but the big question around here is whether Quan Tang was among those seventeen that met their demise."

"Sorry," replied Jensen. "I can't do anything for you there. Quan Tang may have never reboarded the *Rogue Trader* after they refueled in San Juan. We're going through the flight records of planes departing the Luis Muñoz Marín International Airport to see if we can locate him traveling under some sort of alias."

"Let us know if you come up with anything."

"Right," said Jensen, but there was no mistaking the sarcasm in his voice. "Hey, this incident with the VR warhead could have been a lot worse, but I'm going to be running cleanup on this for months. If we're not careful it could become an international incident. If you want to pursue this vendetta with Quan Tang, you are on your own from here on out."

"Come on," coaxed Sheila. "If you play your cards right you could get a promotion out of this—"

"I don't want a promotion," said Jensen. "This line's not clean anymore." The phone call abruptly ended and the phone line went dead.

Sheila sighed and tossed the phone on the bed. Sly sat on the other side of the bed, the hotel room phone six inches from his ear while he dropped a handful of atropine and diazepam pills in his mouth and swallowed them down with a glassful of water. The man on the other end of the line was screaming.

"Maybe you don't understand me," replied Sly to the profane rant. "The helicopter isn't capable of making the flight back. You're going to have to send a flatbed and winch to pick it up at the address I gave you."

Again the screaming began. Sly waited patiently. "Why won't it fly? Probably a bullet clipped a fuel line."

"A bullet?" cried the man at the rental agency. "How in *le diablo* did the helicopter get hit with a bullet?"

"Oh, it got hit with far more than one bullet," replied Sly. "The insurance I purchased will cover that, right?"

The man at the rental agency began swearing. "No it won't cover that! You're going to pay for it."

"Fine, fine," acquiesced Sly. "No need to get your panties in a wad. These sort of things happen all the time."

"Not to me, they don't!"

"Hey, I said I'll cover it. Now send your man over to collect the copter. He shouldn't have any troubles finding it. It's parked on the front lawn of the Hacienda Hotel."

The voice finally calmed a bit. "*Si*, a yellow helicopter on the front lawn shouldn't be difficult to locate."

"Actually," said Sly, "the color of the helicopter is a little bit different than when I rented it. Tell your man to look for a green and black camouflage helicopter. It tends to blend in with the lawn."

Sly hung up as the fellow at the helicopter agency erupted in a tirade of further profanity.

Sheila climbed onto the bed behind Sly and massaged his bulky trapezoids. She couldn't help but notice his hand trembling as he put the phone down. "Hey, you okay?"

Sly grinned. "Of course, that was a piece of cake compared to handling Jensen, which you did a magnificent job of, by the way."

"Good news on the crew of the *Rogue Trader*," said Sheila.

Sly wiped away the sweat forming on his brow. "No casualties?"

"Seventeen casualties, but it seems the world will be a better place without them; murderers and rapists, the lot of them. Jensen had them connected with the murder of Alexander Thomasine and the disappearance of his wife and daughter."

Sly grunted; he had seen articles and photos of Thomasine and his family in the society pages of various rags before they disappeared. "What about Quan Tang?"

"Probably on his way back to Czechoslovakia."

Sly coughed. "Then Fritz and Matthias will be ready and waiting for them."

Chapter 22

Fritz sat in a battered Yugo outside the high stone wall of Quan Tang's gated mansion in the Malesice District located within Prague District Ten. Dusk settled upon the streets and the branches of the overhead beech trees cast skeletal reflections upon the weathered orange finish of the vehicle, the leaves rustling in a cooling breeze that gave relief to the heat of the day.

The rock guitarist sat with a paper plate on his knees, eating a sausage with a side of bread pasted with ketchup and mustard. "You know, in America we put the sausage in the bread with the condiments, to get all the flavors in one bite."

Otka was behind the wheel of the Yugo. "That's foolish," she protested. "The ketchup and mustard are best as a chaser to the flavor of the sausage."

Ignoring Otka's culinary admonitions, Fritz placed the dog in the middle of the bread and folded it over. "It's also more convenient."

Otka gasped. "I can't believe you did that!"

Fritz grinned and then took a bite of the sausage and chewed. "The only thing missing is the sauerkraut."

The Yugo sat up the winding cobble street from Quan Tang's gate, one of a number of other vehicles which lined the streets. A woman with gray hair and a faded floral dress walked a small pug down the stone walk, occasionally stopping to let her canine mark what it presumed was his territory.

"How much more of this surveillance do we need to do?" asked Otka, who followed a delicate bite of her own sausage with an equal portion of condiment-dressed bread. "Budek was not keen on me coming with you."

"I could sense that," said Fritz, "but he needs to concentrate on getting Matthias into Pankrác Prison."

"He says this watching is dangerous and that I would be safer at the church."

"What he says is probably true," said Fritz, "but I needed someone I could trust, and who is familiar with Prague to help me find Quan Tang's compound. Otherwise, I would still be searching for District Ten, let alone this specific street."

Otka's dark eyes surveyed the steep roofs and arched windows of the stone mansion beyond the high wall. "Compound? It looks more like a mansion to me."

"As it should," said Fritz, "but it is very well guarded."

Otka's auburn hair splayed about her shoulders as she shook her head. She was wearing a plain yellow sundress that displayed the hollows where her slender neck met her clavicles. "I don't see any guards."

Fritz handed Otka his binoculars and directed her gaze to the tower of the mansion, which rose higher than the rest of the structure. "See the top floor of the tower: there is a moon-shaped window which is open. Beneath it you'll see a round cylinder poking out. That's the barrel of a rifle. Underneath the two beech trees that line the drive to the mansion you'll find men dressed in patterned gray clothing that precisely matches the bark of the trees they are standing against."

Otka's mouth dropped as she recognized the men standing next to the trees. "You can barely discern them from the bark! They seem to be wearing swords on their backs."

"They are Vovinam adepts," said Fritz, "trained to blend into their surroundings, and deadly with blade and sword."

"So there are just two of them, and a gunman in the tower?"

"During the last six hours, I've spotted five others," said Fritz. "The ones beneath the beech trees were the easiest to spot. There's at least two blending in with the bricks of the wall and three hiding amidst the shrubs. Every three hours they are replaced by another adept. That's the easiest time to spot them."

Otka lowered the binoculars and her dark lashes fluttered. "How will you get past them to reach Quan Tang?"

"That's the thing," said Fritz. "I'm not getting past them."

"You're not?"

"First, I need to see some evidence that Quan Tang is actually inside the compound, or I'll be risking my life for nothing. He probably isn't even here. Quan Tang was spotted by a harbor master in Puerto Rico. That's the last place he's been seen."

"When was that?"

"Two days ago," said Fritz.

"So he could be here already," Otka replied. "We came early this morning. He might have arrived last night."

"He might have," agreed Fritz and he finished off the last of his hot dog. He carefully wiped his mouth with a napkin. "I can think of another reason that Budek didn't want you away from the church."

Otka arched her brow and a faint smile played upon her lips. "Oh, and what is that?"

"You're a beautiful woman. Maybe he senses some competition and wants to keep you away from me."

"He says that rock stars are used to taking any woman that they want. That they have no morals and I should keep my distance or you might take me against my will."

Fritz recalled a number of debaucheries he'd witnessed after shows with the Dregs of Humanity, and the Mix Gäang. "There's certainly some truth to what Budek says, but you have nothing to worry about from me. My mother taught us to respect women."

"Respect is admirable," said Otka and she leaned toward Fritz, "but Budek and I aren't married. He doesn't own me and I'm still free to make my own decis—"

Otka noticed that Fritz's attention was not fixed upon her. Instead he was looking past her and toward the gate of Quan Tang's compound. "Am I being too—"

"There's a black Rolls coming down the road," said Fritz. "It's got armor-plating."

Otka swiveled in the driver's seat. "That's Quan Tang's car."

"So either Quan Tang is coming into town or they've spotted us and this is a clever ploy to make us believe that he'll be inside the mansion," said Fritz.

Otka rested both hands on the steering wheel, still a little miffed that her moment with Fritz had been interrupted. "Are you always this paranoid?"

"It's not being paranoid when you've actually got people out to get you," replied Fritz. "It's merely self-preservation. Quan Tang is devious enough to plant a bomb in a flashpot beneath our stage. Why wouldn't he be devious enough to send his car ahead to see if he can draw me out?"

Otka could find no argument against this. "Maybe you should hit the car now, before it gets behind the walls of the mansion."

Fritz shook his head. "I've got some steel jacketed slugs that might be able to penetrate the windows, but the body's got enough armor on it to resist any of the firepower I've got on me. Even Matthias's ridiculous 454 Casull couldn't punch through that plating. You might find Sly willing to take a wild gamble on a hunch, but I'm more of a planner. I like to tilt the odds in my favor before acting."

"But his mansion is full of Vovinam martial artist fanatics. What kind of chance do you have against them?"

Fritz scratched at the stubble growing on his chin. "A better chance than you might think."

Otka reached out and put her hand on Fritz's shoulder. "Listen, Fritz. You don't have to do this. I want Quan Tang taken down nearly as much as you do. I'm positive that he's the one who sent the state after my father, but what good is revenge if you end up dead, too?"

"It's not revenge," said Fritz. "It's retribution. If we let just one person act against us without retaliating, then all our old enemies will have no fear of doing the same."

The gate opened up for the Rolls-Royce, and the vehicle drifted like a shadow through the gloaming, winding past the hidden sentries and to the great porch of the mansion. "Just how many enemies do you have?"

"More than I can begin to count." Fritz lifted the binoculars to his eyes and peered through them. There was just enough light to make out the figures and faces of the men who climbed out of the car. They were dressed in blue vophucs belted with red, which indicated they were masters in the Vovinam art. They surrounded a man, ushering him up the stairs and through the black-painted double doors of the mansion. For an instant this man turned his head in Fritz's direction, revealing cold flint-like eyes that seemed to pierce the twilight veil and look right into Fritz's soul. The guitarist recognized those eyes, just as he recognized the scar on the chin— the same scar that he had given Quan Tang when they crossed swords once before.

Then Quan Tang's cruel visage was lost in a sea of blue vophucs, which swept him inside the mansion. The doors closed and the chauffeur drove to a detached garage alongside the mansion. He left the car and punched in a security code on the faceplate near the great doors. Once the garage door lifted, the sleepy-eyed chauffeur returned to the Rolls-Royce and eased the great vehicle inside the pristine interior that blazed with bright light. As the garage door closed, this bright light narrowed from a beam to a sliver, then disappeared entirely, devouring both car and driver in its gullet.

Fritz chuckled.

"I'm glad you're finding humor in this," said Otka.

Fritz was perceptive enough to hear the irritation in her voice. "The security code to the garage is all nines and fives. Easy enough to remember."

"The Vietnamese consider fives a most inauspicious number," said Otka. "Nines are considered extremely lucky or an indication of violence."

"It's not surprising that Quan Tang would adopt those numbers," said Fritz. "As soon as darkness settles completely, I'll need you to head back to the church, or better yet, visit your friend's house in District Three. Meet us at four in the morning at Kafka's grave."

"You want me to meet you in the middle of the night at a cemetery?"

"Hopefully, Matthias and Budek will be there with your father, and then we'll figure a way across the border."

"I thought you liked to plan things out."

"Oh, I've got a plan," said Fritz, "but even the best laid plans tend to go awry."

Chapter 23

Matthias was wearing the jumpsuit of a janitor when he entered through the employee entrance of the great courthouses that fronted Pankrác Prison. He wore a photo ID card pinned to the front which identified him as Jirka Michna. Jirka Michna had a bulbous nose and drooping eyes. The only real resemblance was Jirka had long hair about the same color as Matthias's. Matthias hoped that in the eyes of the Czech authorities, all hippies looked alike.

Budek also wore a similar jumpsuit, but his ID possessed his own photo and categorized him as part of the janitorial services. A number of lawyers and civil service drones with ashen faces drained of life filtered from the interior cubicles and offices, crossing the cracked tiles to find their way to their government-assigned tenements—miles and miles of ill-maintained housing tracts that were made unique only by the people that lived within.

"Where did you get these IDs?" asked Matthias, once they had passed by the security guard who gave them only a cursory glance, and made no acknowledgment to Budek's greeting.

"I borrowed yours from Jirka. I paid him twenty of the US dollars that you gave me so that he would stay home from his shift tonight."

Budek had insisted that he needed a thousand US dollars to make bribes and obtain IDs. Matthias was starting to wonder if he had been taken. "Is twenty dollars enough to keep him quiet?"

"Jirka makes about three thousand korunas a year." Budek licked his lips and glanced nervously behind as they negotiated the long hallway which was festooned with tattered communist propaganda.

"Right," said Matthias. "But the exchange rate is what? About three korunas to a dollar?"

"That's the official exchange rate. On the black market it's about thirty korunas to a dollar. So by giving Jirka twenty US dollars, he earns six hundred korunas. That's over two months' wages."

Matthias suspected that Budek was planning on keeping most of that one thousand dollars for himself, but the information he shared about the black market rate of dollars to korunas rang true. Matthias recalled his youth in Berlin and remembered the high value of the American dollar in exchange for bootleg records and American jeans. "What about your ID? Is that doctored, too? You're a big shot around here. Why didn't the guard even acknowledge your existence?"

Budek stuttered an embarrassed response. "I'm not really a big shot. I just said that because I wanted to impress Otka. She's so amazing, I just can't imagine why she'd ever settle for someone who was just a janitor."

They turned the corner down a poorly lit hall and Budek used his keys to give them access to a janitorial closet that contained a variety of cleaning chemicals, mops, and brooms. "Grab a cart. Trust me, if you're pushing one of these things nobody will pay any attention to you—unless they want to yell at you to clean up blood or vomit."

"You know, once we get out of Czechoslovakia, you'll have the chance to reinvent yourself. There's no shame in being a janitor, but if you want to do something else, you'll have the opportunity."

Budek's eyes shifted back and forth as he filled a rolling mop bucket. "It's too late to reinvent myself. The best I can do is lie to Otka ... and myself ... about what I am."

"It's not too late." Matthias grabbed a cart and began loading it with cleaning supplies.

"I don't know about that," said Budek. "I'm just a janitor, what kind of chance do I have with Otka compared to a big time rock guitarist, like your brother?"

Budek was growing increasingly bitter and Matthias thought it best to change the subject. He examined a plastic jug and found the inscription illegible. "What's this?"

"Bleach, and that's pneumonia next to it."

"Maybe you mean ammonia?"

Budek shrugged. "My English needs work."

"Hey, I'm not coming down on your English. I only know a few words of Czech."

Once Matthias completed his disguise with various cleaning agents and scrub brushes, they headed down the hallway side by side.

"To reach Father Lada, we'll need to pass into sector seven, where they keep the political prisoners," said Otka.

Matthias nodded. He knew this. They had been over the plan a dozen times, step by step. Matthias had spent hours memorizing the map of Pankrác.

"Would you like to see the room where the Nazis kept the guillotine?"

"Not necessary," said Matthias. "This isn't a sightseeing tour. We grab Father Lada and get out. Any deviation puts us at further risk."

Budek accepted this with nonchalance. "I spend every evening here and have been to every part of the prison, even the torture rooms. To me, there seems to be no danger."

To Matthias it seemed that despite Budek's familiarity with Pankrác, he was taking this altogether too lightly. "You do realize that if you're caught helping me that you'll likely end up in that torture chamber, sitting in a chair right next to me?"

"Warden Vlach prefers to put his prisoners on a rack and stretch them until their joints pull apart." To demonstrate this, Budek made a stretching motion and a clucking sound with his tongue.

One thing that Matthias had learned over the years was to trust his gut, or maybe it was divine intuition, that informed him that all was not as it appeared. He drew up short while Budek continued to push his mop bucket.

Budek saw that Matthias was not keeping pace and he halted. "What's wrong?"

"We're aborting the rescue," said Matthias. He turned the cart around and began pushing it back the way they had come.

Budek abandoned his mop and bucket and came up alongside of Matthias. "But what about Father Lada?"

"It was Fritz that promised to rescue him. We'll come back when we've got more resources."

"I got you into the prison without one person even noticing you," said Budek. "What better resource could you have than me?"

Matthias began unscrewing the caps on a few of the jugs. "That's just it, Budek. Is security at Pankrác so lax that they don't even know what Jirka Michna looks like?"

"The guards don't pay attention to the janitors," protested Budek. "And besides, I knew that a different guard from day shift would be on duty tonight filling in."

"You're just a janitor," said Matthias. "How did you know that?"

Budek stammered. "I … I … I have the key to the warden's office. Someone has to clean it."

In truth, Matthias had suspicions but as of yet they added up to nothing. Matthias was fishing by putting the pressure on Budek. "Is Warden Vlach waiting for me in the guillotine room? Is that why you wanted to take a detour?"

Budek's silence spoke volumes. Matthias kicked over the cart, open containers spilling their guts and intermingling. An alarm sounded in the distance and he heard footsteps coming down the corridor. Matthias backed away from the upended cart and the growing puddles of cleaning supplies.

He gave the Czech janitor a hard stare. "They're onto us, Budek. You'd better run or you'll be caught."

Instead of running, Budek reached into the pocket of his jumpsuit. His hand came out with a switchblade, but Matthias was already moving. Using his forearms, he pincered Budek's arm. Budek dropped the knife even as the blade flipped open. Budek screamed as Matthias wrenched his arm behind his back and to his shoulder blade.

"Are you worried now, Budek?" asked Matthias. He reached into his overalls and came out with the 454 Casull, which he shoved into the small of Budek's back. "Don't flinch. The trigger is very touchy and this pistol is big enough to take down a bull elephant."

"Let me go," pleaded Budek. "There's still time to escape. I know how to get us out of here."

"Then lead the way," said Matthias, "but remember if you lead me into a trap, you're only one trigger pull from having your spine blown through your belly."

It might have sounded like mere rhetoric but Matthias spoke it with conviction and, in truth, the Casull cartridge carried 300 grains of gunpowder—enough to do just what Matthias threatened.

"There's a hallway behind us that goes to the left. If we pass through the laundry we can leave the prison through the loading docks."

The footsteps drew nearer and they belonged to four prison guards who accompanied Warden Vlach—a man with flabby jowls and a pocked face. They slowed to a stop about a dozen feet from the upended mess of the cart. Vlach spoke to Matthias. "I don't recommend running. There are still the gates and the guards to contend with and they are authorized to use lethal force."

"It's a communist prison in the middle of Czechoslovakia," shrugged Matthias. "Why should I expect anything else?"

Warden Vlack's lips twitched. "I thought it might be helpful if I went over the facts."

"So what course of action are you recommending?" asked Matthias.

"I would suggest that you remove your arm from Mr. Benes's neck and give yourself over into my custody."

"What's in that for me?"

Warden Vlach spread his pudgy hands. "I can make things easier on you if you cooperate. It's inevitable that you become my prisoner. Why fight the inevitable? Think of it as a business decision made between two business partners."

Matthias tightened his forearm beneath Budek's chin, but he kept his 454 Casull hidden from sight behind Budek's back. "I've fought the inevitable all my life. Now, let me pass or I'll break Mr. Benes's neck!"

"I'm afraid that you've misjudged me, Mr. Gantlet. Somehow, I seem to have given you the mistaken impression that I care about what happens to Mr. Benes. Wring his scrawny neck like a chicken. I don't care." Warden Vlach motioned his guards forward. They pulled wood batons from their belt and their booted feet splashed through the puddles, but they failed to realize that Matthias had mixed bleach and ammonia, and they breathed in the resultant nitrogen trichloride. One of the guards failed to make it through and fell against the wall, but the others staggered through the miasma with burning lungs, reeling toward Matthias with black spots before their eyes.

Matthias shoved Budek to the ground and plucked away a baton from the nearest. In their befuddled, barely conscious state, Matthias was able to fell the remaining three with as many strokes. He took a deep breath of clean air and then plunged through the poisonous miasma of nitrogen trichloride and a few moments later he caught up to the fleeing warden.

Warden Vlach reached for a Soviet-made Makarov pistol that he kept holstered at his belt. He thought better of it when Matthias shoved the snout of the massive 454 Casull against his chest.

Matthias reached out and appropriated the Makarov. "I'll take care of that for you."

Vlach cursed and spat. "Mr. Benes told me that he would make you come unarmed!"

"Benes told me the guards had metal detectors and that I should come without weapons. I let him think that I was coming unarmed. Apparently, I made the right decision."

"What are you going to do with me?" asked Warden Vlach.

"You are going to order that Father Lada be released. When we're safely away, I'll let you go unharmed."

"Ludicrous!" protested Warden Vlach. "I could never do such a thing."

Matthias's finger tightened on the trigger of his Casull. "Then I'm afraid our business relationship must come to an abrupt end."

The warden blanched and he had a sudden change of heart. "Wait, wait! Perhaps we can come to some sort of arrangement."

"You're in no position to bargain," said Matthias. He spotted a radio on the warden's belt. "Put out the order now, and have Father Lada brought to the laundry."

"But …" the warden protested, "that would be highly irregular. The guards might find it suspicious."

"Who is in charge at Pankrác? You or the guards?"

Warden Vlach spoke through gritted teeth. "I am in charge."

"And is your leadership so weak that the guards are in the habit of questioning your orders?"

"No," admitted Vlach. "They obey my orders implicitly."

Matthias thumbed back the hammer of his Casull for emphasis. "Then make the call. Tell the guards you plan to put Father Lada to work. Remember, at the first sign of treachery I'll be putting a bullet through your brain."

The rock vocalist hoped that this threat would be enough to forestall any attempt at trickery. Since Matthias only understood a few words of Czech, Warden Vlach might easily order the prison guards to come in force and make escape for Matthias impossible. This was precisely the reason that the warden needed to understand that his personal well-being was dependent upon the personal well-being of Matthias.

The warden unclipped the walkie-talkie from his belt and snapped off some orders in rapid-fire Czech which Matthias had no hope of comprehending. That was when he noticed Budek scrambling off down the hall, clutching his injured. Matthias could easily have shifted his aim and blown a hole through Budek's spine, but Otka's boyfriend had chosen the most strategic moment to make his escape. If Matthias fired while the warden had an open transmission going, the gunshot was sure to alert the guards on the other end that something was amiss. By the time that Warden Vlach finished his conversation, Budek had ducked around the corner into one of the side hallways.

This seemed to concern Warden Vlach as much as it concerned Matthias. "I have no control over what Budek does. He might warn the guards and I would have nothing to do with it!"

"Here's the deal," said Matthias. "You get me and Father Lada out of this prison alive and you get to stay alive. The second a guard tries to capture me or fires a bullet anywhere in my general direction, you will die!"

Vlach's pocked and jowled face was hard and he chewed on his lower lip. "How do I know I can trust you?"

Matthias thought this was rich, considering Vlach made a living imprisoning and torturing political prisoners for the communist regime. Still, he didn't feel he had the time for debate. "I have a reputation for keeping my word."

Vlach fell silent as he considered this.

Matthias nudged Vlach with the barrel of his Casull. "Lead the way to the laundry facilities. I don't want your guards to beat us there."

Though not as strong, the nitrogen trichloride vapors were spreading and Matthias was beginning to see black spots dance before his eyes. It was evident that Vlach was feeling similar symptoms and they hastily beat a retreat from the drifting chemical miasma. Matthias kept one hand on Warden Vlach's collar while keeping his pistol pulled back, in the case that Vlach should make any sudden moves. With the snout of the barrel pulled back a foot, it would be simple enough for Matthias to adjust his aim in the case that Vlach tried to make a grab for the gun.

When a guard approached down the corridor, Matthias slipped the Casull through a slit he had made in the side of his jumpsuit. He kept the snout of the Casull trained on his prisoner, however.

Vlach barked a few stern Czech words at the guard. The guard saluted, turned on his heel and went off on whatever task was appointed him. Matthias considered demanding that Vlach divulge what orders he had given his charge, but then he thought better of it. Perhaps Vlach was laboring under the illusion that Matthias could understand a smattering of Czech. If so, it might be best not to let Vlach know that he was almost entirely ignorant of the language.

They negotiated a series of drab and narrow hallways festooned with more aging propaganda posters. If there was anything that communist regimes seemed to have an endless supply of it was propaganda curriculum. Finally, the scent of bleach and the hot vapor of steam came to Matthias's nostrils and they entered a large room packed with industrial washers and dryers that had been built at least three decades earlier. A number of employees went about their work, spurred on to more energetic efforts by the presence of the warden.

"Over toward the loading dock," directed Matthias. They passed through a labyrinth of wheeled laundry carts filled with laundry in various states of cleanliness and Matthias welcomed a breath of fresh air gusting in from the outdoors. From the loading dock, he could view the cracked concrete of the courtyard, which was enclosed by great walls on three sides. A heavy gate was set into the mortar of the third wall and a guardhouse sat in the lee of the wall, sheltered from the icy winds of winter and in the shade to combat the sweltering heat of the summer.

To Matthias's disappointment, he could find no sign of any vehicle parked inside the wall, but outside the gate he could see vehicles moving past the prison wall. Freedom was within sight. "How many guards in the guardhouse?"

Warden Vlach didn't even find it necessary to glance in the direction of the guardhouse. "Just one: Hnedy Kudrna. He's sharp-eyed, with an attention for details. He could be a problem."

Matthias nodded and leaned against the brick wall next to the open pull-down door of the loading dock. This way his back was not exposed to the fire of Hnedy Kudrna, should the guard figure out what was going on. "Where's Father Lada?"

Warden Vlach's face was stoic, but he wrung his pudgy hands betraying his own distress and belying the demeanor of his features. "Be patient. It takes time to pull a prisoner from maximum security, let alone deliver him to the laundry room."

The laundry room overseer, a slight man in white overalls, with the sickly pallor of a man who rarely ventured out of doors, approached the warden, pressing his hands together in an obsequious manner. "Is there anything that I can do for you, Warden Vlach?"

Vlach fired back rapid-fired insults to the overseer's management skills and the cleanliness of his domain, jabbing a finger in various directions as he pointed out things that were lacking. The overseer replied in brisk tones and then scurried off to rectify the shortcomings that Warden Vlach had identified. It was just a couple of minutes later that a pair of sturdy prison guards ushered Father Lada into the laundry room.

Matthias had studied a series of photographs that Otka Lada had provided him, and the slumping, bruised, and dejected man that stumbled forward on leaden feet scarcely resembled the strong, bold, and confident image that her father had projected in those photographs. His cheek and lips were distended, swollen from harsh beatings, so that Matthias had some difficulty in ascertaining if this was indeed Father Lada or if Warden Vlach had pulled a switch and extricated some other poor inmate out of the torture chamber.

Father Lada's head hanging, the guards pulled the inmate the last few feet to Warden Vlach.

"Have the guards raise his head," said Matthias.

Vlach barked an order and one of the guards, none too gently, grabbed a patch of the father's thinning hair and jerked back his head revealing that, in addition to a broken cheekbone, the inmate had a broken nose. Splotches of purple and blue broken blood vessels underscored both eyes. Even close examination was not sufficient for Matthias to entirely determine whether this was indeed Father Lada. Though Matthias hadn't anticipated such difficulty in identifying Father Lada, Otka had required that he learn a phrase in Czech, forcing him to repeat it over and over until his inflection and accent were performed to her satisfaction.

He repeated that phrase now. "Otka asks where the tire swing hangs."

A glint of recognition and hope came into the inmate's glazed eyes and he mumbled an answer through mashed and distended lips. "On the banks of the little stream."

"What does that mean?' asked the warden.

"Nothing, to you," answered Matthias, and that was the truth. It was merely a cherished memory of Otka's. When she had been a child her father had pushed her on a tire swing over the bank of a creek that they called 'the little stream.' The phrase was designed to ensure that Matthias was breaking the right man out of prison. "Tell the guards to leave Father Lada with you and go back to their posts."

Warden Vlach jabbed his finger out the door of the laundry and barked a few guttural words. The guards pulled away from Father Lada and the priest began to fold under his own weight. Matthias pushed up a laundry cart, so that Father Lada collapsed into the wheeled conveyance among the freshly folded prison uniforms.

Matthias quickly turned his attention back to Warden Vlach and found that he hadn't dared move a muscle during Matthias's brief moment of inattention. One of the guards glanced over his shoulder to witness what had happened, but he caught the stern gaze of the warden and turned his attention forward, departing the room with his companion.

Matthias stood away from the laundry cart now, realizing that it would be difficult for him to maneuver the cart and keep a close eye on Warden Vlach. "Order one of the laundry workers to push this cart to the gate. We're going for a walk."

"Don't you think it will look strange for me to be accompanying a janitor and a laundry worker through the gate with a cart occupied by an inmate?"

"Of course it will look strange," said Matthias. "So your life depends upon just how precisely your prison guards obey your orders."

"You don't understand," said Vlach. "If I allow a prisoner to escape, I will be removed from my position, and maybe even end up an inmate in my own prison!"

"Maybe it would help you to take a look at the big picture, Warden. If you don't help me and Father Lada out of Pankrác, you will be dead. Are you ready to become a martyr for the communist cause?"

Vlach mulled this over for a moment then he raised his hand and called to a fellow who was loading soiled clothing into the barrel of a massive washer.

A few moments later they were descending a concrete ramp from the loading dock and into the courtyard. Matthias kept just a few paces behind the warden. As they approached the guardhouse constructed of concrete blocks, Hnedy Kudrna stepped out, hand on the butt of his holstered pistol.

"Warden, what is the meaning of this?"

Vlach continued forward. "Open the gate, Kudrna."

Kudrna hadn't yet spotted Father Lada lying in the rolling cart. "This is highly irregular, sir."

"The moment that the janitor passes the gate, I want you to open fire upon him," said the Warden in a brisk Czech that would be difficult for even a native speaker to follow. "Until then it should appear as if you will let us pass."

Matthias, of course, understood none of what the warden said. Hnedy Kudrna nodded and returned inside the guardhouse behind the protection of a layer of bulletproof glass. The machinery of the gate hummed and clanked, slowly rolling open.

The laundry worker didn't know what to make of the situation. He fully realized that he was wheeling the beaten and bruised body of a prisoner out of the jail in a laundry cart and he wondered if the warden had set him up to take the fall for engineering an escape. He couldn't, for the life of him, figure out what he had done to earn the attention or animosity of the warden. Matthias could see the laundry worker's nervous glances from the cart to the guardhouse and guessed what the poor fellow might be thinking.

As the laundry worker began to push Father Lada through the gap between the gate and the wall, Father Lada called out a warning to Matthias, for he had heard part of the warden's orders to Kudrna. It was at that moment that Warden Vlach gave out a cry and dove to the ground. This was Hnedy Kudrna's signal, and the sharp-eyed prison guard burst out of the guardhouse firing wildly.

Chapter 24

When the landscape was engulfed completely in darkness, Fritz reached for his rucksack and unzipped it. He stripped off his Count Zero concert shirt and replaced it with one that was black and long sleeved. He was already wearing loose-fitting jeans of black denim and cross trainers that were black, down to tightly fitted laces.

As Fritz changed his shirt, even by the moonlight, Otka couldn't help but notice the pale scars that crossed his muscular and hirsute chest. "Where did you get those?"

Fritz tucked in his shirt. "Get what?"

"Those scars."

The rock musician's face was a mask of shadows. "Each scar comes with a story, Otka. I don't have time to tell them all now."

"Maybe when we escape Czechoslovakia?"

"If you have the time for me." Fritz withdrew a scabbarded thirty-three-inch *katana* from the rucksack.

"Where did you get that?" breathed Otka in awe of the obviously ancient weapon.

"From a very wealthy dealer in Japanese antiquities."

Otka brushed back her hair, her bee-stung lips looking particularly enticing to Mitz in the nighttime umbra. "If he is so wealthy, why is he dealing in antiquities?"

"I don't know how wealthy he was prior to selling me this sword, but I know he was wealthy afterward. This was forged by the master craftsman Koyama Munetsugu in 1847 and carried by Oe Masamichi during the Meiji Restoration."

"You know, Fritz, I've never heard of any of those men."

Fritz grinned and girded on a twelve-inch *yoroi doshi tanto* blade that was meant to punch through armor. "Unless you've studied Japanese history or are a connoisseur of Japanese weaponry, there is no reason you should know."

"I'm afraid that my history classes have been limited to learning the 'glories of communism' The classes here are very wrong, and I'm sure my professors would not deem Japanese history worthy of our time."

"I endured all too many years of communist education in East Germany," said Fritz. "I know exactly what you're talking about."

"See," said Otka, "we do have something in common."

Fritz began to darken his hands and then the area around his eyes with black face paint. "I don't believe I ever said that we didn't have something in common."

"No," said Otka. "It was just me wondering if a preacher's daughter from Czechoslovakia could ever possibly have anything in common with a world famous rock star."

Now Fritz began to roll on a face mask that covered everything but the area around the bridge of his nose and his eyes. "You might be surprised at how much we have in common."

"Wait," said Otka. She reached over and peeled up Fritz's mask, then placed a gentle, lingering kiss upon his lips. "Be safe."

It took Fritz a moment to find words. "I'll see you at four AM at Kafka's grave."

"Keep a low profile. The *policie* are suspicious of nighttime travelers."

Fritz checked the dome light of the vehicle to make sure it was in the off position and then he slipped out of the battered Yugo. Once he left the car, he almost immediately disappeared from Otka's view, blending with the shadows so that he was unseen as he made his way down the street and toward the great stone wall that encircled Quan Tang's compound.

After waiting a handful of minutes, Otka started the engine. She made a sharp U-turn in the street so that she would not actually have to pass by the gate of Quan Tang's mansion and be scrutinized by the hidden Vovinam guards. She uttered a prayer as she drove, begging for the return of her father and for the safety of those who had come to her aid.

While Otka fled District Ten for the sanctuary of her friend's home in District Three, Fritz reached the wall of the compound and by inserting his fingers and toes into the crevices between the stones where the mortar had begun to flake away, he was able to reach the top. Here, he was confronted by shards of broken glass that were mixed into the concrete, and a row of spikes that were tangled with razor wire.

The rock guitarist was well prepared for this obstacle and he produced a pair of wire cutters even while he clung to a projecting spike with his left hand. This would have been better accomplished if he had been wearing gloves, but he had chosen to forego the gloves so that he could more easily climb the wall in the first place. The razor wire cut easily enough, parting with a twang that reminded Fritz of snapping guitar strings. It wasn't a loud noise, but if one of the Vovinam masters were hidden nearby, they might well hear it amidst the sounds of the croaking chorus of frogs that was rising from the ditch that ran along the back wall of the compound. One of the released razor wires whipped across Fritz's knuckles parting the flesh and drawing blood.

The razor wire was the most dangerous of the obstacles and once that was parted, Fritz had enough space to pull himself over the wall. The broken glass was merely a deterrent and the spikes only dangerous if a climber should slip. When he and his brothers had escaped over the Berlin Wall, a chasing East German guard had lost his footing and a barbed spike had gone through his open mouth and punched through his cheek, catching him like a fish on a hook.

Fritz managed to ease over the wall with only a few additional slices from the broken glass and lowered himself behind a clump of narrow-leafed shrubs. If Quan Tang had been entirely fastidious about his security, he would have removed any and all of the landscaping so there was a clear field of sight to fire at any intruders. There were a number of rocked gardens and shrubs that were capable of providing excellent hiding spots as he progressed toward the mansion. However, these shrubs might even now be concealing Vovinam masters.

Having managed to pass over the wall, Fritz was in no hurry to leave his hiding spot. He lowered a set of night vision goggles over his eyes and it captured the ambient and near-infrared light spectrum and intensified them, so that to his eyes the landscape was bathed in an eerie green daylight. The Vovinam guards that Fritz had detected earlier had been depending largely upon camouflaging to help them blend in with their surroundings, but the night vision washed away all that patterning in a luminescent emerald so that, even now, Fritz could make out the forms of a half dozen Vovinam guards hidden about the yard.

There was no turning back now, so Fritz set his sights on the nearest guard, which was about twenty yards away, back pressed against the bole of a tree, hand on the hilt of a *kiem*, a double-edged straight sword with a needle-like point. It was most efficient when used as a thrusting weapon, but could certainly do some damage in slashing attacks.

Fritz crept forward bit by bit, staying in a crouch so that he would appear to be part of the dark mass of shrubbery. It took him twenty minutes to move five feet, but now he was at the edge of the clump of bushes and could not move forward much more without it becoming apparent that he was actually not a part of the foliage.

Though versed in a number of schools, Fritz was a master of Tosa swordsmanship which emphasized efficiency over all else. Surprise and first strike were favored over dueling or defensive stances. The moment the Vovinam swordsman's attention shifted in another direction, Fritz uncoiled from the shadows, rapid footfalls carrying him across the spongy sward. Fritz held his sword in striking position at his waist.

The Vovinam master heard the footfalls and he whirled, his sword rasping from his sheath. He was just a moment too late. Fritz brought his *katana* up in a rising diagonal *kiriage* strike which crossed the collarbone and severed the swordsman's larynx. The Vovinam master crumpled to the ground, twitching and futilely gasping for air. Fritz slipped his *yoroi doshi* beneath the third rib of the fallen swordsman and pierced his heart, ending his silent struggle. He left the body lying in the darkness and took up the same position against the tree where the now dead guard had performed his watch.

As Fritz regarded the fallen body, he noticed that a pair of night vision goggles dangled around the dead Vovinam master's severed neck. Though Fritz had presumed he had the upper hand by virtue of the technology that allowed him to see clearly at night, it was suddenly clear to him that this was not the case. The only reason that he had been able to sneak up on this Vovinam master was that the fellow had removed the spectacles in favor of his natural, but somewhat limited, eyesight. The amplified and luminescent landscape seen through night vision spectacles could induce a headache after continuous use and perhaps that was why the guard had removed them.

The fact that this guard had night vision goggles suggested that perhaps other guards had them as well, and begged the question of just why the other guards hadn't seen him when he slipped over the wall. Granted, it had only been for a moment that he been visible before dropping behind the thick foliage, and even in broad daylight he might have been well enough concealed to be obscured from the vision of all the guards, but if the other guards were wearing goggles similar to his, surely they had seen him cross twenty yards and cut down their brother in arms.

Fritz looked back to the various posts where the other Vovinam masters had been obscured. They had changed their positions, and if he wasn't mistaken they were slowly closing in on him in an ever tightening cordon of flesh and steel. There were at least six swordsmen surrounding him and since stealth was no longer an option for Fritz, he decided to resort to speed.

The Vovinam masters upon the mansion's grounds were merely obstacles. Unless they opposed him, Fritz didn't care if they lived or died. His entire purpose for being there was to bring about the death of Quan Tang—the man responsible for killing his brother. Fritz's bandy legs carried him toward the mansion at an amazing speed.

The cordon of swordsmen abandoned any pretense of stealth and pursued him. A pair of swordsmen moved to intercept and Fritz let his feet carry him directly toward them. At the last moment, he changed his direction so that he would not pass through the gauntlet between them, but moved to his right, where the right-handed swordsmen had a slightly longer stretch to strike him with his *kiem*.

As the Vovinam swordsman lashed out, Fritz executed a *kote*, and blood erupted from the wrist of his enemy's sword hand as a result of the slashing cut. Normally, Fritz would have followed with a thrust to finish his opponent, but any delay would result in him being surrounded and cut down. The wounded swordsman fell, clutching at his spurting wrist, his *kiem* dropping into the grass. The Vovinam master standing next to him leaped his fallen companion, pursuing the intruder, but when Fritz saw how quickly the master moved, he wheeled and thrust upward. The point of his *katana* slid up the breastbone, pierced the larynx and separated the base of the skull from the first vertebrae of the neck. This was a *tsuki* thrust, and though Fritz had performed this exact movement many times in practice, it was the first time he had employed it in actual combat. It was brutally effective, but the pause in his headlong flight had cost him precious moments.

He jerked his blade loose and continued toward the mansion, even as emerald figures closed in upon him like luminescent ghosts. Fritz reached the maintenance door just a pair of paces ahead of the swiftest of his foes and found the door unlocked. He threw open the door and found an unlit vestibule beyond, empty but for benches lined with rows of wicker baskets which contained the personal belongings of each of the Vovinam masters whose duty it was to protect Quan Tang from those who meant him harm.

Fritz took all this in with but a moment's glance. He ducked and spun, his instincts serving him well because a *kiem* bit into the frame of the door, narrowly missing his skull. Such confined spaces made it difficult to employ his *katana*, a weapon which, when one included the leather-wrapped tsuka around which Fritz's fist was firmly wrapped, was well over three feet in length. Normally, it didn't behoove a warrior to assault an enemy with a weapon which was inferior in length to the one that his foe bore, but there were exceptions to the rule. For just a moment, the Vovinam master's sword was wedged in the wood of the door frame, and Fritz ducked beneath the stuck blade, drawing his twelve-inch *yoroi doshi* and driving it beneath the swordsman's exposed armpit and through to the heart.

The swordsman stiffened and gave a wheezing death rattle before he lurched away, his weight tearing the *yoroi doshi* from Fritz's grasp, so that the blade stayed caught between the dead man's ribs.

Still, there were three foes left, and they thought they saw an opening, so they moved forward, the closest delivering a sharp thrust that was intended to skewer Fritz through the heart. The German rock musician twisted sideways and the point of the double-edged *kiem* pierced his shirt, the narrow blade cutting a furrow across his chest. Fritz delivered an over the head thrust that sent the point of his *katana* through his enemy's throat. The *kiem* tore out through Fritz's shirt, leaving a bloody, but shallow, line in his flesh. Fritz ducked low beneath the sword which was still jammed in the doorframe, and retreated into the vestibule, even as a pair of blades licked after him but failed to find his flesh.

Behind him, Fritz heard the mechanical sound of a magazine being slammed home. Without hesitating, he threw himself over the bench, knocking loose his goggles, and that's when bullets began to fly. Fritz recognized the juddering sound of a Skorpion machine pistol. He'd encountered more than a few of them on his previous trip to Czechoslovakia and its small size and easy concealability made it a favorite of the Palestine Liberation Organization as well. Its drawbacks were that it was so lightweight that it made it almost impossible to accurately aim the weapon when it was firing on full auto—and when firing full auto, its ten- or twenty-round magazine lasted about one second.

At short ranges it was a fearsome weapon, and muzzle flash spattered patterns of light into the dim recesses of the vestibule, while bullets sprayed wildly. A few bullets ricocheted around the room, splintering benches or throwing baskets of clothing on the floor, but most of the bullets flew down the central corridor of the chamber and mowed down the two Vovinam masters who were pursuing Fritz through the doorway.

Though Fritz had come armed for battle with Vovinam masters, he had not neglected to bring his trusty Colt Anaconda. The moment the Skorpion machine pistol rattled to a halt, Fritz rolled out from hiding and located the guard, form illumined in the background glow of a stained glass lampshade. Instead of seeking cover before changing magazines, the gunman either figured that he had killed the intruder, along with two of his fellow guards, or he simply thought he could swap out the empty banana magazine of ammunition before Fritz realized that he had a moment to make a move. Fritz didn't try for any fancy shooting; he fired center-mass into the darkness of the gunman's shape, the .44 magnum pistol rocking in his hands. The gunman lurched backward at the impact, even as he jammed the banana magazine home. However, the massive shock of a pair of magnum slugs ripping through his chest prevented him from pulling the trigger, and the Skorpion clattered along the tile floor even as the gunman fell, spasming in his death throes.

Fritz leaped to his feet. A quick glance showed him that his dislodged night vision goggles had a cracked lens. Time was of the essence now. His presence was known and Tang's Vovinam guard would be prepared for him. However, he paused long enough put his foot on one of the dead Vovinam masters and tear loose his *yoroi doshi*. As he plunged deeper into the mansion, he leaned down and scooped up the Skorpion machine pistol, thrusting it into his belt so that it rode alongside his *katana*. Not nearly so elegant a weapon as the blade forged in a former century, but it might have its uses.

It seemed that Quan Tang preferred his abode cloaked in twilight, for the long halls, punctuated with alcoves of Vietnamese hand embroidery, were illuminated only by footlights set into the lower wall, and a few lamps cloaked in stained glass, which cast colorful mosaics upon their immediate surroundings. This made for spectacular mood lighting, but it also provided shadow and darkness which Fritz used to conceal himself.

Fritz's hand went to his chest and came away bloody, but the wound was not serious nor life-threatening. He heard footsteps along the bamboo flooring and sank into an alcove splashed with rainbow hues of refracting light. Without pausing, he removed a life-size embroidery of a somber Buddhist monk from the wall and draped it over his body, and he waited, listening to the creak of footsteps, measuring the pace by the progression of each footfall. Each tread was measured and just by the sound, Fritz knew that the Vovinam master traveled lightly, with his weight evenly distributed. The Vovinam devotee was wary and on his guard.

Fritz had spent years studying the art of stealth and the sword—something of an obsession, really—since his most unstealthy departure from East Berlin all those years ago. His instructors had emphasized that even masters of stealth could be undone through a sharp eye, bad luck, or the slightest misjudgment. This, Fritz had just experienced for himself, because he had horribly misjudged his strategy in approaching the mansion by assuming he would be the only one taking advantage of night vision technology. Much of stealth involved fooling the visual senses by blending into the surroundings, or in other words, providing something that hostile eyes expected to see in normal circumstances. This often meant camouflage patterns to blend with foliage or desert landscapes or dark clothing to blend into the night. In this case, the embroidered tapestry of the Buddhist monk was exactly the same thing that this Vovinam master saw each and every time that he passed this particular alcove. So when he glanced into the alcove and saw that same tapestry, his eyes snapped forward again for just a moment, until his brain, a moment later, formed the idea that there was something peculiar about the monk this time—that it's form was more three dimensional than usual and that the visage of the monk, though somber, was not of the same cast.

This moment of realization was long enough for Fritz to leap from the alcove and wrap a thick arm around the Vovinam master's throat. Before the Vovinam guard could react, Fritz thrust the *yoroi doshi* beneath the swordsman's ribs and into his liver. Bile gushed out across Fritz's bloodied fingers and Fritz stifled the death cry of his foe as the Vovinam master's knees buckled.

Fritz quickly stripped off the martial artist's indigo vophuc before it could be further soiled by bile and blood, and he attired himself in the Vovinam uniform, finishing the ensemble by tying the red belt around his waist which indicated that he was a master of the Vovinam martial art. Close up, no one would be fooled into thinking his Teutonic features resembled those of a Vietnamese, but in the shadows it might afford him a few precious moments to close the distance.

Fritz wiped the *yoroi doshi* clean on the T-shirt of the dead Vovinam master, dragged him into the alcove, and then threw the tapestry of the Buddhist monk across the crumpled form. He doubted the corpse would stay hidden for long, but he had tarried here long enough. He continued down the corridor dressed in his newly appropriated and bloody Vovinam uniform. Unfortunately, he was wandering blindly inside the corridors of the mansion and he needed to locate Quan Tang and get out.

He headed up a flight of stairs and a uniformed man called from the top of the steps in Vietnamese. Fortunately, Vietnamese was one of the languages that Fritz spoke very well and though he affected a German accent when speaking English, he was capable of flawlessly pronouncing all but a few words and phrases in Vietnamese.

Fritz continued up the stairs as he responded. "We've a report that the intruder fled back toward the wall. Is Mr. Tang safe?"

"He's in the vault. Nothing short of a Russian tank could get to him."

The high forehead and straight nose of Fritz's German features emerged from the shadows, but before the Vovinam guard could react, Fritz thrust him through the heart with the *yoroi doshi*. He wrenched the twelve-inch blade free and caught the tottering body before it tumbled down the steps. Instead of letting it fall, he pushed the body down in the wide corridor of the second floor.

"In the vault," muttered Fritz as he leaned over the body. "Just where is the vault?"

The Vovinam master gave no reply. His eyelids fluttered closed and the breath wheezed in his throat as he gave his death rattle. Fritz didn't waste any more time with the fallen foe and he continued around a bend in the corridor, where he saw two vophuc-clad Vietnamese guarding a doorway.

The nearest called out to him. "Where's Thuc?"

"His heart gave out on the stairs," said Fritz, and his brisk pace turned into a run, even as his *katana* rasped from its lacquered wooden scabbard.

Chapter 25

At the moment that Warden Vlach shouted a signal and fell to the ground, Matthias reacted, and made a diving roll that slammed into the laundry cart and pushed it through the gate, even while knocking over the bewildered laundry worker who had been pushing the cart with the dazed Father Lada still inside.

Bullets spat from Hnedy Kudrna's pistol, slicing the air where Matthias had stood just a fraction of a second before and then pounding the concrete wall of Pankrác Prison as they carved a trail toward Matthias, where he was sprawled between the wall and the gate, one leg inside of the prison and one leg outside, and his back propped against the wall.

Matthias leveled his Casull while crying out to the laundry worker to hit the ground. It may have been the language barrier or perhaps the laundry worker just panicked, but he lurched in front of Matthias, blocking his line of fire so that he could not hit the Czech sentry that had burst from the guardhouse. Matthias barely restrained himself from pulling the trigger. Hnedy Kudrna seemed less concerned about the laundry worker and two bullets caught the poor fellow in the chest.

Things were happening so quickly that Matthias barely registered what had happened. Staying alive in a firefight required undistracted focus on the target and the moment the laundry worker's body was out of Matthias's line of sight, he eased back the trigger. A three-foot-long gout of flame blew from the snout of the Casull and a bullet pounded through Hnedy Kudrna's chest, hurling him back through the door of the guardhouse.

Kudrna's last action before departing the mortal coil was to reverse the direction of the opening gate, his hand slapping the mechanism so that the great gate began to grind toward Matthias, threatening to crush him between a concrete wall and a ton of rust-flecked steel. Then the last spark of life left the Czech prison guard and he fell face first upon the floor into a crimson pool of his own blood.

Warden Vlach scrambled toward a narrow defile between the guard-house and the prison wall, hoping to make it through and then take refuge behind the relative safety of the guardhouse. Matthias was tempted to put a bullet through his back, but he figured it was more important to get out of the way of the gate which was threatening to crush him. Adding to that danger was the boom of gunfire from a couple of prison guards on the loading dock. These were the same prison guards that had delivered Father Lada and that Warden Vlach had ordered back to their posts … or so it had seemed to Matthias at the time. Apparently, Warden Vlach had realized the limitations of Matthias's Czech language abilities and exploited them by telling the prison guards to pretend to leave and return shortly. Matthias also had no doubt that the warden had make arrangements with Kudrna, the sentry, to begin firing upon his command.

Chunks of asphalt exploded near Matthias and the gate was within inches of turning him into a eunuch. With amazing alacrity, Matthias lifted his legs and cartwheeled onto the street, a ton of steel grinding to a halt as it pressed flat against the prison wall. Bullets clanked against the bars of the gate and ricocheted through as Matthias leaped to his feet and grabbed hold of the laundry cart.

Still dazed, Father Lada was again trying to climb out of the cart. Matthias figured he could make better time pushing the father than trying to support or carry him. "Stay inside!" He gave the cart a push, the sudden acceleration toppling Father back into the laundry cart. Then Matthias was pushing the cart down the cracked sidewalk at breakneck speeds, the wobbling wheels threatening to tear off at any moment.

With Budek, Matthias had scouted all the streets surrounding Pankrác Prison and so he was familiar with this road and knew that Budek's mo-torcycle was just around the corner. It would only be a matter of a minute or two and the prison would disgorge a stream of guards to recapture their escaped prisoner and kill the man who had helped him escape. Matthias sent the cart careening around the corner, and one of the wheels broke loose and went tumbling under a nearby automobile. However, Matthias compensated for the missing wheel by lifting and pushing the cart at the same time. When Matthias and Father Lada reached the cracked concrete where Budek's battered Jawa had leaned on its kickstand, they found that it was gone.

Now, Father Lada climbed from the unsteady cart. "Who are you and where are you taking me?"

"Matthias Gantlet, and I won't be taking you anywhere unless I can find us a vehicle."

Beneath the swollen and bruised brow, Matthias thought he saw a glint of recognition in the father's eye.

"You … you're Fritz's brother."

"That's right." Matthias cast about for a likely vehicle. There were plenty of puny European automobiles which might serve, but they would require hotwiring and though Matthias had hotwired vehicles before, it took him a little bit of time, and that was more time than he figured they had before a horde of prison guards descended upon them. The prison wall loomed over them, and once the guards marshaled themselves, a number of them could gather upon the wall and fire down upon them. If possible, it would be best to lose themselves in the maze of surrounding streets and then find themselves a vehicle to steal. However, the broken laundry cart was of little use now, and Father Lada was in no condition for a sprint through traffic and back alleys. Still, Matthias didn't see how they had much choice in the matter.

"Fritz is a good man," said Father Lada.

"Yes, yes he is," agreed Matthias, and he pointed. "Let's get moving— across the street and down that road there. Can you walk?"

"Just barely," said the father, but when his weight fell upon his right leg, he cried out in pain. He fell heavily against the trunk of a car. "They struck my leg with a crowbar. I think that it might be broken."

An angry voice called out to them, and a middle-aged man wearing a threadbare suit crossed through traffic toward them. "What are you doing to my car?"

Matthias didn't understand the words, but he deduced the meaning just the same. He didn't know enough Czech to answer the question, though. Fortunately, Father Lada understood and spoke Czech just fine. Father Lada, still leaning against the car, spoke rapidly and the owner of the vehicle responded in a consonant-heavy staccato.

Father Lada turned to Matthias. "Do you have American dollars?"

"Yes."

"Give five hundred of them to this man. He's going to let us borrow his car."

Matthias fished some greenbacks out of his pocket. "Five hundred? Isn't that the equivalent thirty thousand korunas?"

"We have the entire contingent of Pankrác Prison guards breathing down our neck. Do you really think it's the time to bargain?"

Matthias slapped five or six bills into the automobile owner's out-stretched hand—he didn't take the time to make an exact count. "No. I think it's a great bargain."

Father Lada worked his way to the passenger side of the orange four-door Skoda, while Matthias snatched away the keys.

With a great effort, the father managed to pull open his door. "Punch him!" he called to Matthias. "The authorities need to be convinced that you stole his vehicle!"

Matthias had just sent a prison guard to his grave and he balked at shedding unnecessary blood, but nevertheless he realized that if the prison guards weren't convinced that the vehicle had been taken by force they might hold the owner, search him, and discover his sudden windfall. He struck the owner a sharp blow, but pulled his punch so that he merely split flesh and didn't break the cheekbone. The Czech stumbled and fell in the street, and then Matthias slipped behind the wheel.

The 1174 cc motor in the trunk roared to life and Matthias yanked the wheel and lurched into the street, cutting off a vehicle coming the opposite direction, before he lurched down a side street. Gunfire rattled from the walls of Pankrác, chasing the orange Skoda down the street, spattering against the cobblestones. A couple of rounds punctured the trunk and one passed through the rear windshield and out the driver's side window near Matthias's head as he veered around a corner and out of sight of the prison.

Matthias cycled through the gears with as much speed as he could. "This thing's as slow as a tractor."

"Yes," agreed Father Lada, "but still much, much faster than carrying me over your shoulder."

Matthias's concentration was fierce as he weaved between automobiles and watched for pedestrians darting across the cobbled lane. The streets were narrow and lined by parked vehicles, and there were far too many delays for Matthias's liking.

"Do you happen to have a cigarette?" asked Father Lada. "I haven't been allowed to smoke since they threw me in jail."

"Not me," grinned Matthias. "Those things will kill you!"

Father Lada, despite the pain he was enduring, laughed uproariously. "That's funny from a man with a death wish!"

Matthias spun around another corner, the trunk engine whining. "Death wish? What are you talking about?"

"Anyone who breaks into a communist prison, with nothing but a pistol and his intestinal fortitude, to break out a worthless worn-out priest has a death wish!" The priest coughed harshly, his body wracked by the strain.

"Your daughter doesn't seem to think you're worthless. She wanted you out of prison and she can be very persuasive when she puts her mind to it."

"Otka ... she is just like her mother—headstrong and with no thought of the consequences. There is no room for women like that in Czechoslovakia—at least a communist Czechoslovakia."

Matthias negotiated a series of hair pin turns, trying to put as much distance between them and Pankrác as quickly as the Skoda's feeble engine would allow. "What happened to Otka's mother?"

"She spoke her mind, was arrested by the *policie* and we never saw her again. Word came to us that she died in a woman's work camp, but some nights I have dreams that she is still alive and that she is bitter that I have done nothing to help her. Perhaps the next life will be a happier one."

"Perhaps?" asked Matthias. "Aren't you the priest? Shouldn't you be reassuring me that the next life will be a much better one?"

"Forgive me," said Father Lada. "I did not mean to sound as if my faith is wavering. I know that in the glorious resurrection all this pain and misery will seem but an instant. The Lord will make all right, and bloody-handed murderers like Warden Vlach and his ilk will burn in hellfire."

Matthias was silent as he considered his own fate. Would the Lord consider him a bloody-handed murderer at the judgment day? Certainly he had shed enough blood. When had he ever turned the other cheek? Always, blood had followed blood.

Father Lada seemed to know, intuitively, what the rock musician was thinking. "You're wondering what will happen to you when you die, perhaps?"

Matthias slowed up to allow a mother and child to safely cross the street, before he cut down a side alley that was lined with garbage bins and smashed crates. "Are you a mind reader, Father?"

"A priest is the physician of the soul," said Father Lada. "Just like a doctor would examine the body for sickness to heal, it is my job to examine the soul so that Christ might heal the soul through the miracle of atonement."

"I've sent a lot of bloody-handed murderers to hell," said Matthias as he eased the Skoda in between a mound of garbage sacks and across shattered slats and lumber. "It only seems fair that I join them there, eventually." Matthias heard the hissing of air from a punctured tire that must have gained a nail or two. "The authorities know we're driving an orange Skoda, so we're going to have to find another vehicle or at least a place to lay low until tonight."

"What's happening tonight?" asked Father Lada after he recovered from a coughing fit.

"We're meeting my brother Fritz and Otka at Kafka's grave. Then we're all getting out of Czechoslovakia!"

Father Lada nodded. "If you don't have any cigarettes, then perhaps you have some painkillers?"

"That, I can help you with," said Matthias as he fished a bottle out of one his pockets.

Father Lada opened the bottle and found a rainbow of assorted pills. "What are these?"

"Antibiotics, painkillers, valium, antihistamines, cyanide ..."

"Cyanide?"

"Just kidding about the last one. You want two of the blue pills— should help to take the edge off some of the pain in your leg."

"And just about everywhere else," groaned the father.

Chapter 26

Fritz's headlong charge carried him beneath the swinging *kiem* of the Vovinam master, and his sideways stroke plunged the point of his blade through his enemy's neck. Without pausing, he swung his *katana* to the fore, in the nick of time to deflect a downward blow by the second Vovinam guardian. Then Fritz's momentum took him past the second guard, cutting a ribbon of crimson through flesh with the razor edge of his *katana*.

Both Vovinam devotees crumpled. Wounded and dying, they leaked out their lifeblood upon the bamboo floor. One of them reached for a pistol shoved into the waist of his indigo uniform, but Fritz reversed his momentum and hewed off the rising hand before the pistol could be aimed.

"Where is Quan Tang?" demanded Fritz.

"Inside," gasped the Vovinam master who had lost his hand. "You'll never reach him. The vault is four inches of steel."

"We'll see about that," said Fritz. The door in front of him was heavy and well made. It was not the door to a vault, so Fritz presumed that the safe room where Quan Tang had taken refuge must be deeper into the house. He put the heel of his foot to the door and the frame splintered, so that it tore loose from the wall, hanging drunkenly. A second application of boot knocked the door to the ground. Fritz heard shrieks and he saw two Vietnamese girls clad in nothing but silken robes fleeing toward the tiled bathroom.

Fritz knew that these were probably unfortunate girls, just like Ket Nien, who had been seeking a better life outside of Vietnam. Instead they had been forced into prostitution and told they needed to work off the debt they had incurred by being smuggled into Czechoslovakia. It was a debt that Quan Tang would never allow them to pay off, because he would keep adding to the total by charging for food, lodging, and whatever amenities he provided for them. Fritz pointed his bloody sword in their direction. "Out the front door, now! Do as I say and you won't be harmed!"

They saw Fritz's black clad form, face masked and sword bloody. They shrieked in terror, clutching at each other for comfort and safety. Still, they were too fearful to make a run for the exit, lest they should pass within striking distance of the gory *katana*.

Fritz cast his eyes about the chamber, seeing the expensive carpets and four poster bed that hung with great swags of crimson. "Where is the vault?"

One of the girls mustered the wherewithal to lift a trembling hand and point toward a great walk-in closet. "Behind the clothing at the back of the closet."

Fritz was satisfied that neither of these girls was any danger to him, so he turned his back and strode into the closet. "Go now. Get as far away from here as you can. Quan Tang will die tonight. You are released from your debt. There is a woman named Lieu Vang who runs a laundry on Myslíkova Street. Find her and she will be able to give you some help."

As he moved deeper into the closet, he heard their scurrying footfalls as they crossed the carpets and over the fallen door. His hearing muffled by the racks of clothing within the closet, he could still perceive their horrified gasps as they saw the still-twitching remains of the Vovinam guard he had slain in the hall. Even out from under the thumb of Quan Tang their futures were grim and uncertain. The Czech government would not be sympathetic to their plight. It was only generous people like Lieu Vang and her underground railroad that would provide women like this a place to stay and food to eat while they created false identification papers and found them legitimate places of work.

The door to the vault was hidden behind a rack of clothing, which rolled out of the way, taking a portion of false wall with it. The vault door was impressive: the hinges hidden behind the surface of the door, and when he rapped upon the steel surface he could tell that it was at least a foot thick. True, this door was impervious to his sword or handgun, but he'd come prepared for such a possibility. Fritz placed a magnetic thermite charge at the seam of the vault door where he estimated the hinges would be set. Thermite, in and of itself, was not explosive, but it was mixed with various pyrotechnics so that it would ignite easier. It burned at 4,500 degrees and often threw off molten slag, so Fritz backed out of the closet and across the room as the thermite flared blinding white, burning its way through the steel skin of the vault door.

The sound of the burning thermite was not so loud that it would alert the other guards inside the mansion, but still Fritz took up position at the doorway, watching the corridor for the unwelcome arrival of any more of the Vovinam masters. Fritz didn't know how many others might be lurking about the grounds, looking for him even now. Even though the burning thermite didn't produce enough volume to give away his location to the other guards, the sound of the two-thousand-pound vault door falling to the floor sure might. It crashed through the reinforced floor, cracking concrete and buckling floor boards, its impact reverberating throughout the mansion.

Quan Tang did not waste any time going on the offensive. A spray of bullets greeted Fritz as he ducked through the closet and stood to the side of the vault. The bullets chewed through a rack of Italian suits, turning them into rags under the withering hailstorm of lead, and the wall behind began to crumble. Fritz removed an M84 stun grenade from his belt and tossed the flash-bang grenade into the vault. There was a tremendous boom and a flare of white light that lit up the vault with incandescent brilliance. Fritz expelled a deep breath and then came around the corner into the vault.

At first, Fritz thought his gambit had failed, because Quan Tang was sitting on the floor of the vault with a French MAT 49 machine gun clenched in his hands, looking directly at the doorway. Then Fritz realized that those eyes stared blindly; Quan Tang's vision and hearing had been muted by the flash-bang grenade, temporarily obliterating a pair of his critical senses. Fritz knew that he had a couple more seconds at best, and though the Vietnamese crime lord had been blinded and deafened, he hadn't taken leave of his other senses.

Quan Tang slammed a fresh magazine of thirty-two nine-millimeter rounds into the forehandle of the machine gun and began spraying the opening in the vault, a scathing blast of lead beneath which nothing could possibly survive. Fritz, however, had already moved past Quan Tang. The ringing ears of the crime lord had been unable to detect Fritz and now the German rock guitarist withdrew his *katana* and lifted it for the killing stroke. The MAT 49 clacked as the last round was fired, and Quan Tang released the empty magazine, letting it fall to the vault floor next to him where a phone rested, the receiver off the cradle.

The crimelord's vision must have cleared, and perhaps his hearing was returning, because he seemed to realize that there was nobody standing in front of him and no bullet-filled corpse either. He slowly rotated his head until, through bleary eyes, he could make out the form of someone standing behind him. Tang let his machine gun slip out of his hand. "Fritz Gantlet? It must be you. No one else could slay so many of my Vovinam lackeys using their favored weapons."

Fritz's eyes were cold pieces of flint. "You killed my brother. Your day of reckoning has come."

"I don't deny it," said Quan Tang, "but believe me when I say that nothing personal was intended. It was merely a business decision. If I let you waltz into the country that I make my home and dismantle my livelihood and slice open my chin without any repercussions, then I look weak. In my line of work, appearance is ninety percent of the battle. I swim in a pool of sharks and they all want a piece of what I have. If I look weak for just a moment, they will snatch what is mine away from me."

Fritz knew that Quan Tang was stalling for time, but for some reason he felt like he needed to hear what the crime lord had to say. What was he hoping to hear? That Quan Tang was sorrowful for taking Otto's life? "If it wasn't personal, why did you fly all the way from Czechoslovakia to witness the explosion?"

Quan Tang shrugged in a nonchalant fashion that made even Fritz's icy blood boil. "I like to closely oversee these matters. It was a botched assassination. That explosion was meant to kill every one of you."

Fritz spoke through clenched teeth. "Unlucky for you that it didn't."

Quan Tang did not stir from his position kneeling upon the floor, for he knew that the slightest provocation would result in his death. "Listen to me, please. I am a wealthy man, and though I know money can never reimburse you for the loss of your brother, I want you to name a price— blood money to recognize the fact that I have wronged you. Just give me a number and I will get you the money."

Fritz's movement was swift and the sword blade descended with precision. There was a spray of blood and Quan Tang's head went rolling across the floor. So clean was the stroke that it wasn't until a few moments later that Tang's body collapsed from its kneeling position. "It's nothing personal," muttered Fritz to the headless cadaver, "but there's no amount of money that would afford me solace for the loss of my brother."

With practiced movements, Fritz cleaned the blood from his blade and sheathed his *katana*. There had been too much noise and the time for subtlety was long gone. Fritz picked up the MAT 49. It was a well-built machine gun that was tightly constructed in order to keep out dust and grit—ideal for desert and jungle warfare. It was a larger and much more accurate gun than the Czech Skorpion machine pistol that Fritz had thrust through his belt and there was a row of loaded magazines laid out on a teak side table.

Fritz shoved a number of these magazines into the tunic of the indigo vophuc which he still wore, and then he slung the MAT 49 over his shoulder. That was when he heard someone shouting in Vietnamese through the receiver of the phone. He picked it up and held it to his ear, speaking in Vietnamese. "If you are looking for Quan Tang, you'll find that he is permanently unavailable. His crime syndicate is now disbanded. Go home and find some honest work."

"This is Duoc Tang—Mr. Tang's son. Now tell me where my father is or I can guarantee that you will be a dead man."

"As soon as we're born, we're dead men," said Fritz. "Quan Tang is dead and unless you want to join him before your time, you'll forget you ever talked to me."

Fritz yanked the phone cord out of the wall and moved past the tattered rags of a wardrobe that had cost hundreds of thousands of dollars. He heard the voices of Vovinam warriors and Quan Tang's Czech enforcers, alike, crying out as they reached the top of the stair and began down the corridor. He had no more grenades and didn't want to be delayed in a time consuming and bloody gun battle, so Fritz crossed into the bathroom, treading across the tiled floors and past the great iron tub and the waterfall showers to a great, arched mosaic window of stained glass, through which the murky light of the moon filtered into the somber shadows that lingered within.

Picking up a heavy bench that rested nearby, Fritz swung it at the window and cleared away the leaded glass, then followed the rainbow cascade of shards by leaping through and onto the sloped roof a story below. He landed cat-like and ran across the peak of the roof like a crazed tightrope walker. Even as he ran he could see the figures of Czech and Vovinam guards moving in the darkness of the mansion's grounds. In addition to the staccato of machine gun fire, they had heard the crashing of glass and they were doing their best to locate the source of the sound.

Since some of them were equipped with night vision goggles, it was only a matter of moments before they caught sight of him. Fritz saw the stuttering flare of a machine pistol a moment before he heard the gibbering report. Bullets chewed up the roofline just behind him and then Fritz ran out of roof. He leaped across the void, bullets whistling around him, and then landed on the roof of the adjacent garage, finding some cover in the valley of a projecting dormer. Bullets shattered the glass of the dormer's window and then for a moment the barrage of lead stopped while the gunman, ostensibly, took a moment to swap his empty ammunition box for a full one.

Fritz took advantage of this momentary lull and dove in through the wreckage of the window frame, crawling further into the loft of the garage as a renewed barrage ate through the shingles, and bullets smashed through in a haze of splinters. It wasn't but a few seconds before Fritz came across the chauffeur who was huddled on the floor in the fetal position, trying to make himself as small a target as possible to avoid the indiscriminate bullets flying through his modest home in the loft of the garage.

Their eyes met for just a moment and then Fritz continued on past to the head of the descending stairs, content to let the chauffeur live. It was a mistake, because every one of Quan Tang's men was a killer, even the lowliest errand boy and chauffer. Fritz caught a flicker of movement out of the corner of his eye as the chauffeur reached for a pistol shoved behind a cedar chest. It was only the fact that the chauffeur had to reach for the weapon which saved Fritz's life. Even as the chauffer's hand closed around the grip of the pistol and he began to swing the snout toward Fritz, the German rock musician squeezed the trigger to the MAT 49 he'd taken from Quan Tang and sent three rounds crashing through the chauffeur's ribcage.

The chauffeur gurgled and slumped against the chest, even as he reflexively pulled the trigger of his pistol, taking a chunk out of the plasterboard. Then the pistol fell from his fingers and his eyes went glassy.

Fritz went softly down the stairs lest there was some other employee who had residence in the garage that his footsteps might alert. His efforts at stealth may have been completely wasted because another barrage of bullets began from outside, covering the sound of his foot treads. Fortunately, most of these seemed to be aimed into the loft. The overhead lights flickered as bullets plowed through the upper reaches of the garage and Fritz found the stately black Rolls-Royce that he had seen earlier, parked next to a sleek yellow Maserati. Thankfully, there was no sign of any other employee.

There was really only one viable option and Fritz plucked the key to the Rolls-Royce off the wall and slipped behind the wheel. He locked the doors and started the engine, revved the motor and then sent the black behemoth plowing through the garage door and into the teeth of a barrage of machine gun fire. Bullets knocked the flying female Spirit of Ecstasy ornament off the hood, but the armored grill and hood sent the majority of the gunfire ricocheting away, and even though a half dozen bullets pocked the glass of the windshield, none of them penetrated.

Fritz knew full well that the term bulletproof glass was something of misnomer. Bullet-resistant might be more accurate. Nothing was completely bulletproof, but depending upon the velocity and type of round being fired, some glasses provided excellent protection. He accelerated through the storm of bullets and they rattled against the side of the car like hailstones on a tin roof as he passed through the gauntlet of gunmen.

"A Gantlet through the gauntlet," muttered Fritz to himself, and he grinned as he hurtled down the drive and toward the great wrought iron gate. It was a massively built gate that even a barbarian horde or tons of hurtling Rolls-Royce Phantom might have difficulty breaching, but it wasn't much of an obstacle if one had the key to open it. Fritz reached up to the overhead visor where a remote with a numbered pad was clipped. He knew that there was no remote for the garage door, because he had witnessed the chauffeur step out of his vehicle and punch in the code on the keypad mounted at the front of the garage. The gate, however, was a different matter. It had opened automatically when the Rolls-Royce had approached and Fritz was gambling his life on the hope that the code to open the outer gate was the same code that was used for garage.

Fritz held the Rolls-Royce steady with one hand, even as it was rocked by gunfire from both sides, and he punched in the numbers. "Three nines, three fives. Inauspicious violence. How appropriate!"

For a moment nothing happened and Fritz braced himself for impact with a ton of wrought iron metal, but just when he had abandoned the hope of the code working, the gate began to slide open. He was approaching too fast and the gate opening too slow. A gunman stepped in front of the Rolls-Royce and blazed away, lead spattering the windshield and hood, and the gunman lit up in the blinding strobe of the muzzle flash. The gunman didn't move away fast enough and the Rolls-Royce clipped his legs, shattering them and sending him spinning away.

Fritz adjusted the course of the Rolls-Royce and sent it through the narrow gap between the gate and wall. Metal shrieked and sparked and then the Rolls-Royce burst from the compound and onto the narrow lane. The vehicle was going too fast to make the sharp turn onto the cobbled lane and its momentum took it over the far sidewalk and onto the slope of the lawn beyond. Fritz spun the wheel, and the Rolls threw up clots of sod as it sloughed around and back onto the lane. The gel tires of the Rolls-Royce sagged as a spray of bullets blew out a few compartments, and then the black Phantom disappeared over the rise and into the deepening umbra of night.

Chapter 27

Fritz trudged up the ancient hill on the eastern side of Prague, climbed over the low stone wall that took him into the Jewish cemetery and then continued past the right side of a darkened ceremonial hall until he reached a sign that read Sector 21. This he could barely discern by the glimmer of the moon which only occasionally penetrated the veil of clouds cast upon the sky.

Wisps of fog lay near to the ground and Fritz imagined them as specters of the many souls buried at the cemetery rising up to haunt him. He turned right and headed toward the rugged wall surrounding the sector. When he could go no further, he walked along the wall until he reached a sign indicating the end of the sector, and here he found a tall and narrow headstone rising up and facing the wall.

Through the spectral mists, Fritz could see a memorial plaque mounted on the wall opposite the gravestone, featuring the name of Kafka's friend Max Brod who published Kafka's work posthumously. Fritz circled around the gravestone and just casually noted the Czech inscriptions, before his eyes darted elsewhere, searching the murky shadows cast by the multitude of gravestones. He was a few minutes behind schedule and it concerned him that neither Otka, Matthias, Budek, nor Father Lada was there. A multitude of different possibilities played through his mind and few of them were good.

Then he heard a stirring amidst the tarry umbra a dozen gravestones away. Fritz reached for the MAT 49 which he had stowed beneath his jacket. One of the interesting features of the machine gun is that its front handle, in which the magazine of bullets was inserted, folded forward for easy stowage. Fritz snapped the forward handle back into firing position and kept his finger alongside the trigger even as he ducked behind Kafka's gravestone.

A husky, but decidedly feminine, voice called out to him from the tenebre. "Fritz, is that you?"

Fritz breathed a sigh of relief. "Otka! I was worried that something had happened."

Otka emerged from the shadow. She stepped slowly, hesitantly—a hazy figure of languorous beauty and she moved into Fritz's arms, embracing him. "I don't like graveyards during the broad light of day, but in the night they are absolutely dreadful."

"There's nothing to fear from the dead," said Fritz, even though sometimes in the darkest of nighttime dreams he had been haunted by the faces of those he had sent on before. "It's the living we need to worry about."

Otka's dark orbs gazed hopefully into Fritz's steel gray eyes. "Have you heard from Matthias? Were he and Budek able to retrieve my father from Pankrác?"

"I haven't heard anything at all," admitted Fritz. For a moment he had been distracted from his concern for his brother by Otka's close proximity, the warmth of her body, and the subtle scent of perfume that she wore, but her plaintive voice brought him back to the harsh reality of their situation.

The sound of heavy footsteps and harsh breathing alerted Fritz and he dragged Otka down into the depths of shadow and night, peering around the corner of Kafka's gravestone until the wan light of the moon revealed Budek trudging along the wall, one hand trailing along the rough stone.

Fritz rose from concealment. "Budek! Where's my brother and Otka's father?"

Budek's eyes were dark-rimmed and bloodshot. "You asked us to do much alone. It's as though Warden Vlach knew that we were coming. He was ready for us and killed Matthias and Father Lada at the gates as we tried to escape."

Pain and anguish stabbed at Fritz's heart. He had sought revenge for the loss of one brother, and in accomplishing that he had paid the price with the life of another brother. Otka pulled her knees to her chest and began to sob.

"How did you escape?" demanded Fritz.

Budek shook his head, his face angular and sharp, his expression hidden by the veil of night. "The bullets—they missed me somehow, and I stumbled through gate before it closed."

Fritz seized Budek by the lapels. "Are you absolutely sure they are dead?"

Budek's expression was haunted and fearful. "The warden's guards blew their brains out on the pavement after they fell."

Otka could not restrain herself any longer and she gave out an anguished cry. "Why? Why did I not leave well enough alone?"

Budek looked accusingly at Fritz. "If we had your help within the prison, we all might have made it out alive. Instead, you were pursuing some vendetta with a Vietnamese crook."

The words resonated in Fritz's mind and a horrible guilt churned in his gut. For the moment he pushed it aside. There would be plenty of time to wallow in his guilt later. He had a responsibility to keep the rest of them alive long enough to escape Czechoslovakia.

"We must hurry," urged Budek. "I was as careful as I knew how to be, but still they might have followed me somehow."

Some stray thought niggled at the back of Fritz's mind. "How did the warden know you were coming?"

"When he caught us he didn't say much, but he knew that you had flown into to Czechoslovakia from Austria, said that he has friends in Austria that informed him. That was before Matthias tried to make a move for the gate."

Fritz processed this for a moment. "That means they've probably discovered our ultralights by now, so that's not an option for escape."

Budek shrugged. "I don't know how to fly one, anyway."

Fritz's face became as hard as granite. "If you want to get out of Czechoslovakia you may have to do a lot of things that you've never done before. Are you prepared to go the distance?"

Otka rose, steadying herself on Kafka's gravestone. "My father is dead. I have no family. There's nothing here for me in Czechoslovakia. Death is preferable than staying any longer."

This pronunciation seemed to make Budek's decision a simple one. "I attempted the impossible in the hopes that I could once again see Otka smile with the same happiness that she possessed before her father was taken away. I have failed and seen two men die in that attempt but, for Otka, I would attempt the impossible again and again. Even if it costs me my own life."

Now, Fritz was plunged into even greater depths of guilt. How lightly he had come in and stolen kisses from Otka, while Budek was risking his life to save Otka's father! Not only had his foolish quest for vengeance cost Matthias's life, but could he so blithely take Otka away from a man who had risked so much for her? "I've got Quan Tang's Rolls-Royce Phantom and a full tank of gas. The upside is that thing can resist a lot of punishment and still keep rolling. The downside is that, given Quan Tang's relationship with the authorities, the *policie* have surely been notified that I stole the Rolls-Royce and they will be on alert for it."

"A Rolls-Royce doesn't exactly blend in," said Budek, his voice sour. "I hope you'll come up with some better options than that—and in a hurry. We don't have time to stand around this graveyard. The *policie* could be on their way right now! I've got a friend that lives near the Zelivskeho Metro stop, not far from here. He's been bugging me to trade him my motorcycle for an old Yugo he owns."

Otka's brow furrowed. "You promised me you were going to stay away from that loser!"

Budek put a reassuring arm around Otka's shoulder. "And I have been, *miláčku*" he insisted. "But we really need a different vehicle right now, and he's got one."

"And he's willing to make that trade in the middle of the night?" asked Fritz.

"Rybar is usually up until dawn drinking whiskey and playing cards, anyhow," said Budek. "It's the daytime that he sleeps."

"How does Rybar pay his bills?" asked Fritz.

"When he plays cards, he bets for money or sometimes for things, which he sells on the black market when he wins."

"How often does he win?"

"Enough to drink whiskey and smoke cigarettes all evening," said Budek. "What more could you ask for?"

"I could think of a few things," said Otka.

"If Matthias were here he could have hotwired a car for us," said Fritz, "and we wouldn't have to risk human contact to get ourselves a vehicle, but it seems like our best option."

Budek cast his gaze upon Fritz's blood-splashed shoes. "I'm sorry about your brother, Fritz. I really am." He shifted his gaze to Otka. "I'm sorry about your father, too. I really did my best to get him out."

Otka blinked tears that dripped from her long lashes as she embraced Budek. "I know that you did everything you could."

"We can't all get to Rybar's place on the motorcycle," said Fritz.

"You'll have to drive the Rolls-Royce," agreed Budek. "Park by the Metro entrance and Otka and I will meet you once we've made the trade."

"You sure you won't need my help with Rybar?" asked Fritz.

Budek waved his hand in a dismissive gesture. "That Yugo he owns runs fine, but it's a piece of junk. He'll jump all over it when I agree to give him my Jawa in exchange for it. Rybar I can handle."

Budek's Jawa motorcycle was pulled up next to the black Rolls-Royce in the parking lot of the Jewish cemetery, and Otka climbed onto the bike behind her boyfriend, clasping him around the chest as he fired the engine and released the kickstand.

Fritz hadn't failed to notice that Budek seemed to be calling the shots now, and he couldn't say that he was comfortable with it. The Yugo might get them to the border, but they lacked papers, and no border guard would let a man without papers cross unmolested into Austria. Alone, Fritz figured he could cross the border on foot, but with Budek and Otka in tow, success became much less likely.

After following Budek and Otka down the hill, the Jawa peeled off down a narrow side street and Fritz continued a block or two and parked near a long line of drab three-story buildings, with slitted and barred basement windows.

His long and varied training in the martial arts had taught Fritz much patience, but even so, as he waited in the Rolls-Royce, he found himself fidgety and restless. Finally, after about ten minutes he decided that rather than this restlessness being a lack of self–control, it was his subconscious telling him that something was wrong. He turned off the headlights of the Rolls-Royce and kept the interior in blackness while he watched the thin early hour traffic of mostly small, communist-made vehicles. A mid-sized *policie* vehicle passed slowly by and Fritz watched carefully to see if there was any hesitation in the driving pattern of the police vehicle. Indeed, there was a slight pause, but then the *policie* continued down the road about thirty feet and paused again, continuing this same pattern, as if checking license plates and tags in a periodic fashion.

Surely Quan Tang's son and his people would have reported the stolen Rolls-Royce by now, so Fritz didn't understand why the *policie* vehicle had continued on—unless perhaps there was some reason that Duoc Tang wanted to handle this affair in-house. Perhaps it would be perceived as a sign of weakness if it should come out that Quan Tang had been beheaded in his own home—a place where he should have been most secure.

The *policie* passed on, out of sight, but still Fritz was uneasy. Every minute that he waited here meant precious time that was not being used in getting themselves closer to the border. Fritz checked his pocket watch. Over twenty minutes had passed. He realized that it could take some time to make a trade of vehicles, but he thought that perhaps Budek and Otka had run into some sort of trouble. Unfortunately, he did not know the exact location of Rybar's apartment, and finding it in a four or five block radius in the unfamiliar city of Prague might prove time-consuming and difficult. For the moment, Fritz resolved to stay put for ten more minutes, and if Budek and Otka hadn't made an appearance, he would take action. So he sat and let the pit in his stomach gnaw at him. It was his fault that Matthias was dead. Vengeance hadn't been worth the cost of yet another of his brothers' life.

Before ten minutes had passed, Fritz noted some unusual movement in the street traffic. A number of the cars that passed were larger sedans of a similar make and with tinted windows. When Fritz compared license plates, he realized that though he had seen multiple cars of the same make, he was seeing some of them repeatedly. A pair of these cars pulled in alongside of him, blocking him in, and even as Fritz turned the ignition, the lock of the front passenger-side door clicked into the open position and a young Vietnamese man with a large mole at the right corner of his lip slipped inside.

The Vietnamese man held a German Walther PPK leveled at Fritz's chest. "Let me introduce myself. I am Duoc Tang and I am here to require justice for the murder of my father."

Fritz saw now how Duoc's men had kept up a distraction—a parade of cars—to keep his attention diverted even while Duoc crept up to the Rolls-Royce and used one of his father's keys to slip into what should have been a nearly impregnable fortress of bulletproof glass and armor plating.

"The *policie* tipped you off to my location," said Fritz.

Duoc Tang gently laughed. "No, Mr. Gantlet. The *policie* are a resource which I am not afraid to use, but in this case it was a Mr. Budek Benes who contacted me and negotiated a deal."

"Budek? What sort of deal did he negotiate?"

"He feels you are a rival for the affections of a Miss Otka Lada. By removing you from the picture, his path to winning Miss Lada is unimpeded."

Fritz scowled. "Except for the fact that he'll be executed for attempting to break Otka Lada's father out of Pankrác Prison. That might put a crimp in his plans of wedded bliss."

"I hate to be the one to disillusion you, Mr. Gantlet, but your 'facts' are incorrect. Mr. Benes cut a deal with Warden Vlach to deliver your brother Matthias to him. Matthias has created some past enmities with various communist governments and such a capture would undoubtedly bring plaudits and advancements within the government ranks."

"But Matthias was killed, not captured."

Duoc Tang shrugged. "Either result is a feather in the cap of an ambitious communist bureaucrat. My sources have yet to confirm the details."

"You say you seek justice," said Fritz, "but it was I who came seeking justice when your father killed my own brother, Otto."

"But that was in retribution for the disruption and deaths that you caused to my father's prostitution and slavery ring. You see, it is a vicious cycle. Eye for an eye, tooth for a tooth, and a death for a death—but I am not here to play word games with you or even pretend that I am in the right. In fact, you did me a favor, but no good deed ever goes unpunished."

Fritz could see a dozen men gathered outside the Rolls-Royce, some carrying machine guns and others with sword blades sheathed across their backs. "How did I do you a favor?"

"As long as my father was alive, I was only second in command. I didn't dare kill him myself because he commanded the respect and loyalty of his people. You took care of that problem for me."

"So why not let me go on my way?"

"You already know the answer to that," replied Duoc Tang, and his lips turned in a wry smile. "Would my father's men consider me a leader that demands respect if I did not exact swift and brutal vengeance?"

Duoc pulled the trigger of his Walther and the bullet sped unnerringly for the heart. Fritz slammed against the car door at the impact, and saw the smoking hole in his chest pocket.

Duoc saw that his shot had been precise, right to Fritz's heart, and though he was extremely satisfied with his handiwork, he was a man of detail and was about to put two rounds into Fritz's head when all hell broke loose outside.

The boom of a gunshot resounded in the Prague street, echoing off the walls of the surrounding buildings, so that it was difficult to pinpoint the source of the gunfire. The sound was somewhat muted inside the cab of the Rolls-Royce Phantom, but suddenly two of Duoc Tang's men dropped in the street.

Duoc shouted, though his men standing in the street were unlikely to hear him. "Fools! I told you never to stand too close together."

Blood dripped from the hole in Fritz's shirt, and Fritz was slumped against the inside of the driver's door. Despite the gunfire outside, Duoc was not going to leave without ensuring the successful assassination of Fritz Gantlet. He shoved his Walther forward so that the snout of his pistol was about a foot away from the guitar player's head. Just as Duoc was about to pull the trigger, the bulletproof windshield caved inward as if hit with an invisible sledgehammer. Fragments of glass sliced Duoc's face and a bullet took off the tip of his nose, passed through the interior of the vehicle and cracked the back window without passing through.

Duoc knew now that the bulletproof glass was not sufficient against whatever firepower was being used against him and he threw himself into the footwell of the Rolls-Royce. The vehicle was armored all the way around, designed to stand up against grenades and even shaped landmines, so he was confident that he would be better protected down low.

A gunshot boomed again. This time the sound was not muted. Another of Duoc's guards was struck and he fell heavily against the door of the Rolls. Now his men scattered for cover. A gun fired twice more. One of his Vovinam masters fell forward on his face even as he tried to run. The second shot missed a fleeing Czech gunman and caved in the brick wall where it hit.

There was a moment's reprieve and Duoc realized that he had better act quickly. With a hole smashed through the front windshield, the mysterious gunman could fire through or even toss a grenade inside. What he thought had been a virtual fortress was now a cubicle of death. Still, he could make the vehicle's armor plating work for him.

With great effort he forced open the passenger door, pushing away the body that had fallen against it. Duoc clambered out of the car, using the open door as shield against further gunfire. But instead of gunfire, he caught sight of something lofting through the darkness toward each of his two support vehicles which were parked across the street. They were grenades, but each of them fell short of the cars and then they exploded, lighting up the streets, caving in the doors of his men's vehicles and shattering windows.

Duoc began running down the street, his scattered men darting behind him as he made a run for the corner, where he had hidden his own vehicle.

A grenade came wobbling through the air, skipping down the street after him and then it exploded, taking down a half dozen of his men with shrapnel, but amazingly Duoc found himself unscathed. The grenade had not been thrown far enough for him to be within the initial radius of the explosion, and his men, accidentally serving as human shields, seemed to have absorbed the shrapnel that might have hit him.

Duoc disappeared around the corner and a long-haired apparition strode down the street, loading fresh shells into a massive 454 Casull pistol. It was Matthias Gantlet. He paused at the open door of the Rolls-Royce and peered inside. "Fritz?"

Fritz had his shirt up and was prying out bloody fragments of his Lang eighteen-carat gold pocket watch out of his chest, where they had been imbedded by Duoc Tang's gunshot.

"Are you all right?" asked Matthias.

"Thanks to grandfather's pocket watch," said Fritz as he ruefully examined the debris of the watch, "but the bullet hit me so hard over the heart, that I must have blacked out for a few seconds. Tang's son may not have been able to kill me, but he does have the power to stop time."

"Yeah, well let's get out of here before the clock starts ticking again."

"No chance of that. I assume that the shooting was your handiwork?"

"Yeah, you like it?"

"Very much. That grenade throwing needs some work, though."

"I can't for the life of me seem to hit what I'm throwing at," admitted Matthias. "But it bought us a little time. I'm going after that runt that shot you, be back in a few minutes."

Fritz shook his head, remembering how just a few moments ago he had thought himself responsible for Matthias's death. "I'm just glad to have you back in the land of the living. Let him go. We've got to concentrate on getting out of Czechoslovakia."

"What do you mean land of the living?" asked Matthias. Before Fritz could answer, his brother turned and killed two of Duoc Tang's already wounded men, who had recovered enough from the initial shock of their shrapnel wounds to point their pistols in Matthias's general direction.

"Budek told me that you and Father Lada were killed in the rescue attempt."

Several of Tang's men climbed from the grenade-damaged wreckage of their car and began firing at the Rolls-Royce. Their bullets hammered against the armored plating and the driver side windows of the vehicle, ricocheting away across the pavement or into the air. Matthias waited for a lull in the barrage and sent just one shot winging across the street. It blew through one gunman's chest and the bullet continued through the side of the car, killing the driver who still remained behind the wheel. "Budek's a lying sack. Don't trust a word he says."

Fritz picked the last piece of gear out of his flesh. "A bit too late for the warning, little brother. Budek's the one who sold me out to Quan Tang's son."

"The runt who just shot you?"

"One and the same. Understandably, he didn't care for me offing his father." Fritz dropped his shirt. "Well, actually, he thanked me for doing him a favor and then tried to kill me."

Across the street, the remaining gunmen piled into the last car and it squealed off as fast its driver could take them. Tactically, it was advantageous for the enemy combatants to leave the field, so Matthias didn't fire after the vehicle in the case that it might disable their transportation, leaving the four or five gunmen to throw bullets in his direction.

"So, if Budek lied to me about you being killed, what else did he lie about?" asked Fritz.

"I told you ... probably everything."

"Does that mean that Father Lada is still alive?"

"Did Budek tell you that the father was dead?"

"Yes," said Fritz. "Yes, he did."

"Well, in that case, you know that the opposite is true. Not only is he alive, but I've got him hidden around the corner in a Skoda."

With the revelation that Matthias and Father Lada were both alive, Fritz felt as though a great weight had been lifted from him, and he chuckled in giddy relief.

"Where's Otka?"

Fritz made a face as he heard sirens in the distance. "That's the problem. I bought into Budek's lies. He's with Otka and supposedly trading in his Jawa for a Yugo at this very moment."

"What he was really doing was making an excuse to get her away, while Duoc disposed of you. Still, in order to win Otka over, he has to sell the lie. He may actually be at least pretending to make the trade."

Fritz climbed out next to Matthias and together they fled the growing cacophony of the sirens, away from the crimson-spattered bodies, through the shifting shadows and to the Skoda where Father Lada anxiously awaited.

He anxiously gripped Matthias's arm as the vocalist opened the door. "Where is my daughter?"

Fritz climbed in the back of the Skoda and unlimbered the French MAT 49 just in case they needed some firepower. "Good to see you again, Father Lada. We're going to need to make a quick stop to pick up Otka."

"Is she safe?"

"She's with Budek at some fellow's house—a fellow named Rybar."

Father Lada frowned. "Budek? What does that worm want with my daughter?"

Matthias steered the Skoda in a quick U-turn. "I think you know the answer to that, Father. Otka is an attractive woman, and Budek has been doing everything in his power to win her over."

Fritz rolled down his window. "Including selling out her father."

Father Lada put a hand on the dash to steady himself. Whether it was Matthias's driving or the news that his daughter was with Budek that caused him to seek some stabilization, it was difficult to say. "Where is this Rybar?"

Fritz listened to the sirens and directed Matthias to take a right ahead. "We think he may be within a couple of blocks of here."

Matthias spun the wheel to the right.   "The bad news is that Budek is the one who told us that, so Rybar may live miles from here … or he may not even exist at all."

"Otka seemed to know of him—to have met him," clarified Fritz. "So his existence isn't completely a figment of Budek's imagination."

Matthias scanned the vehicles parked along the streets where squalid tenements reached five and six stories into the air. "If we want to find Otka, we need to spot Budek's Jawa."

"That boy was always trouble," muttered Father Lada. "Always a little too eager to please and full of dubious stories that he thought might impress whomever it was he was talking to—and he's always had an interest in Otka. When he was just eight years old he pulled a handful of flowers from Widow Kot's garden and gave them to Otka—claimed he had cultivated them himself and told Otka that he was growing a whole garden full of flowers just for her."

Colorful lights splashed against the walls of the tenements at the intersection ahead and with wailing sirens a pair of police cars sped by.

Fritz checked the road behind them and found it clear. "This part of the city will be crawling with police shortly. The longer it takes us to locate Otka, the more likely it is that you'll end up making a return visit to Pankrác—along with the rest of us."

"Warden Vlach would love to get his hands on us again," commented Matthias. He silently prayed that he would be led through the maze of city blocks so that he might be able to find Otka. Matthias turned off the headlights and crossed the intersection, noting a cluster of *policie* vehicles halted around the scene of the gun battle near the Metro stop and the shattered wreckage of a number of empty vehicles that had taken bits of shrapnel from Matthias's grenades. There were some streetlights at the intersection, but the bulbs had burned out six months ago and hadn't yet been replaced, so Matthias sent the Skoda gliding through an umbral twilight cast through dusty windows from the still-burning lights of a few night owls in the surrounding tenements. He took a right at the next block and it turned out that he was proceeding the wrong direction down a one-way street. Fortunately, there was no traffic about and Matthias took the next left without encountering any oncoming vehicles.

The sirens wailed in the backdrop of the night, reminding them that any moment they might encounter the police.

Fritz kept vigilance to the sides and rear of the vehicle. "We need some sort of system for methodically searching this area of the city."

Matthias laid on the brakes of the Skoda and brought the vehicle to a sudden halt. His prayer was answered. "There's a motorcycle parked behind that Dumpster in the alley."

Fritz peered into the darkness of the alley. "Where?"

Matthias leaped out of the Skoda and his form became shrouded in the darkness. His footsteps took him into the alley where he, indeed, found a Jawa motorcycle with a license plate that identified the motorcycle as belonging to Budek. Not far down the alley was a back door to the tenement which was propped open a crack by an old brick jammed between the door and the frame. A faint light seeped out into the alley and he could hear the rumble of a bass speaker.

Fritz followed Matthias down the alley. "Is that Budek's bike?"

"Same tear in the seat, same license. It's his. I'll back the Skoda into the alley and you see if you can find Otka."

This sounded like a wise plan to Fritz. He handed his MAT 49 machine gun to Matthias. "You might need this." He handed his *katana* to Matthias next. "This might also arouse some suspicion."

Matthias slung the sword over shoulder. "I'll be right here waiting for you. Don't take too long."

Fritz pushed open the door and found himself in the vestibule of a stairwell. Bags of refuse were thrown into one corner and a couple of young men were smoking cigarettes on the stair. They looked up from their animated conversation when Fritz entered.

The German guitarist spoke to them in fluent Czech. "I'm looking for Rybar's card game."

The first had a scraggly beard with patches that wouldn't evenly grow. "That's a private game, mister. Only personal friends of Rybar get an invite."

Fritz thrust a hand into his pocket and produced a handful of brightly colored one-hundred and five-hundred koruna notes that Otka had traded on the black market for US currency that he had given her. "Rybar may be more interested in these personal friends than me, but I enjoy a good game of taroky so I have a tendency to overlook his lack of sincerity."

The second smoker on the steps grinned, revealing several missing teeth. He motioned up the stairs. "Then by all means, join the game. Second floor, apartment two hundred seven. But you already knew that, right?" Scraggly Beard stubbed out a half-smoked cigarette and carefully placed it in the pocket of his jacket and they moved aside to allow Fritz to pass. The German musician shoved his hand inside his jacket to secure the bills in a different pocket from which he had drawn them.

As he passed, he heard the rasp and click of a switchblade. Fritz was ready for this. He found it curious that Scraggly Beard was extinguishing a half-smoked cigarette. Obviously, if he was leaving his cigarette half unsmoked he was planning to do something else. Fortunately for Fritz, Scraggly Beard had frugal tendencies and despite the prospect of a pocketful of korunas, he didn't want to waste a few grams of tobacco. He was unlikely to ever smoke that saved cigarette.

Fritz swiftly thrust his twelve-inch *yoroi doshi* into the Scraggly Beard's kidney and ripped out the blade, striking his second attacker, the one with the missing teeth, hard in the ribs with his elbow. A switchblade and a partially-opened pocketknife clattered down the stairs. Fritz whirled, opening the jugular of the second attacker, and the body tumbled down the stairs in a bright arterial spray.

Fritz paused to clean and resheath his *yoroi doshi* then continued up the stairs. The groans and gurgles of the dying covered by the sound of the music which grew more intense each step that he climbed. Clearly, Fritz had underestimated the greed of the two men watching the stair. He had figured they would be content to let Rybar fleece him in a game of taroky and then take their share. Instead, they had figured they would cut the money out of the newcomer without the benefit of a card game. Now, Fritz had made a mess and it was only a matter of time before someone discovered the bodies and informed Rybar or the police—and since the police were congregated only three blocks away, it would only take a couple of minutes for them to arrive once they received the call.

Rybar's apartment was not difficult to find. The smell of hashish and the sound of bootleg concert recordings lingered in the corridor and reverberated through the walls. Fritz rapped on the door and a moment later it opened about six inches, a chain between the wall and door still providing the meager illusion of security.

Bloodshot eyes peered through the crack. "I told you already, we will not turn the music down. If you call the police I will personally pay a visit to your wife while you at work and show her how a real man ..."

The time for subtlety was long past and so Fritz put his shoulder hard into the door and pushed. The chain tore loose, taking a chunk of frame with it, and the door smashed into the man speaking, breaking his nose and throwing him against the far wall.

Fritz didn't waste a moment forcing himself into the apartment, which was thick with marijuana vapors intermingling with the smoke of tobacco and chicory cigarettes. The card table was thick with half-full bottles of wine and beer, trays of smoldering cigarette butts, and carefully guarded piles of winnings alongside a stack of well-worn cards. A number of non-card players inhabited various beer-stained and well-worn chaise lounges, inhaling from elaborate water bongs, clutching beer bottles and cigarettes or each other in drug-addled passion.

The man with the broken nose fell into the corner behind the door, clutching at his bloodied face and swearing in Czech. Fritz spotted Budek gesticulating wildly as he spoke with a bearded fellow wearing a shirt with open lapels and a gold chain around his neck, and despite the loudness of the music, he could overhear some of their conversation.

"I don't understand, Rybar," said Budek. "Before you said you'd do a straight across trade for my Jawa. Now you want my Jawa and five hundred korunas?"

Rybar idly scratched his beard in a practiced movement that was designed to telegraph the idea that he really had no investment in the conversation, one way or the other. "It's simply that the value of my Yugo has changed since we spoke last."

"No it hasn't," protested Budek. "It's still the same piece of junk that it was three weeks ago."

"So it is," agreed Rybar, "but I sense that you need the Yugo more than you needed it last month, so now I'm willing to give you my Yugo in exchange for your Jawa and for six hundred korunas."

"But it was five hundred korunas a moment ago!"

"And now it's seven hundred korunas and your Jawa. Take it or leave it."

Budek clearly wasn't happy, but he pulled loose a wad of korunas from his pocket and peeled off seven hundred notes. "Fine!"

Otka's mouth fell open, as she had never seen Budek with that much cash on hand. "Where did you get that money?"

Rybar raised an eyebrow. "It seems that my friend has come into some money! I'd heard word that you've been spreading some cash around, Budek. Did you find that engagement ring you were looking for?" Rybar broke off from the conversation as he finally heard the groanings of the man with the broken nose and turned to see the stolid form of Fritz Gantlet striding toward him. "Who is this lunatic?"

Budek's forehead creased. "Fritz, I thought that you were waiting in the Rolls for us."

"Rolls-Royce?" interjected Rybar, with great interest.

"You seemed surprised to see me," said Fritz as he tapped the bloody hole in his breast pocket. "Maybe you were expecting Duoc Tang to shoot me in the heart?"

"Duoc Tang? I'm sure that I don't know what you're talking about."

Fritz hauled off with a right-handed haymaker that snapped back Budek's head and sent him reeling to his knees. Otka shrieked and Fritz took her by the wrist. "Come on. We don't have much time."

"But why did you hit Budek?"

"He sold your father and Matthias out to Warden Vlach, and then he sold me out to Quan Tang's son."

Otka's auburn hair swung about her shoulders as she twisted. "Budek, is this true!"

Budek was on his hands and knees, blood dripping from his mashed lip. "He's gone insane. Whatever you do, don't go with him! He just wants you for himself—to use you and discard you. That's what rock stars do! Me, I want to marry you. I even bought a ring!" He fished out a small case from his pocket and held it out.

Otka hesitated.

To Fritz it was clear that Budek had rehearsed at least a portion of that speech, though it was likely going down under much different circumstances than Budek had imagined. Fritz relinquished his grip upon Otka's forearm. "You can stay if you want, Otka, but your father is waiting for us, with Matthias, and we have very little time."

"But they're dead! Budek told us th ..."

"Exactly," interrupted Fritz. "Budek told us a lot of things that weren't true. He figured if your father was sprung from Pankrác that he wouldn't have a chance at you and he made a deal with the warden to turn Matthias over to him."

Otka's eyes turned to fire. "Is this true, Budek?!"

Under Otka's withering gaze and the weight of so much fact, he could no longer hold the pretense. "I only did it for us! Can't you see that I love you!" He thrust forward the box with the wedding ring.

Otka slapped the box aside, so that it spun across the floor. "I never want to see you again, Budek Benes!"

She and Fritz proceeded to the door of the apartment where the doorman was struggling to his feet. He reached underneath his shirt and Fritz could see the form of a pistol outlined underneath. Fritz pulled loose the Czech Skorpion machine gun pistol and was the first to pull the trigger. The short barrel wasn't enough to hold the aim steady, so it chewed a bloody trail from belly to skull and then into the plaster of the wall before Fritz threw aside the weapon. The doorman collapsed, eyes rolled up into his skull, but his hand still clutching the handle of his pistol in a death grip.

"But I love you, Otka!" wailed Budek as he crawled across the floor, extending his hand in one last appeal for mercy. Otka was shocked by the grisly death of the doorman and only later would she recall that final pitiful plea, but for the moment Fritz took her hand and guided her from the apartment and down the corridor.

When Fritz had left, Rybar picked up the small case and flipped the lid open, examining the diamond ring inside. "Very nice, Budek. Since you won't be needing this, I'll be hanging onto it. I need something to reimburse me for the damage done to my apartment."

Budek pushed his back against the wall and sat on the floor, trying to douse the flow of blood from his mouth. "I didn't do any damage to your apartment. It was that lunatic, Fritz Gantlet."

Rybar scratched at his beard. "Ah, yes, but it was you that brought Fritz Gantlet here, wasn't it? I did not invite this Fritz Gantlet. He was your guest and therefore you are responsible for any damage that he caused. And think of poor dead Miroslsv. How are his wife and children going to survive now that they no longer have a provider?"

"Miroslsv isn't married," said Budek.

"Nevertheless," said Rybar. "I'm going to have to pay to have his body properly disposed of. I'll be keeping that seven hundred korunas that you gave me for the Yugo. Just to help defray my expenses, mind you."

Chapter 28

A glow on the horizon indicated the coming of dawn, the sunlight slowly encroaching upon the firmament and pushing away the darkling void. Matthias drove while Fritz rode shotgun, and Otka and her father occupied the inadequate rear seat of the Skoda. Father Lada's breathing was heavy and labored, and it was apparent that the tortures he had endured during his imprisonment were causing him great pain. Otka did the best to make her father comfortable, but the jarring of the vehicle over the potholes of the poorly maintained roads was a constant aggravation to his injuries.

Matthias kept a circumspect pace as they wound through the bewildering mazes of Prague's streets and finally emerged through the sprawl and into the countryside. They indirectly retraced their path toward Ivan, avoiding E65 which could have returned them to the Lada church and household within three hours, in favor of a series of back country roads.

"The *policie* will doubtless set up a series of checkpoints along all the major roads looking for someone who might have been involved with the massacre of Quan Tang's men near the subway entrance," coughed Father Lada. "Perhaps, Fritz could pull off a convincing Czech accent, but Matthias can barely speak a word of the language. It wouldn't take long for us to be undone."

Otka thumbed the collar of her father's prison grays and noted the numerical assignation on the back. "Speaking of which, perhaps we should find you a change of clothes. Only a blind policeman could miss the fact that you are an escaped prisoner."

"We've also got bullet holes in the car," noted Fritz. "It's best we stay just as far away from the police as we can."

More than once they caught sight of checkpoints at intersections ahead and were able to slip down a secondary road. Often, when the clouds opened up in the heavens, they drove without lights, depending upon the light of the moon to show their way, until the clouds again obscured its luminescent face and forced them to use the headlights of the Skoda. They finally came into Ivan through Velky Dvur.

"We've still a long ways to the border," said Otka. "Swing by our home and I'll fetch us some food and pick up a few things for the journey."

"Sorry," said Fritz. "You're going to be traveling with nothing but the clothes on your back. The authorities may not have made the connection between Quan Tang's death and Matthias helping Father Lada escape from Pankrác, but I would be very surprised if they weren't watching the church for him to make a return."

Father Lada shifted painfully in his seat. "So why bother bringing us back to Ivan at all? Isn't it dangerous?"

"It is dangerous," agreed Fritz, "but we're not crossing the border by Skoda or on foot. Matthias and I came into Czechoslovakia by air and there's room enough for one passenger on each of our ultralights. We'll wait until evening and make a night flight to Austria."

"Where did you hide the ultralights?" asked Otka.

Fritz peered across the farmlands. "We landed in a field over by the tributary."

"Won't they have found your ultralights?"

"It's possible," admitted Fritz, "but we hid them quite well in the adjoining forest."

During the drive, most of the conversation had been in Czech so Matthias gleaned what he could from the gestures and the few words that he knew of the language and just ignored the rest, concentrating on the driving and keeping them out of any spots where they might make contact with the police. They were driving a car reported as stolen and the word was out. Czechoslovakia was enemy territory and though they had been fortunate to elude the police thus far, they were up against the resources and might of the entire Czechoslovakian communist machine. The clock was ticking and the longer they stayed within the borders of Czechoslovakia, the smaller their chances of staying at large became.

Instead of passing by the yellow church that Father Lada and Otka called their home, and crossing the main bridge over the tributary, which was the way that Fritz and Matthias had originally hiked into Ivan, Father Lada showed them a little-used bridge further down the river, which rested at the edge of a vast piece of farmland. This took them down a narrow road between thickly grown arbors and eventually terminated at the edge of a field of sugar beets. Matthias pushed the Skoda down a dirt path at the perimeter of the field until they met an ill-maintained road at the other side of the field. A half dozen workers were in the field plucking weeds and they looked on with some curiosity as the Skoda rattled over the bumps, leaving a trail of rising dust in its wake.

"We're going to have to switch vehicles," said Matthias. "I can hotwire something."

"I don't want to resort to stealing," said the father. "Most Czechs are good, hard-working people and taking a vehicle from them might cause great hardship."

"I understand that," said Matthias, "but our lives are on the line here. I'm betting that just about everyone in Ivan has been notified that they need to be on the lookout for you or your daughter. If you walk up to them and purchase a car, they are going to turn around and alert the authorities."

"There are friends that I can trust," said the father.

"Well, I hope that your judgment is better than Otka's, because Budek was just about the worst friend that I could imagine."

Though Matthias spoke to Father Lada in English, Otka heard her and Budek's names mentioned in conjunction and she rapidly began to quiz Fritz on just what had been said. Fritz happened to strongly agree with Matthias's estimation of Budek's character and he was happy to repeat it in Czech for Otka.

Otka considered the translation for a moment and appeared unhappy, then the hint of a smile formed at the side of her lips. "It seems that my judgment is improving, seeing that I most recently made friends with Fritz and Matthias Gantlet. However this turns out, I don't want you to think for even a moment that I am not most grateful for what you and your brother have done for me and my father."

Matthias understood none of this and he continued his conversation with Father Lada. "Do any of these friends have vehicles they would be willing to sell?"

"I think so," said the father. "We've got another three hundred kilometers to go before we reach the Austrian border. It would be best to do it in another vehicle."

"How about a place to hide? Would any of them have a place to hide us?"

"Novak Lukes has hidden Vietnamese girls who escaped from the service of Quan Tang. He can be trusted. He has a small non-collective farm about ten kilometers from here."

Matthias peered through the dusty windshield. "The government allows farm ownership?"

"There are limitations on the amount of land one can use, and they only cede poor or tired farming land, saving the best for the collectives—and in Czechoslovakia no one truly owns anything. If your farm becomes too productive or too successful, they seize it and put it under the control of the collective."

Under Father Lada's guidance, they continued on a series of back roads until they found a small plot of weedy land obscured by surrounding trees so that only glimmers of sun could penetrate the foliage. Some rangy goats wandered the property, content to munch on the weeds, and a small lady in a large-brimmed hat worked over a garden patch that was centrally located in order to maximize the sunlight.

Matthias pulled the Skoda deep into the thicket of weeds and trees at the edge of the property.

"Well done," commended Fritz. "No one will ever find this Skoda for at least a hundred years. Problem is, we'll still be trapped in it when they find it." He tried to push his door open, but failed. "Can anybody get their door open?"

With some effort, Otka managed to shove away some brambles with her door and slide out the back just as the small woman came rushing over, brushing dirt from her calloused hands. "Otka Lada? Is that you? Are you unharmed? Why in heavens did you drive right into the trees?"

"Mrs. Lukes, what a pleasure to see you!" greeted Otka.

Now that she was in the shade, Mrs. Lukes took off her sun-bleached hat. "We've been worried for your welfare. We've seen very little of you since the authorities took your father away. Have you heard how he is doing?"

"He is very ill, Mrs. Lukes. Do you think that you could do something to help him?"

"I'm not sure what I can do," said Mrs. Lukes, "but I will do whatever I can. Are the authorities allowing him any visitors, now?"

"Not exactly." Otka motioned to the car, and a beaten and battered Father Lada crawled out. "He's escaped from prison, Mrs. Lukes, and we need a place to hide."

The Lukeses had five children from the ages of six to eighteen who were quite curious to see the spectacle of the vehicle that had been jammed so far into the brush. However, Mrs. Lukes shooed them away and told the oldest son to escort their visitors to the fruit cellar. "The old one—out by the knotted apple tree," she specified.

Once Arnost heard these words, a light went on his eyes and he understood the gravity of the situation. He seemed all skin and bones and he motioned with one lanky arm for the four new arrivals to follow him. "Come this way!"

As they went around the side of the peeling and faded house, Matthias glanced back and noticed that the rest of the children were quickly transferring brush from a burning pile and mounding it up around the rear of the Skoda so that it would be completely invisible to anyone who did not take the time to dismantle the pile and peer beneath. He couldn't help but admire the efficiency and bravery of even the tow-headed six-year-old girl that pitched in as readily as the other children.

"I like these people," said Matthias.

"They are good, good people," agreed Father Lada. He staggered along with one arm around Fritz, who supported him as they traversed the uneven ground toward a knotted and twisted apple tree that spread its gnarled limbs in a great umbrella. Underneath the shelter of its claw-like branches, Arnost squatted, his fingers pushing into the carpet of fallen leaves and yellow sod. He lifted up a piece of plywood that was hidden beneath and revealed a set of cracked concrete stairs that descended into the dank earth.

Fritz helped Father Lada down the steps and into a cellar that had been upgraded with a pair of lightbulbs and a ventilation pipe that pushed through a ceiling consisting of creosote-soaked boards supported by a number of randomly scattered beams and four-by-four pillars. Fritz set Father Lada down upon the single cot and the priest gratefully reclined onto it. Matthias found a spot on the floor next to several tins of grain and leaned against the dirt wall.

Otka pulled up a tin and used it as a stool, surveying the jars of canned meat, fruit, and vegetables. "At least we won't be hungry!"

Fritz shook Arnost's hand, to which bits of earth still clung. "Thank you for your help. We'll be leaving this evening."

"Where will you go?"

"Somewhere outside of Czechoslovakia," said Fritz. "I won't give you any details."

Arnost nodded to Fritz and then Matthias. "The two of you look like those rock stars from the Gantlet Brothers. I have some bootleg records ..."

"With all those bootlegs floating around, it's a wonder that we ever make any money," said Fritz.

Arnost's eyes widened. "You mean ... you actually are Fritz and Matthias?"

"Impressive. Most people can't keep track of which brother is which," said Fritz. "I can't tell you how many times people have mistaken me for Mitz, when I'm clearly the better looking of us two—"

"Why are you in Czechoslovakia? Shouldn't you be ... partying and hanging out with beautiful women?"

"The Gantlet Brothers' idea of a party is a little different than most bands." Fritz made the slightest of nods in the direction of Otka. "But we're hanging out with at least one beautiful woman."

Arnost smiled appreciatively, acknowledging that Otka's beauty had not gone unnoticed. "I see her at church, but that Budek Benes is always bothering her."

Fritz displayed a split knuckle on his right hand. "See this?"

"What happened?"

"I got this punching Budek Benes in the face."

Arnost laughed. "I wish I could have seen that."

"So, Arnost, we're going to need another automobile. Do you have anything that we can purchase from you, or should we be talking to your father?"

"You should be talking to me," said Arnost. "I have a Tatra 613 that I've been working on in the shed."

Fritz's brow furrowed. "Isn't that a luxury car? I thought that only government officials got their hands on those."

"Almost any car is too expensive for us peasants to own," said Arnost, "but I rescued this from the junkyard by paying the owner one hundred korunas."

"One hundred korunas? What kind of shape was it in?"

Arnost waved his hand. "There was a reason it was in the junkyard, you know. The frame was bent and a lot of the panels were crushed from a head-on collision, but the engine is in the rear and it was intact. It's a V8!"

"So this vehicle is in running condition?"

"It runs perfectly. I straightened the frame with a sledgehammer, and replaced the broken panels, myself."

"What are you boys chattering about over there?" called Otka.

Fritz glanced over his shoulder and smiled. "I'm trying to arrange for some transportation."

"It needn't be anything as ostentatious as that Rolls-Royce you showed up with last time," teased Otka. "I know you are trying to impress me, but anything with four wheels and an engine will make me happy."

"What's wrong with the Skoda you brought in?" asked Arnost.

"A few bullet holes. Nothing that some putty won't fix. The main problem is that the automobile has been reported as stolen."

Arnost raised his eyebrows. "You stole it?"

"Not exactly. Matthias paid the owner for it, but then that fellow reported it as stolen."

"Why would he do that?"

Fritz deflected the question. "It's complicated—something to do with a prison break from Pankrác and a bunch of angry prison guards. The point is, we can't use the car any longer. You can keep it, but if you show up in Ivan, driving it around, the authorities are undoubtedly going to ask you some questions."

"I can take it apart and sell the pieces on the black market. Only a few of the pieces have serial numbers and they can be filed off."

Fritz reached for his wallet. "How much do you want for the Tatra?"

"I don't know," hedged Arnost. "With all the work I put into it, maybe a thousand korunas."

"Sorry," said Fritz. "I don't have that many korunas. How about a thousand US dollars?"

Arnost's eyes almost fell out of his head. "Are you serious?"

Fritz knew full well that this was the black market equivalent of thirty thousand korunas, but he did appreciate what this family was doing for them and he could afford to be generous. Fritz counted out ten hundred-dollar bills and handed them to Arnost. "Be careful how you spend those. You don't want to attract any attention."

Arnost reverently folded the bills and placed them in his pocket. "Matthias is the singer, right?"

"That's right," said Fritz.

"If I didn't know better I would have thought that he was a mute. He hasn't said a word since he got here."

"He's just depressed because his throwing skills are severely lacking," said Fritz. "He threw three grenades and none of them hit the mark. Bodies all over the place."

Arnost was dismayed. "Innocent people?"

"No, they were all trying to kill me, but the big shot bad guy got away."

"I had no idea he was such a poor thrower."

Fritz put a finger to his lips. "It's a well-kept family secret. When we escaped over the Berlin Wall, Matthias—for the life of him—could not get the grappling hook to stick."

Matthias scowled. "You seem like you're in an awfully good mood, Fritz. Just what it is it you and Arnost are talking about?"

Fritz shrugged. "I'm just pleased to find out that you and Father Lada are alive and well. After that piece of good news, nothing can kill my good mood—not even being stuck in a cellar for the rest of the day."

Father Lada managed a smile on his bruised and beaten countenance. "He was also regaling Arnost with stories of your poor throwing ability."

"Hey," said Matthias. "I saved your life, didn't I? If it wasn't for me, Duoc Tang would have put more than just one bullet into you."

Fritz spread his hands wide. "I'm not complaining, little brother, just having a little fun at your expense."

"Set up a code with Arnost so when he comes to inform us of nightfall we don't accidentally shoot him. Then pipe down so I can get some sleep. You can tell everybody about how I couldn't throw a grappling hook over the Berlin Wall after I've had some shut eye."

"I don't recall that getting the hook over the wall was really the problem," replied Fritz. "I seem to remember that you threw one grappling hook completely over the wall—rope and all."

"It got away from me," said Matthias. "And that was how many years ago, and you're still busting my chops for it?"

"I'm just glad to have you around," said Fritz. "I'll take first watch."

Matthias began drifting off to sleep. "Good. Wake me up when it's time for me to take over."

It seemed just a few moments later when Fritz was shaking his shoulder. "Matthias, it's your turn. I can't stay awake much longer. I'm starting to hallucinate shadows into Czech storm troopers."

"Get some rest. I'm on it." Matthias shook off the heavy grasp of his deep slumber, rose to his feet and took the MAT 49 which his brother shoved into his hands.

Only one of the overhead bulbs burned, and the rest of the cellar was in shadows. Father Lada slept fitfully on the cot, and not far away Otka was stretched out with a thin blanket pulled over her recumbent form. Her face had relaxed in slumber and the lines of concern faded away under Morpheus's influence, a few strands of her auburn hair falling across her features. Matthias stretched his legs and crossed to the dark well of shadows at the base of the concrete steps. "Fritz, what's the code that you set up with Arnost?"

He turned and found that Fritz was already asleep. Matthias paced the cellar for a few minutes and then sat on the steps. He could hear the cackle of the chickens somewhere above. He began to think of his wife and his children Anna and Jacobbe, both named in the memory of his parents, and the hours slipped past. Matthias's reverie was broken when the satellite phone in his pocket rang. He unzipped the pocket and answered. "Mitz?"

The gravelly voice on the other end had a heavy Czech accent and certainly didn't belong to Mitz or any other of Matthias's brothers. "Aah, so that crashed ultralight does belong to the Gantlet Brothers. I'd received all kinds of reports about how Fritz and Matthias Gantlet had infiltrated into Czech territory and been causing all kinds of trouble. Which one am I speaking to, by the way?"

"Matthias. And who am I speaking with?"

"Ludvik Kolka, lieutenant of the Státní bezpečnost in charge of border security."

"The Czech secret police?"

"Perhaps you are familiar with our work?" mocked Kolka.

"Let's cut to the chase," said Matthias. "Is there some reason you're calling? Because I'm on a very tight schedule. I'm catching a flight out of Austria in a few minutes."

"Is that so? Because I have witnesses that spotted you inside the borders of Czechoslovakia less than an hour ago."

Matthias couldn't help but notice that this was suitably vague. There was no detail about just where this witness might have seen them. Kolka might be fishing for information, seeing if he could break Matthias's bluff. "You better have their eyesight checked."

"So, you're telling me it wasn't you in that Skoda you stole outside of Pankrác?"

"You're wasting my time," said Matthias. "Go ahead and keep that ultralight. Someday maybe you'll need a quick flight out of Czechoslovakia."

"It's in no shape to go anywhere," said Kolka.

"Why do you think we left it behind?"

"So, how did you get out of Czechoslovakia?"

"What, so you can plug the holes? Nice talking to you, Ludvik." Matthias hung up the phone and wondered just how much of his story Kolka bought.

"Who was that?" rasped Fritz. He was just coming out of sleep and he rubbed at his eyes with the fierceness of a bear coming out of hibernation.

Matthias held up the phone. "The Czech secret police. Apparently, they found your missing phone and put two and two together."

Now Fritz was awake and his gray eyes focused with great intensity. "What about our ultralights?"

"Oh, yeah ..." Matthias halted before he continued his sentence. "Actually, I'm not sure on that one. He specifically mentioned finding a broken ultralight, but he didn't say anything about a second ultralight—and I didn't ask him."

"So you think it's possible that he found just one of our ultralights, when yours was less than a hundred yards away?"

"It was pretty well hidden," said Matthias, "but I thought yours was well concealed, too."

"Maybe this fellow you talked to ..."

"Ludvik Kolka," interjected Matthias.

"Maybe this Ludvik Kolka was playing a game—hoping he could lure you out of hiding to use the second ultralight, which he purposely failed to mention."

"Maybe," said Matthias. "I don't suppose that it matters much anyhow. One ultralight is not going to be enough to get four of us over the border, unless we make three trips. We were going to have to cross the border some other way, anyhow."

"I can slip over on foot," said Fritz, "but it's a whole different endeavor when I've got someone else with me."

"And Father Lada can barely stay upright, let alone run across a no man's land between borders. You know, if my ultralight is still hidden I could fly Father Lada over the border. It would probably be the easiest way for him to go."

Fritz looked back at the slumbering forms of Otka and her father. "If I know Father Lada, he will never allow it. He'll refuse to cross the border until he knows that Otka is across."

"There's got to be some way to persuade him of the practicality of him flying over."

"Do you know how many enslaved Vietnamese girls he risked his life to help? Those were total strangers. Otka is his own flesh and blood. Father Lada won't even take practicality into account."

"The odds of getting him over the border any other way are very small," said Matthias.

Fritz acknowledged this with an open-palmed gesture. "This all may be a moot point, anyhow. If that second ultralight isn't still hidden in the forest, then none of us are flying out of here."

"And if it is?" asked Matthias.

"Then we need to find a way to make it happen," said Fritz.

"Then you'll talk to Otka about it?"

Fritz glanced back at the sleeping brunette. "If I get a chance. There's not a whole lot of opportunities for privacy down here."

A muffled rapping came from above.

"Who's the best guitarist in the world?" called Fritz.

A vague and indistinct voice called back. "Michael Schenker!"

Matthias glanced over at his brother. "There is some room for argument on that one. You know, some people put you in the same class as Schenker."

"Nice of you to say," said Fritz with a jerk of his head up the stairs. "Now if I got a response like Double R Townsend of Strychnine, I would know that we've got trouble."

"You know, Sly's run into Brent Mickelson. Says he's a stand-up guy."

"That may be true, but Double R is not a stand-up guy," said Fritz. "Have I told you about the time he stole my guitar and tried to sell it back to me at twice the price?"

"Does this story end with Double R having a broken nose?"

"Don't I wish," fumed Fritz. "You know, I pride myself on keeping a calm demeanor, but that's the one guy that can play my last nerve like the virtuoso guitar player that he is not!"

The overhead plywood scraped away and the dying light of the day filtered in. Arnost's shadow stood at the top of the stair. "Daylight's almost gone. It's time for you to be on your way. You ready to take a look at your brand new Tatra 613?"

Arnost pulled the Tatra out of the shed for them, its motor alternately rumbling and spitting as the Czech proudly stepped out of the driver's seat and waved his arm toward his handiwork. The Tatra had been reconstructed from the panels of many other junkyard Tatras and so the car was a patchwork of different colors and panels that either didn't quite fit or were not installed properly.

"That's quite a car," said Matthias.

"All I care about is that it runs," answered Fritz, so that Matthias could barely hear his brother over the rumble of the Tatra.

Matthias nodded and smiled broadly. "That's the part I'm worried about."

The roar of the engine woke Otka and her father and they slowly emerged from cellar. As a mantle of darkness settled upon the farm, they crawled into the backseat. They said their good-byes to the Lukeses and expressed their sincere appreciation. Then Matthias took the driver's seat and Fritz rode shotgun next to him.

Matthias shifted into gear and put both hands upon the wheel. "Let's take this baby for a spin!"

The Tatra coughed, belched black smoke, and they lurched down the driveway. The sky was a glowering, overcast gray as they negotiated a series of back roads that took them toward the field where Fritz and Matthias had made their initial touchdown inside the borders of Czechoslovakia.

"It's the perfect night for a covert flight," said Fritz, "but the weather looks like it will be a bit wetter than when we came in."

Indeed, the clouds were thick and heavy and threatening to empty their swollen bellies. As they drew within a mile of the forest where they had hidden their ultralights, Matthias extinguished the headlamps of the Tatra and pulled into the narrow cleft that was the mouth of an old road, which had fallen into disuse and become overgrown. A cloud of smoke drifted across them as Matthias killed the engine.

Fritz opened the door and was momentarily enveloped in the haze. "I think we're burning more oil than we are gas."

"Where are you going?" asked Otka.

Fritz renewed the dark camouflage which he had smeared his skin with when infiltrating Quan Tang's mansion. "I'm going to do a bit of reconnaissance. I'll be back within the hour."

Otka opened up her door and stood next to Fritz. "Do be careful!"

Fritz's response was not audible to Father Lada's ears, but when Otka returned to her seat there were smudges of black upon her lips. Matthias noted this and covertly motioned to her. For a moment she was perplexed and then she understood, and discreetly began to wipe away the smudges with a handkerchief.

Her father was not fooled. "Otka. There seems to be a bit of camouflage on your face. Did you plan to do some reconnaissance, also?"

For a moment Otka was tongue-tied and unable to formulate a response.

"It's an entirely different kind of reconnaissance," said Matthias over his shoulder. He patted the dashboard. "Nothing like stealing a few kisses after a luxurious ride in a Tatra 613 that's been patched together with chewing gum and baling wire."

Father Lada chuckled. "In Czechoslovakia, we have to be resourceful. If you can't find the necessary parts, you find something and make do. Arnost is a resourceful young man."

"As long as it gets us where we're going, then I have no complaints," said Matthias. "And Arnost has my utmost admiration."

"So these ultralights you flew into Czechoslovakia—how did you avoid being caught by our air defenses?"

"If you fly low enough to the ground you can avoid being detected by radar," explained Matthias. "However, when you fly low you run the risk of being spotted by people on the ground. That's why it's important to fly on a night with plenty of cloud cover and very little light."

"These ultralights each have two seats?" asked Father Lada.

"Yes," said Matthias. "Arnost made us some garbage sack ponchos, but I have a feeling that it's going to be a very wet flight."

Father Lada rustled through a bag in the backseat. "I only see two ponchos here. I'm afraid that half of us are going to be very wet."

It seemed they waited in the darkness for many hours, but in reality Fritz was back before the hour was up. He moved quietly and unseen through the darkness so that he seemed to appear suddenly at the door. Matthias was startled and before he recognized that it was Fritz, he had his 454 Casull out and leveled, finger lying alongside the trigger.

He lowered the gun and let Fritz inside, the inner door panel falling off and exposing the gears for lowering and raising the windows. "What did you find?"

"The coast is clear and we've got wings."

Father Lada smiled. "That is good news." He lit up a cigarette he had bummed from Arnost and sucked the tobacco in like a hungry baby at a bottle.

Matthias coughed. "I hope that's your last cigarette."

"It will be," promised Father Lada. "If we make it into Austria, it's a new life for me. I'll never smoke another cigarette." He shifted in his seat and groaned.

Matthias opened his pill bottle, fished out a pair of tablets and handed them back to Father Lada. "Take these for the pain. We've got a long flight ahead of us and it won't be very comfortable for someone with a hairline fracture of their femur."

Father Lada gulped them down. "Bless you, Matthias!"

"We can drive right into the forest," said Fritz, "and remove the camouflage from the ultralight."

With a great backfire, Matthias turned the engine over, coaxing it to life. When the clatter of the engine seemed steady enough, Matthias backed the car out of the overgrown defile and headed down the road. He pulled on Fritz's blood-spattered night vision goggles, peering through the cracked lens, and proceeded without the use of the headlamps. The Tatra was so loud that it made any attempt at stealth untenable, but if they traveled in the pitch-darkness, it would be difficult to locate them should the Czech secret police have left some sort of surveillance.

Once they reached the field, Matthias sent the Tatra jouncing off the road and brought the vehicle into the umbra beneath the overshadowing boughs of the forest, but not so deep inside that the vehicle would be inextricably captured by the trunks and foliage. Matthias killed the engine and joined Fritz in the trees. Fritz used a flashlight with a narrow beam to examine the floor of the forest.

"This is where we hid my ultralight. You can see where they dragged it out. They must have hauled it off somewhere."

Matthias proceeded deeper into the forest and a mound of foliage reared up before him. He began removing boughs and branches. Fritz joined him, and then Otka was beside them helping remove the camouflage. In a few moments, Matthias breathed a sigh of relief as they uncovered the framework of his ultralight.

"How is it that they missed this?" asked Otka, using her German so that Matthias could understand her.

Earlier, the idea that the secret police had discovered one of the ultralights, but not the other, seemed more likely to Matthias. Each ultralight had two seats, so it was very much possible that Matthias and Fritz had flown in together on a single aircraft, but now—witnessing, again, the proximity of the two crafts—it seemed implausible that the secret police hadn't done a thorough enough search to uncover the second ultralight. "Fritz, hand me your penlight."

Matthias took the proffered penlight and played it over the body of the ultralight. "We'll need to fill up the tank."

"I'll get the Gerry Cans." Fritz returned to the Tatra and with some great difficulty managed to open the obstinate trunk. He softly called to Father Lada. "How are you doing, Father?"

"Whatever your brother gave me is starting to work. I can't feel anything."

"Good," said Fritz. "Once we get Matthias's ultralight clear, we'll help you into it."

"Otka goes first," insisted Father Lada. "Then me."

Fritz didn't reply, but hoisted a pair of full five-gallon cans out of the front boot. He returned to the ultralight with the intention of filling the tank, but Matthias halted him.

"We've got a problem." Matthias was lying on the ground and he twisted the head of his flashlight, broadening the pencil beam so it would illuminate a larger section of the ultralight's undercarriage.

"What are we talking?"

The blue beam showed a pound of plastic explosives tied to the undercarriage just beneath the fuel tank. "Lieutenant Ludvik Kolka has been playing us or he's hedging his bets. We've got a bomb here that's hooked to the altimeter."

Otka peered down at Matthias, the lines of her face veiled in auburn hair and darkness. She spoke in German. "What did you say about Ludvik Kolka? My father has had dealings with him before. Lieutenant Kolka suspected him of being involved in spiriting girls away from Quan Tang and sending some of them across the border, back to Vietnam."

Matthias reached up into the wiring. "Kolka found Fritz's lost phone and called me. He led me to believe that they'd found only one of our ultralights."

Otka's mouth fell open. "He knew who you were?"

Matthias pulled loose the altimeter wire. "After Budek ratted us out, we weren't exactly traveling incognito anymore. Kolka seemed to have put two and two together. The altimeter on this bomb guarantees that he kills us when the bomb goes off, since it won't blow until we're in the air."

"Can you deactivate it?"

"Not that hard," grunted Matthias. He disconnected the bomb from the altimeter and rolled to his feet, a pound of plastic explosive with a blasting cap thrust into it, cradled in one arm, and a long coil of blasting cord trailing out. "Problem is, if Kolka was hedging his bets, he probably put a couple of guys on surveillance. They probably heard the Tatra and called it in. We may be having visitors soon."

"Where's the other ultralight?" asked Otka.

Matthias raised an eyebrow and glanced in his brother's direction. "I take it that Fritz has not had the opportunity to talk to you?"

"About what?" questioned Otka.

"Lieutenant Kolka hauled off the other ultralight," said Fritz. "It wasn't in flyable condition, anyhow."

Otka's voice took on a strident tone. "So just how did you plan on getting us all out of here?"

"Matthias is going to fly your father out of here," said Fritz. "You and I are going to take the Tatra to the border."

"The border protected by barbed wire, machine gun towers, and land-mines?"

"If things look too risky, Matthias will fly back in for us after he gets your father to safety."

"But you've only got one phone," said Otka. "How will Matthias know? And he'll only be able to take one of us back with him."

"We've got to play the hand we've been dealt." Matthias handed Fritz his satellite phone. "I can pick up another one of these when I get to Austria."

"You're forgetting something," said Otka. "My father will never allow you to fly him over the border unless I'm already across."

At that moment, Father Lada emerged, tottering from the darkness. "My leg actually feels pretty good."

Fritz stepped up and caught Father Lada as his eyes fluttered closed and he began to collapse toward the earth. He threw the father over his shoulder in a fireman's carry and took a few steps to the rear seat of the ultralight. "Otka, help me strap your father in."

"What's happened to him?"

"We knew he would object to going first, but we also knew that he wasn't healthy enough to cross the border on foot, if it came to that. We fed him enough Valium to knock him out for the next three or four hours."

"Maybe longer," said Matthias. With the brush cleared away, he spun the propeller and the engine roared to life. He climbed into the seat in front of the unconscious father and began to taxi across the rough field. "I'll call you in about five hours, Fritz."

"We may just beat you across the border," said Fritz.

"I hope so!" Matthias waved and brought the ultralight onto the farm road that bordered the tract of cultivation. He urged the ultralight forward to greater speed, and that was when he saw a convoy's worth of headlights coming at him head on, and at breakneck speed.

Matthias increased the speed of the ultralight, loose gravel crackling and spitting beneath the tires, and the headlights loomed larger. Some enterprising secret policeman leaned out the window of the foremost vehicle and fired a couple of shots in Matthias's direction, but the automobile he was in hit a pothole and he was catapulted from the car, only to be run over by one of the vehicles in the rear of the convoy.

With a head-on crash impending, Matthias wrestled back the yoke of the ultralight and the aircraft lifted into the air, its wheels actually rolling up the windshield of the front vehicle, and then Matthias and Father Lada, head lolling to one side, were up and over the convoy. Matthias could afford a free hand now, and he pulled loose his Casull hand cannon and fired downward, leaving a trail of bullet holes in engines, roofs, and through a windshield, before the cylinders of his pistol went empty and he was out of range, soaring into the night sky.

The Casull was not meant to be fired one-handed and Matthias's wrist stung as he pushed it, still smoking, back into its holster. Father Lada began snoring behind him. Apparently the dosage of Valium had been so strong that the father had slept through the entire take-off and the ensuing gunfire. Matthias twisted in his seat and it appeared to him that the father hadn't been hit by any flying lead. Matthias banked the ultralight toward the Austrian border and scanned the ground for any signs of Fritz and Otka, but he couldn't see either one.

The convoy had halted, headlights lancing into the darkness at odd angles. One of the cars was on fire and Matthias could see the figures emerge from the vehicles, some temporarily limned in the light of the fire or the headlights as they formed a perimeter. Then the stutter of machine-gun fire sounded in the night, accompanied by the strobing muzzle flash. The ultralight was nearly invisible in the overcast night and so the bullets sprayed into the sky did not reach their mark, and Matthias rapidly flew out of range. Just as the ultralight passed out of sight of the jumbled and burning convoy, Matthias heard the roar of the Tatra that indicated Fritz and Otka were on their way.

Matthias smiled. It was going to be a long night.

Chapter 29

Fritz sent the Tatra barreling down the night roads—no headlights, and squinting through his damaged night vision goggles so he could navigate. Otka sat beside him in the front seat, biting her lower lip in a most fetching way, despite the odd luminescent spectrums that were revealed to Fritz's eyes.

"Do you think that Matthias and my father got away?"

"Oh yeah," said Fritz. "And Matthias managed to buy us some time by dumping a few bullets into the convoy."

"What are we going to do now?"

Fritz patted the dashboard. "We're going to ride this Tatra as far as she'll take us down every back road that you know—as long as it takes us closer to the border of Austria. We'll have an advantage, running without lights."

"If only the car weren't as loud as a jet engine," said Otka. She fell silent for a few moments. "What do you think our chances are?"

"Well, we've got the entire secret police and the Czech army looking out for us. I'd say our chances are better than most."

"You're not answering my question," said Otka.

Fritz searched the roadway ahead, the goggles amplifying the ambient light and magnifying it for his right eye. "This isn't my first border escape, Otka. The odds are always against the individual who dares stand up against the communist machine, but if you carefully follow my instructions, I'm confident that we can make this happen."

"Do you have any more of those goggles?"

"Do you think I'd be wearing this pair if I had another set?"

"No, I suppose not," said Otka. "They make you look kind of goofy."

"I was going for the mad scientist look," said Fritz. "Let me know if you want to borrow them. I'm sure they would look much better on you."

"Are you flirting with me?"

"That's the general idea," said Fritz. "Are you liking it?"

In response, she reached over and stroked his curly locks, where they emerged beneath the band of his night vision goggles. "Thank you for risking everything for my father and me."

Though Otka's beauty had distracted Fritz for a few moments, his mind grew heavy again as he recalled the horrific event that had brought him to Czechoslovakia. How could he pretend to such confidence in crossing the border when he had been unable to do the slightest thing in order to save Otto from a death that had come instantaneously It would be no different for him and Otka should a well-aimed rifle spit a bullet that took them through the vitals.

"What's wrong?" asked Otka.

"How long have you known me?"

"About two days," said Otka, "but ..."

"But already you can read me. I was just thinking about Otto."

Otka didn't cease stroking Fritz's hair. "Some things are out of our hands. Only God can sort them out."

"That's what bothers me," said Fritz. "We grab for what happiness and what justice we can for a few moments of our existence, then our life is whisked away like dust in the wind."

"You're quoting song lyrics from American bands. My English is nearly non-existent and even I recognize that."

"I've studied the philosophers," said Fritz, "but Kansas ranks among the best."

"This life isn't all there is, Fritz. It's a school ... a proving ground that God has sent us to."

"And how do you know this?"

"My father may be foolish enough to smoke two packs of cigarettes a day, but he is wise in many ways."

"So you learned this from your father. Mine taught me little of spirituality and my mother was afraid to speak of it for fear word might leak out to the authorities and our family be blacklisted from holding any position of importance. And my father is gone now—dust ..."

"...in the wind," completed Otka.

"I like to think that I'll see my father and Otto again someday, but perhaps my faith is lacking. What does your religion say will become of them?"

Otka hesitated and Fritz regretted asking the question for he recalled the teachings of some religions which stated unless a person was baptized before death that they would burn in an eternal torment. "Never mind. You don't have to answer that question."

"Fritz," soothed Otka. "I know what the teachings are, but I have to believe that the Lord will be more merciful than that."

Periodically, jets screamed overhead, racing toward the border and they saw three or four helicopters, rotors beating the air and searchlights illuminating the dark bellies of the clouds that populated the veiled sky. A half dozen times, Fritz turned the Tatra down driveways, side cuts, or side roads to avoid being seen by oncoming vehicles which they could spot by the distant glimmer and aurora of headlights. These many detours slowed their progress toward the border, but shortly prior to two AM, on foot, they approached the border through a thick copse of trees. The floor of the forest was laden with a round-leafed ivy, the roots of which threatened to tangle Otka's feet. She was traveling blindly, hanging onto Fritz's belt as he led the way through the anthracitic umbra. They halted at the edge of the forest and Fritz pushed his broken goggles back into the curly mass of his hair. They crouched at the edge of a ridge. At the bottom, loops of razor wire curled across the landscape and beyond that lay a barren field that had been defoliated with poisons and planted with landmines. Past this field of death was a forty-foot tower of iron and stone. At the top was an enclosed chamber to provide heat to the contingent standing guard, but outside of this chamber was a pair of mounted machine guns and a great spotlight which swept the no man's land of the minefield. A thousand yards down the declivity, in either direction, stood more towers.

"They're serious about keeping people in," said Fritz.

A fighter jet howled overhead, flying along the border.

"They're still looking for Matthias and your father," said Fritz.

"Don't you think that they've already passed over the border?"

"If all went well," said Fritz. "They should be safe in Austria by now. I think we should take it as a good sign that the jets are still out looking for them."

"Unless they're looking for us," suggested Otka.

"Not with jets," said Fritz. Then he heard the thumping of rotors and from the west he saw a pair of Russian-made Hind helicopters pushing along the border, their searchlights lighting up the slopes and the forest. "Those helicopters, on the other hand, they're looking for us."

Fear washed Otka's features. "People say that they have infrared lenses aboard those helicopters. There's no way we can hide from them!"

Fritz's face was impassive as he considered this. "Infrared detects variations in heat. Move back into the woods and scoop as much earth over you as you can. The coolness of the earth will disguise the heat of our bodies."

For just a moment Otka was frozen into place and then she leaped back into the scrub brush, and threw herself onto the ground. The earth here was a combination of decaying leaves and loam and Fritz began shoving the dirt over Otka's body. When she was mostly covered, he lay in the concavity he had dug out in procuring earth for Otka, and he pulled the edge of the cool earth down over his body. The Hind helicopters grew nearer and Fritz's efforts hadn't been enough to completely cover himself in earth, but he ceased his efforts and did not move as the blinding sweep of the helicopter's spotlights swept across them, turning the forest into a blazing tableau of brilliance and stark shadow. It only lasted for a moment and then the twin helicopters moved past, leisurely inspecting the landscape, slowly shrinking from sight, and the cacophony of their rotors gradually subsiding.

Fritz rose from concealment and shook off the earth. He reached down and helped Otka from her makeshift grave.

"It worked!"

"They'll be back," said Fritz. "We need to cross the minefield before they make another pass. If they catch us out in the open, we won't be so fortunate." He watched the pattern of the lights from the watchtowers. There was a certain corridor which they rarely seemed to pass over. Maybe this was intentional—as they hoped to drive escapees into the heaviest concentration of landmines, or perhaps it was simply because the spotlights had a limited arc of rotation.

Fritz unlimbered his bag and fished out several lengths of hollow aluminum tubing which he began to fit together. At the end of this he clipped on a disc-shaped sensor pad. He fitted an earpiece into his left ear and plugged it into the device.

"Please tell me that's some sort of short-range teleportation device that can pop us over the border," said Otka.

Fritz glanced up and saw the faintest hint of a smile on her camouflage-darkened features. "Don't tell me you're a fan of science fiction?"

"I do like the Star Trek show." Otka seemed embarrassed by her admission.

Fritz chuckled. "Me, too. The original series for me—"

"There's more than one Star Trek?"

"I'll show you when we get to the United States." Fritz passed his newly assembled device over his sword blade and a tone sounded in his earpiece. "This is a metal detector."

"That's what I figured," said Otka.

"Stay right behind me and step exactly where I step," said Fritz.

"I won't let you out of my sight," promised Otka.

They crept down the slope, making good time until they reached the eight-foot-high coils of razor wire which looped across the terrain. Fritz unfolded a pair of clippers from his belt and began to slice a pathway through the barbs. He began to inch his way through the tangle, trimming the wires until he had burrowed through to the other side. Despite his best efforts, he still emerged with a few nicks and cuts. "Please hand me the metal detector, Otka."

In a moment, the Czech girl pushed through the long apparatus and Fritz slung it over his shoulder, while he took in the barren landscape ahead—shafts of brilliant light sweeping across tufts of yellowed grass which had been poisoned by periodic applications of defoliant. "You next."

Otka wriggled her way through the tunnel Fritz had cut, coming out the other side unscathed, except for the piece of wire that caught on her jacket and cut through the sleeve. She took a deep breath and smiled gamely. "You sure do know how to show a girl a good time."

"First date is surveillance on Quan Tang's mansion, second date is crossing a minefield. Wait until you see what I've got in store for date number three."

"I'm hoping it's a quiet dinner in Austria," said Otka. "A girl can only take so much excitement."

Fritz swept the sensor of the metal detector across the earth in front of them and proceeded into the minefield. "Remember, walk in my foot-steps."

A tone sounded in Fritz's ear and he halted, Otka running into him. Fritz stood his ground, checked again, and then detoured around the mine. A few steps later they encountered another mine, and their next detour sent them into the path of a third mine. Eventually, these detours sent them out of the corridor that Fritz had determined was safe from the il-luminating beams of the spotlight. The great beams swept within feet of them now, and as they proceeded across the field, Fritz did everything he could to push their steps back into the strip of darkness that lay between. However, it was this very strip that seemed to have the heaviest concentra-tion of landmines.

Each step was potentially lethal, but Fritz kept faith that his metal detector would lead him safely. Still, he couldn't help but start when some-thing vibrated at his belt.

Otka put her hand on Fritz's shoulder. "What is it?"

"It's my phone," answered Fritz, with a grimace. He carefully lowered the sensor pad of the metal detector onto a safe patch of ground and put the phone to his unencumbered ear. "This better be good," he said into the mouth piece.

"Am I interrupting some sort of romantic interlude?" asked Matthias, whose voice crackled over the phone.

"If you consider crossing a minefield romantic," replied Fritz.

"Not high on my list. The skies were full of low-flying jets and I had to take a few detours. We just dropped onto Austrian soil, and it took me a little while to locate a satellite phone. I'd be happy to hop back into enemy airspace and pick up Otka for you."

"She's in the middle of the minefield with me, so there's no place to land."

"I'll need something more serious than an ultralight to extract you. There's a military base a few miles from here. If you don't mind an international incident, I might be able to steal an armed attack copter."

"That raises a whole host of problems, that could make us dead or imprisoned for life. No. Thanks for the offer, but we've got this one under control."

Otka tugged on Fritz's sleeve. "How's my father?"

Fritz relayed the question.

"He woke up as I landed. He's having his leg set and cast even as we speak. If his temper is any indicator, I expect him to make a full recovery. He was mad as a nest of hornets when he found out that Otka was still in Czechoslovakia—threatened to kill me about twelve different ways."

"Good new," chuckled Fritz. "Take care, little brother. I'll see you soon."

"Godspeed," said Matthias. "Give me a call as soon as you can and I'll arrange for a ride."

Fritz closed the connection and replaced the phone.

"How is my father?" asked Otka.

"Under medical supervision and getting a cast on his leg. Matthias said that he slept through the entire flight."

"How much Valium did Matthias give him?"

"Not quite enough. Apparently, Matthias is on his list of people he would like to strangle. Your father is not happy that we sent him on ahead, instead of you."

"Father's got a temper," said Otka, "but he's also got a great capacity for forgiveness. He'll get over it."

"I'm sure that seeing you safe and sound will help the matter considerably," said Fritz. A beam of light swept to within three feet of them and they caught their breath as it lingered, watching the motes of dust that were captured within its unblinking stare. Then the beam of light moved away and they began to breathe again.

"I don't know how long it will be before those Hind helicopters make a return visit," said Fritz. "We best get moving again."

This was easily said, but the fact was that progress across the minefield was painstakingly slow. Still, they kept picking their way through the treacherous no-man's land, threading between thick clusters of mines and the roving spotlights that drew near to their position innumerable times, so that the ambient light illuminated the fraying threads upon Otka's black sweater. Doubtless, if it were not for their dark clothing and the fact that their skin was smeared with black, they would have been discovered even though they never fell directly in the beam of a spotlight.

They were between the guard towers when Fritz's phone began to vibrate again. Fritz couldn't afford to be distracted, so he reached for the phone and killed the call, then resumed his careful sweep of the earth in front of him, discovering a pair of mines with a few scant inches between them. He took a careful step forward and whispered to Otka. "Directly in my footsteps. Don't step outside my footprint."

Otka exhaled slowly and placed her foot precisely in the spot that Fritz's had vacated. Fritz's phone began to vibrate again and for a moment Otka's concentration was disrupted. Her foot turned on a rock, she lost her balance and grabbed at Fritz's jacket to keep her from toppling onto the mine. Fritz's stance was wide enough that he was not pulled down by her weight, but as he reached out to support her, the pad of his metal detector swung freely, passing inches over the pressure trigger of the mine before glancing against the earth.

Once Otka was righted and steady, Fritz reached for the phone and answered in a low voice that would not carry far beyond them. "Now is not a good time. We're trying to cross a minefield."

"Ha," came the gravelly response of Lieutenant Kolka. "I suspected that you not already in Austria! You'll find I am not so ea ..."

"Please leave a message at the tone," continued Fritz, and he uttered a low tone that imitated that of an answering machine just before turning the power off.

"Who was that?" whispered Otka.

"Lieutenant Kolka, expressing his best wishes."

"So, he knows where we're at?"

"Not precisely," said Fritz. "And I doubt if he's got the equipment on hand to triangulate our signal."

Fritz checked the metal detector and swept the forward terrain, then moved into a gap between mines, Otka following him closely. In the distance they began to hear the thump of rotors beating the air.

"The Hinds are coming back," said Fritz. They were still a hundred yards away from the top of the ridge on the other side of the valley, and here were a number of shrubs that marked the edge of no-man's land. How far the minefield extended up the ridge Fritz could not say for certainty. Austria wasn't concerned about its citizens escaping and so they had no razor wire or fences delineating their border. Still, though it was just a few seconds sprint to the safety of the border, one misstep would result in death or dismemberment. The hardscrabble earth beneath them didn't afford them enough loose loam to cover their bodies and conceal their heat signatures from the approaching Hinds.

Otka didn't lose her nerve, but panic was written on her features. "What do we do?"

Fritz motioned toward the base of the guard tower. "We're close to the tower, we might be able to make it into the shadow before the Hinds get here." He shifted the sweep of his metal detector and they began to make sideways progress, working their way around several buried mines so that when finally the pair of Hinds drew near, Fritz and Otka were nestled at the stone base of the tower, in which the metal tripod supports of the structure were firmly implanted.

Digging into his pack, Fritz produced a large chunk of plastic explosives, with a coil of wire dangling from the detonator thrust into the clay-like substance. This was the same bomb that Matthias had removed from the ultralight—a present from Lieutenant Kolka. Fritz pushed the explosives firmly against one leg of the tower.

"What are you doing?"

"Just in case we need a distraction," said Fritz. "Let's hope it doesn't come to that."

The Hinds hovered in the air, massive wasps with four-barreled 12.7mm belly guns, and pylons full of rocket pods. They moved forward in concert with an agonizing leisure that left the two fugitives in suspense. As they advanced, Fritz and Otka moved around the stone base of the tower, always keeping out of the line of sight, so that their heat signature could not be picked up by the Hinds' onboard sensors.

As if understanding this possibility, the pilots of the Hinds split their trajectory, each making an arc around the tower in opposite directions. However, each support of the tripod tower was built on three joined stone pads that were about ten feet in height. There were deep crevices between the pads, and Fritz and Otka pushed as far as they could into one of these fissures. Fritz could feel Otka's body trembling against his as they squeezed together in the dark recesses of the cold stone.

Then the Hinds choppers moved on to the next tower. Still, Fritz and Otka did not dare move until the choppers were long out of sight and Fritz's mouth happened to find Otka's while they waited in the darkness, and they assuaged their fear with the sweetness of a few stolen kisses.

"What will happen to us when we are out of Czechoslovakia?" murmured Otka.

Fritz thought that it was just like a woman to want to talk about the future when they were in the middle of a minefield, but he was the one who had opened that door by stealing that first kiss. "I think maybe a proper date would be in order. Something that doesn't involve minefields or machine guns ..."

He let his words trail off, because he heard a clamor of commotion from far above in the enclosed portion of the tower, next to where the machine gun and spotlight were mounted. Somebody was angry and was venting their rage over a two-way radio, and the captain of the guard tower was, in turn, venting his spleen on his subordinates. Footsteps clanked on the metal planks far above and commands and threats were shouted.

Otka could more easily understand the voices than Fritz. "Lieutenant Kolka is spreading the word. He wants us found!"

"That's our cue to leave," said Fritz. They quietly crept from the deep crevice and began to cross the last leg of no-man's land, the coil of wire unspooling from Fritz's belt. Fortunately, the concentration of mines seemed to thin out as they approached the Austrian border, but Fritz refused to let a false sense of security urge them to reckless speeds, and though they made faster progress, with the specter of the guard tower looming behind them, it still seemed agonizingly slow.

They passed beyond the defoliated zone and through a sparse scattering of scrub brush as they picked their way up the slopes. That was when they heard the pounding of the Hind helicopters, yet again.

"They're coming back!" said Otka.

"Maybe I was wrong about them triangulating the signal from the cell phone," said Fritz. "They seem to know that we're in the area."

Otka cast her eyes up to the ridge of the slope that they were climbing. "We must almost be across the border ..."

Fritz agreed, but there was no fence on the Austrian side, no line drawn in the earth, so it was difficult to tell where exactly that border might be. There might be enough soil here on the slopes to dig themselves in again, conceal themselves from the infravision of the Hind choppers, but the volume of the Hinds' rotors was rapidly increasing, indicating that the Russian helicopters were closing in upon them fast.

"There's some trees beyond the ridge," said Fritz. "They might provide some cover for us." He kept the metal detector running, and passed it over the earth in front of them as they moved higher on the ridge, but they moved forward recklessly, not giving the detector sufficient time to respond and counting on the hope that they were well beyond the minefield, for they hadn't encountered a mine for the last hundred feet they had traveled.

The Hind choppers came in low, kicking up a storm of dust and wind as they came to a halt, hovering near the tower and rotating as they scanned the fields for heat sources. Fritz and Otka were at the top of the ridge now, but still fully exposed. Fritz was sure that they would be discovered any moment.

"Make for the woods," he called to Otka, but he stopped and knelt in the tall grasses upon the ridge.

"What are you doing?"

Fritz broke the back panel off his satellite phone. Inside was nestled a very large, but powerful battery. "Get into the forest, now!"

"But ..." Otka broke off as she saw one of the Hinds swinging around.

The four-barreled belly gun of the Hind chopper began to bark, spewing light and bullets that chewed up the slope toward their position. Fritz touched the battery leads to the wire he had trailed behind him, and it sent a current down the wire, which triggered the blasting cap shoved into the plastic explosives at the base of the guard tower. There was a great explosion that turned the supporting metal leg of the tower into shrapnel that spattered the closest Hind chopper, splaying the windshield of the cockpit and sending the chopper reeling drunkenly away.

The tower toppled, the machine gunner leaping from his nest and falling forty feet into the minefield, breaking both legs. The tower smashed into the rotor of the second Hind chopper. The rotor broke into a hundred pieces, fragments bursting through the guardhouse atop the falling tower and killing the commander. Then, inextricably entangled, the tower and the Hind tumbled to the ground, triggering a landmine that blew a hole through the belly of the chopper and killed three of the crew.

The remaining Hind careened through the air, its tail rotor dipping dangerously low, so that it skimmed a few feet above the naked earth. To Fritz's eye it looked as though the pilot would pull out of his spin—unless he could do something to keep the pilot off his game. Fritz reached for the French MAT 49 he had removed from Quan Tang's grip, unfolded the forward magazine and emptied all thirty-two rounds into the gyrating copter. Bullets chewed through the side of the chopper, causing havoc within, and then a pair of bullets clipped the control rod which connected the swash plates to the blade grips. Immediately, the pilot of the Hind lost control of the chopper and it went down in a great flurry of dust and dirt, coming to rest upon its side, its rotors bent and broken. Amazingly, it seemed to have avoided triggering any mines when it went down. Still, any of the crew daring to venture outside might make an untimely misstep and Fritz figured that this might keep the surviving occupants of the helicopter sequestered inside the bullet-riddled shell of the aircraft.

Fritz stood, and traced Otka's path, a furrow through the grasses, into the forest. As he walked, he replaced the heavy battery into the brick-shaped cell phone. He saw a sylph-like form detach from the shadow of a tree and Otka rushed into his arms. "We made it!"

He did indeed figure that they had passed over the border, but in case the Czechs proved overzealous and might consider pursuing them across the border, he wanted to put as much distance between themselves and Czechoslovakia as quickly as possible. Fritz kissed Otka, but didn't let his lips linger overlong. "Best we get out of the area. The Czech military won't be happy about the loss of two Hind choppers and Austria won't be happy about the commotion at its border, either."

"Do you dare risk using the phone?"

Fritz answered by dialing Matthias's newly acquired phone. "We're over the border and we need a lift."

"I'm already on the way," said Matthias. "If you travel due south you'll hit the Thirty. I'll be watching for you and flash my headlights three times."

"How do you know where we are?"

"I've been cruising the border and when I saw and heard the explosions, I knew that a Gantlet Brother had to be nearby."

It took Fritz and Otka less than ten minutes to find the dark concrete ribbon of the Thirty and, indeed, a vehicle approached, flashing its light three times. Fritz sent a return signal with a flashlight and an open-bed Halflinger pulled to the side. Matthias leaped out of the fiberglass cab and embraced Fritz and Otka. "Good to see you both in one piece. I've got a private flight booked for tomorrow morning, which will take us back to the States. Hopefully, we can get out of Austria without any foreign entanglements."

"You might want to get on the horn to Jensen and see if he can iron things out for us."

"Are you making that call?" said Matthias. "Because I don't want to be the one to tell him we've been traipsing around Czechoslovakia causing international incidents."

"I'll play you a game of Klootschieen to decide who makes the call," challenged Fritz.

"You think that just because I misplaced a few grenades that you can throw a lead ball farther than me?"

Fritz grinned. "I don't ever remember you outthrowing me in Klootschieen."

"That's because the only times we played were in East Germany, before our escape, and I was littler than you."

Suddenly, Fritz's phone began ringing. He looked at Matthias. "I guess it's not you calling me."

Matthias smiled. "You think it's Kolka calling to congratulate you on your escape?"

"I doubt if it's congratulations that he's offering." Fritz answered the phone, however. "What do you want?"

Lieutenant Kolka's harsh voice crackled over the phone. "You've been very troublesome, Mr. Gantlet, and my superiors will be very upset unless I can bring you back—dead or alive. It doesn't much matter how."

"I'd like to remind you, Mr. Kolka, that people who cross me end up dead—or haven't I amply demonstrated that?"

"That you have, Mr. Gantlet: wholesale slaughter in mobster Quan Tang's own home, and the loss of two Hind assault helicopters and a guard tower. You have the attention of my superiors."

Fritz's eyes narrowed as something occurred to him. "You sent the Hinds back for us after you triangulated our general position from your brief phone call."

"You must be referring to the 'answering machine' that received my call," said Lieutenant Kolka. "That was quite a humorous joke. I and my comrades enjoyed it immensely."

"Glad I could be of some amusement," muttered Fritz. He cocked his arm back and sent the phone hurtling high into the air. It spiraled over the tree tops and deep into the forest.

Matthias arched an eyebrow as he considered the impressive throw. "Forget that game of Klootschieen. I'm just going to concede right now and make that call to Jensen."

There was a hiss and a rumble, then a flicker of light in the night sky, then the forest exploded into splintered trees and a great ball of flame and smoke. Branches and clots of earth rained down, pelting Otka, Fritz, and Matthias.

"What was that!" exclaimed Otka as she ducked for whatever cover the Halflinger afforded her.

Fritz opened the door of the vehicle that many people referred to as the "Austrian Jeep" and climbed in after her. "It was a missile. It occurred to me that Lieutenant Kolka was being just a bit too chatty. He had somebody triangulating our signal while we were talking."

Matthias swung into the driver's seat and gunned the engine. "We really must have ticked off the Czechs for them to authorize a cross-border missile strike."

Otka was wedged on the bench seat between the two Gantlet Brothers and she peered anxiously through the broad windshield, looking for the glimmer of another rocket in the sky. "Stealing my father from a high-security jail and destroying a couple of their helicopters seems to have pushed them over the edge."

Matthias pushed the Halflinger to its top speed, slowing only for turns, so that he didn't capsize the top-heavy vehicle. He recalled the day that he and his brothers had escaped from East Germany. "Say good-bye to Czechoslovakia, Otka. You may never see it again."

Chapter 30

Arturo Sippo, concierge of Boston's secretive Black Cemetery Hotel, raised one bushy eyebrow as he encountered Mitz's dismay. "I believe that your instructions were precisely stated as 'Give him whatever he wants, but make sure he doesn't leave here.' I am sure that I fulfilled that injunction most precisely."

"But Thin Dai has run up a bill of thirty thousand dollars with this Madame Wong's Parlor. What could she possibly be selling that ..." Mitz broke off as he saw a pair of slender Asian beauties in provocative clothing descending the cage elevator to the lobby.

Sippo turned and waved them in the other direction. "Out the back door, ladies. The lobby is off limits to practitioners of your most venerable of professions."

They giggled and waved, but complied by heading down the hallway to the back entrance.

"Don't tell me that those were employees of Madame Wong's parlor," said Mitz.

"Indeed," said the concierge, "but being mute about their profession will hardly change the facts. Also, there is a considerable charge for the daily deliveries of cases of chilled Kristal."

Mitz snarled as he reached for his wallet. "I should have just shot that conniving little son of a ..."

Sippo waved a finger. "Profanity will gain us nothing, Mr. Gantlet. Have I not fulfilled a very difficult request with the utmost of discretion?"

"That's debatable, Mr. Sippo." Mitz counted out cash for the sizable bill, including a generous stipend for the concierge to help ensure his silence. "Please inform Mr. Thin Dai that he is free to depart immediately, and that if he doesn't keep his nose clean we will be back to collect on the bill he racked up while he was here, plus a pound or two of flesh taken out of his hide."

Arturo Sippo smiled as he collected the stack of bills. "Indeed, I will be most happy to convey your message. Mr. Dai's presence has grown most tiresome."

Chapter 31

Sly pulled his low-slung canary yellow Ferrari 328 GTS into a parking slot in front of a jumble of high-end Santa Barbara condominiums that overlooked the broad ribbon of sandy coastline. The roof panels of the Ferrari were absent and the wind-tossed forms of Sly and Mitz hoisted themselves out of the low seats. The air was filled with the tang of saltwater and a warm breeze blew in off the Pacific Ocean, the low rumble of the incessant surf and the cry of the wheeling gulls in the background of their hearing.

"So this is where Ronny lays his head?" asked Sly.

Mitz checked the map. "According to this and the employment form he filled out for Gantlet Productions."

Sly bent over coughing, then stood upright and began striding to the concrete stairs. "He's certainly made himself scarce since we went after Quan Tang."

Mitz strode alongside of his brother. "Jensen was kind enough to do a covert check on Ronny's account and it seems that he came into twenty thousand dollars shortly after Matthias and Fritz headed to the airport to catch Quan Tang. He's spent most of it since then, but ..."

"That's all it takes to sell us out, now? Twenty grand? At least Ostkopf held out for a hundred grand."

"Fat lot of good it did him," said Mitz.

Sly gripped the iron rail hard, leaning on it a bit as they walked down the flights of concrete steps. "How about Ostkopf's wife?"

"Her cancer is in remission, and it turns out that Harold had a two-million-dollar life insurance policy. If she can manage without her husband, she'll be okay financially."

Sly grunted. "Two million dollars in exchange for your spouse—not a trade off I'd be willing to make, but I guess fate has its own way of figuring things out."

"Yeah, and Thin Dai gave us enough of a clue to figure things out—once we realized that the clown hawking hamburgers was Ronald and not Krusty, then we just had to put our minds to the people that knew Fritz and Matthias were going after Quan Tang on his plane."

"It's not a big surprise that Ronny got in over his head gambling. He was always bragging about his latest Vegas trip."

Sly grunted. "But the way I heard Ronny tell it, he was always coming back a big winner."

Mitz surveyed the network of palm-flanked walkways to pick out the best path to Ronny's condominium. "It seems those stories were greatly exaggerated—or at least, he neglected to tell us about the many times he lost money gambling."

They climbed a series of steps, which took them through a tiled pool area which was shielded by an overhanging ceiling of colored glass, which splashed odd hues across the waters and a pair of early morning swimmers. They emerged into a light breeze and a walkway which overlooked the frothing azure waters of the ocean from steep on the hillside.

"Nice view," said Sly, and he coughed. "And I was referring to the ocean—not that surfer girl paddling out into the breakers." He emptied a few atropine pills into his palm and swallowed them dry.

Mitz paused for a moment and saw the distant sun-darkened form of a woman riding a board out to catch a wave. "Ronny's condo should be to the right and up that ramp."

They trudged up the ramp and Mitz knocked at the red-painted door to Ronny's condominium. There came no reply.

"How do we know that Ronny's not climbing over the balcony right now?" asked Sly.

Mitz took out a set of lock picks and began to ply the locking mechanism. "We don't."

Sly went barreling down the ramp to circle to the opposite side of the building, in case Ronny was attempting an escape, and in a few moments Mitz had the door open. He strode into a haze of marijuana smoke, and a jumble of pizza boxes and empty TV dinner trays. "Ronny! It's Mitz. I'd like to have a few words with you."

There was a cry of something that might have been terror at the back of the apartment and as Mitz rounded the corner he caught a glimpse of a bulbous-nosed Ronny, frantically scrabbling to open the sliding glass door to the balcony. His hair hung in lank strands and his eyes were bloodshot as he threw open the door and staggered toward the rail, shrieking. "No, don't kill me. I'll pay Biggs next week. Honest ..."

Ronny lost his balance and struck heavily against the iron rail and it tore loose from its moorings. Hands flailing wildly for some sort of purchase, Ronny plummeted from the third story like a wounded bird, his blond hair streaming in greasy wavelets. He landed on his shoulder and neck and by the time that Sly reached him, life was already fleeing his body, crimson blood leaking into the pattern between the cobblestones of the walk.

His eyes seemed to focus for just a moment as he saw the bearded rock musician lean over him. "Sly! I'm so sorry, brother. I needed the money so bad ... so bad. I didn't think it would hurt anything if Quan Tang escaped for just a few more days and I ..." His breathing was ragged and the light began to leave his eyes. "I had Biggs's fingerbreakers coming after me ..."

"I get it," said Sly, "but you should have come to us if you were between a rock and a hard place."

Ronny's eyes glazed over and Sly's features were impassive as he rose. He looked up to find Mitz standing at the hanging railing three stories overhead. "You pitch him off?"

"Nah, he was stoned out of his mind and scared of some guy named Biggs—probably his bookie."

A helmeted cyclist stopped his bike to gawk at Ronny's lifeless body and a pair of female joggers in Spandex shorts, tank tops, and shaded visors halted their run to gasp in shock at the gory sight. Sly ignored them. "What's your schedule looking like this afternoon, Mitz?"

"I've got a date with a certain supermodel named Cindy Warner tonight. Until then, my schedule is open."

"You want to help me dismantle this bookie named Biggs?"

"I'm game," answered Mitz.

Chapter 32

Broward, Florida, One week later

Dressed in a black suit coat and tie, Sly coughed and cleared his throat as he went to the podium which was set up beneath the gazebo of the Forest Lawn Memorial Gardens. A light breeze rippled the palms and nearly a thousand people were stretched out across the grounds to pay their respects to Otto Gantlet, who had lived a short but eventful life.

Blake Hawkins prowled the edges of the crowd, fending off the paparazzi with menacing glares and stern words of warning. He towered over one brave photographer and put a massive palm over the lens of his raised camera. "You can take pictures after the memorial. Until then, if I see you snapping just one shot, I'll crush your camera, and after that I'll crush you."

For the briefest of moments, the cameraman thought of voicing his defiance, then wisdom took the better part of valor and he decided for discretion. "Yes, sir."

Usually Sly was verbose and never lacking for words, but today emotion choked him up and he could manage only three words. "I'll miss him."

He stepped down into the waiting embrace of his wife Sheila and Jim Striklawn, lead guitarist of Devil's Venom, took his place. "First we lost Cliff in that bus accident ... and now we've lost Otto—two great bass players. I'll drink a toast to them tonight."

"He'll drink far more than one toast," Matthias murmured to his wife, Courtney, who stood next to him. Jacobbe and Anna lingered in front of them, wondering at the ornate closed casket, which was engraved with a gilded G and airbrushed with artwork from each of the Gantlet Brothers albums.

Members of Queensryche, Iron Maiden, and The Cult stood up to pay their respects. One tattooed millionaire who was used to spending time behind the microphone came to the podium, his long brown hair swinging as he leaned forward. "Otto saved my skin. If it wasn't for him, I wouldn't be alive today. I don't know how many other people are alive because he was willing to put his life on the line for them, but I've heard rumors that he helped locate a nuclear bomb that was set to detonate in a major city at two minutes to midnight. If that's true, he may be responsible for saving millions of lives—and he was willing to give his own life in return. That's the most any of us can hope for … to die with their boots on like Otto Gantlet."

Father Lada was the only clergy the Gantlet Brothers were well acquainted with, so they had asked him to conduct the ceremonies, and now he emerged from the crowd, leaving the sides of Fritz and Otka, and resumed the service, speaking in heavily accented English of a loving Heavenly Father who would welcome the deceased into his arms in the afterlife.

Mitz leaned toward Matthias. "Do you think there is an afterlife?"

Matthias shook his head. "I don't know, but I can only hope so."

"He wasn't baptized, none of us were. Isn't that a requirement for not burning in hell?"

"It seems as though it depends upon whom you talk to. You're asking for answers I don't have."

"You better figure it out, then," said Mitz, "because who knows which one of us is next?"

After the services, they removed themselves to Otto's grave and watched the gilded casket as it was lowered into the cold earth alongside a granite grave marker that was carved in the shape of a Gibson flying V bass guitar—the guitar which Otto preferred to play. Built into a nearby alcove was a speaker system that looped the recorded music of the Gantlet Brothers, including a never-released song which they had slated for their next album, but now would forevermore only be heard graveside of Otto Gantlet. The bass rumbled, the guitars wept mournfully, and Matthias's voice oozed pathos in a musical symphony that seemed a fitting epitaph to Otto's life.

Fritz scanned the crowd and saw a lean figure dressed in black leave the cemetery's grounds and climb onto a motorcycle. "There's Legion Tate."

Otka shielded her eyes from the sun and caught a glimpse of the hollow, haunted visage. "The famous guitar player, Legion Tate? Why didn't he say hello to you?"

Fritz frowned. "He's got his own demons to fight—feels like he needs to do it himself."

"He shuts everyone else out," said Mitz. "Just try reaching him on the phone. You can leave messages until you're blue in the face and he won't even acknowledge them."

Cindy Warner clutched at Mitz's arm. She looked radiant even in the black funeral gown, a hat the shade of midnight, clipped into her lustrous hair. "It's enough that he was here, Mitz. When's the last time that he came out of hiding?"

Mitz caressed Cindy's hand. "You're right. It's been years since anybody's sighted him."

A black man as tall as Blake Hawkins wound his way through the crowd, accompanied by an equally striking woman with almond eyes and curly hair the color of a tropical beach, and one arm in a sling. The man's physique was that of an Olympic diver, and his eyes the color freshly-minted copper pennies. He clasped Sly's hand and then kissed Sheila on the cheek. "I'm truly sorry for your loss. If you ever need anything, do let me know."

Usually Sly had a smart comeback, for the two of them were famously competitive, but today Sly was somber and muted. "Thanks, Dillon."

"I recognize that woman," said Sheila. "I've seen her file somewhere. She does corporate surveillance and sabotage—Toi Lahayne, I think."

Sly regarded his wife blankly. "What woman?"

Sheila squeezed her husband's arm. "You really must be in the first stage of grieving if you didn't notice a woman like that."

Dillon slipped through the crowd with his beautiful, handicapped companion and he came face to face with the scowling visage of Blake Hawkins, who had placed himself in Dillon's path.

Dillon raised an eyebrow. "Can I help you?"

"You bothering my...Dillon? I didn't recognize you all spiffed up and with a beautiful woman on your arm—makes you look almost respectable."

Toi Lahayne patted Dillon on the arm. "I know, isn't it bizarre what a little soap and a nice suit can do for him?"

"Hey!" objected Dillon. "If I recall, you liked me just fine before you ever saw me in a suit."

Blake looked thoughtful. "I didn't know you were friends with Sly as well as Matthias."

"Sly is one of the most dirty rotten, scoundrels I've ever had the displeasure of knowing" said Dillon, grasping the hand of the mocha-skinned woman accompanying him, "but, yeah, we're friends. Just don't ever tell him that. It might go to his head."

Blake grinned. "I won't breath a word."

A few of the mourners had begun the wake prior to attending the services and they were already deep in their cups. A fistfight broke out between the singer for Strychnine and a roadie for Night Ranger over who owed a bar tab from nine months earlier.

Lightning flashed in the distant sky as a cold front came in, and thunder rolled across the assemblage of mourners. A few moments later, fat, warm raindrops began falling and the crowd dispersed as lightning struck near the grave marker of Otto's Gibson guitar, the resulting thunderclap nearly bursting the eardrums of all those standing near.

It was a fitting ending to Otto's memorial services.

Chapter 33

One month later, London, England

Matthias was sitting inside the Swan gazing out over the mist-shrouded and drizzle-spattered Thames, poking idly at a mixture of onions, oatmeal, and congealed blood before pushing it to the other side of the table, eschewing the abominable concoction called black pudding in favor of the smoked bacon and poached eggs that came with the overpriced Bankside Breakfast he'd ordered. To the west he could see the Millennium Bridge, rising up from the fogs like some sort of ghost ship adrift from its moorings, and to the east was the Southwark Bridge, which carried a steady stream of vehicles that appeared to float through the haze on concrete and steel that seemed to hover in the air of their own gravity-defying volition.

At his feet was a battered guitar case, which had been stripped of all its tour stickers so it would appear as nondescript as possible. Matthias's hair was tucked beneath the collar of his bulky leather jacket, which likewise gave no indication that he was a member of the Gantlet Brother band. He was finishing off the baked beans and chestnut mushrooms when his satellite phone rang. Matthias quickly answered it, speaking in low tones that would be difficult to overhear by the over-attentive waiter.

"You got anything for me?"

Though he didn't identify himself, either, it was Jensen's gravelly voice that responded. "We've got an agent that picked her up leaving the Savoy where she was registered under the name of S. Chamberlain, which is a known alias of Monica Killingsworth."

"Do we know where she's headed?"

"Our agent is monitoring a wide range of transmissions and Killingsworth received a call directing her to the London Fencing Club for an 'engagement.' If you beat her there you might be able to prevent the 'engagement' from occurring."

Matthias speared the last mushroom. "That's just fine and dandy, but where can I find the London Fencing Club?"

"Where are you situated?"

"Near the Southwark Bridge."

Matthias heard Jensen conferring with Meriweather and the rustling of pages which he presumed were maps before Jensen's voice returned full force. "Skip the Southwark and take London Bridge across the Thames. These roads are a convoluted mess."

Matthias threw a twenty-pound note, depicting William Shakespeare, on the table and grabbed his guitar case, slinging it over his shoulder before fishing his keys out of his pocket. The waiter began to object to his abrupt departure, and reached out to stop him. "But, sir. I haven't made up the check yet!"

Matthias shouldered him aside. "Your money's on the table."

"Was there something wrong with the meal?"

Matthias declined to make a comment on the black pudding and pushed his way out the door. "I think you'll find your tip most generous."

Sitting a few feet away was an 850 cc Norton Commando motorcycle and Matthias climbed on and fired the engine. He still had Jensen on the phone. "What's she driving?"

"A BMW motorcycle, license LL34JMB."

Matthias jammed the satellite phone between the brake cables that strung down his handlebars and left the connection open as he goosed the gas, spinning the motorcycle around in a haze of blue rubber smoke, so that he faced south on Emerson. He put his weight down on the seat of the Commando and in a few seconds he leaned the bike around the corner so that he was heading east on Park Street, splitting the traffic and riding the gutter between the street and sidewalk.

He'd been haunting London for the last two weeks, getting familiar with the roads and waiting for Killingsworth to surface. Getting across the Thames took a bit of a detour, which carried him around the walled courtyards of the London College of Advanced Studies and then hurtling toward London Bridge. Matthias was going one hundred when he crossed the Thames, his long brown hair unfurling from beneath his collar and tangling in a wild flurry behind him. Then he was rocketing down Bishopsgate, past the corner tower of Liverpool Street Station, threading between taxis and buses and steering clear of a pair of cyclists who were braving the rain.

Through the howl of the motorcycle's engine and roar of wind, Matthias could hear Jensen directing him. "Turn left on Shoreditch!"

Matthias complied, making a left hand turn near the Drunken Monkey tavern, weaving through traffic that carried him past car dealerships, Turkish restaurants, and establishments of a more dubious nature that inhabited the underbelly of every major city. A large building inhabited the center of the roadway ahead, and the streets formed a large roundabout so that traffic veered around through the structure. Matthias followed the road left and back onto Old Street which was flanked on the right by an impressive row of oaks.

"Turn right on B144," shouted Jensen.

Matthias didn't see the street sign. "I'm passing Helmet Row!"

There was a pause and Matthias slowed his motorcycle. "You've gone too far," said Jensen. "You're a couple of blocks past B144."

Matthias spotted a gap in traffic and did a U-turn which took him up the sidewalk under the overhanging trees which momentarily sheltered him from the incessant drizzle. He slipped back onto the roadway in time to avoid an oncoming pedestrian bearing a brightly colored umbrella and made his way back to the intersecting road which he had flown past a couple of minutes before. Following Jensen's directions, Matthias circled around Saint Luke's Garden and pulled down a narrow road between the Langton Arms apartments and a brick recreation center with a black metal stair that took visitors to the London Fencing Club. However, as Matthias slowed his pace he thought he saw a motorcycle parked in the alley between the older architecture of Langton Arms and the adjacent eleven-story Burnhill House, which was an example of the blocky sort of architecture that could be found anywhere in the world.

The black-painted gate that protected the alley was ajar and as Matthias parked his Commando and approached it, he could see the lock lying on the ground, smashed by a single bullet. Matthias carefully surveyed his surroundings as he approached the motorcycle. It was indeed a BMW motorcycle and the yellow license plate matched the one that Jensen had given him.

Matthias hovered his hand near the engine and felt the warmth radiating, indicating the bike had not been here for more than a few minutes. Still, that might have been long enough for Killingsworth to accomplish her hit. He unlatched the saddlebag and inside were a half dozen thirty-two-round magazines that Matthias knew, from experience, slipped nicely into the foregrip of an UZI mini-machine gun. He reached inside his bulky leather jacket and pulled loose his Casull pistol. As his eyes shifted upward, he noticed some color and movement in the puddle beneath the saddlebag.

From behind him, not in the direction of the Fencing Club at all, a woman clad in a black leather riding suit strode around the corner of the Langton Apartments. She wore a bright red motorcycle helmet, the tinted visor ov which was tilted upward revealing the icy blue eyes and dark lashes behind. Her mini-submachine gun was already leveled and she fired an entire burst into Matthias before he could turn and fire. Matthias pitched to the ground, his jacket nothing but tattered shreds and he vainly gasped for air as he lay by the BMW, but his lungs would not function. Black spots swam before his eyes as the woman stepped over his body, dropped her empty magazine into her still open saddle bag and pushed another into the handle of her UZI.

Before Matthias's vision faded to black, he saw those merciless eyes spare him the slightest of glances. She saw the gleaming Casull lying a half dozen feet away. "Nice gun," she commented, her voice tinted with a Bristol accent. "A little overlarge for my tastes, but a fine piece of handiwork." She stepped over him and climbed onto her motorcycle. It roared to life and she sped off, leaving Matthias in a cloud of rubber smoke.

A few moments later, Matthias stirred. With a great groan he hoisted himself to his feet, cracked and shattered ceramic plates falling out of the tatters of his leather jacket. These, along with the Kevlar lining, had saved Matthias from dying, but his torso was a mass of bruised and battered flesh. He staggered to his Commando, forcing himself to put one foot in front of the other, his limbs not wanting to cooperate with his mental commands. Finally, he reached his motorcycle and he fired the engine and turned it in hot pursuit of Monica Killingsworth.

As he sped away, he heard a cry from the London Fencing Club. "Murder! Elias Cranston has been murdered!" Apparently Matthias had been too late to stop the killing, and nearly on time for his own. As he sped back the way he came, pieces of shattered ceramic spilled out the rags of his jacket and bounced erratically along the roadway.

Matthias saw a flash of movement as Killingsworth scraped around the corner, turning left onto Iron Monger's Row, leaving composite from her knee pads on the pavement. Wearing nothing but Levi's on his legs, Matthias couldn't afford to take the turn at such a speed or such an angle, so as soon as he flashed by the leafy bowers of St. Luke's garden, he laid into his brakes, then took a sharp turn that put his knee within inches of the pavement. He righted his bike and gunned it down Iron Monger.

Already Killingsworth was leaning right and onto Lever Street, a block away, and as soon as Matthias reached the turn, he saw that the assassin was splitting off onto Dingley Place where it Y-ed away. She was taking a quick succession of turns, but Matthias wasn't sure that she yet realized that he was pursuing her. She had left him for dead and perhaps these quick maneuvers were merely part of her planned get away from the scene of the crime. Probably, she had a vehicle stashed somewhere nearby, would strip out of her leather motorcycle outfit and hit the road in something less conspicuous in the case that anyone had witnessed her assassination of Elias Cranston.

Indeed, once Dingley Place turned a corner, it became a narrow street bordered by a brick warehouse on one side. Killingsworth pulled up to slatted double doors that were painted black and held a small sign that read FIRE EXIT: KEEP CLEAR. These doors opened up just as Killingsworth approached and she gunned her motorcycle through and into a courtyard beyond. As soon as she slipped through, the doors closed again and Matthias pulled his Commando up short about a hundred feet down the street. He had already been caught by surprise once and so he halted behind a squat black vehicle in case Killingsworth might have noticed him following and leap out firing another magazine from her UZI.

Already, Matthias could hear sirens blaring as squad cars departed from the nearby Shoreditch Police Station, dispatched to the scene of the murder. Jensen's voice crackled over the satellite phone. "What's happening?"

Matthias leaned toward the cell phone. "I got there too late. I'm in pursuit of Killingsworth." He cut the connection so that he wouldn't be distracted and he climbed off his bike. At the moment, he was running on adrenaline and his muscles hadn't stiffened up yet. He was sure he would feel the pain even more intensely later. The drizzle spattered Matthias as he approached the double doors. They shifted slightly and a gunman with short-cropped hair and a scar across his nose leaned out. Matthias was ready and he fired two shots that blew through the intervening slats and pounded through the chest of the gunman. Even as the gunman fell, Matthias burst through the double doors and into the courtyard beyond. A burn barrel flared, incinerating a leather jumpsuit and melting a crimson helmet, a jerry can of gasoline stood nearby.

Monica Killingsworth was stripped to a halter top and a pair of Lycra shorts, her blonde hair still pinned to the back of her head. She was climbing into an orange Peugeot and reaching for her UZI which was on the roof of the vehicle. When she saw Matthias, she leaped inside the cab, dragging the UZI with her. The engine of the Peugeot started and it lurched toward Matthias, even as Killingsworth ducked low in the cab, using the engine block as cover.

Matthias dove to one side and the Peugeot barreled over the dead body of her accomplice, smashed one of the slatted doors to splinters and rammed into the brick wall, vapor filtering from beneath the crumpled and rubble-spattered hood. Matthias sent a shot into the side of the vehicle, rupturing the gas tank, so that the volatile fluid belched out. Without so much as blinking an eye, Matthias kicked over the burn barrel. A flaming helmet spilled from the barrel, and rolled next to the vehicle, which went up in a ball of roiling flame, Monica Killingsworth trapped inside.

He saw movement for a moment, but then nothing moved inside the Peugeot except for the flickering tongues of all-consuming flame.

Chapter 34

Cromwell Jensen met Matthias at the Fort Lauderdale International Airport as he emerged from the boarding tunnel. His suit was different than the last time Matthias had seen him, but it still fit poorly around Jensen's broad shoulders, and then hung loose around his middle. "Good to see you in one piece, Matthias."

Matthias groaned as he stretched his torso. The twelve-hour flight from the UK had been unkind and his body was an ache of battered flesh. "My bruises have bruises. I might need a wheelchair to get me to the parking lot. So, who was this Elias Cranston that I was too late to save?"

"A wealthy industrialist who was buying up some diamond mines in Nigeria. His business partner thought it would be more profitable without Cranston taking a share of the profits, so he started asking around—looking for a top-notch assassin to off his partner. Apparently, he was somehow able to make contact with Killingsworth."

They started walking across the vast tracts of tiled lobby. "Your wife and kids are waiting for you in the pick-up area. They're excited to see you."

"I'm looking forward to seeing them. Thanks for getting me out of Britain on the down-low."

"Thanks for taking care of Monica Killingsworth for us. Sometimes it works better if we stay on the periphery of events. The Brits don't like it when we meddle with things on their soil. This way, if they discover that you were involved, we're one or two steps further up the chain of plausible deniability."

"You figure out just who Killingsworth was?"

Jensen shrugged his thick shoulders. "We're getting the information secondhand. We don't have any of our guys with direct access to the evidence, and her body was burned to a crisp. We have no dental records to compare and no DNA to match her with—just another soulless assassin working under an assumed identity. Cut one down and another ruthless killer pops up to take his or her place. Some days it all seems so futile."

"Rough week, Cole?" asked Matthias.

"Rough enough," said Jensen with a sigh. "I'm just glad to put this mess in the rearview mirror."

"Me, too," agreed Matthias. "Me, too."

Chapter 35

Three years later

Otka Gantlet triggered the remote on the visor of her BMW and the wrought iron gate in front of her home rolled open. She pulled the vehicle through and up the bricked drive, pulling to a stop in front of a broad doorstep with an overhanging veranda which was flanked by a pair of brass lions.

She set the emergency brake and stepped out of the car, then opened the rear door to unbuckle tow-headed, one-year-old Rosette Gantlet from her baby seat. Otka's pregnancy had lent some pleasing curves to her slender figure—at least Fritz seemed to be pleased, so that was what counted. Either way, she turned heads when she went for her early morning runs through the breezy Fort Lauderdale Hills where they had set up their home.

She hoisted Rosette from her seat, and the toddler giggled and grabbed a handful of her mother's long auburn hair. "Careful, Rosie, you're going to pull Mommy's hair out by the roots!"

Otka carried Rosette past the brass lions and pressed one palm against a reader set next to a great oak-paneled door inset with the Gantlet coat of arms which had been modernized with the addition of a pair of crossed guitars next to the crossed sword blade and pike. Dead bolts released and the door popped open an inch so that Otka was able to put her shoulder against the panels and shove it open.

The sound of the electric guitar wafted to her ears, indicating that Fritz was working on his latest masterpiece of lead fretwork. "Fritz! Can you give me a hand? I've got a trunk full of groceries."

The interior of the house was a curious mixture of Oriental and Grecian architecture and decoration. Ancient weapons were framed and encased behind thick panels of Plexiglas, this to discourage little fingers because already Rosette could climb like a monkey and had been known to mount the leather recliner and pull herself onto the mantle of the great stone fireplace that was the centerpiece of the center room.

Fritz appeared and unslung his axe, carefully resting it in the cradle of a handy guitar stand. "Did you bring me something to grill?"

"I sure did!" Otka leaned in and gave Fritz a kiss.

Rosette switched positions and held out her arms. "Papa!"

Fritz took his little girl and kissed her on the forehead. "Did you miss your daddy?"

"It still amazes me every time that I go into the store, just how much there is," said Otka. She spoke in odd sort of English that reflected both a Czech accent and the German accent which Fritz spoke with. "You get these American idiots that talk about the wonders of Socialism, but they've never seen it in action. We'd wait in line for three hours to get our hands on three or four cans of peaches. Here, I walk into the store and there's a hundred cans of peaches just sitting on the shelf!"

"It's the idea of Big Brother taking care of their every need, lifting their responsibilities that lures people into Socialism." Fritz lifted Rosette onto his shoulders and she laughed, using his ears as makeshift handlebars. "Everyone equally sharing sounds like a great idea, except the folks in power take the lion's share and distribute the scraps to everyone else, and no one has any incentive to work hard. Have you seen my satellite phone?"

Otka furrowed her brow. "Last I saw it, Rosette was running around with it while you were weeding."

Fritz chewed on the inside of his cheek. "It's probably buried in the garden somewhere. The house phone is dead. I need to call the phone company. What about your satellite phone?"

"In my purse," said Otka and she leaned in to kiss him again, "which is in the trunk with the groceries that you need to bring in!"

Fritz grinned. "Perfect. I'll kill two birds with one stone."

Otka waggled her finger. "Oh no, there will be no killing anything today—especially innocent birdies."

Fritz lowered Rosette to the ground and she ran off after a toy doll she spotted sitting underneath the coffee table. "It's just an English expression."

Otka lowered her brow and peered through the screen of disheveled reddish hair that Rosette had pulled over her face. She wrinkled her nose. "I know." She reached into her pocket and pulled out a small box. "Guess what I picked up this morning?"

"A small box?" guessed Fritz.

Otka rotated the cardboard container, displaying it to her husband. "Yes, I picked up a box. Isn't it nice?"

"Okay, I'll bite. What's inside?"

Otka carefully slipped the lid off, revealing an eighteen-carat-gold pocket watch. "It's your grandfather's Lang pocket watch. It took nearly two years to reconstruct everything, but there it is—almost as good as new." She flipped the lid open and Fritz saw that it was keeping time.

"I had no idea … I thought the parts were still sitting in a box at the back of the workbench." He examined the workmanship and was amazed to see that there was no sign of the damage the bullet had wrought. The craftsmen who repaired the watch must have cannibalized other Lang watches or even reproduced some of the parts to make it whole again. Fritz closed the lid of the watch and swept Otka into his arms. "I want you to know that even though Grandfather's watch hasn't been keeping track, that the last two years have been the best of my life."

"And why is that, Fritz?"

"It just might have something to do with this auburn-haired beauty that I ran into in Czechoslovakia."

"Oh, really? Tell me about her."

"She's very beautiful, brave, and kind."

Fritz kissed his wife and finally grabbed the key to the BMW then passed the guarding lions, leaving his wife to keep an eye on Rosette. Before he popped the trunk, he could hear Otka's phone buzzing. Nestled among the bags of groceries, he found Otka's black leather Gucci-like purse. It was a knock-off, because Otka insisted it was ludicrous to pay that much money just for a brand name. He rifled through the contents of the purse until he uncovered the phone.

"If you're trying to get a hold of Otka, you'll have to give me a minute," said Fritz as he answered the call.

"Fritz!" It was Matthias on the other end. "Thank God you're all right. Are Otka and Rosette with you?"

"They're in the house." Fritz turned, looking down his bricked drive and the high foliage-lined fence of wrought iron. Beyond he had glimpses of a woman in a neon sports bra going for a jog with her schnauzer. A dark blue Sedan cruised past. "What's up?"

"Get them someplace safe. I just got word from Jensen that Quan Tang's son has been identified as having entered the country. I was getting nothing but ringing on your home phone and the same with your satellite phone."

Fritz shoved aside a couple bags of groceries, lifted the flimsy presswood flap that hid the spare tire and pulled loose a .44 Colt Anaconda, one of several that he owned, that was holstered alongside it. "It's probably in the carrot patch. That one I can blame on Rosette, but I'm beginning to think that it's no accident that my phone line's dead—especially if Duoc Tang is in town. How sure is Jensen?"

"His partner, Meriweather, estimates a seventy-eight percent chance that the identification is correct."

"How does he come to the figure of seventy-eight percent?"

"Beats me, but he's proven reliable before. I say we take this seriously."

Fritz narrowed his steel gray eyes and he saw a second sedan pass by the gate. This was a different vehicle, but he could see that the interior was packed with men wearing suits, and they appeared to be of Vietnamese persuasion. They also appeared too old and not so genial as the Mormon missionaries canvassing the neighborhood, which Fritz had encountered on previous occasions. Since Otto's death, Fritz had taken the time to speak with all the religious persuasions that came to his gate. "Meriweather is right, again. Looks like Duoc is gathering his forces. How far away are you?"

"About thirty minutes."

"Get here as soon as you can and bring plenty of firepower. What are Sly and Mitz up to?"

"Mitz is in Paris and Sly won't be any help. I talked to Sheila this morning and he's not doing well at all. The tumor is causing hallucinations and his lungs are a mass of scar tissue from inhaling that nerve gas off the coast of Puerto Rico."

"Is that why his health has been so bad?"

"He didn't tell anybody, but that's why he was running through bottles of diazepam and atropine. They're both used to treat the tremors caused by the nerve gas."

"We'll go check on Sly as soon as we get this Duoc Tang situation resolved. For now, it's on you," said Fritz. "Get here as soon as you can."

"I'm bringing Blake," said Matthias. "Hang on, big brother!"

Fritz saw a pair of Vietnamese suits cross the street toward his gate. When they crossed, they clutched their sides, indicating that they were holding concealed weapons in place. They looked up and saw Fritz watching them from his position by the BMW at the top of the brick drive. Fritz lifted his Colt Anaconda into view and suddenly they scrambled for cover, hands dipping beneath their suit coats for their ill-concealed weapons. Fritz lined up his sights and slightly led one of the thugs, predicting his path of flight. Just as a mini-MAC submachine gun came out of the thug's jacket, Fritz squeezed the trigger and the thug crumpled to the street, blood spraying from his skull.

"Aiming too high," muttered Fritz and he wondered if the sights had been jogged by riding in the trunk of the BMW. He heard the rattle of a machine gun, and he saw branches and leaves as they were clipped from a palm at the edge of his property. Then the bullets that weren't diverted by the branches or absorbed in the trunk of the palm pounded the side of the BMW, leaving a wild pattern of bullet holes that stitched across the metal.

Fritz could see a pair of gunmen had taken position on the slope of a neighbor's lawn, but he had no time to return fire. While the first gunman reloaded his mini-MAC, the second gunman unleashed another torrent of lead. The thugs were using the Model 11 Ingram's with the short barrel, also known as the Mini-MAC, and they had foregone the use of the wire shoulder stock so they could conceal their weapons more easily. This meant it was hard to aim the Ingrams because of the kickback and the short barrel. Still, they put a lot of lead into the air and they could blow out a box of thirty rounds in less than two seconds. Even an inaccurate gun at a bit of a distance might be able to put a couple of rounds in the right place, and at short range they could chop a man in half.

So instead of returning fire, Fritz ducked and found shelter behind the engine block of the BMW. Bullets punched through the car, and rattled around inside, but didn't penetrate through the other side. The Ingram 11s used a less powerful short round than their bigger brother, the Ingram 10. Now a gunman at the gate opened up and sent bullets skipping off the bricks of the drive, and then chewed up the trunk of the BMW, spraying milk and eggs instead of Fritz's blood.

Fritz crouched alongside the car and sighted down the barrel of his Anaconda. For just a flash the head and shoulders of the gunman passed into his sights. He aimed just a fraction lower and pulled the trigger twice. The first bullet spanged off a wrought iron post, bending it, and the second slipped by it and pounded into the chest of the gunman.

For the briefest of moments, the assault stopped and Fritz dashed from behind the engine. Immediately the assault began again, but by this time Fritz was passing between the brass lions. Bullets rang against the great beasts, but none found Fritz as he kept up his low sprint and then rolled through the front door of his abode. He slammed the door shut and bullets pounded against it, but he had little fear because the wooden panels of the door concealed a two-inch steel plate.

"Fritz! What's going on out there?" called Otka.

"It looks like Duoc Tang's decided to come after me."

Otka came into the vestibule, clutching wide-eyed Rosette. "Why now? It's been two years!"

As if in answer, the telephone began to ring. Fritz and Otka stared at each other. The phone had been out for hours. Why was it ringing now?

"Stay low," advised Fritz. "We should be pretty safe inside the house. I spent a fortune having steel plating installed inside the walls and all the windows are bullet-resistant, but they might have something heavier than the mini-MACs they've been firing."

Otka nodded and retreated to the sunken living room, but here were a series of glass panels that overlooked the terraces of the backyard. In back, the fences were brick and lined with angled spikes, but she could see suited forms crawling over those walls, and carefully pulling themselves past the spikes. One of these thugs sent a burst toward the house. A hail of lead spattered against the glass, scarring it in a dozen places.

"Take Rosette to the bedroom and into the vault. You'll be safe there."

"What about you?"

"I need to slow them down long enough for Matthias to get here."

"What about the police?"

"I'm sure Matthias has already called them. If I can keep these guys busy for ten minutes, we should be free and clear."

The phone continued to ring and the answering machine picked it up. "Now is not a good time. We're trying to cross a minefield," intoned Fritz's recorded voice. "Please leave a message."

Duoc Tang's voice came over the speaker of the message machine. "Pick it up, Fritz. I know you're there. It was my machine gun fire that sent you scurrying inside like a scared rabbit."

Fritz looked at Otka and jerked his head toward the bedroom. "Get in the vault. I'll take care of Duoc."

Otka disappeared into the center of the house with Rosette and as Fritz triggered a secret panel in the floor of the living room, he answered the phone. "What do you want, Duoc? I thought you'd be content to rule the criminal empire that you inherited from your father. The criminal empire that you only run because of me, I might remind you!"

Duoc chuckled harshly. "My old benefactor and nemesis—all in one. It's a joy to be speaking with you once again."

"Pull your men out now and get out of the country," replied Fritz. "Do that, and I'll let you live. You have my word."

"You're in no position to dictate terms, Mr. Gantlet. I've made an agreement with the some of your local criminal organizations that I've had dealings with in the past. Part of our agreement involves wiping out you and your family."

At least Fritz knew Duoc's intentions now. Duoc was dead-set on killing them all. "Why hassle with any of this? It's only going to look bad if you go limping back to Czechoslovakia to run your father's criminal empire."

"That's the problem," said Duoc. "My father's empire has dwindled to a small fiefdom. The other criminal organizations don't respect me. They think that I'm only in charge because of a fickle twist of fate and they've been chipping away at my territory, pushing me out until I'm barely considered a dabbler anymore."

"I had nothing to do with any of that," said Fritz. He lifted the lid of the secret compartment in the floor and revealed the same 7.62mm SIG Swiss-made machine gun with which he had chased away Duoc's father's men a lifetime ago in Massachusetts. Fritz still considered it the finest machine gun ever built and it was very rare, having been produced only in small quantities. "Head back home and take care of your business."

"You had everything to do with it!" snapped Duoc, and even over the phone line the hatred in his voice was intense enough to peel fresh paint. "When you escaped me, it made the other bosses think that I was weak— that I couldn't handle my own business—and when they scent weakness they attack like jackals. You gave me my father's empire, but in the same stroke you took it away from me."

If the stakes weren't so high, Fritz would have felt some irony that he was serving the function of therapist and advisor to a Vietnamese criminal boss. Fritz plucked up a box of ammunition, which held four belts of two hundred fifty rounds. "They're like any bullies. They'll back off when you show them your strength."

"That's exactly what I'm doing," said Duoc. "I've made a list of each instance where I've lost face and I will rectify each instance with blood and fire. I'm starting with you and your family. I will make an example of each and every person that has slighted me."

Fritz glanced over his shoulder and saw that one gang member had managed to impale himself upon the spikes that thrust up from the walls surrounding his home. Still, he could see at least three of them creeping up the terraces. More bullets spattered against the windows and this time they webbed and cracked beneath the duress. "That's got to be a long list, Duoc."

"I'm starting at the beginning," replied the gang boss.

Fritz started up the stairs, the Swiss machine gun over his shoulder, phone held to his ear with one hand, and a box of a thousand rounds in his other. Bullets tore into the concrete siding of the home, and they rang against the two-inch steel plates inserted between the double-stud construction. "You'd best make quick work of it, Duoc. The police will be here in a few minutes."

"I've taken measures to delay them. Did you know that there is only one road in and out of Coral Heights?"

Fritz climbed into the turret that rose above the roof of his home. This contained his office and library and had a large, round, multi-paned window which overlooked the neighborhood. Through these bullet-resistant panes he could see that Duoc had assembled a veritable army to wipe him out. There were numerous vehicles parked along the streets and squads of Vietnamese gangsters that were gathering around his home and encroaching on his property. "I knew that."

"That road has effectively been blocked with vehicles that have been destroyed. It will be at least an hour before the police arrive. By that time you, your wife, and your baby will be ashes."

Fritz scarcely paused in his office. A brace of Anaconda pistols with gold inlaid grips stood on a pedestal just beneath his Koyama Munetsugu *katana* that hung on the wall above them. The walls contained a row of platinum-record awards and to the left of them hung a Death Machine tour jacket. He reached for a rope hanging from the ceiling and pulled down a ladder which he used to climb into the attic above. Here the roof was lined with steel and there were a number of loopholes cut just beneath the overhanging eaves of the roof all the way around. "What makes you think you can kill me, Duoc?"

"I shot you in the heart two years ago," said Duoc. "You've been living on borrowed time ever since."

Fritz cut the connection and tossed the phone on the floor. He set his SIG 710 on a tripod, attached the belt of two hundred fifty rounds and lay on the floor behind the gun, peering down the barrel and through the loopholes. He started with the nearest targets: the thugs climbing up the terraces of his meticulously manicured gardens, heedless of the carefully cultivated plants they were crushing beneath their foot treads. With the selector switch on single fire, Fritz carefully sighted and put a bullet through the brain pan of the thug closest to the house. He switched the selector to fully automatic and put a three-round burst into the chest and belly of a second thug who tried to cross an open expanse of lawn.

The last thug took cover behind a rock-walled terrace and didn't dare show himself, but Fritz had plenty of other targets. Another trio of thugs had thrown a ladder against the outside of the brick wall at the rear of Fritz's property and they were scrambling over the top. The last man to the top of the wall thought it wise to provide some cover fire, so he lowered his Ingram and sent a blast of bullets rattling ineffectually against the side of the house. Fritz returned fire, scathing the wall clean with about forty rounds of ammunition—a solid four seconds worth of trigger pull. It was at that moment that the hidden thug rose up with a grenade in his hand, arm cocked back to throw.

Fritz stayed on the trigger and swept the snout of the machine gun toward the newly exposed target, throwing up clots of earth until finally bullets stitched across the grenadier's chest. The grenade, however, had already left the man's hand and it bounced up to the rear deck before exploding, turning the steps into splinters and rupturing a dozen planks.

Now, Fritz turned his facing. There were far too many of them, and they were coming from all directions. He sent a pair of suited thugs scurrying for cover as they tried to scale the side wall and then he looked toward the front of the house. Through the screen of palms he could glimpse a half dozen cars parked in the street. Hiding behind the cars were mobs of Vietnamese thugs culled from local gangs, and they could scarcely be seen behind the strobing muzzle flash of their machine guns. They peppered Fritz's home with hundreds of bullets, tearing off scraps of siding and webbing the windows. He squeezed the trigger of his machine gun and mowed through branches, bursting windows of the automobiles and sending bullets slicing through the vehicles. Only the framework and engine block provided much protection against the SIG rounds, and a half dozen thugs fell dying and wounded before Fritz's machine gun ran dry.

With efficient movements, Fritz fed a second belt into place and prepared to renew the assault. The suited thugs were fighting for space behind the engine block or scrambling for boulders or even fire hydrants in a desperate attempt to find cover. Then, from the slope of a neighbor's yard, from behind an ivy-shrouded boulder, came a flash of a rocket-propelled grenade. It pounded into the side of the house and exploded, blowing through the wall of the house. Fritz knew now that his time was, indeed, running out. The RPG-7s out of the USSR were capable of blowing through twelve inches of tank armor. The two inches of armor in his turret would be about as effective as tinfoil against such a weapon.

He hoped that Duoc had already expended the largest of his artillery and that this round that had blown out the side of his house had been the only rocket-propelled grenade in Duoc's arsenal. Still, it might be wise to put some suppressive fire on that boulder, in the case that the thug who had fired the weapon was reloading his launcher right now with yet another warhead. Otka and Rosette were beneath a ten-inch vault door set in the floor of the closet, which dropped them into a safe room buried in the earth. The walls of the safe room were two-foot-thick concrete. They would be safe against all but a direct hit against the vault door, but Fritz knew that he had to hold out long enough for Matthias to arrive and chase away Duoc and his armed goons, or else Duoc might have enough time on his hands to crack that vault door and kill Otka and Rosette. It was all too fresh in his memory, how Sly had lost his first wife Aaliyah and his son Aksel to a jihadist hit squad. It was no wonder that he'd been reluctant to have another child with Sheila.

Fritz squeezed the trigger and scathed ivy from the boulder behind which the gang member with the rocket-propelled grenade launcher had fired. After about three seconds and forty bullets, he eased off and then waited to see if the man would dare show his face. That was when the house was hit again with a grenade launcher, this time from the west. The kitchen blew into a shrapnel of splinters and glass and the explosion picked up the refrigerator, threw it through the intervening wall and into the sunken living room, where it spilled its guts across the floor.

A few moments ago, Fritz had been confident that he could hold off the hired hit squad long enough for Matthias to arrive, but now his hopes of keeping the wolves at bay long enough to save Otka's and Rosette's lives were fading. Already, he had determined that he might well die in the attempt to keep them safe, but now he realized that in order to distract the wolves long enough, he might need to take the fight to them. Apparently, Duoc Tang had more than one rocket launcher and if Fritz held his position, Duoc's hit squad would turn the house into a pile of rubble.

Fritz could not fire in all directions at once and so he adjusted his sights and put a dozen rounds into the tank of the nearest sedan, ripping it open so that gas gushed across the pavement. The Swiss machine gun belched more bullets and Fritz sent them skipping off the concrete. None of them sparked, but the bullets fanned beneath the vehicle and took down two thugs that were hiding behind it.

Now, Fritz jerked his sights back toward the boulder and saw a thug with a rocket launcher step out from behind his cover. The thug placed the rocket launcher on his shoulder and leveled the warhead at the tower where Fritz was firing from. Fritz squeezed the trigger of the Swiss machine gun and chewed up the landscape before pushing a half dozen rounds through the grenadier's body. It was too late to keep the rocket launcher from firing, but the warhead flew as the grenadier pitched backward, and the rocket-propelled grenade went high, arcing over the top of the house, passing over the backyard and landing in the green belt of palms just over the back brick wall. The brick wall crumbled as the warhead exploded, and a pair of the Vietnamese gang members were pulped by the explosion.

Fritz fired the last of his belt into the string of vehicles along the front of the property, toppling part of a palm tree onto the top of a car. The thugs saw the palm tree falling and it did not catch any of them beneath its falling bole, but as they scattered away from the tree they left their cover behind the engine and Fritz shot down a pair of them. The third, who had elected to stay behind and take his chances, was unharmed by the tree, even though it crushed the top of the cab.

It was the work of a few seconds for Fritz to load the third belt into the feeder. He fired from yet another loophole, endeavoring to cause as much mayhem and damage as he possibly could. The thick screen of lead that he was laying down would discourage the second rocket launcher to fire any more missiles in the direction of the house, for at least as long as the barrage of bullets lasted. Bullets gnawed the pavement, and to create further distraction Fritz spent a few moments firing at the base of a water hydrant, eating away the pavement that kept it moored and then sending it spinning away in a gout of water and ricocheting bullets. Then he spent a few seconds gnawing up a couple vehicles the wolves were using for cover, and sent clots of earth and rock flying at the base of the boulder at the corner of the block.

Fortunately, all the neighbors had sprinted for cover at the first sound of gunfire and the only people left out of doors were men who wanted to do Fritz and his family harm, so Fritz could unleash the machine gun with wild abandon. When finally his gun chattered to a stop, Fritz fed in the last belt and waited for someone to get brave enough to pop their head out of cover and take a shot at the house. A thug with an Ingram MAC-11 finally pulled together enough moxy and stood up from behind a bullet-mangled vehicle and spewed a volley of bullets in Fritz's direction. These were stopped dead by the two inches of steel plate inside the wall, and Fritz let the thug fire away. He knew that those short rounds were unlikely to penetrate and do him any harm. Instead, he waited, hoping that this lack of retaliation would encourage bigger fish to swim out of their holes.

Indeed, after about ten seconds of non-retaliation, he saw a head emerge from behind the stone at the corner. Through the screen of mist cast by the gushing water hydrant, Fritz could see the thug resting a rocket launcher on the top of the stone.

Fritz grinned and muttered as he sighted down the barrel of his machine gun and pulled the trigger. "I've got you now, sucker."

The face dissolved in a blaze of muzzle flash and bullets but still the rocket-propelled grenade fired, its flight going awry and soaring thirty feet into the side of a dark green sedan. The sedan erupted into a ball of flame, casting shrapnel in all direction. Several of the gunmen toppled, pieces of metal lodged in their flesh. Flaming debris hurtled high into the air and then plummeted in trails of oily smoke. Some of the debris dropped into the pools of gasoline formed by the ruptured gas tank Fritz had caused earlier. The gasoline immediately ignited and the bullet-riddled vehicle went up in a deadly conflagration. Fritz caught sight of a flaming gunman fleeing the intense heat, his clothing, hair, and flesh afire. It was a mercy when Fritz finished his life with a half dozen rounds from his Swiss machine gun.

Adding to the utter chaos, Fritz continued to pour machine gun fire into the scattering ranks of the enemy, until every last bullet of the belt was gone. With no more ammunition for the Swiss machine gun, Fritz was considering his options when he heard the whoosh of a rocket-propelled grenade and, through one of the loopholes, caught a glimpse of something fired from well down the road.

He rolled through the open hatch of the attic, dropping awkwardly into his office below. Even before he struck the bamboo floor of his office, the attic blew into splinter and wreckage. Beams fell, and the steel plates that sheathed the roof ruptured, raining down on the roof of the house. If not for the steel plating in the floor of the attic, Fritz would have surely been incinerated by the inferno, but now that same steel plating threatened to kill him, as heated plates loosened by the explosion pelted down through the pulverized ceiling of his office.

One plate narrowly missed slicing off the top of Fritz's head and another fell between his legs, the heat of the plate scorching his pants as he crawled through the wreckage. His ears were ringing, so he scarcely realized that his phone was next to his palm and ringing as well. The explosion had left Fritz stunned and disoriented, so he absently picked up the ringing phone.

"What do you want?"

Duoc Tang's voice came through the telephone speaker and filtered through to Fritz's muted hearing. "I want you dead! Why are you still alive, Fritz Gantlet?"

"I'm just stubborn that way." Fritz noticed a wetness at his ear and when he pulled away the phone he discovered blood on the receiver. His eardrum had been ruptured by the explosion.

"I just want to assure you," said Duoc Tang, "that once you're dead, I will kill your wife and daughter, just like you killed my father."

"Leave them out of this," croaked Fritz. "I'll give myself up, if you swear that you'll leave them untouched."

"How much mercy did you extend to my father? I'll extend the same amount of mercy to your wife and daughter."

"I did you a favor," said Fritz. "You admitted the same to me in Prague. Now do me a favor. I'll give my life in exchange for my wife and daughter."

There was a pause as if, perhaps, Duoc Tang was considering the bargain. Finally, the Vietnamese mobster responded. "I truly wish that I could accept your offer, Fritz Gantlet, but I have let you go unpunished for too long. For two years I have let you live in peace and because of this I have lost the respect of my rivals. To regain their respect, I must show no mercy. Anyone that dares cross me must know that I will not only kill them, but their loved ones as well. You will be the example of that, and others will fear me when they think of you and what happened to your family."

Fritz found his tour jacket among the rubble and pulled it on. For the moment the firing had ceased and he wondered if he could buy time by continuing his conversation with Duoc Tang. Of course, Duoc Tang was probably thinking the same thing. Even now, Fritz suspected, Duoc Tang's men were converging on the house, entering through the hole in the kitchen wall, and fanning out, searching for him. "You're forgetting an important part of the equation, Duoc."

"Oh," responded Duoc Tang, his voice dry as the summer Sahara. "What is that?"

Fritz zipped up his jacket and found the gold-inlaid pair of Anaconda magnums that had fallen to the floor. He pinched the phone between his left ear and shoulder while he spoke. "I've got three brothers that will take you and every last felon of your organization down—from your hired killers to your number runners, your pimps, and even your errand boys."

"Let them try," said Duoc Tang. "There's a Lieutenant Kolka who is very anxious to have the Gantlet Brothers set foot on Czech soil again. Your escape was very embarrassing to him."

Fritz loaded his guns with .44 shells and holstered them. "As it should be. He did cause an international incident by shooting rockets over the border, after all."

"My point is that your brothers will not find it so easy to put foot on Czech soil."

"I suspect you're hiding behind a phalanx of lackeys, Duoc Tang, so I don't know if I'll be able to kill you, but my brothers can dismantle your organization without ever crossing the Czech border."

Duoc Tang's voice was arch and superior. "How so?"

Fritz stood and slung his Koyama Munetsugu *katana* over his shoulder. "They'll kill you before you ever leave the United States of America." He dropped the phone among the wreckage and crushed it underfoot.

As he left the office, he crept down the stairs, staying close to the wall, which was lined with the original artwork from various Gantlet Brother album covers: from the eponymously titled first album, past Point of Destruction, Death Machine, Matter of Splatter, and Walking on Thin Ice—a Vallejo painting which showed Cindy Warner on an ice floe that was splitting beneath her, clawed hands thrusting up from the revealed chasm beneath. Fritz could only hear from one ear, and the ringing in his right ear masked his own foot tread so he could not tell—except by his practiced footfall—if his feet were stepping silently. So, when he rounded the curved wall of the stair and found himself facing three Vietnamese gunmen, he was not aware of their presence until the moment he laid his eyes upon them.

The trio of gunmen, however, seemed to be just as surprised as Fritz, so apparently he had descended the stairs with enough stealth to keep his presence a secret. Each of them held a pistol or an Ingram machine gun in their hands, but as they raised their weapons, Fritz moved like a jungle cat into the midst of them. His sword blade flashed from his scabbard, striking in the same movement. A severed hand bearing a pistol went tumbling through the air, spraying a crimson mist.

"He's still alive!" called a machine-gunnist and he fired his MAC-11. A fraction of a second before he pulled the trigger, Fritz went into a low crouch, and the short rounds spat over his head, peppering the second pistolman, so that his chest erupted red blossoms and he pitched backward, his gun spitting bullets into the ceiling.

Fritz spun around, his sword blade describing a glittering arc that took out the machine-gunnist at the knee. The muzzle flash of the MAC-11 burned Fritz's face, but the burst of bullets seared past him, stitching across the floor. Fritz reversed the edge of the *katana* and struck again as he rose to his feet. The blade shuddered in his hand and then his gory work was finished. He performed a sharp movement which sent the blood spraying from his *katana*.

Through the roar of his impaired hearing, Fritz thought he heard the crunch of breaking glass underfoot. He turned his head and saw four men approaching from the vestibule. The front two carried machine guns and the pair in the rear held a gas-powered concrete saw and a cutting torch. In that instant, Fritz realized that Duoc Tang had known all along about the vault beneath the house and had come prepared to cut Fritz's wife and daughter out of it, so he could ensure their deaths.

It was poor form to treat such a fine piece of craftsmanship in such a manner, but Fritz relinquished his grip upon his Koyama Munetsugu *katana* and let it drop to the floor, even while both hands went for his brace of Anaconda magnum pistols. Unfortunately, the machine-gunnists already had the drop at him, and lead pounded him backward even as he fired. He didn't have the advantage of being ambidextrous like Mitz and bullets hammered him in a constant stream so he couldn't do much in the way of aiming, but he began to pull the triggers on both guns, hoping against all hope that some of his own bullets would find their target.

Darkness closed around Fritz's vision. When he awoke, he didn't have any sense of how long he had been unconscious, but he still gripped his Anaconda pistols, and both were entirely empty. Apparently he had shot every single round before passing out, or even after he had lost consciousness. His tour jacket was a ruin of tattered leather. The ceramic plates were pulverized into dust and the Kevlar panels were singed and torn. Each time Fritz tried to breath it felt as if a hundred-pound anvil was sitting on his chest.

He slowly, painfully pushed himself into a sitting position and found that not all the bullets had sprayed his torso. At least three bullets had torn his jeans and creased his legs and a bullet had torn through his left bicep, making the arm all but useless. Fritz looked toward the vestibule and saw four men scattered across the floor and leaning against the wall. Blood puddled the stone floor, and bullet holes gaped in walls and flesh alike. With twelve shots Fritz had managed to kill all four men, even while being hosed with 9mm bullets.

Beyond the vestibule, the front door hung open, the dead bolts cut with a torch. Past the bullet-mangled BMW, Fritz could see more thugs making their way through the wreckage-littered landscape. "Matthias," muttered Fritz, "where are you?" Now Fritz whispered a prayer. "Lord in Heaven, please let my brother arrive in time to save my wife and daughter."

When these whispered words had passed Fritz's lips, a resolve fell upon him and he knew what he must do. He had to buy Otka and Rosette just a few more moments.

He crouched and resheathed his *katana*. He found a pair of fresh magazines for the Ingram MAC-11s thrust into the belts of the dead men, and he went to the door bearing a machine gun in each hand. He fired at the approaching gunmen, knocking down one of them before a hail of bullets responded. Fritz pulled his arm and head back behind cover and let the bullets gouge the siding and pound into the walls of the open vestibule.

As soon as there was a moment of reprieve, Fritz thrust the snout of the MAC-11 out the door and let the enemy know that he was still alive. In a few moments the magazine was empty and he threw the machine gun aside. With one fully loaded machine gun left, Fritz formulated a desperate plan to take the fight away from the house, away from Otka and Rosette, and out into the open.

More bullets pounded into the house and ricocheted around the vestibule. Then, in a moment of respite, Fritz burst across the doorstep, between the brass lions that were pitted with bullet marks, and down the driveway into the midst of the advancing enemy. He fired the MAC-11 with his injured left arm, holding the machine gun close to his side for support as he let a stream of bullets precede him. It took less than two seconds to empty the thirty-round magazine, but he covered nearly twenty yards in that time span. Still, he was ten yards away from reaching the nearest of his enemies when they recovered from their surprise and returned fire at the sprinting target.

Fritz let the MAC-11 fall from his unsteady grip and clatter on the bricks of the drive. He unsheathed his *katana* and a storm of bullets sliced through the remnants of his no-longer-bulletproof jacket, and through his body, so that his last steps became unsteady and reckless. He plunged into the ranks of the enemy, his sword stroke taking off the head of the gang member who was unfortunate enough to be in the path of Fritz's *katana*. Then, Fritz tumbled to the ground, his life seeping from him even as his blood filled the grout between the bricks.

Chapter 36

Matthias peered through the windscreen of the Bell 222 helicopter as he piloted it over Coral Hills. A bandolier of grenades lay across his shoulder and his 454 was thrust into the gunleather at his belt. Great plumes of smoke spiraled into the air ahead and as Matthias came over the crest of the jungle-covered hill, he saw the cause of the first plume. In the roadway was an old school bus which was turned across the concrete in a narrow part of the road, which had no shoulders—just a ten-foot-deep ravine on one side and a steep slope on the other. An explosive of some sort had been detonated at the center of the bus, so that the roof was peeled away, the windows shattered, and belching black smoke. As it came into sight, Matthias could see that the bus was still burning. Even the tires were alight, puddling the pavement with melting rubber which sent out an oily vapor.

Four police cars were caught on one side of the improvised barrier unable to progress any further into the Coral Hills development. Police stood outside their vehicles radioing for fire trucks and a bomb squad to investigate whether a second explosive might be set to detonate should they attempt to push the bus out of the way.

"Looks like Duoc Tang went all out," said Matthias. "He's blocked off the entrance so the police can't help."

Blake grunted and rubbed at his bristling Mohawk as Matthias tilted the copter so he could get a better view. "Back in my not so good days, I did something similar when I wanted to make sure I had enough time to break into the vault of a rival drug-runner. I dropped an electric pole over the entrance and exit to the street."

"How did you get out?" asked Matthias.

"There was an eight-foot-radius storm drain that ran right underneath the warehouse. That got me and my crew four blocks away to catch a ride out of town with a half million in cash and the drug kingpin's daughter—

who came willingly."

Several of the police officers pointed at the Bell helicopter as Matthias sent it buzzing past. "That's a story I won't tell Vera."

"Oh, she knows the story. There's nothing I haven't told her about my sordid past, and if I had to do it again, I would have left the daughter behind. She was so much trouble that I had to pay her father to take her back."

Matthias laughed, and Blake pushed open the hatch, warm air buffeting them inside the cockpit.

"The members of my crew were the only ones that made any money off that heist."

Matthias piloted the helicopter over the rolling hills and well-appointed homes with lush emerald lawns and sparkling turquoise swimming pools. He kept the Bell just high enough to avoid the network of electrical wires that climbed the hills by means of large towers.

Blake reached into the back of the aircraft and began to unlock a hard-shelled case. "How close are we?"

"I'm not sure," admitted Matthias. "I've always visited Fritz's place by automobile, but I see two more columns of smoke. I'm betting that the closest column is Fritz's house."

Blake scowled and lifted an M2 .50 caliber machine gun, locking it onto a pintle which Matthias had welded into the helicopter—one of a few custom modifications he had introduced to the craft. "I don't like the sound of that. Hopefully, he got himself and the family into the vault underneath the house."

"You know about that?"

"It's hard not to," said Blake. "The workmen were digging a giant pit before they poured the foundation. I ran a work permit up to Fritz one day and couldn't help but put two and two together."

Matthias was pushing the helicopter past two hundred sixty miles an hour, the maximum speed rating of the craft, and the body of the helicopter shuddered and groaned with the strain. "Yeah, well, I wonder who else put two and two together. There was a whole work crew that knew about that vault and it wouldn't have taken more than a few hundred dollars or even a few free beers to loosen that fact to one of Duoc Tang's associates. I'm thinking that's why Duoc Tang is taking such extreme measures to make sure the police don't have quick access to Fritz's house. Tang wants time to take that vault apart."

Blake cocked an eyebrow at Matthias. "So you don't think it was me that sold Fritz out?"

"You I trust, Blake."

"Why not hit Fritz and his family when they're away from the house—shopping or something? Somewhere Fritz doesn't have the protection of his home?"

Matthias shrugged. "Duoc Tang's coming in from Czechoslovakia. Maybe he didn't feel like he had the luxury of surveilling Fritz's home and waiting for a chance to hit the whole family at once. This way he gets to control the time table and he's done a pretty good job of controlling the battlefield by blocking off the entrance to Coral Heights."

This seemed to satisfy Blake and he fed a belt of massive .50 caliber shells into the machine gun. "Just give me a target, Matthias. Just give me a target."

Black smoke seemed to grow until it enveloped half of the sky, and somewhere beneath the roar of the overhead rotors, the rattle of machine gun fire came to their ears. They came up over the rise, Matthias bringing the helicopter up higher to avoid a network of electric wires, and they saw the battle zone stretching out beneath him. Portions of Fritz's home had been blown away by rocket-propelled grenades and the house was aflame, the winds swirling the smoke into a great column. Vehicles were stretched around the perimeter of the house, their bodies so riddled with bullets that they looked like Swiss cheese. Some were aflame, and blood-spattered bodies lay on the pavement.

Still, suited figures scurried from cover to cover, a group of Vietnamese gang members working their way across the front lawn and firing at the front of the house.

Blake jabbed a finger toward the front lawn. "There's Fritz!"

A small figure sprinted from the doorway of the smoking ruins of the house, machine gun blasting, and then the gang members returned fire, bullets spewing and empty casings glittering in the air. Matthias saw a blade flash, a head go rolling, and then Fritz was down. Matthias stifled a cry. "Hang tight. I'm going in!"

Blake saw the flare of rocket fire, and then another close on its heels. He was about to voice his concern, but Matthias saw them, too, and sent the helicopter jigging away with such force that Blake was almost torn from his seatbelt. Matthias was familiar enough with the Stinger anti-aircraft rockets. They used a two-stage rocket thrust. The first carried the warhead off the shoulder-fired launcher and then the second thruster engaged, pushing the missile up to twice the speed of sound—about eight times faster than the helicopter could travel.

Matthias knew he had just a matter of seconds to evade the stinger missile before the second stage kicked in and blew them to kingdom come. His flight took him back toward the electric tower, the rotor blades cutting dangerously close to the power lines while Matthias sent the Bell 222 climbing. As Matthias attempted the dificult maneuver, the roar of the .50 caliber machine gun filled the cockpit, empty casings ricocheting against the windshield and rattling beneath Matthias's feet. Blake managed to hit the first oncoming missile and it went up into a super-heated blossom dangerously close to the helicopter, the shock wave pushing the craft through the air.

With every bit of skill he knew how to muster, Matthias hung onto control of the craft, bringing the helicopter just beyond the screen of high tension wires. The second stinger missile followed, plowing into the wires, and the warhead detonating, blowing apart the tower. The power in every home within a six-mile radius blinked off, and Matthias took the helicopter up and over the devastation, heading back in the direction of the anti-aircraft fire.

"Nice shooting!" called Matthias.

"Nice flying," muttered Blake.

"If it wasn't for that extra boost of the shock wave, we wouldn't have gotten past the high tension wires in time to stop the second missile."

"All part of the plan," said Blake, but he and Matthias both knew that it had been sheer luck or divine intervention.

Matthias sent the helicopter hurtling forward at full speed, diving toward the hillside where he had first seen the eruptions of the rocket launcher.

Blake's brow furrowed. "What are you doing?"

"Ramming ourselves down the throats of those men with the stingers before they can get more missiles loaded. If we don't take care of them now, we won't have a second chance."

Blake nodded and sighted down the barrel of his machine gun. Duoc Tang had come well prepared. Not only had he blocked off access and egress, but he had anticipated police helicopters and taken measures to keep them from interfering with his vengeance. Blake pulled down his sunglasses to protect his watering eyes from the hot wind and then he saw a group of men perched on the hillside, nestled at the base of a trio of towering palms. Indeed, they were hastily loading second rounds onto two separate stinger anti-aircraft shoulder launchers. Blake breathed out, squeezed the trigger and unleashed a blistering torrent of hot lead, and when finally, a minute later, he eased off the trigger and the blinding muzzle flash cleared from his vision, he saw nothing but mangled trees, and the bullet-riddled cadavers of men sawed in half. "I got 'em!"

Matthias responded by veering from his suicide course toward the hillside, pulling away just in time to avoid collision with the severely pruned cluster of palms. He zoomed low over a neighbor's red-tiled mansion and he could see the fearful faces of its owners peering from behind plate glass windows.

As soon as more targets came into sight, Blake began to fire the .50 caliber, scattering the gathered might of the gang, so that when Matthias brought the helicopter down on the slope of Fritz's front lawn, the gang members surrounding Fritz had fled over the wall, leaving their dead and dying behind.

As soon as the helicopter settled to the ground, Matthias unbuckled his harness and leaped from his seat. "You stay here and keep the fleas off!"

Blake kept a sharp eye out in case he needed to dust any gang members from the walls or fence. "Gotcha, boss!"

Matthias ran to Fritz and knelt down beside him. By the amount of blood running between the bricks, Matthias estimated that Fritz must have already lost at least two or three quarts of blood. His brother's torso was a mass of gristle and flesh that reminded Matthias of ground hamburger. He couldn't even begin to estimate how many hundreds of bullets Fritz must have taken. Matthias had witnessed much death and dying, and immediately he knew that Fritz had no hope of surviving.

Fritz's eyes fluttered open and stared. "Otto?"

"It's Matthias, Fritz. I'm here for you."

"No, standing behind you," said Fritz. "It's Otto. I'm guessing that he's here for me."

Matthias couldn't help but look over his shoulder because he, also, felt a familiar presence. When he looked, though, he saw nothing but heat rising from the pavement. "Do you still see him, Fritz?"

"He's holding out his hand. Wants me to come with him."

Matthias had an inkling how much pain his brother might be in, and though he selfishly wanted Fritz to stay with him for a few more minutes, he realized that at this point death might be a welcome reprieve. "Then go with him—go with Otto."

"Not yet," grimaced Fritz. "Otka and Rosette, they're in the vault. Take care of them, keep them safe. All I was trying to do was buy enough time to save them—my beautiful wife and daughter. Enough time for you to get here."

"I'm here now," choked Matthias. "I promise I'll keep an eye on them."

With every bit of effort he could manage, Fritz reached up and clasped Matthias's forearm. "Do something else for me."

Smoke drifted across the lawn. "What's that, Fritz?"

"Let it go. Don't go after Duoc Tang. It's a vicious cycle. If you kill him, it will only cause someone else to come after you and your family. Just let it go."

Matthias's jaw tightened. "I can't let this go unanswered Fritz. You know I can't do that."

Fritz's eyes rolled back into his head. His body convulsed and a death rattle passed from his throat and over his lips, the last vestiges of his once-vibrant life fleeing the broken shell of his body. Matthias felt grief and anguish convulse his own body. He closed his brother's still-open eyelids and stood, the weight of the world upon his shoulders.

He heard Blake calling out to him. "The gun's jammed and we've got a car on the move!"

Matthias looked past the sagging fence and saw a rental car cruising down the street. The window unrolled and Duoc Tang leaned out with a machine gun in hand. He opened fire at Matthias, who, in his anger, stood his ground. Much of Duoc Tang's gunfire was absorbed by the screen of foliage and ricocheted off the wrought iron fence, but other rounds spattered around Matthias's feet and another split his pant leg, searing his calf. Matthias plucked a grenade from his bandolier and drew his arm back, estimating the speed of the vehicle and throwing far ahead of it, over the gate, and timing it perfectly so it dropped through the window as Duoc Tang pulled back inside to reload his machine gun.

A moment later the car erupted, glass shattering, and sheet metal bulging outward as the explosion pulped the occupants of the vehicle. The rental vehicle drove through the water of the still-gushing hydrant and onto the great boulder at the corner, where it flipped onto its side and sparked to a halt. No one emerged from the black pall of smoke that billowed from the wreckage.

"Sorry, Fritz. I just couldn't let Duoc Tang off the hook."

Blake came up alongside of Matthias, cradling a full-sized UZI. "I thought you couldn't throw. That was a one in a million toss."

"One in a million toss for a one in a million brother," said Matthias. "I just couldn't let it go."

"Couldn't let what go?" asked Blake, who hadn't been privy to the words spoken between Fritz and Matthias.

The sound of sirens filled the air. Apparently, the police had pushed aside the bus blocking the road and now a dozen police vehicles came rushing into the area, lights flashing. "I'll tell you later," said Matthias. "Let's see to Otka and Rosette."

Blake knelt down next to Fritz and checked for a pulse. He shook his head when he couldn't find the faintest tremor of a heartbeat. "Let me get a blanket out of the emergency kit so we can cover your brother. I'm really sorry we couldn't get here in time."

"We did the best we could," said Matthias. "He's gone on to a better place."

"You sure about that?" asked Blake, who seemed surprised Matthias would make such a pronunciation.

Matthias recalled how Fritz had seen Otto waiting for him. "Now, I'm sure about that." In a daze, he turned toward the smoking ruins of the house, entering past the bullet-scarred lions of brass, over the dead bodies in the vestibule, past the cadavers at the bottom of the stairs and into the spacious bedroom. Fritz's emergency generators were already kicking on and so the intercom hidden behind the mounted Les Paul guitar was functioning.

"Otka, this is Matthias. You can come out now. It's safe."

"Is that you Matthias?" answered Otka.

"No, it's your grandma," replied Matthias.

An expertly concealed panel in the floor slid open revealing stairs into the vault below and Matthias steeled himself for the hard news that he bore. Still, those words did not even have to pass his lips, because the moment Otka emerged and saw the anguish upon Matthias's face she knew that Fritz was dead. Somewhere, Grandpa Gantlet's gold-plated pocket watch continued to tick, counting down the seconds, minutes, and hours until the next Gantlet would be called home.

The End.

Books from Pulpwork Press:

Derrick Ferguson
Dillon Series:
Dillon and the Golden Bell
Four Bullets for Dillon
Dillon and the Pirates of Xonira
Dillon and the Voice of Odin

Joel Jenkins

Dire Planet Series:
Dire Planet
Exiles of the Dire Planet
Into the Dire Planet
Strange Gods of the Dire Planet
Lost Tribes of the Dire Planet

Tales from the City of Bathos Series:
Escape from Devil's Head
Through the Groaning Earth

The Gantlet Brother Series:
The Nuclear Suitcase
The Gantlet Brothers Greatest Hits
Gantlet Brothers: Sold Out

Damage Incorporated Series:
The Sea Witch

Denbrook Supernatural:
Devil Take the Hindmost

Children's Books:
The Pirates of Mirror Land

Arthurian Fantasy:
The Island of Lost Souls

Collections:
Weird Worlds of Joel Jenkins

Biography:
One Foot in My Grave: One Man's Battle Against Cystic Fibrosis

Josh Reynolds
Dracula Lives!

Percival Constantine
Love and Bullets
Outlaw Blues: Infernum
Myth Hunter
Dragon Kings of the Orient

Anthologies
How the West was Weird, edited by Russ Anderson
How the West was Weird 2 edited by Russ Anderson
PulpWork Christmas Special 2011
PulpWork Christmas Special 2012

Coming Soon
How the West was Weird 3
Lone Crow Collected by Joel Jenkins
Denbrook Knights by Derrick Ferguson
The Vril Agenda by Josh Reynolds & Derrick Ferguson

For more information on these and other titles or for online ordering
visit us at PulpWork.com or find our titles at Amazon,
KoboBooks.com, and BarnesandNoble.com

www.ingramcontent.com/pod-product-compliance
Lightning Source LLC
Chambersburg PA
CBHW052017020726
47501CB00004B/1108